Desire never deceives…

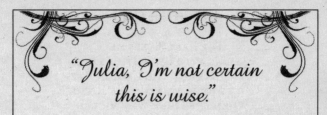

"Julia, I'm not certain this is wise."

She gave him a speculative look. "To be comfortable?"

"To tempt me."

A thrill shot through her. Yes, they were in mourning, yes, sorrow radiated from him, but she still had power over him. She flung the neckcloth aside and cupped his face between her hands, her fingers dancing along the back of his neck. "I missed you so much."

She tilted his head down, rose up on her toes, and planted her mouth on his. His arm snaked around her, drew her nearer. His tongue slid between her lips as he adjusted the angle and took the kiss deeper. She fairly melted against him.

Hunger. Urgency. A compelling need. They were all there. In him. In her. As though death hovered nearby, waiting, as though with enough passion and desire they could ward it off. A low growl vibrated through his chest, shimmered through her breasts, which flattened against the linen of his shirt.

The heat between them intensified. His hands traveled over her back, her hips, cupped her backside, pressed her even closer . . .

By Lorraine Heath

ATTENTION: ORGANIZATIONS AND CORPORATIONS
HarperCollins books may be purchased for educational, business, or sales promotional use. For information, please e-mail the Special Markets Department at SPsales@harpercollins.com.

Lorraine Heath

The Earl Takes All

AVONBOOKS

An Imprint of HarperCollinsPublishers

This is a work of fiction. Names, characters, places, and incidents are products of the author's imagination or are used fictitiously and are not to be construed as real. Any resemblance to actual events, locales, organizations, or persons, living or dead, is entirely coincidental.

AVON BOOKS
An Imprint of HarperCollins*Publishers*
195 Broadway
New York, New York 10007

Copyright © 2016 by Jan Nowasky
ISBN 978-0-06-239103-2
www.avonromance.com   MAY − 3 2016

All rights reserved. No part of this book may be used or reproduced in any manner whatsoever without written permission, except in the case of brief quotations embodied in critical articles and reviews. For information address Avon Books, an Imprint of HarperCollins Publishers.

First Avon Books mass market printing: May 2016

Avon Trademark Reg. U.S. Pat. Off. and in Other Countries, Marca Registrada, Hecho en U.S.A.
Avon, Avon Books, and the Avon logo are trademarks of HarperCollins Publishers.
HarperCollins® is a registered trademark of HarperCollins Publishers.

Printed in the U.S.A.

10 9 8 7 6 5 4 3 2 1

If you purchased this book without a cover, you should be aware that this book is stolen property. It was reported as "unsold and destroyed" to the publisher, and neither the author nor the publisher has received any payment for this "stripped book."

For the awesome Jessie Edwards

Prologue

On the cold and dreary evening of November 15, 1858, Edward Alcott's life turned gray. The only thing that saved it from going completely black was Albert. At the age of seven, older than Edward by only an hour, his twin had become the Earl of Greyling that night when their parents were killed in a horrific railway accident.

Days later, Albert held Edward's hand as they sat dutifully in front of the caskets that contained whatever remained of their parents. During the evening of the day their parents were buried, Albert crept into Edward's bed so neither of them would feel so lost and alone. While they traveled to Havisham Hall, where they became the wards of the Marquess of Marsden, Albert unwittingly offered a distraction, providing a place for Edward to vent his anger and frustration over life's unfairness. They constantly shoved and slapped at each other until the solicitor traveling with them separated the boys. After they were abandoned so far from home, left in the marquess's keeping, Albert assured

Edward all would be well, that they began life together in the womb and, therefore, would always remain together. Albert had been his anchor, his solace, his one constant in all matters, all things.

And now *she* was stealing him away—with her silken black hair and her startling blue eyes and her sweet laughter and her gentle smile. Lady Julia Kenney. Albert was blinded by her beauty, her grace, and her attentions, allowing her to take up far too much of his time with rides in the park, rowing on the Thames, theater, dinners, and—God forbid—poetry readings. She was pulling him away from those closest to him, causing him to put aside his love for drinking, whoring, gambling, and traveling. In six weeks the Duke of Ashebury, Viscount Locksley, and Edward were going on a trek through the Far East. As far as Edward was concerned Albert should be going with them. He had been planning to go with them until Lady Julia asked him not to leave. Without so much as the blink of an eye, Albert had adhered to her wishes and cancelled his plans to travel with them.

She had managed to effectively wrap his brother around her littlest finger without much more than an occasional batting of her eyelashes and a fluttering of her fan. It was not to be tolerated. A woman should not have so much influence and control over a man's life.

Edward wasn't certain why he'd followed her out of the festive ballroom and into the quiet shadows of the garden, why he'd stopped to watch as she left the path and disappeared into the thicket of rose-adorned trellises and boughs. He knew only that he couldn't lose Albert to her.

He hesitated but a minute before darting into an area where the shadows were heavier, the glow from the gaslights lining the path held at bay. Proceeding cautiously until his eyes adjusted to the gloom, he finally saw her leaning back against the brick wall. Her lips slowly curled up to reveal her winsome smile. She looked so bloody glad to see him.

In spite of the gray darkness, as he stepped nearer he could see the adoration in her eyes. No other woman had ever looked at him as though every breath she took was for him and him alone, as though she existed only for him and his pleasures. It caused a tightening in his gut, a heady sensation of supremacy and purpose.

"I thought you'd never get here," she said in a whispered voice that belonged to angels.

Temptation such as he'd never known tore through him, leaving him powerless against her siren's call. He didn't understand it. In all of his twenty-three years, he'd never had a woman create such a maelstrom of confusing and uncomfortable emotions. He should leave now while he could, but she drew him in as though she had been created by the gods for him and no other.

With one hand, he cradled her face, felt the rapid thrum of her pulse against his fingers, and stroked his thumb along her smooth cheek. She released a soft sigh; her eyes turned languid.

He knew it was wrong, knew he would regret it, but he seemed incapable of rational thought or action. Leaning in, he took what he had no right to possess; he claimed her mouth as though it belonged to him, always had and always would belong to him.

She sighed again, a softer, warmer mewl that traveled through him, caused him to harden with such desire that he nearly doubled over. Drawing her in closer, he angled his head, took the kiss deeper, sweeping his tongue through her luscious mouth. She tasted of rich champagne with a hint of strawberries. Her slender arms came around his neck; her gloved fingers plowed through his thick blond curls. Her sigh this time turned into a welcoming moan. The passage of time seemed to come to a standstill like the clocks at Havisham Hall. No ticking, no movement of the hands, no tolling of the chimes.

He wanted to stay here forever. Wanted the night, and every night that followed, to belong only to them.

Drawing back, he held her languorous gaze. She touched her fingers to the wisps of hair at his temple, such a soft caress. It almost wasn't one at all. She smiled tenderly. "I love you so much, Albert."

His brother's name on her lips was a punch to the gut that nearly took him to his knees. Her welcome hadn't been for him. Her passion, her spark, her desire, hadn't been for him. What a colossal fool he was to have imagined, even for a second, that they had been. Not that he was going to reveal to her exactly how she affected him, how badly he wanted her.

He forced himself to grin devilishly, triumphantly. "If you really loved him, wouldn't you be able to tell us apart?" Ashe and Locke could. Even the mad Marquess of Marsden, who had served as their guardian, could distinguish them.

"Edward?" she rasped, looking as though her dinner would soon be making a second appearance.

Her obvious revulsion delivered a hard blow to his pride, but keeping his expression impassive, he offered an exaggerated bow. "At your service."

"You beast." Her gloved hand met his cheek with such unexpected force that he staggered back.

He regained his footing, cocked his head. "You enjoyed it, Julia."

"It's Lady Julia. When I marry Albert, it'll be Lady Greyling. I shall insist you address me properly. And I most certainly did not enjoy it."

"Liar."

"Why would you do such a horrid thing, take such advantage? How could you be so cruel and deceitful?"

Because he'd never been able to deny himself anything he wanted, and he'd quite suddenly wanted her. Desperately.

"What's going on here?" a deep voice asked.

Edward spun around to see Albert standing a few feet away, a quizzical look on his face. Not angry, but with an almost innocent expression, as though it would never occur to him that Edward would do something as dastardly as kiss his betrothed.

"I was waiting for you as we planned," Julia said sweetly, moving in against Albert's side, looking up at him with complete adoration that merely served to grind salt into Edward's wounded self-esteem. "Edward happened along, began telling me more details about the journey to the Far East that he and the others have constantly been discussing. It sounds as though it'll be the adventure of a lifetime. He'd so like for you to go."

Edward hated being grateful for the lie she spun, but he knew that Albert would never forgive him if he learned how he had taken advantage of Julia. He wondered why she hadn't confessed the truth, why she hadn't taken the opportunity to create a chasm between the brothers that nothing on heaven or earth would have ever breeched. But more, why was she now encouraging Albert to go with him?

"You're adventure enough for me." Albert shifted his gaze to Edward. "I've told you that I have no interest any longer in traveling. I don't appreciate you going behind my back to use Julia to try to persuade me to change my mind. Now I'd welcome your taking your leave so my little tryst in the garden with Julia can continue as intended."

"Albert—"

"Be on your way, Edward."

The impatience mirrored in his twin's voice warned Edward that if he continued on this course, he would gain nothing except distancing himself from his brother. After giving them a slight bow, he strode away from the couple, the roses, the shadows.

He needed a glass of scotch. A bottle would be better. He needed to drink himself into oblivion until he could no longer remember the warmth of Julia in his arms or recall how glorious it had felt to have her mouth moving beneath his. He needed to forget that he had ever—for the briefest of moments—wanted her for himself.

Chapter 1

Mr. Edward Alcott, brother to the Earl of Greyling, met an untimely end during their recent travels in Africa. Sadder still is the knowledge that he failed to accomplish anything of note during his twenty-seven years upon this earth.

—*Obituary in the* Times, *November 1878*

HE needed scotch—badly.

But duty required that he stand outside the residence at Evermore, the ancestral estate in Yorkshire, and express his gratitude to the few lords and ladies who had attended his twin's funeral that afternoon.

"Awfully glad it wasn't you, Greyling."

"Such a fine dancer, although he did tend to hold the ladies scandalously close during the waltz."

"Shame he had to go before amounting to anything."

"Drank me under the table more times than I can count, I tell you."

The acknowledgments continued, painting the portrait of a wastrel and scoundrel. Not that he'd ever before minded how the earl's younger brother was viewed, but today it bothered him, perhaps because the epitaphs expressed were so damned accurate.

His childhood friends, the Duke of Ashebury and Viscount Locksley, stood nearby garnering their share of condolences, as everyone knew the four of them were as close as brothers, having been raised by Locksley's father. Although he'd had very little opportunity to visit with them before the funeral, he wished they were both climbing into their own conveyances right about now, but along with Minerva, Ashe's wife, they were staying the night. Julia had extended the invitation, thinking her husband would welcome more time with them. She couldn't have been more mistaken, but he knew she'd meant well.

Graciously expressing her appreciation to those who had come, she was a vision of loveliness even draped in black. She had handled most of the arrangements, sending out the mourning cards, informing the vicar of how the service was to progress, ensuring that refreshments were on hand for their guests before they began their trek home. He'd barely had occasion to speak with her throughout the day, not that he would have known what to say if he had. Since his return, they'd had far too many moments of awkward silence. He knew that needed to change, and quickly.

As the last of the carriages finally rolled down the

drive, Julia wandered over, slid her arm around his, gave a slight squeeze. "Rather glad that's over with."

Even swollen with child, she was the most graceful woman he'd ever seen. Reaching up, she placed her black-gloved hand against his cheek. "You look tired."

"It's been a long week." He'd returned from his travels ten days ago. Most of his grieving and mourning had occurred during the long and arduous journey home. For him, today was simply a formality, something to get through before moving forward.

"I could use a good stiff drink," Ashe said as he, his wife, and Locke joined them.

"I know just where to find one," he assured his longtime friend. After leading the group into the foyer, he placed a hand on Julia's lower back. "Will you ladies excuse us for a bit?"

She hesitated, a thousand questions swirling in those lovely blue eyes of hers. He didn't mean to dismiss her, but he was desperate for a drink and hoped she mistook his craving for wanting time alone with his friends. After searching his face for what seemed an eternity, she nodded. "Yes, of course." Turning to Minerva, she smiled softly. "I'll ring for some tea."

"We won't be long," he assured the women, before heading down the hallway, his two friends not even half a step behind.

Once he entered the library, he charged forward to the sideboard, poured scotch into three tumblers, and dispensed them before holding his up. "To my brother. May he rest in peace." He downed the contents of his glass in one long swallow.

Ashe merely took a small sip, then arched a brow.

"That's hardly likely to happen, is it? What the bloody hell are you up to, Edward?"

His body froze while his mind reeled with the possibility of denying the accusation, but too much was at stake. He walked to the window and spied the spire of the village church where only a few hours earlier the funeral service had been held in his honor. Visible in the distance, ribboning through the rolling hills, was the road over which the black and glass hearse bearing the French-polished casket with its elaborately carved moldings and gleaming metal handles had journeyed, while mourners followed, to the family mausoleum. "When did you figure out I wasn't Albert?"

"Shortly before the funeral began," Locke said.

"Did you say anything to Julia?"

"No," Ashe assured him. "We thought it best to hold our suspicions until we had them confirmed. What the devil is going on here?"

"I promised Albert as he lay dying that I would do all in my power to ensure Julia did not lose the babe she carries." During their short marriage, she'd lost three, never carrying any of them to term. "Pretending to be my brother seemed the best way to go about it. I need to know how you deduced the truth. If Julia suspects—"

"Have you lost your mind?" Ashe bellowed.

"Lower your voice," he ground out. He didn't need the servants to overhear.

"Do you truly believe that you can fool Julia into believing you're Albert?"

He'd been doing it for a little over a week already. Had convinced everyone: the servants, the vicar, the few mourners, Julia. But not these two, and that was a problem. He spun around. "Albert gave me no choice if I am to honor his request."

"Surely she is far enough along now that she is past the point of a possible miscarriage," Locke said, standing shoulder-to-shoulder beside Ashe, as though together they would be better able to convince him of his foolhardiness, as though he wasn't already perfectly aware of it.

Edward glowered at him. "Can you promise me that? Can you guarantee it? You know how much she loves him, how much he loved her. If she learns that he was the one killed, will she not crumble? Will she not make herself ill with grief?"

In answer, with a heavy sigh, Locke moved off to the sideboard, grabbed the decanter, and poured himself more scotch. Although Edward knew he'd made his point, he took little satisfaction in it.

"Do you have any idea what this deception will do to Julia, how she will feel when she learns the truth?" Ashe asked.

It was all he'd thought about as he trudged through the jungle with his brother's body in tow, as he sailed across the blue waters toward England, as he rode in the wagon that transported the wooden box that held the Earl of Greyling. "She'll think worse of me than she already does. I expect she'll attack me with the handiest object that can inflict a mortal wound. And she'll be devastated, her heart will be crushed, and her life will go dark."

"Which is the very reason you must tell her now before you take this deception any further."

"No."

"Then I bloody well will," Ashe said, heading for the door.

Darting in front of him just as he reached for the latch, Edward cut him off. "Touch that door and I'll lay you flat."

Ashe glared at him. "I refuse to let you do this."

"You may be of the higher rank and older, but this matter does not concern you."

Shaking his head, Ashe squared his jaw. "It bloody well does concern us. Locke, inform him that he's a fool and cannot do this."

"Unfortunately, I agree with him."

Clearly stunned, Ashe twisted around. The man whom he'd mistakenly believed to be his ally sat with one hip perched on the edge of the desk, glass of scotch in hand. "You don't think this is a bad idea?"

"I'm convinced it's the worst idea an Englishman has had since one decided to go crusading. But he's correct. It's not our business, and we don't have a say in the matter."

"You might not care about Julia, but I do."

"But if Edward has the right of it and telling her causes her to lose the babe, the last gift Albert will ever bestow upon her, how will you feel then?"

Ashe's shoulders slumping slightly, he stepped back. "I loved Albert like a brother."

"But like a brother is not the same as being a brother," Locke said. "Not to mention neither of us was there when Albert drew his last. We didn't hear his final words nor did we witness the desperation that might have laced them."

Be me, he'd gasped. *Be me.* Edward had never realized how much power two small words, four letters, could hold.

"Do you have to always be so bloody logical?" Ashe asked.

Locke raised his glass. "I wouldn't complain if I were you. My being logical contributed to you gaining your wife."

Shaking his head, Ashe turned his attention back to Edward. "Have you truly thought this through? How far along is she? Somewhere between seven and eight months? You're looking at several weeks of pretending to love Julia when the two of you have never gotten along, when all of London knows you can hardly stand to be in the same room with her," he said, getting to the crux of what he surely believed was the challenge Edward had set for himself.

If only it was that uncomplicated. After that blasted, ill-conceived kiss in the garden years ago, she'd never taken kindly to him, had barely tolerated his presence. Not that he blamed her. During the intervening years, his behavior had been less than exemplary. "I have considered it from every angle."

Balling his hands into fists, Ashe scowled. "I can see nothing but disaster on the horizon if you follow this course."

"Disaster on the horizon I can deal with when it arrives. My concern presently is avoiding disaster *before* the babe arrives. I know it won't be easy—the past ten days have been horrendous, trying to behave around her as Albert would, and I know I've not managed completely because she studies me as though I'm a puzzle with a piece that doesn't quite fit. So far, I believe, Julia has kindly chalked my odd behavior and requests for solitude up to my grief. Yet I know I can't use that excuse much longer, so I need to know what gave me away. How did you deduce it was me and not Albert wandering around today?"

"I don't know that I can help you with this," Ashe said. "Deceit does not sit well with me."

"And you think it sits well with me?" Edward asked, the pain and agony from weeks of deliberation, guilt, and doubt slicing through his voice. "I convinced him to go with me because I selfishly wanted one last trip together. I wanted him to put me before her. And it cost him his life. All I can do now is strive to ensure it doesn't cost him his child. It's all that's left of my brother. I would have given anything to be the one we laid in the vault this afternoon. But that I cannot change. So I am left with only the ability to keep my promise to him. No matter the cost, no matter how mad it seems, I know no other way to ensure Julia does not lose this child. So help me. If you truly loved Albert as you claim, then help me."

With a deep sigh, Ashe walked to the sideboard and poured himself a generous amount of scotch. "We've known you since you were seven. While your looks are identical, your mannerisms are not. You don't rub your right ear."

"Ah, damn, yes." He did so now, pulling on it until it hurt. When he was five, Albert had lost hearing in that ear after Edward shoved him into a frigid pond. Afterward, it pained him from time to time and he would rub it, especially when he was contemplating a matter—usually trying to determine the best way to bring Edward to task for some misconduct.

"And you toss back far too much scotch, far too quickly," Locke said. "I don't suppose you've stopped doing that."

"No, but I only do it after she's gone to bed."

Ashe narrowed his eyes. "You don't go to bed with her?"

"God, why would I? I'm certainly not going to cuckold my brother even if he is dead."

"I can't speak for Albert, but whether or not I make love to my wife, I sleep with her nestled within my arms."

"Because you're disgustingly in love."

"So was he."

Edward shook his head. "They have separate bedchambers. I'm safe there."

Ashe tilted his head. "So do we."

With a harsh curse, Edward filled his glass to the brim with more scotch, walked over to the seating area by the fire and dropped into a comfortable chair. Surely, Julia would have said something if he was supposed to be in her bed. Unless she was crediting his absence as a need to grieve alone. How long before his odd behaviors caused her to worry, added strain to the situation, burdened her until he caused to happen exactly what he was trying to prevent?

Ashe and Locke joined him, taking nearby chairs. Neither appeared pleased to be there but at least they were no longer looking at him as though he were as mad as the Marquess of Marsden.

He stared into the writhing flames of the fire, imagined his eternity would be spent thrashing about in the ones ignited in Hell. "I thought about staying in Africa, sending her a telegram with an excuse for our delay, but I knew Albert would haunt me if I left her alone as her time carrying his child neared an end. I'm well versed in the dead haunting the living."

"My mother's ghost screeching over the moors is nothing but my father's madness," Locke said.

"Still, I grew up with it." Edward glanced over at the two men who had been like brothers. "Do you know if Albert had a special endearment for Julia?"

Both men blinked, looked at each other, seemed at a loss for words. Finally, Ashe said, "He's the sort who would have had one, but I never heard him call her anything other than Julia."

"Neither did I," Locke admitted. "It was probably saved for intimate moments."

Bloody hell. He'd had such confidence that he could adequately imitate his brother, but they were unveiling countless things he never considered. For the short term, he'd succeeded. For the long term, it was going to require more awareness and effort. "I haven't sorted through his things. Merely packed them up." He'd had both his trunk and Albert's placed in the bedchamber that had been his when he visited. To be gone through later. "Perhaps I'll find a letter he penned that can provide some answers." A letter possibly unfinished that would tear at his gut. Death left much undone.

"Have you contemplated," Ashe began slowly, tapping his finger against his half-empty glass, "that you are going to have to abstain completely from any sexual encounters? Considering your past and your appetites, that's going to create quite the challenge, which I honestly don't know if you're up to meeting. But should she hear of you fornicating about, thinking it was Albert being unfaithful to her, *that* could very well cause her to lose the babe."

"I considered that and I plan to be as chaste as a monk." He released a self-deprecating laugh. "It might not be as hard as you imagine. None of my previous conquests were here today. And some of them were ladies." He'd noticed their absence, along with the absence of tears. Not a single one shed for Edward. Christ, attending one's own funeral was an incredibly humbling experience.

"Edward—"

"Greyling," Edward said, cutting off Locke. "If my ruse is to have any chance at all of succeeding, you must both acknowledge me as the Earl of Greyling, call me either Greyling or Grey, as you did Albert when it wasn't only us about. Except now you must do it even when we're alone. Lest you slip when we're not." And he needed to stop thinking of himself as Edward. In manner, thought, and deed, he had to become the Earl of Greyling. At least until Julia delivered the heir.

Then he would be obliged to do what he did best: give her another reason to hate him by revealing the truth, breaking her heart, and shattering her world.

Chapter 2

*I*N death, it seemed Edward Alcott was accomplishing what he'd not been able to in life: He was causing Julia to lose Albert. Since his return, Albert seemed to welcome any excuse not to be in her company. She despised that she was experiencing petty jealousy toward a dead man because all of her husband's focus was on him, that she'd begun to doubt herself and question her husband's love for her.

She rather wished now that she hadn't encouraged him to go, to take one last trip with Edward, but she knew how much he'd enjoyed traveling before she came into his life. Bless him, he'd always sensed how much she worried that something awful might happen while he was away, so he'd curtailed his exploits, which had created a fissure between the brothers. She'd thought the trip would do them all a world of good, might make Edward more accepting of her. It was no secret among the aristocracy that they didn't quite approve of each other. It saddened her that they'd not been on good terms when he parted this earth.

Suddenly she became aware of a hand closing around hers on her lap and squeezing.

"Where have your thoughts gone?" Minerva asked.

Tea had been prepared and brought to them, but it had grown cold with neither of them touching it. "My apologies. I'm being an awful hostess."

"Posh. Under the circumstances, you shouldn't feel as though you need to be a hostess at all. You looked so sad just then. I think it's more than the funeral or Edward's death that's troubling you. I'm here to listen if you want to talk."

It seemed at once a betrayal and a weakness to voice her doubts, but perhaps another's perspective could shed some light. "Albert's not been quite himself since he returned."

"No doubt grief taking its toll," Minerva assured her.

"That's what I've been telling myself. But he's been so distant, offering and accepting no affection whatsoever. And that is so unlike him. Although I'm a beastly woman for finding fault with his lack of attention during a time such as this." But how could they console each other when he took all his meals in his room, had yet to visit her bed?

"You're not at all beastly, but I do doubt he's in an amorous mood, considering the circumstances."

"I don't expect him to make love to me. I know I'm hardly attractive in this condition, swollen with child as I am, and as you say, he is distracted, but a gentle kiss would be welcomed." Even a smile, a soft touch, a reassurance that he still cared for her. After months of being separated, when he'd finally arrived home he just stood there staring at her as though he hardly recognized her. She was the one who had wrapped her arms around him, the one who had squeezed. His only words had been, "I'm sorry."

Then he'd marched into the residence as though that were enough.

"Have patience," Minerva suggested. "The brothers were extremely close."

"I know they were. But we were separated for four months. It was supposed to be only three; however Edward's death delayed Albert's return. Not that I'd realized Edward was dead. The telegram Albert sent merely read, 'Delayed. Return as soon as possible.' It wasn't until he arrived in a wagon bearing a wooden box that I learned the truth. That in itself was odd—not sharing his burdens."

"He probably didn't want to worry you, not in your delicate condition."

"Yet I want to be there for him. We've always had the sort of marriage where our joys were doubled and our burdens halved. But that's merely a small indication of how he changed while he was away. During this week, I've had moments where I felt as though I don't even know him at all any longer. Which is ludicrous. He's my Albert."

"Which, my dear, is what you must focus on. He no doubt feels as though he lost half himself in those jungles. The twins, I know, seemed to have a special bond, an attachment far more intimate and stronger than that found between other siblings."

"I know you're right. I just feel as though he's keeping me at a distance."

"Men are odd that way, striving to never show any weakness. I suspect he fears needing you and so he pretends he doesn't. The very last thing he needs is for you to be pushy. It'll just make him dig in his heels. Men are stubborn that way. Patience is all you require. He'll come 'round."

She hoped so, as she truly didn't like this . . . oddness in their relationship. Made her feel out of sorts.

"How are you feeling with the babe?"

Welcoming the change in topic, Julia couldn't stop herself from smiling as she folded her hands on her belly. "Wonderful. Happy about my condition in spite of the sadness over Edward's passing. I do believe this one is going to stay around to play in the nursery." She glanced at the clock on the mantel. "I think we've given the gentlemen enough time with their scotch. Shall we join them?"

As she and Minerva strolled into the library, the gentlemen stood, the somberness about them as they sat remaining with them, maybe even closing more tightly around them.

"Our apologies for being gone so long," Albert said. "We got caught up in reminiscing. Time got away from us."

"We thought as much," Julia said. "Dinner will be served shortly. Perhaps we might all like to take a moment to freshen up before."

"Splendid notion," he said, then tossed back the amber liquid that remained in his glass. With a grimace, he clenched his jaw, gave his head a barely perceptible shake. It occurred to Julia that Albert never seemed to relish spirits with the enthusiasm of his brother.

Setting his glass aside, he joined her, offered his arm, and she inhaled his familiar tangy bergamot scent. They left the room in silence, with the others following behind just as solemnly. Because the duke and viscount were more family than friends, Julia had arranged for their bedchambers to be in the family wing, just down the hall from the master suite.

As they reached her door, she turned to her guests. "Shall we plan on meeting back in the library in half an hour?"

"That should be sufficient time," Minerva said. "It's not as though we'll be changing out of our crepe."

No. Julia would give Edward the full six months of mourning due him as her husband's brother. She would go into labor wearing black.

"Grey," Ashebury said with a nod to Albert, before nudging his wife down the hallway.

"Thank you, Julia, for everything," Locksley offered quietly before heading to his room.

Albert opened the door to her bedchamber and followed her in. It was the first time he'd been in the room since his return. She didn't know why her stomach fluttered with the thought.

Glancing around, his gaze seeming to dart past the four-poster bed, he walked over to the window, looked out on the dark clouds gathering in the distance. It was a cold, dreary day but at least the rain had held off. "I've not had a chance to thank you for everything you did for . . . my brother. The service you arranged was lovely. You went to a great deal of bother to give him a nice send-off."

Cautiously, she approached, stopping just shy of touching him. Quite honestly, he looked as though he could easily shatter. "I'm sorry more people didn't come." She'd been appalled that so few of the nobility had attended the service. If not for the servants whom she'd required to attend, the church would have been embarrassingly near empty. "I think with the distance and the storm threatening—"

"I think Edward wasn't as well-liked as he thought."

"We received many letters of condolence. I placed them in a black box and put it on your desk, so you can read them at your leisure. I think you'll draw comfort from them." He'd been too sorrow-filled, lost in his grief, to pay much attention to correspondence, so she'd seen to it for him.

"I'm certain I will." He shifted his gaze to hers, and as always she found herself falling into the dark depths. "You're very thoughtful."

"You say that as though you're surprised."

He gave his head a quick shake and looked back out the window. "No, I just . . . I can't seem to regain my footing with my brother gone."

"You will." She rubbed his upper arm. "You will. But speaking of footing, I must sit down. My feet are killing me."

He swung around. "You're in pain? Why didn't you say something?"

"It's only my feet. They've begun swelling of late. I just need to put them up—Albert!"

He'd swept her up into his arms as though she weighed no more than a feather pillow, as though she wasn't this ungainly creature. Then he was glancing around as though he didn't know quite what to do with her now that he had her. Her heart was hammering, her fingers clutching his shoulders. He'd not carried her since their wedding night, and when he'd set her on the bed—

She warmed with the memories of their coming to-gether as man and wife. Surely, they were not now on the verge of engaging in frenzied lovemaking.

In long, sure strides he headed to the bed and placed her on it as gently as though she were hand-blown glass. With a swiftness to his actions that she'd not seen since he left for his trip, he shoved pillows behind her back. "Are you comfortable?"

"Yes, but a chair would have sufficed."

"Where's your button hook?"

"Top left drawer of the dressing table, but if I remove my shoes I won't be able to get them back on for dinner."

"You can go barefoot. No." He gave his head an-other shake, began walking away. "You're not going to dinner. I'll have a tray brought to you here."

"I can't ignore our guests."

Coming to an abrupt halt at the foot of the bed, he glowered at her. "They're not guests, they're family. They'll understand or they'll damned well answer to me."

She couldn't stop herself from staring at this man, her husband, unable to recall a single time when he'd been so forceful. She couldn't quite fathom why she found his behavior—him—so appealing at that moment. She'd always been attracted to him, but this was something more. He always deferred to Ashebury, for instance, had never stood up to him. Not that he'd had a reason to, but still.

Sighing, he plowed his hand through his hair before taking a step nearer and wrapping his long, thick fin-gers around the bedpost. "We don't want to risk you losing the babe."

Regretfully, she nodded. "I am rather weary. It's been an exhausting few days. Still, I shall feel like such a terrible hostess."

"I imagine they'll enjoy having a bit of time to visit without my morose presence."

His words startled her. "You're not going to join them?"

"I'm not going to leave you here to dine alone after the trying day you've had, not when you're experiencing discomfort that came about because of my brother's actions."

"I'll be fine."

"Fine isn't good enough."

For a moment she thought he was blushing before he turned away.

"Let's get those shoes off," he said.

She watched as he strode to her dressing table, shrugging out of his jacket as he went and tossing it onto a nearby chair. With his jacket gone, she could see clearly that during his few months away, his shoulders had broadened and his skin had become bronzed by the harsh African sun. She was taken aback that at a time such as this, she should feel such a magnetic pull toward him. How selfish she'd been earlier to want his attentions when he was giving her far more now than she'd expected. She wanted things between them to be as though he'd never left, but she realized that the usual ease they experienced with each other might be slow in coming. However, she had to believe it would return.

He sat on the edge of the mattress and skillfully used the hook to loosen the buttons on one shoe and then the other. Setting the hook aside, he gently tugged off her left shoe. She grimaced with the discomfort, then sighed with relief as her toes were free to wiggle about.

"My God," he said.

"I know. They're hideously swollen. I fear my ankles rather look as though they belong on an elephant."

"You should have said something sooner," he chastised, slowly easing her other foot out of the shoe.

"Don't be cross."

"I'm not cross," he said, refusing to take his gaze from the trunks that were her ankles. "I'm worried about you, Julia."

"The swelling is to be expected. I don't think I'm in any danger of losing the babe."

He nodded toward the side. "Pass me one of the pillows you're not using."

With extreme tenderness, he placed it beneath her feet. "Need to get a bit of blood flowing, I think," he said.

He placed both hands around her ankle, slid them up beneath her skirt and over her knee until he reached the tie of her stocking. Her breath caught and held as she waited. Having his fingers so near the apex of her womanhood was sweet torture. He slowly loosened the ribbons, then even more slowly rolled the silk down past her toes and set it aside. His hands journeyed up her other leg, and she nearly melted on the spot. It was ridiculous how desperately she wanted his hands on her. When the other stocking was cast aside, he returned his attention to her first leg and began kneading her calf. His hand glided up to the back of her knee, his fingers massaging there for a moment before beginning the journey back toward her ankle. "Tell me if I hurt you."

"It feels lovely." The skin on his palms and fingers felt coarser, not as smooth as it had been before his journey. She imagined he'd gone a good deal of the time without gloves. If he had worn them, his hands wouldn't be so tanned now. "I may find myself grateful for the swelling. You've never rubbed my feet before."

He stilled a fraction of a heartbeat before continuing the fluid, soothing motions, offering her an apologetic smile. "What a cad I am."

She laughed lightly at his teasing. She'd missed it. Missed this. Simply being with him, no expectations, no burdens. "You also never used profanity in my presence."

"It seems Edward's bad habits became mine during our travels."

"You must have seen some amazing sights."

Moving his hands to her other ankle he nodded. "We did."

"I wish I could have journeyed with you."

"You wouldn't have much liked it when Edward broke an egg into your shoe and insisted you walk about with the muck in there."

"Are you joshing?"

He lifted his eyes to hers, and for the first time she saw no sadness, and she was filled with hope that perhaps the mourning would not last the remainder of his life. "Prevents blisters."

"How did he know that?"

He shrugged. "Read it somewhere. He was always reading, trying to ensure our journeys were as comfortable as possible."

"You had a good time when you were with him."

"I did. It was the best . . . until it wasn't."

She wanted to give him a bit of cheer during this dark time. "I thought we might name our son after him."

His gaze went to her belly, then he looked away. "No. We'll not name the Greyling heir after such a selfish bastard. He's to be named after his father, as he should be."

She didn't know what to say to his harsh words regarding Edward. He'd never shown any anger toward his brother. Not when Edward stumbled into their residence three sheets in the wind. Not when he held out a hand for more money because he'd frittered away his allowance. Not when large men knocked at their door because he had amassed large gambling debts. Albert indulged his brother, seemed to think his irresponsible lifestyle was harmless enough. He'd never had a bad word for Edward. Until now. It was so unlike him.

She could sense him withdrawing into himself. She didn't want to lose him, not again. As he continued massaging, his hands periodically disappearing beneath her skirt, a little bit of naughtiness took hold of her. "You are my husband. It is perfectly acceptable for you to lift my skirt over my knees."

"I don't need the temptation."

As inappropriate as it was during this time of mourning, she couldn't help but feel a little thrill. "Are you tempted?"

"A man is always tempted when a lady reveals her ankles."

"Then I'm nothing special."

His hands stopped, his eyes captured hers. "I did not mean that. Other ladies no longer tempt me."

She smiled softly. "I know. I was merely teasing, striving to make you laugh, relieve your burden for a bit."

"Eventually, we will laugh again. Just not today." He patted her ankles and stood. "I should let the others know we won't be joining them for dinner."

"My feet aren't as swollen. If I sit with them resting on a little stool—"

"No, it'll be better if we dine alone. I won't be long."

He snatched up his jacket before leaving her room. With a sigh, she sat back farther into the pillows and wiggled her toes. *If we dine alone.* His wording did not escape her. Now that Edward was laid to rest, perhaps her husband would finally return to her.

SHE had the tiniest toes. Even with feet and ankles swollen, it was obvious that her toes were small and delicate. Why the bloody hell should he find them so intriguing?

As he strode into the library, he was grateful to find no one was yet waiting on him. He crossed to the side table, poured himself an unhealthy amount of scotch and tossed it back. He had to take care with his words, had to ensure he gave her no cause to doubt Greyling's devotion to her. He couldn't mention other ladies' ankles or thighs or lovely attributes. He could give no indication that he remained a man who found other women attractive. Although at that moment he couldn't think of a single woman other than Julia who appealed to him. Still, he needed to tamp down all natural urges, in order not to find himself taking advantage of this situation. He quickly drank another tumbler of scotch.

Even the urge to drink to excess had to be curbed. He could get by with it for a couple of days, chalking it up to grief, but he doubted Julia had ever seen Albert deep into his cups. And if he himself were drunk, he could very well make a ghastly mistake and reveal who he was. Although it was likely that could happen if he was sober.

He wandered to the desk and grazed his finger over the shiny ebony box. He'd noticed it earlier but assumed it always sat on his brother's desk. In the past, he'd often visited his brother at the estate, but never really lived within the residence, especially after Albert married Julia. The manor had been closed up when their parents died, so when Albert reached his majority, he'd come to Evermore, hired new staff, and opened the place back up. Edward knew a few by name, but most he couldn't have cared less about. Knowing Albert, he'd probably known them all. God, he'd stepped into a quagmire. He was going to have to tread so very carefully.

He returned to the table, reached for the decanter, paused with his fingers wrapped around the delicate crystal—

With a harsh curse, he picked it up and slung it against the wall, taking no satisfaction when it shattered into shards and sent amber liquid raining down along the dark paneling.

"Not so easy being your brother?"

With another harsh curse, Edward spun around to face Locke, grateful it wasn't Ashe standing there with his wife. He almost blurted that Julia had tiny toes, as though Locke would give a fig. "She's exhausted; we won't be joining you for dinner."

"You're afraid we'll slip up."

He plowed his hand through his hair. "More afraid I will."

"Tug on your ear," Locke said as he casually strolled nearer. "When you reach for your hair, tug on your ear."

"Right." He did so now, knowing it was too late. Albert tugged before he spoke, not after.

Locke planted his hip on the edge of the desk. "I suspect she's stronger than you give her credit for."

But she had the tiniest, most delicate toes. And such silken skin. Whatever had he been thinking to skim his fingers over her calves, across the backs of her knees? "Can't risk it. The babe is all that remains of my brother."

He couldn't explain the hole that now resided within him, the place where Albert had been. He needed this child to survive as much as Albert had wished that it would.

"I was a babe when my mother died," Locke said quietly. "I grew up with a father who perpetually mourned her loss. Nothing replaces such a loss."

"I'm not expecting the child to be a substitute, but I owe Albert this small sacrifice. My mind's made up, and while you're very skilled at laying out your arguments, on this matter, nothing will sway me."

Locke glanced over at the mess left by the hurled decanter. "You might want to reel back your temper a notch."

Edward chuckled harshly. "More than a notch, I'd say." Albert never displayed a temper.

Hearing footsteps, he glanced toward the doorway in time to see the duke and his duchess enter. Locke was halfway correct about Edward's reasons for not joining them for dinner. He feared the duchess would figure him out. She was too sharp by half.

"The affairs of the past few days have worn Julia out," he told them. "She and I will not be joining you for dinner."

"I assume she'll have a tray in her bedchamber," the duchess said. "Perhaps it would be best if I joined her there, gave you gents a little more time to catch up."

He tugged on his ear. "I appreciate the offer, but I think we've caught up all that we need to. I left my wife alone for far too many weeks. I intend to make that up to her now. We'll see you at breakfast."

He caught a spark of approval in Ashe's eyes; not that he was seeking approval, but apparently he'd managed to conduct himself more as his brother might. Now if he could just do the same without stumbling through the maze that had been Albert's life with his countess.

Chapter 3

Julia's feet were feeling so much better. Albert's massage had done wonders. It had also helped that once he left, she called for her maid and changed from the stiff black crepe into her softest nightdress and wrap. Although she enjoyed visiting with their guests, she welcomed the opportunity to simply relax with her husband.

Sitting in a plush chair near the fire, she set her feet on a low stool and curled her toes. Unfurled them, thought of the callused hands that had stroked her with such surety, as though he'd rubbed her feet a thousand times before, when he'd never once performed that intimate and luxurious service for her. She imagined those abraded hands skimming over all of her, how marvelous the different textures would feel, what a very different experience it might be. She rather hoped they wouldn't go completely soft before they made love again.

Hearing the click of the door opening, she looked over to see her husband stride in with two wineglasses dangling between the fingers of one hand and two wine bottles caught in the other. He staggered to a stop and stared at her, his gaze running the length of her as though he'd never before seen her in a nightdress and wrap. Perhaps it was simply that her condition was not as disguised as when she wore a dress. Self-consciously she tugged on the sides of her wrap, trying to close it over her belly and breasts, but it refused to cooperate. "I've become huge while you were away."

"No, not at all." With his elbow, he closed the door before bringing the wine and glasses over and setting them on the small table before the sofa. She could see now that one was a bottle of red, the other white. "Our guests were completely understanding, and the servants should be bringing our dinner any moment now. I thought we might enjoy a spot of wine while we waited."

"I'm not convinced spirits are good for the babe."

He suddenly looked incredibly uncomfortable, as though he'd forgotten about her condition. "You're absolutely right. Not certain what I was thinking."

"No reason you can't indulge."

He wasted no time pouring red into a glass, lifting it toward her in a salute before taking a sip and walking to the fireplace. He looked at the fire, darted a quick glance to her, and returned his gaze to the fire as though not quite sure what to do with his eyes. "How are your feet?"

"Much better. It helped I think to change into something not quite so confining. Since it was to be only the two of us here, I didn't think formality was required."

"Of course it's not."

Shoving herself to her feet, she was grateful the

swelling had dissipated completely and she was able to glide toward him without any limping or discomfort. She couldn't be completely certain, but it appeared he'd ceased breathing as she neared. "You should be as comfortable," she murmured, taking his glass from that marvelous hand that had touched her so intimately and placing the wineglass on the mantel.

Slipping her hands beneath the opening of his unbuttoned jacket, she glided them over his shoulders, tugging off his coat. "You've broadened a bit while you were away."

"Trekking through the wilds is strenuous work."

The jacket began to fall. She caught it before it hit the floor and tossed it onto the nearest chair. Slowly, she freed the buttons of his black waistcoat. "Your skin is darker."

"The African sun is harsh."

She lifted her gaze to his. "I could always tell you and Edward apart because he wasn't nearly as fair as you. Did you blister when you arrived?"

"No."

She eased off the waistcoat, pitched it onto the jacket. Lowering her gaze, she began unknotting his neck cloth.

"Julia, I'm not certain this is wise."

She gave him a speculative look. "To be comfortable?"

"To tempt me."

A thrill shot through her. Yes, they were in mourning, yes, sorrow radiated from him, but she still had power over him. She flung the neck cloth aside and cupped his face between her hands, her fingers dancing along the back of his neck. "I missed you so much."

She tilted his head down, rose up on her toes and planted her mouth on his. His arm snaked around her, drew her nearer. His tongue slid between her lips as he adjusted the angle and took the kiss deeper. She fairly melted against him.

Hunger. Urgency. A compelling need. They were all there. In him. In her. As though death hovered nearby, waiting, as though with enough passion and desire they could ward it off. A low growl vibrated through his chest, shimmered through her breasts, which were flattened against the linen of his shirt.

The heat between them intensified. His hands traveled over her back, her hips, cupped her backside, pressed her ever closer. The hard rigid length of him pushed against her belly, driving her mad with want and desire. It had been so long, too long. Once they knew she was with child, he'd insisted they refrain from any intimacy for fear his ardor might cause her to lose the child. Oh, he'd kissed her, held her, stroked her on occasion, but not like this. Not with this fierce need. She wasn't certain what they'd shared had ever been as primal as this—as though he'd returned from his travels uncivilized, in need of taming.

A knock on the door had him lurching back as though he'd been caught doing something he shouldn't. They were both breathing rapidly, heavily. Horror was reflected in his eyes.

"My apologies," he rasped.

Disappointment slammed into her because he was retreating, was regretting what had just passed between them. "None is needed. You're my husband."

"But the babe." His gaze dipped to her belly. "Did I hurt the babe?"

"Your son is a bit stronger than that." Still, she took a step back as well and bade the servant to enter.

More than one came in carrying trays bearing an assortment of covered dishes. Julia sat as a maid set a tray in her lap. Albert had retreated back to the fireplace, was gulping his wine with vigor while a young maid set his tray on the low table.

"Will there be anything else, m'lord?" the first maid asked.

Staring at the fire, Albert merely took another swallow of wine.

"No, that'll be all," Julia said.

The servants left, closing the door in their wake. Her husband stayed as he was.

"Albert?" He seemed lost. "Albert," she said more sharply.

He finally jerked his head toward her, his brow furrowed so deeply it had to be painful.

"Sit, eat," she told him.

"Are you certain I didn't hurt you?"

"It was quite lovely actually. It's been so long. I was beginning to fear you hadn't missed me as much as I missed you."

"Trust me. Not a night went by that I didn't drift off to sleep without thoughts of you."

"I'm selfishly glad to hear that. Were you tormented by those thoughts?"

"In ways you cannot possibly comprehend."

She was being beastly to take such satisfaction in knowing thoughts of her had plagued him, but it was so incredibly satisfying. She smiled softly. "Let's eat, shall we?"

He gathered up the clothes she'd strewn over the chair, took them to the bench at the dressing table and then dropped into the chair that put him the length of the short table away from her. She had hoped he would sit on the sofa, on the corner nearest to her. Perhaps he hadn't because he feared she'd be a distraction.

She'd feel a bit better about things if she had the sense that he welcomed the distraction. Instead she was left with the awareness that he regretted it.

*T*HANK *God for the knock on the door.* That was all that ran through Edward's mind. *Thank God, thank God, for the knock on the door.*

He'd been on the verge of lifting her into his arms and carrying her to the bed. For the first time since his return he hadn't been consumed with guilt, buried in grief. Instead, he'd been lost in passion, desire such as he'd never known. Her fragrance, her heat, her softness. It didn't matter that it would have been the worst possible thing he could have done. For a moment she'd served as a blessed distraction. The fire in her kiss—

Good Lord. Where the devil had that come from? Certainly there had been a spark that night in the garden, but what he just experienced had fairly consumed him. Maturity and knowledge gained had replaced innocence and naiveté. A lethal combination that could send his good intentions to perdition.

With an unsteady hand, he reached for the wine, began pouring, saw her arch a delicate brow, and refrained from refilling his glass to the top. Being alone with her in a bedchamber was proving to be incredibly dangerous to his ruse. But how to avoid it? He had to recall that she held no affection whatsoever for Edward, that the kindness she was showing him, the temptations she offered, were merely offered because she believed he was Albert.

This was Julia—who had kicked him out of his brother's London residence because he arrived home in the early hours in an inebriated state that she didn't fancy. Julia—who had encouraged Albert to reduce Edward's allowance so he couldn't indulge to his heart's content in wine, women, and wagering. Julia—who always looked at him as though he were something she'd recently scraped off the bottom of her shoe.

Julia—who had arranged an elaborate and elegant funeral for a man she couldn't tolerate. Who had seen to a few guests without complaint even though it had exhausted her. Who had kissed him as though no one in the world were more important to her. Who had initiated the kiss. He'd never had a woman do that before. It was incredibly intoxicating.

If she had hated him after the encounter in the garden, she was going to hate him doubly so when she learned the truth and recalled this kiss. He had to avoid his lips coming within a hairbreadth of hers, lest he forget again that he was not the one she loved, the one she desired, the one with whom she'd exchanged vows.

Looking down at his plate, he bit back a curse. Garnished fish. Of course, on a day like today, the cook would have prepared Albert's favorite. Edward had never developed a taste for it. He preferred his meat red and bloody.

"What were you reminiscing?"

He jerked his head up, saw Julia studying him as though once again beginning to have doubts about him. "Pardon?"

"In the library. You said that you and the others were reminiscing. About Edward, I assume. Did it help to recall happier times?"

It might have, he thought, if that had indeed been what they were discussing. While he hoped to minimize his lies to her, he couldn't eliminate all the little white ones. "A little."

"Share something with me."

If I could sip on your mouth whenever I wanted, I could do without wine. "Such as?"

"Something about Edward. A pleasant memory. We never really spoke much about him except when you expressed your worry that he would come to an untimely and unpleasant end, or when I lost patience with his . . . questionable activities."

Albert had worried over him? He knew his brother had not been happy with the way he led his life, but he hadn't known he actually worried over him. Whenever Albert had taken him to task, he'd simply viewed it as an older brother being disappointed or needing to control a younger one. Yet, he'd promised Albert if he took the journey to Africa with him, that when they returned he would settle down, marry, and seek a position in Parliament. He hated that he couldn't be certain it was a promise he would have kept. He would have said anything to get Albert to go with him. That truth pained him now: that he might not have been completely honest with the one person who had always been absolutely forthright with him.

She was waiting expectantly for him to tell her something about a man she disliked, and for the first time that he could recall, he wanted her to have a favorable impression of him. "Edward didn't like being the second son."

"I suspect most second sons don't," she said gently, no disapproval in her tone.

Before he left on his trip with Albert, she'd only ever spoken to Edward with disapproval threaded through her words. He didn't like that he now enjoyed the soft tenor of her voice, that he was suddenly finding it very easy on the ears. "Ironically, though, he had no desire whatsoever to be earl."

"Too much work," she said with a smile.

He found himself returning it, only a slight lift of one corner, but it was more than he'd ever thought he would experience again. "Exactly. You knew him very well."

"Not really. I regret that now. But we digress. Something pleasant."

Something pleasant. The fish definitely didn't fit that category, and while he'd only managed a few bites without gagging, he set his plate aside and snatched up his wineglass while he still had an excuse for indulging. "At first we didn't like living at Havisham Hall. It didn't take us long to determine that something wasn't quite right. None of the clocks worked, not a single one ticked. The manor was as large as Evermore, but there were only half a dozen servants. We were forbidden from entering a good part of the manor, many of the rooms locked. So Edward began plotting our first expedition." He smiled at the memory, the seriousness of it. In this story at least he would be himself.

"You told me once that the marquess had stopped all the clocks when his wife died."

Edward's smile withered. Damnation. How was he to know what Albert had shared and what he hadn't? Surely she would give an indication if she knew this story. "The marquess stopped a lot of things when his wife died. Living, mostly."

"I can imagine that. I don't know what I would have done had it been you who died in Africa." She shook her head. "I'm sorry. I didn't mean for us to go there. We're at Havisham Hall."

Still, her words merely confirmed that his present course was truly the only one open to him if he wished to honor the vow he'd made to Albert. While he might not have been a man of his word before, he damned well planned to be one now. "I don't know why we got it into our heads that we could go exploring only at midnight. It wasn't as though anyone was truly about during the day to interfere."

"More forbidden at night, after you all were supposed to be abed, I imagine. That's when I would have gone," she said with a tantalizing wicked upturn of her lips.

He fought not to stare. At that tempting luscious mouth and at the sparkle in her eyes that hinted she'd have been right there alongside them, sneaking down dark corridors with only a single candle to light their way. He didn't much like discovering that she was comprised of unexplored facets. He liked even less that he found himself wanting to explore them. He merely wanted to walk in his brother's shoes until his heir was born, walk cautiously forward without taking any side jaunts. Getting to know Julia better had not been part of his plan. Still, he had to acknowledge she had the right of it. "More adventuresome as well when we were in danger of getting caught, as the marquess roamed the hallways at night. I often heard his soft footfalls going past my bedchamber door, so the thrill of escaping back to our beds unscathed was a driving force," he admitted.

Her smile blossomed into something that caused a tightening in his chest. "And did you?" she prodded.

"Do you want me to spoil the story by giving you the ending to our adventure?"

She reduced her smile a fraction. "Now you sound like Edward with his obsession for storytelling."

Damnation. He'd slipped. He'd always enjoyed weaving tales. Albert always preferred a more direct approach, never taking the time to enhance the narrative.

"He was always so good at it," she continued.

He blinked, wondering if he'd heard correctly. "I didn't think you noticed."

"I loved listening to his stories. It's the reason that I always held a dinner party when Edward and the others returned from one of their adventures. I knew he would never bother to share his exploits with me, but he would weave a mesmerizing tale for others, for an audience. It didn't hamper his storytelling to know I was in the back of the room, although I tried not to let on how much I was enjoying it, lest he decline the next time I invited him."

"I didn't know." He'd assumed she'd always done it for the attention it brought to her. The Countess of Greyling managing to provide London Society with a night of entertainment courtesy of the Hellions of Havisham—as the four of them were often called.

She lifted a delicate shoulder. "I have a few secrets."

He found himself wanting to uncover every one, although he suspected for the most part they were innocent, trivial, while the one he now held from her was horrendous. "He thought you had no interest in his trips. If you had merely asked—"

"He'd have said no. You know he would have. Edward had no wish to please me, to please anyone other than himself. It inflated his self-esteem to have an audience, and so I provided it. And in return, I got a little something for myself. Hearing about the adventures."

She was wrong. Had she asked, he would have woven the tales for her, just for her. How was it that they managed not to know each other at all, when Albert had been so important to both of them?

"Now finish sharing your memory," she prodded, interrupting his thoughts.

"If I tell it like Edward might have, well, it's only because I had two months of listening to him prattle on. He does like hearing the sound of his own voice."

She laughed lightly. "That was always obvious. He was never lacking in confidence."

Her tinkling laugh served to lift a fraction of the pall of sorrow that had enveloped him with Albert's death. How odd that it was she, rather than Ashe or Locke, who would provide a spark of hope that a time would come when he wouldn't feel as though he'd gone into the vault with his brother. He wished he could tell her the truth now, wished they could share their memories of Albert.

"Arrogance, more like," he offered. "He never doubted that we could break undetected into the large salon."

"That was your first expedition?"

"Yes. He drew up a plan of the residence and our route—not a direct one, of course. That would be too boring. It included lots of twists and turns. He'd managed to sneak into the housekeeper's room after she'd gone to sleep and nicked her keys. He led the way with a candle. We were terrified."

"But you saw it through."

"We did. The walls were mirrored. Ashe squeaked like a mouse that had been trapped by a cat when he caught sight of his reflection. It was eerie. Chandeliers and candelabras unlit, serving as anchors for cobwebs. No light except for the solitary candle. There were dead flowers in vases. Dust covered everything. Musty odor was thick on the air. I don't think anyone had been inside the room in years. That's what we discovered on each of our adventures: a room abandoned, no longer used. But we got bolder with our explorations, always found something that made us glad we'd ventured forth. I think that's the reason, when we were old enough, that we began exploring the world." He looked toward the fire. "Edward started it all. Had we ever gotten caught, we might not have begun to think we were invincible." He turned his attention back to her. "Still, most of the memories are good ones."

She was studying him again, as though striving to figure him out. "I'm glad you have them."

With a nod, he finished off his wine and stood. "It's late. I'll see to having the servants come clean up the mess so you can retire. I also want to check on our guests."

"Will you come back and sleep with me tonight?" Her eyes held such doubt, and he knew it had cost her to ask. He was also acutely aware that she shouldn't have to plead with him for anything. Albert would grant her anything she desired. He was failing miserably at the task he'd set himself.

He hesitated. "I don't think it's wise with the babe."

"I think we're safe if all we do is hold each other. Until you went on this trip, I'd forgotten how much I disliked sleeping alone."

"Yes, all right." Then, although the words were a lie, he knew he had to say them. "I've missed holding you."

She gave him that smile again, the one that tore a hole in his chest while managing at the same time to make him grateful she bestowed it. Before all was said and done, she was going to be the death of him.

HE was going to sleep with her. But first he needed some scotch. With any luck, Ashe and Locke were still up, they'd join him, and he'd have an excuse for not returning to her bed until he was well and truly foxed.

He caught them and Minerva on his way down the wide sweeping stairs as they were on their way up. "Care to join me for a drink before retiring?"

He'd even welcome the duchess. She had a reputation for favoring spirits, for favoring all things wicked, which was one of the reasons she was an excellent match for Ashe.

"It's been a long day, Grey," Ashe said. "We plan to depart early tomorrow, so I think Minerva and I are better served calling it a night."

"Sleep well, then."

As the couple walked past him, the duchess reached out and placed a comforting hand on his arm. "In taking care of Julia, don't forget to take care of yourself."

He grinned. "I'm about to take care of myself in the library." As soon as the words were out, he knew they were ones that Albert would never speak. Fortunately, Minerva hadn't been familiar enough with Albert to know that. Ashe, however, scowled and shook his head before placing his hand on the small of his wife's back.

"Let's go to bed, sweetheart."

He waited until they disappeared down the hallway to turn his attention to Locke. "Ashe was correct. While Albert and Julia have separate bedchambers, my brother did sleep in his wife's bed. She just mentioned that she missed her husband being there. My following through on that particular habit of his necessitates a drink first. I prefer not to drink alone."

Crossing his arms over his chest, Locke leaned back against the banister. "You're going to go to Julia's bed reeking of whiskey?"

"I was thinking more along the lines of scotch. I need to dull my senses so I don't do something stupid."

"Dulling your senses *is* doing something stupid."

He wanted to slam his fist against a wall. He hated when Locke was right, but he saw no other option.

"She's a woman. If I climb into bed with her, my cock is going to react."

"She'd expect that. You're supposedly her husband."

Plowing both hands through his hair, he hissed a vile curse before admitting, "I don't know how to sleep with her."

Locke stared at him. "Christ, Edward—Grey—you're not a virgin."

"No, but what do I do with my hands?"

"Pardon?"

He splayed his fingers. "Do I cradle her breast? Cup her backside? I don't know what she expects."

Locke shrugged nonchalantly. "Just hold her."

Easier said than done. Albert had never shared the intimate aspects of his relationship with Julia. Wouldn't she be suspicious if he did something his twin had never done, reacted in a way that Albert never had? The intimacy of being beneath the sheets with her, even if his body wasn't joined to hers, made him break out in a sweat. "I'm going to give myself away."

"Don't overthink it. Assume she's in need of comforting, reassurance that nothing changed between her and her husband while they were separated."

"Everything changed. That's the bloody problem." Giving his ear a hard, unforgiving yank, he shifted his gaze toward the foyer that branched into multiple hallways, one that led to the library and solace. With a deep sigh of longing, he turned back toward the bedchambers and, with Locke beside him, began trudging up as though climbing a treacherous and demanding mountain. "Will you be departing early as well tomorrow?" he asked.

"Long journey back to Havisham."

"I haven't even asked after your father," he said as he came to a stop outside his bedchamber door. He'd call for a bath before going to his brother's wife for a long, interminable night.

"He deteriorates a bit more each day," Locke said. "You should come to see him once Julia delivers the babe."

"Are you going to tell him the truth of things?"

He nodded. "I want to ensure that during whatever time remains to him, he's mourning the proper loss. Your secret will be safe. Out on the moors, he has no one to tell."

"Except for the ghost of your mother. I thought I saw her once."

Locke gave him a laconic grin. "Everyone thinks they've seen her. It's just a wisp of fog. Ghosts don't exist."

"Still, I can't help but believe that if I look out toward the mausoleum, I'll catch a glimpse of Albert watching. I don't want to let him down."

"Then tonight hold his widow a bit more tightly than you think you should."

With that bit of advice, his friend turned on his heel and headed toward his bedchamber, leaving Edward to stare after him. In all the days, hours, and minutes since Albert's death, he'd been so consumed with his own guilt for his role in what came to pass that he'd never once thought of Julia in that solemnized term: a widow.

Chapter 4

WITH a low fire simmering on the hearth and one lamp casting a low glow from its place on the bedside table, Julia lay beneath the blankets, her hands clutching them to her chest as she listened to the familiar noises coming from Albert's bedchamber. Was he having a bath prepared? There were so many comings and goings that she didn't see how it could be anything else.

She would have dearly loved to slip out of bed, go into his room, kneel behind him and scrub his back, would have enjoyed feeling the quivering in his chest with his satisfied groan. Eventually she would move on to more interesting aspects of his body. He would kiss her, his nimble fingers working free the buttons on her nightdress. Before long they would be in his bed, with his still-wet body gliding over hers. She loved contemplating the notion of how badly he would want her.

But she couldn't bring herself to do it. Not when she'd never done it before, and there seemed to be this odd strain in their relationship. While she had not expected it to be so, she was experiencing butterflies worse than the ones that had fluttered about on her wedding night. This was Albert. She knew what to expect. Only she didn't. Four long interminable months had passed since he'd been in her bed. If she were honest with herself, she'd forgotten things that she had thought to always remember: the feel of him, the scent of him, the warmth of him.

They weren't quite as comfortable as they'd been with each other before he left. She knew grief was a consideration, the upheaval in their lives created by the death of his twin. Always, Edward was there hovering, so they'd been unable to relax into each other.

Then there were the changes in her, in the shape of her body as well as in the fabric of her being. She could be laughing one moment, weeping the next. Her lady's maid had begun treading lightly around her because she never knew when Julia might lash out. It was unsettling to feel as though sometimes she had little control over herself.

Perhaps the changes in her deserved more credit for this distance between them.

As the minutes stretched out, she began to wish she'd called for a bath, although she'd bathed that morning and washed up before donning her nightdress.

Why was he taking such care in his preparations if they were merely going to sleep? Yet she couldn't deny the little shiver of pleasure that coursed through her at his thoughtfulness. Albert was always thoughtful, sometimes too thoughtful, as though he feared with a misstep that he might lose her love. That was impossible. She would never love another as she loved him. She'd begun to fall for him the moment he'd first waltzed her over the dance floor.

The door separating their bedchambers opened, and the butterflies launched into a frenzied flight moving from her stomach into her chest. She watched as her husband walked into her room, wearing his dressing gown sashed tightly at his waist. He gave her a small smile before striding over to the fireplace, taking the poker, and stirring the logs on the fire.

"Are you cold?" he asked.

She realized he was delaying coming to her. Perhaps he, too, had noticed that things between them weren't all they should be. "I won't be once you're in bed with me."

Setting aside the poker, he came to the bed, his gaze on the lamp. "Do you want the light?"

"No."

He extinguished the flame, and the shadows moved in, dancing in rhythm to the flames cavorting on the hearth. He untied the sash, shrugged out of the dressing gown, and tossed it toward the foot of the bed. At the sight of his bared chest, her mouth went dry, the butterflies fluttered lower, and she cursed herself for not asking that the light remain.

Sliding between the sheets, he settled onto his back. She rolled over to her side, placed her hand on his chest, welcomed the warmth of his skin. "You've never not worn a nightshirt to bed."

Beneath her splayed fingers, he stiffened. "It was unbearably hot in Africa. I became accustomed to sleeping in the nude."

She trailed her fingers up his chest, down to the waistband of his drawers, which she assumed he'd worn out of consideration for her sensibilities. "Perhaps after the babe is born, we'll both sleep in the nude."

Grasping her wandering fingers, he jerked his head to the side. Even with the shadows, she could feel the intensity of his stare. Her cheeks grew warm as she forced a brave smile. "I think it would be lovely."

Bringing her hand to his lips, he kissed her fingertips. The butterflies settled, warmth sluiced through her, tears stung her eyes at the tenderness of his action.

"I know I've not been myself."

"Shh. It's all right," she cooed. "Our being separated was more challenging than either of us expected, I think. I hadn't anticipated being uncomfortable with you when you returned."

"I don't mean to make you feel uncomfortable."

His hand was still curled around hers, holding tightly. The bond was there, it would always be there. "I don't mean to imply you're at fault. It's merely the circumstances and going so long without having you about . . . to be quite honest, I've forgotten things that I never thought to forget. What it's like to be with you. I got rather accustomed to caring only about my own needs, my own wants. I only had to see after myself. Now that you're home, I have to settle back into being a wife. It's not that I mind. I don't feel burdened by it. It's simply that I feel a bit awkward sometimes because I'm not quite sure how to act or what to say."

Rolling onto his side, he pressed his forehead to hers. "I'm sorry that I'm not the man you married."

"You don't have to apologize. Don't you see? We changed somewhat and now we just have to get to know each other again."

Leaning back, he cradled her cheek. "You're so . . .

insightful. I thought I was the only one feeling as though I didn't know you any longer."

Reaching up, she brushed his hair back from his brow. "The only thing that hasn't changed is that I love you beyond all imagining."

He pressed a kiss to her forehead. "You humble me."

Dropping his arms around her, he pulled her into his chest. That broad, wonderful chest. "It's been a long day. What say we sleep for a bit?"

Nodding, she tried not to be bothered that he hadn't confirmed that he loved her. Before, whenever she professed her love for him, he was quick to reassure her that he loved her as well. In retrospect, she dearly wished she'd not encouraged him to take the sojourn with his brother.

THE *baby gorilla peered out through the underbrush.*

"She's adorable. Look at those huge brown eyes. Ladies will fall in love with her."

"Don't get too close."

"We're fine. She's a sweetheart. Look how eagerly she came to me."

"You always had a knack for charming the ladies."

"We should take her back with us. Think of the attention we'd garner. And Julia would adore her."

"I'm not certain that's a good—"

The frightening growl ripped through the dream, jerking him awake as it had every night since Albert's death. He was sitting up, breathing heavily, drenched in sweat. He had no memory of pushing himself up, the remnants of the nightmare causing uncontrollable tremors to ratchet through him.

"Albert?"

"Apologies for disturbing you. Go back to sleep." Tossing back the covers, he lunged out of bed and strode to the fireplace. The flames were low, on the verge of sputtering out. Kneeling, he carefully set a log on the dying embers, added kindling, watched as it sparked. He was cold, so blasted cold, as cold as his brother was now. He needed to get warm, needed his teeth to stop chattering.

He needed the horrendous nightmares to stop. He felt as though he couldn't draw in a breath, as though the oppressive heat of the jungle were suffocating him. Why had they wandered away from camp without their guides? Why did Albert have to be so damned observant and spot the baby gorilla? Why did he have to notice everything? Why hadn't Edward had his rifle at the ready rather than slung uselessly over his shoulder?

"Here, sip on this."

With a great deal of effort, Edward looked over at the small hand extending the glass, lifted his gaze to blue eyes filled with worry and concern. "Where did you get that?"

"Edward's room. It's scotch. It'll help calm you."

How long had he been lost in the aftermath of the dream? And how the devil did she know that she'd find scotch in *Edward's* room? Taking the glass, he downed half the contents in one long swallow, welcoming the burning in his throat as it went down, the heat spreading out through his chest.

"This is the reason you haven't been sleeping with me, isn't it?" she asked.

It wasn't, but still he nodded.

"Were you dreaming of Africa?"

He turned his attention back to the fire. "I can't stop seeing it. That last afternoon. The sunlight dappling through the leaves, the din of insects and wild creatures going about their day. The jungle is seldom quiet. All the minutia of that moment mocks me. I remember it in such vivid detail."

"You haven't told me exactly what happened. Tell me now."

"Julia—"

She placed her hand on his shoulder, gave it a gentle squeeze. "Unburden yourself."

He shouldn't, but it was eating at him.

"We, uh . . ." He cleared his throat. "He, uh . . . It was early afternoon. We'd been trekking through the jungle, stopped to eat, to have a spot of tea. I heard something, went to investigate, rifle in tow. He came along. He spotted it first. He was always so good at that. Spotting things . . . even when we were lads . . ."

His voice trailed off and he became lost in a whirlwind of memories that went back for years. She rubbed her hand in a gentle circle over his shoulder. "What did he spot?"

"A baby gorilla. It was small, with such huge eyes, so damnably cute."

Her fingers flinched, and he knew his use of the word "damnably" had taken her by surprise. He had to remember that Albert never used profanity or vulgar language with her.

"He approached it, knelt on one knee, and began to play with it. I just stood back watching. He looked happy, smiling, chuckling low. He was actually tickling the thing. I was so incredibly glad that we were there, that we'd made the journey together . . . then there was this terrifying . . . roar is the only way to describe it. I could swear the earth trembled. Then this monstrous gorilla swept up my brother and hurled him against a tree as though he were nothing, a scrap of paper lying about. I don't know how many times he slammed him to the ground before I was able to shoot the beast through the back of his skull. But it was too late. My brother was already gone."

She wrapped her arms around his shoulders and squeezed tightly. He was trembling, brought his hand up and dragged it over his mouth. "Oh, Albert, how dreadful. I'm so so sorry. I don't know what else to say."

"There's nothing to say. I think the first blow did it." A lie. But he didn't want her to know the truth of it, not when it was actually her husband who had lain there all broken and dying. "He didn't suffer overmuch. He might not have even known what was happening. It was quick." He took in a shuddering breath. "I should not have shared such a ghastly thing with you in your condition."

"I know you think otherwise because of the babes I lost, but I am not so delicate as all that. You must share everything with me. You mustn't keep it to yourself."

He finished off the scotch, set the glass aside.

"Steadier?" she asked.

Remarkably, he was, and he didn't think it was so much due to the scotch. He forced himself to meet and hold her gaze. "Yes." He was no longer trembling, his teeth no longer chattering. The chill in his bones had faded away. "Thank you for the scotch. It was exactly what I needed."

"I tried to wake you up when you began thrashing about."

He'd been thrashing about? "Did I hurt you?"

Shaking her head, she brushed the damp hair back from his brow. She had such gentle fingers. "No. But it tore at my heart to see you suffering so."

He did not deserve to have her experiencing any sort of mental anguish on his behalf. He didn't deserve her worrying over him. "It might be better if I slept in my bedchamber until the dreams stop."

Yet how could he give up the comfort she offered, here kneeling beside him, rubbing her delicate hand in circles over his shoulders and back. Her bare hand on his skin felt so damned good. He didn't deserve to be touched, didn't deserve to be comforted.

Your husband is dead because of me, he wanted to shout. He had to pretend for a little while longer, had to be stronger than he'd ever been. He wished Albert were here so he could punch him, for old times' sake. He wished he were here so he could tell him about all the confusing emotions rioting within him. *Ever notice how tiny your wife's feet are?*

"God, I miss him," he croaked. "I miss him so damned much."

"I know," she cooed, wrapping herself around him as though she were a cloak to protect him from the harsh elements. "I know."

Only how could she know? Albert had been a part of him, connected to him through tragedy and triumph. And now he was gone. It was as though a sledgehammer had suddenly struck his chest to bring home the reality—

A fluttering at his lower back caught his attention. "What the devil was that?"

Julia unwound herself from around him, took his hand and placed it on the mound of her belly.

"Julia—"

"Shh, wait," she said so softly that he almost didn't hear her over the crackling of the fire.

Then he felt it beneath his palm, a slight undulation, which caused his mind to empty of all thoughts save one: This was yet another moment he was stealing from his brother.

She smiled sublimely. "That's your son."

His brow furrowed. Earlier she'd referred to the child as a son. "How do you know it's a boy?"

"I just know. Women know all manner of things. I also know that this one is going to stay with us. When the nightmares come, just know that very soon you will be holding a new life."

A knot lodged in his throat, his chest tightened to such an extent that he feared he might never again breathe. Bending slightly, he pressed a kiss beside the place where her hand rested over his. He lifted his gaze to hers. "No matter what happens, Julia, no matter how much you may find me changed, know that there is nothing in this world that I want more than I want this child to be born healthy and strong. There is nothing I want more than for you and him to be well and happy."

As he laid his cheek against her, felt her fingers combing gently through his hair, it occurred to him that never in his life had he spoken truer words.

𝓔DWARD awoke with the realization that his cock obviously cared not one whit whose luscious backside it was pressed against, or how inappropriate it was to be nudging a woman he should never desire.

When they returned to the bed in the early hours of the morning, his arms went around her and he wanted her near, wanted to offer comfort to her as she had offered it to him. Not that she was aware she was in need of comfort, but she would be eventually. Perhaps if he were tender now, she would be more willing to accept his condolences later.

He'd been able to ward off any recurring nightmares by focusing on how soft and pliable she felt in his arms. Her rosewater fragrance. Whenever the image of her naked in the bed had danced through his mind, he shoved it aside, although it kept teasing him from a distance. She was his brother's wife. He'd failed miserably, striving to recall any one of the countless other women he'd been with over the years, and his last thought before drifting off had been of Julia's small feet cupped in his large hands.

He'd betrayed Albert in the garden that long ago night. He certainly wasn't going to betray his trust in death. He was merely going to carry through on his promise and then be done with her.

Lifting up slightly, he gazed down on her profile. She looked so innocent in sleep, with one hand curled on the pillow, the fingers of her other hand interlaced with his and resting just below her breasts. He could feel the movements of her soft breaths. He had an insane urge to lean over farther and press a kiss to her slightly parted lips.

Last night she'd nearly brought him to his knees with her kindness. He'd not expected that, had been unprepared for it. He was going to have to remain ever vigilant lest he become so comfortable around her that he revealed his true self, gave himself away.

Her eyes fluttered open and he stared into the depths of a vast ocean in which he could easily drown. "Morning," she said softly.

He wanted to draw her in closer, stay with her for the remainder of the day. Instead, he cleared his throat. "I should probably check on our guests."

"Probably. I'll be down after breakfast."

Before he could decipher that statement, a knock sounded on the door.

"There it is now," she said. "I told Torrie not to let me sleep in."

"I'll see you later, then," he said, pressing a quick kiss to her temple before leaving the bed and going into his chamber.

As he heard her bade her maid to enter, he leaned against the closed door and breathed a deep sigh. He'd managed to get through the night without giving himself away, although there had been moments when he'd dearly wanted to confess all. He had to remind himself that she was only being kind toward him because she believed he was Albert.

Shoving himself away from the door, he yanked on the bellpull to summon his valet and then immediately stilled. When had he begun to think of Marlow as his valet and not Albert's? He supposed it was a good thing that he was settling into the role. He simply needed to remember that none of this was permanent. Once the heir arrived, he would merely serve as guardian over his nephew's domain until he reached his majority. Then he would carry on with his life. He didn't need to get too comfortable here.

Julia was so certain she was carrying a boy. Surely women sensed those things. He wouldn't even consider that his brother's heir would not be arriving shortly.

After his valet prepared him for the day, Edward made his way down to the breakfast dining room. Ashe and Locke were already seated at the table. They both looked up, studied him hard, and he wondered if he'd sprouted a pair of horns.

"How was your night?" Ashe asked.

"Restless. Julia is having breakfast in bed."

"So is Minerva. That is what ladies do."

As he went to the sideboard, he almost asked if that was true of all ladies. His associations with women usually didn't offer the luxury of lingering until breakfast. He wondered what else he didn't know about them.

He almost took the chair beside Ashe before remembering that his place was now at the head of the table. He'd avoided this moment, taking meals in his room. He could feel Ashe and Locke studying him, wondered if they could sense the battle with which he was grappling. He had to take that chair as though he had sat in it the entirety of his adult life. Avoiding their gazes, setting down his plate, he dragged the chair back and dropped into it, once again hit with the devastation of loss. Would he ever sit here and not feel like a usurper? *It's only temporary until the heir is born.*

As casually as possible, he began slicing the ham. "What else do ladies do?"

"Keep us gents waiting," Ashe said, as though unaware of the emotions rioting through Edward, as though accustomed to Edward sitting at the head of the table.

"Drive us to madness," Locke said at the same time.

Grinning, Edward shifted his gaze between his friends. "We obviously all view women differently."

And the servants had ears, even if they were supposed to keep their mouths shut. He wished he could send the butler and footman from the room. Instead, he sipped his tea and refrained from adding more sugar.

"I know the extent of your grief is immeasurable," Locke said quietly. "If you like, I could stay a couple of days to help you get the estate's affairs in order after your long sojourn."

"That's kind of you, but unnecessary. I feel up to the task of meeting with the steward later this morning." On more than one occasion when visiting, Edward had sat in the library and observed Albert handling his estates. While impatient, ready to be off carousing, surely he'd retained a bit of knowledge.

"Well, if you find yourself in need of assistance, don't hesitate to ask," Locke insisted.

"Afraid I can't offer you the same consideration," Ashe said. "I find managing estates to be a bit more formidable than Locke does."

"It gets easier over time. It also helps if you grew up there. While I'm sorry you didn't get to live on your estates until you reached your majority, I am grateful you were both about Havisham to stop my life from being so lonely." With a slight grin, he looked at Edward. "Do you remember when your brother found a way for us to get up on the roof?"

They'd only been at Havisham for a few days. "We were planning to run off. He was hoping to get a glimpse of Evermore so we'd know in which direction to go."

"It was my first real adventure. I was terrified I was going to slide off."

"You wouldn't have gone far. We were all joined with a rope tied about our waists."

"All that ensured was that we would all slide off together."

"Which was the point," Ashe said. "If one of us went, we all went."

"That is not how my brother explained it to me."

Ashe shrugged. "But that was the truth of it. We became fast friends so quickly. Remarkable, really."

They had become more than friends. Nearly brothers.

"Do you remember when the Gypsies came through?" Locke asked. "Your brother wanted us to leave with them."

"He fell in love with one of the girls," Edward admitted. "She let him kiss her. He worried for the longest time that he'd gotten her with child."

"From a kiss?" Ashe asked.

Edward grinned. "We were ten. What did we know? He finally gathered up enough courage to ask the marquess."

Locke's eyes widened. "That's the reason he took us to a tenant's farm to watch a pair of horses breeding?"

Edward chuckled. "I suspect so, yes. I remember all the questions we had afterward. Not that we dared ask him."

"He would have done better taking us to a brothel," Ashe said.

"We were lads. They'd have not let us through the door. Besides, I have such lovely memories of time spent with the farmer's daughter years later."

"She was sweet," Ashe said with a grin.

"But she only liked novices. Told her I was my brother, so I got to experience her twice. Thought he'd be mad at me for denying him his turn with her. Then I found out he was spending time with a tavern girl in the village."

"He never was one for competing," Ashe said.

"When he put his mind to it, though, he could drink us all under the table," Locke pointed out.

"Then the next morning when we were all sick as dogs, he'd walk about gloating," Edward reminded them, smiling at the memory.

"He was obnoxious about it," Ashe recalled.

"I would have been as well if I suffered no ill effects."

"How did he manage it?" Locke asked.

"I'm not convinced he actually drank," Edward admitted.

"But I saw him downing the swill."

"He sipped, he never downed. He filled the glasses, only made it appear he was filling his own."

"You really think he pulled one over on us?"

Edward nodded. "I do. My brother was not always a paragon of virtue."

"I should say not," Ashe began. "Do you remember the time . . ."

JULIA heard the laughter as she neared the breakfast dining room. Smiling, she leaned against the wall and absorbed the sweetness of joy, so grateful for it, so glad that Albert had his friends to distract him from his sorrow. It was odd how she could distinguish Albert's laughter from the others'. It was a bit deeper, a little more free, as though he enjoyed life a bit more than they did.

It was marvelous to awaken in his arms. They would move forward one day at a time and eventually the grief would ebb away, although she was beginning to realize that she might not have the exact Albert she'd had before. How could she? After months apart, she wasn't exactly the same either. Never before had she been completely without male supervision. Although she'd missed Albert dreadfully, she'd found her time alone quite liberating.

At the click of approaching footsteps, she glanced to the side and smiled at Minerva.

"Are we hiding out?" Minerva asked as she neared.

"I'm eavesdropping on their laughter. I feared it might be a while before any was echoing through the residence again."

"Something about masculine laughter is very satisfying."

"I can't recall Albert ever being quite so boisterous."

"They're different when no ladies are about."

"I rather regret that we'll be disturbing them, but I suppose we must."

"Before they discover we're out here listening. I don't think they'll appreciate our taking advantage."

Albert most certainly would not. With a deep breath, Julia led the way into the dining room. The laughter immediately abated, replaced by the scraping of chairs over flooring as the men came to their feet.

"We didn't mean to disturb you," she said as she crossed over to be nearer to her husband. He appeared less troubled, more himself, and she was grateful for the friendship he'd developed with these men.

"We were finished," he assured her.

"It was good to hear you laugh."

"Our youth provided ample opportunity for such. We were recalling some of the jollier moments."

"But we must away now," Ashe said. "While the weather holds."

Coaches were brought round, trunks loaded, and in no time at all they were standing outside with the chilled wind whipping around them.

"You will send word if you need anything," Minerva said to her.

All she needed was time alone with her husband. He was speaking with the duke and viscount, so serious again. "I will, thank you."

As their guests climbed into their respective carriages, Albert came over to stand beside her. "It's cold out. You should be inside."

Slipping her arm around his, she was aware of him stiffening. "The sun is peering through the clouds. I could do with some sun."

He lifted a hand as the drivers urged the horses forward. She waved, wondering if things would ever again feel normal. They stood there, facing outward for the longest time, until the coaches were out of sight.

"What now?" she asked, hoping he wouldn't retreat back into his rooms.

He kept his gaze on the road, and she wondered if he wished he were in one of the carriages. "I'm meet-

ing with Bocock in a bit. I need to prepare for that."
With her arm nestled in his, he began escorting her up
the stairs. "I know I've already said it once, but I can't
thank you enough for handling and arranging everything so expertly. I don't know how I would have managed without you."

"I hope you never have to find out."

There was the flinch again. If she hadn't been
touching him, she wouldn't have been aware of it. She
thought they'd reconnected in the early hours of the
morning, but right then she felt a chill coming from
him that was colder than the air whipping around them.

Chapter 5

*H*E'D often sat in his brother's office, in a nearby chair, sipping scotch and listening with half an ear while reading or plotting his next adventure as Albert discussed his estate with his steward. So Edward was familiar with Bocock, thought he had an understanding of everything that was within the Earl of Greyling's purview. But after an hour discussing matters with the steward, he realized with startling clarity that he hadn't a bloody clue regarding everything that required an earl's attention.

When the door opened, he was grateful for the reprieve as Julia strolled in. He and Bocock came to their feet.

"Sorry to interrupt," she said softly, smiling serenely, "but I might take a leisurely stroll to the village."

He might have told her to go on if she didn't look so hopeful. Albert would have accompanied her, which meant he needed to do the same, had to give the impression that he looked forward to being in her presence. "A lovely idea. I'll accompany you. We shouldn't be much longer here."

"Then I'll wait, shall I?"

Apparently she was fond of rhetorical questions, because without giving him a chance to respond, she settled into a nearby chair, folding her hands on what remained of her lap. He forced himself to smile, to look pleased, when in truth he wished she wasn't here to witness his bumbling about. Bocock might not notice it, but she no doubt knew every variance of her husband's mannerisms. Had she sat in on these discussions before?

But he couldn't worry about her at that moment. He had to ensure the estates were well managed for the nephew to whom she would soon give birth. Only a few more weeks and he would no longer have to pretend to be the earl. Yet still he would oversee the properties and incomes until the boy reached his majority. The sooner he had a good grasp of everything involved, the sooner he could make certain his brother's legacy remained intact. He retook his seat. Bocock did the same.

"Looking over the reports here, I notice it's been a while since Rowntree has made any payments," Edward said.

"Yes, m'lord. As we discussed before you left on your travels, Rowntree believes that since three generations of his family have shepherded on that land, it belongs to him now, and he should not have to pay for the right to graze his sheep there. You were of a mind to be lenient in hopes that he'd come around. He hasn't. As a matter of fact, two other tenants have not paid recently. I fear you may be losing control."

May be losing it? It was bloody well gone. Had Albert truly believed leniency was the way to go? He knew Albert avoided confrontation whenever possible, but in this case it simply wasn't possible.

"Are you rethinking your stance, sir?" Bocock asked, and Edward heard the disrespect in his voice.

"Watch your tone, Bocock. You're not the only steward in the land."

"Apologies, m'lord. I didn't mean to question—"

"I have no problem with you questioning me. I pay you to oversee matters, keep me informed, and advise me. But I won't tolerate any snide retorts." He slapped his palm down on the ledger. "Nor will I tolerate any man who does not pay what is due."

Bocock straightened as though Edward had shoved a poker down his spine. "I'll speak with Rowntree."

"I'll handle Rowntree. You speak with the others. I expect payment. I expect it timely or I'll know the reason why. If it isn't a damned good one, I'll help pack them up and send them on their way. Just as you are not the only steward, they are not the only farmers."

"With all due respect, m'lord, tenants are harder to come by. Factories and such offer a man a better living."

"Then the land can lay fallow, although I suspect there are a few industrious souls left who would welcome the opportunity to work outside rather than in cramped quarters. If not, perhaps I'll work the land myself."

Bocock's brow furrowed, his eyes blinked. "You're a lord."

As though that explained it all. "I intend to ensure the next Earl of Greyling inherits well. I will do whatever necessary to secure his future."

"Of course, m'lord."

Edward closed the ledger and pushed it across the desk to where the other man sat. "I think we're done here."

"When will you be speaking with Rowntree?"

"This afternoon."

Bocock smiled. "Not letting any grass grow beneath your feet."

"I've learned of late that life is precarious. It's best to see to matters straightaway." Edward came to his feet.

Bocock shoved himself out of his chair, clutching and unclutching the brim of his hat. "Once again, m'lord, I'm sorry for your loss. Not easy losing a brother."

"No, it's not." But he'd wallowed enough. Now he had to see to the future of his brother's child. "We'll meet again in a fortnight, see where things stand."

"Very good, m'lord." Turning to go, he tipped his head toward Julia. "Good day, Lady Greyling."

She pushed herself out of the chair, an ungainly move that Edward should not have found endearing. "Give my best to your wife, Mr. Bocock."

"I will indeed, m'lady."

With that, he walked from the room. Edward should have been able to breathe a sigh of relief, but Julia approached, so he kept up the façade that he hoped to God mirrored his brother's.

"I've never seen you quite so forceful," she said, her eyes sparkling with admiration.

"I'm all for leniency until someone takes advantage. Then my assertive nature breaks through."

She released a small laugh. "I rather liked it."

He couldn't deny that her words pleased him. "I

can't let the tenants think they're in charge. However, I do want to handle this matter with Rowntree posthaste. Perhaps you should go to the village without me."

"I'll come with you to Rowntree's. We can go from there."

Every inch of him shouted that it was a bad idea. But he couldn't continue to make excuses not to be in her company. "Splendid. I assume it's unsafe for you to ride a horse in your condition."

"Yes, I've not risked riding since I discovered I was with child. We'll need a carriage."

"I'll have one readied. Will leaving in half an hour suit?"

"Perfectly."

He waited until she left the room before walking over to the sideboard and pouring himself a finger of scotch. Just enough for fortification.

An afternoon spent with Julia. How could anything possibly go wrong?

He downed the amber liquid in one quick swallow, all the while thinking: Let me count the ways.

JULIA fought to quell her disappointment that her husband had arranged for the cabriolet to be readied and for a groom to sit beside her, serving as driver, while Albert sat magnificently astride a horse and led the way. Why was he discarding her? Every time it seemed as though they were returning to the closeness they had once shared, he retreated. While she was certain it was quite ridiculous, she was beginning to wonder if Edward had disparaged her to such an extent on their sojourn that Albert had fallen out of love with her.

The hood of the carriage was raised, buffeting her from the winds, so she couldn't blame them for the tears pricking her eyes. She'd had such hopes for the outing. Now she rather wished that she had simply gone by herself. On the other hand, she wasn't certain that Albert had ever cut such a fine figure on a horse, and when she wasn't being unreasonably hurt—for surely she was being unreasonable—she had to admit to taking great satisfaction in observing the confidence with which he rode.

She'd always enjoyed riding, but didn't dare while she was with child. She wanted this child beyond all reasoning, but she was growing rather weary of all the pampering, especially when it was providing opportunity to put distance between her and her husband.

She wanted to scream. Perhaps she was simply going mad, imagining slights that didn't truly exist.

He turned up a road, and they followed. She could see the small house in the distance, the sheep dotting the hill. She was familiar with Rowntree and his family. She brought baskets of food to all the tenants at Christmas.

Albert held up a fisted hand and the groom brought the carriage to a halt. Her husband circled his horse around and came back to the carriage. "Stay here," he ordered, before dismounting and handing the reins to the groom.

Then he was striding to the cottage. Rowntree stepped out. Although he was nearly as tall as Albert, he was considerably wider, but comparing the two men, she could see clearly that Albert was all muscle and sinew, strength and firmness, while Rowntree had begun to acquire a portly look.

Hearing the tenor of their voices, but not the words, she nearly clutched the groom's hand when it became obvious that Rowntree was becoming belligerent. Suddenly, Albert grabbed the man by the front of his coat and slammed him against the front of the cottage. As Albert leaned in, Rowntree's eyes grew wide and round. Albert's voice was so low that Julia could barely hear it, but still it sent a fissure of unease through her. It must have done the same for Rowntree, as he began frantically bobbing his head. Albert released him, stepped back, straightened the lapels of the man's coat, and patted his beefy shoulder. A few more words were exchanged before the earl spun on his heel, strode back to the carriage and took the reins from the groom.

He held her gaze, brown to blue, and it struck her that he'd never looked at her quite so intently, as though needing to gauge her reaction in order to ensure he pleased her. "Would you still like to go to the village?"

She nodded. "I was thinking a nice cup of tea and a pastry might be a pleasant way to while away the afternoon."

He gave her a small grin. "I could use some whiling. Let's be off, then."

Mounting in one fluid movement that had her heart fluttering, he took off while the groom urged their horse to follow. In their time together, she must have seen her husband get on a horse a hundred times, two hundred, so she had no idea why at that moment she considered it one of the most sensual actions she'd ever witnessed. Perhaps because during his absence her life had been so incredibly chaste. She'd certainly not looked at other men or sought out a replacement for him. She'd never been drawn to another man as she was to him. From the moment he'd been introduced, he had completely captured her interest.

Only once had her attention ever waned and then only for the space of a kiss in a garden that never should have happened.

When they entered the village, he brought his horse to a halt in front of the tea shop, dismounted, and walked the horse back. Holding the reins out to the groom, he said, "You can return the horse to Evermore now. I'll drive the carriage back."

"Yes, m'lord." The cabriolet rocked as the groom exited.

Albert came around to her side and extended his hand. She placed hers on it, felt the strength and sureness of his fingers closing around hers. "I thought—"

She stopped, feeling like such a ninny.

Angling his head slightly, he arched a brow. "You thought what?"

Studying his beloved face, she wondered why she was filled with so many doubts. "I thought you'd chosen to ride the horse because you didn't truly want to go on the outing with me."

Lifting her hand, he pressed a kiss to the back of her gloved fingers. "I'm sorry, Julia. It never occurred to me . . . I wanted to portray a position of authority. I thought being on a horse accomplished that better than being in a carriage."

She touched her fingers to his jaw. "You looked magnificent. It did frighten me, though, when you grabbed him."

"He wasn't listening. I had to be more forceful. And

to be honest, it pricked my temper when he said I wasn't the man my father was."

"What did you say to him?"

"That the land he lived on belonged to the Crown and had been placed in the Earl of Greyling's keeping centuries ago. He was there by my good graces and my good graces alone. If he didn't pay what was owed, I would personally pack up him along with his family and cart them off the land. He assured me he would be making restitution within the fortnight and would not be troubling me again."

"And you believed him?"

"I gave him the benefit of the doubt. If he lied, at the end of the fortnight he's gone. And nothing on God's green earth will put him back in my good graces. I'm not the vengeful sort, but neither am I very forgiving when I'm wronged."

She'd never known her husband to be so powerful, so determined. This was an aspect to him she'd never seen. It quite fascinated her. "I've never witnessed you conducting your business before."

"Perhaps it's best if you don't in the future. I wouldn't want you thinking me a tyrant."

"On the contrary, I respect how you look after what's yours. And I am yours."

He suddenly appeared uncomfortable, was possibly blushing. Or was it merely the chill in the air?

"We should have some tea now," he said, helping her out of the carriage.

Offering his arm, he led her into the shop. Above the door, a bell tinkled.

A matronly woman trundled over and curtsied. "Oh, Lord Greyling, I'm sorry for your loss."

"Thank you, Mrs. Potts. The countess and I are in need of some refreshment."

"Certainly, m'lord. I have your favorite table right over here." Mrs. Potts made a sweeping gesture with her arm, and a young lady sitting at a small table in the corner by the window gathered up her cup and plate and hurried off.

Albert pulled out the chair for Julia and assisted in seating her before taking his place opposite her at the small square linen-covered table. The scent of cinnamon, butter, and vanilla hung heavy on the air.

"Will you be wanting your usual lemon tart, m'lord?" Mrs. Potts asked.

"No, actually, in memory of my brother I'll go with his favorite: strawberry."

"And your ladyship?"

"I'll have the same."

"What sort of tea might I bring you?"

"Darjeeling."

"Your lordship?"

"The same."

"Be back in a trice." She scurried away.

Julia began removing her gloves.

"You didn't have to go with strawberry," Albert said.

"It's my favorite. I love strawberries. In summer when you're not looking, I gorge. I wonder what else Edward and I might have had in common."

Looking out the window, he removed his gloves and stuffed them in the pocket of his coat. "Not much else, I suspect."

Mrs. Potts returned with the teapot and pastries. After the proprietress left, Julia poured tea for her husband and herself. "I love the fragrances in this place."

"Always makes me hungry," Albert said.

"I don't suppose you had many pastries in Africa."

He shook his head. "Let's not talk about Africa. What did you do while we were away?"

"I don't even know where to begin." She'd longed to share so many moments with him, but now that he'd asked, words failed her. She took a sip of her tea, gathering her thoughts. "I changed, Albert."

He angled his head slightly. "Pardon?"

"I've worried that you sensed it, that I'm not exactly as I was when you left, and that's partly responsible for this . . . awkwardness between us."

"My distraction has nothing to do with you."

"I know that's what you say, and I have no reason not to believe you, as you've never lied to me, but I am also not as I was. While you were away, I did things . . ."

He narrowed his eyes. "What sort of 'things'?"

A fissure of annoyance wove through his voice, and she had the sense that he was striving not to erupt with rage.

"For the first time in my life, I answered to no one save myself. First there were my parents, and I had to obey them without question. When they died of influenza, my cousin immediately took control and dictated every aspect of my Season and what was expected of me."

"What was expected?"

"To marry by Season's end. Thank God, I met you. I adore you, you know that. I considered myself the most fortunate girl in the world because I was able to marry for love. But I went straight from my cousin's household into yours—"

"You found your husband to be a dictator?"

"No, of course not, but everything I did was with the intention of pleasing you, making you proud, ensuring you were glad that I was your wife. Suddenly, when you left, I had no one to answer to. No one cared if I slept until the afternoon. I got dressed in the morning and that was it. I didn't change for dinner or to take a turn about the garden or for afternoon tea. It was liberating."

"My, my. You behaved quite wildly."

The heat warmed her face. "You're mocking me."

"No." A corner of his mouth hitched up ever so slightly. "Well, maybe just a tad. Surely you did something a bit more daring than not changing your clothes."

She took a bite of her tart. "I read *Madame Bovary*."

He stared at her as though he didn't know who she was. "Did you enjoy it?"

"Would you think less of me if I did?"

He laughed, a deep rich sound that seemed to echo through her soul. Reaching out, he skimmed his thumb along the corner of her mouth. When he brought his hand back, she saw the small dab of strawberry jam that Mrs. Potts used on the tarts when she had no fresh fruit. Holding her gaze, he closed his lips around the edge of his thumb. "I would not."

Her stomach tightened with his actions as much as with his words. "Have you read it?"

"I have."

"Did you enjoy it?"

"I found it . . . provocative."

"Have you read all the books and magazines in Edward's room?"

He narrowed his eyes again. "How do you know about the things in Edward's room?"

"I was bored one afternoon. The maids had left the door open, and I thought if I just stepped inside that I might gain a better sense of him. I simply wanted us to get along."

"That's how you knew about the liquor kept in the room."

She nodded. "He kept it hidden away in a small cabinet. I know I should have respected his privacy—"

"The room is in your residence. He didn't own it. You had every right to enter the bedchamber. To be quite honest, I suspect he would have taken immense satisfaction in knowing he'd shocked you."

"But he didn't. I expected to find liquor about. I half expected a woman secreted in the wardrobe to be awaiting his return."

He grinned. "Did you, now?"

"He seemed to have a bevy of followers, but then so did you. It still amazes me that you put all that aside for me."

He turned his attention back to the window. "It was not as challenging as I expected it to be." Swinging his gaze back to her, he pinned her to the spot. When had he acquired the ability to hold her captive with little more than his eyes? "His reading preferences didn't make you want to take him to task?"

Slowly, she shook her head. She could admit the truth because this was Albert, and they were always honest with each other. "Just as you stated with *Madame Bovary,* I found everything quite provocative."

"You read them all?"

"I had a considerable amount of time alone. I had to fill the hours with something."

His eyes filled with remorse. "I'd not considered, when I decided on this journey, that you would be lonely."

"I wasn't lonely, not really. I missed you terribly, but at the same time, I felt as though I came into my own. I made all my decisions without your counsel. I gained confidence."

"I never noticed you lacking in confidence."

"Sometimes I had doubts, but I didn't say anything, as I didn't want to appear weak. You're so strong. You deserve a wife who is your measure."

He studied her as though she were an odd specimen of insect he'd discovered beneath a rock. "You humble me."

Once again he turned his attention to life beyond the window, as though she had made him uncomfortable with her confession. "The sun has begun its retreat. We should probably be away."

When he had her settled in the carriage, he removed his coat and began draping it over her as though it were a blanket.

"You'll catch your death," she told him.

"I've been colder." He tucked the edges of his coat between her and the seat.

"Albert, I feel as though I said something wrong."

Lifting his gaze to hers, he cupped her cheek with one gloved hand, and she desperately wished he hadn't yet put on the leather. She wanted his warm skin against hers. "You're not at fault. I'm feeling a bit melancholy. I thought I knew all there was to know about you. I'm discovering I know nothing at all."

She released a self-conscious laugh. "You know everything. I know I may have changed a bit, but I'm still the woman you married."

Removing his hat, he pressed his forehead to hers. "If only I were the man you married."

Cradling his face between her gloved hands, she urged him back until she could meet and hold his gaze. "Our time apart had a greater effect on our relationship than I anticipated. We need only to reacquaint ourselves. Our time together last night, then this afternoon, is a beginning. Before long, it shall be as though we were never apart."

"Don't wear black to dinner tonight."

"I want to give your brother the respect he deserves."

"Trust me, Edward would be delighted if you wore something other than black. It's so dreary. He would want you out of mourning, at least when we're in residence."

"Are we dining formally this evening?"

"Yes. Perhaps you're right. The sooner we put the grief behind us, the sooner we'll find our way back to each other."

He skimmed his finger lightly over her chin before moving around to the other side of the carriage and climbing in with far more muscled grace than the groom who had been seated there on her journey here. Lifting the reins, he flicked them, causing the horse to take off at a trot.

Wrapping both her hands around his upper arm, she relished the strength she felt there. She knew that things between them would never be as they'd been before he left, but that didn't mean that different wouldn't be better.

Chapter 6

*S*HE'D enjoyed the reading material he'd secreted away in his room. Standing at the window in the library, sipping scotch, Edward smiled with the realization that Julia Alcott, Countess of Greyling, wasn't quite as prim and proper as she appeared. Her eyes had darkened with longing when he'd taken the strawberry jam from the corner of her mouth to his tongue, and while he knew it was impossible, he could have sworn that it was a much sweeter taste having been against her skin.

From the moment she married his brother, he'd been as off-putting and obnoxious as possible, wanting—needing—distance between them so he wasn't tempted to do something he shouldn't. Not that he thought she'd ever dishonor her vows, but seeing desire mirrored in her eyes today had been like having a sharp lance piercing the center of his chest. He wanted that desire to be for him, but if he were honest, he was merely serving as a proxy for his brother—and everything she felt, everything she said, everything she did, only came about because she thought she was in the company of her husband. When she learned the truth, her heart was not only going to break with the news, but her hatred for him would increase tenfold. He should make an excuse to avoid her tonight. The tart hadn't agreed with him perhaps. He was tired, he was weary. He was jealous of a dead man.

He was a fool to think he could spend considerable time in Julia's company with no repercussions to his own sanity.

Hearing footsteps, he glanced over his shoulder as she walked into the room. What a mistake it had been to encourage her not to wear black. Better to be constantly reminded that he was merely playing a role, one that would garner him no applause or standing ovations when he took his final bow. But he was just so blasted tired of the sadness.

She'd selected a deep violet velvet that dipped low to reveal her collarbone and plump cleavage. Although her hair was up, curling tendrils framed her lovely face. He'd always thought her beautiful, but the few passing years had removed the sparkle of youth and replaced it with the glow of maturity. Serenity. Confidence.

"I don't recall you indulging before dinner," she said.

"Another bad habit developed during my travels. Would you like some?"

"I doubt it's good for the babe."

Did that mean that she would have joined him if she weren't with child? He'd never considered that perhaps she had a taste for spirits as well. "One sip."

She was near enough now to take the glass from his hand. Near enough that he inhaled her fragrance. Roses. Unfortunate, as the rich sweetness always reminded him of that night in the garden when he had thought to take her mouth with no consequence. He watched as she carried the glass to her parted lips, tipped it slightly so the amber liquid flowed into her mouth. Why did he find the slow movement so riveting, so sensual? The delicate muscles at her throat shifted slightly as she swallowed, smiled, handed the glass back to him.

No cough, no sputtering. She looked out the window. "You never asked me to join you before."

"For which I heartily apologize. I didn't think you'd enjoy it, but I daresay I believe you've indulged before."

"On occasion. My little secret." She slid her gaze toward him, her eyes twinkling. "A countess should be above reproach."

"On the contrary. A countess should be able to do as she wishes. At least mine should."

With a small laugh, she looked back out the window. "I love winter."

He leaned his shoulder against the wall. "I would have thought you'd favor summer."

"I enjoy summer, but I like the bleakness of winter. It allows for much contemplation."

"You fancy your thoughts more than I fancy mine, then." She turned to study him, and he feared he'd given too much away. He kept himself busy with wine, women, wagering, and traveling so he wouldn't have to examine his life too closely. He'd never possessed much in the way of ambition, other than to have a jolly good time and live with no regrets. Yet still the regrets were there, and a good many of them involved her.

"My lord, dinner is served," the butler announced. Edward hadn't even heard Rigdon enter.

Setting aside his glass, he offered his arm to Julia, relishing the feel of her fingers coming to rest in the crook of his elbow. "I believe I failed to mention that you look lovely tonight."

"It's nice to be out of black, although I didn't want to go with anything too bright."

"A commendable compromise."

"You're teasing now."

She pressed her cheek to his arm, her rose scent wafted up, and it was all he could do to carry on through the doorway and not stop to kiss her. In her condition he could not take things further. Besides, if she'd been struck with the same awareness that night in the garden as he had, she'd have not married his brother.

When they walked into the dining room, the chair at the head of the table didn't loom quite as large as he'd expected. It had helped matters that he'd dined in the breakfast room that morning, had taken his place at the head of that table. It wouldn't be quite so uncomfortable doing it here.

Because he had dined with his brother, he knew that Julia preferred to sit at his right rather than at the foot of the table, so he escorted her there now, pulled out the chair for her, helped her settle, refrained from taking the chair opposite her, instead opting for the one that marked his brother's place. It merely provided him with her profile. He much preferred his view from the other chair.

Wine was poured, the first course brought out. To ensure he made no blunders, he needed to control the direction of the discourse. "Surely you did more than read while we were away." She blushed a delicate pink hue, and he wondered if she'd done the same while reading *Madame Bovary* or any of his magazines with the risqué stories. "How else did you fill your day?"

Delicately, she pressed the napkin to her lips. "I practiced my water coloring. I'm much improved, and I've been working on something special."

"I hope you'll share it with me."

His answer pleased her. It was dangerous to please her too much, to have that smile directed his way.

"I'd rather wait until I'm further along."

"Whenever you're comfortable." He sipped his wine, savored the flavor, trying not to recall the essence of the kiss she'd bestowed on him last night. Kissing her was not going to cause her to lose the child. He was going to have to come up with another excuse to avoid those lips, a reason that wouldn't cause her to doubt herself.

Swirling the wine in his glass, he longed to down the entire bottle but knew he needed to limit himself, keep his wits about him. He was too stiff, too formal with her. He needed to stop thinking that he should relax, so he could relax.

"Do you think Locksley will ever marry?" she asked.

He was grateful for a topic that had nothing to do with them. "If he wants an heir, he must marry."

"That's such an unromantic reason to wed."

"Still, it is reason enough for many lords. Wanting to play matchmaker?"

Pursing her lips together, she shook her head. "No. As much as I like him, I wouldn't wish the life he offers on any woman. When you took me to Havisham to meet his father, I thought I might go mad during the short time we visited. I can't imagine what it would be like to live there all the time. It feels so abandoned."

"It's not that bad."

"Because you were young. Boys. Always able to find adventure. But for a woman, I think it would be a very lonely place indeed."

"Do you find Evermore to be a lonely place?"

"No, I feel as though I belong here. It's my home. I take joy in it. I don't know how a woman would ever make Havisham a home."

He tapped his finger against his wineglass. "It would take a special woman. But then to be honest, I never expected Ashe to marry either."

She took her wineglass, inhaled the bouquet, set it aside. "Do you think Edward would have ever married?"

Slowly he shook his head. "No."

"I find it rather sad that he died without ever having been in love."

"I didn't say he'd never been in love."

Her eyes widened. "Who?"

"Someone he couldn't have."

"She was married, then."

"She could have been a servant."

"No, had she been a servant he would have married her simply to shock all of London."

He grinned. "You knew Edward better than I thought you did."

"I would not have put it past him to marry a woman of ill-repute or at the very least a woman of scandal." She was smiling as though she rather enjoyed the notion of him doing it.

"I didn't realize you gave him that much thought."

She blushed. "I didn't. Just something that occurred to me at some point. He never much cared what people thought."

I cared what you thought. And fearing she'd think the worse, he'd behaved in a manner that ensured she did. "I suppose he did enjoy doing things he ought not."

"Therefore, I can draw the conclusion that the woman he loved was married. Otherwise he'd have wed her."

"Love is a rather strong word."

"You're the one who used it first."

"I misspoke. More like, infatuated. Besides, a good wife is not supposed to question her husband."

"We long ago established that I'm not always a good wife." She swirled her wine, inhaled again, set the glass aside. If he had to guess, he'd say she missed wine, but he had to admire her strength in not indulging. Her gaze came back to him and he felt it like a punch. "You didn't marry me simply to gain an heir. You love me."

Was that doubt in her voice? He didn't love her, but he wasn't going to lie to her either. "Every Earl of Greyling married for love."

Her brow furrowed. "How do you know that?"

"Marsden told us."

"How did it even come up?" Skepticism laced her voice.

"When our parents died, we lost a good bit of our history. That's something one doesn't really consider, how much one learns through stories shared. It bothered Edward, the things we didn't know. How did our parents meet? What was Father like as a student? Every night before we went to bed, Edward would insist that we share something our parents had told us and he would write it into a journal. When we ran out of stories, he began to ask Marsden to share what he knew. I think that's why Edward enjoyed weaving elaborate tales. He didn't like the idea of history not being passed on. He probably would have made a passable minstrel."

"What became of the journal?"

He shook his head. "I don't know. I haven't thought about it in years."

"Maybe you'll find it when you begin going through Edward's things."

Not likely. He'd given it to Albert for safekeeping, to be passed on to his heir. Maybe when he went through Albert's things. "Perhaps."

"Speaking of Edward's things . . . I would be happy—no, happy is not the correct word. I wish it didn't have to be done, but I could sort through Edward's belongings, spare you the sadness of it."

It was an odd thing to realize how involved she was, how conscientious she was of lightening his burden. Her husband's burden. He couldn't forget who she was truly assisting or thought she was. Still, of all the women Edward had been with over the years, not one had ever seemed to care about any burden he might carry. They were only interested in what being with him might gain them. Even if circumstances were different, he wouldn't have known how to accept her generous offer, but he did know it wasn't Edward's possessions that needed going through. He also knew that eventually she would be the one to go through things. Perhaps they would go through them together.

If she didn't hate him with every breath she took.

"I appreciate the offer but I'll see to the task."

"What about his residence in London? I suspect you'll want to get his possessions out of there as soon as possible."

"I don't see the need to rush."

"But you're shelling out money on a lease that's no longer needed."

"I can well afford it." The words came out too tart. He softened his voice. "I have no desire to leave you alone until after the babe is born. And you certainly have no business traveling to London."

"You could send word to the servants to simply pack up his things—"

"No!" He still needed his own London residence, as he intended for her and the child to live in the dwellings that belonged to the earl. "It's a matter that can wait. As I'm finished with dinner, if you'll excuse me—"

Her hand came to rest over his, causing the rest of his words to back up in his throat.

"I'm sorry. I don't mean to push. I know going through his belongings will only bring home that he is truly gone. You'll take care of it when you're ready to face it."

"When we go to London for the Season will be soon enough I think."

With a gentle nod, she gave him a soft smile. Why did she have to be so blasted understanding? "I'm going to the library for an after-dinner drink," he told her.

"I'll come with."

Not what he wanted. He needed some time alone to regain his balance. "But you're not drinking."

"I know you like to use the time after dinner for quiet reflection. I'll read." Her hand had yet to leave his, and she gave it a tender squeeze. "I've had far too many nights without you of late. I promise not to intrude."

How could she not intrude, he wondered, when they were sitting in opposite chairs before the fireplace in the library, he with his scotch—half the amount he would have poured had she not been there—and she with *Wuthering Heights*? While he stared at the low flames sending out their warmth, he inhaled her rose fragrance, heard her quiet breathing. He was quite simply so aware of her presence that she might as well be sitting on his lap. Not that she'd be reading if that were so. He'd have his lips on hers, his hands gliding over her back and shoulders. His fingers would unfasten the back of her gown, peel it down until—

"I think you should record your reflections."

With horror that his errant thoughts might have been revealed on his face, he jerked his attention to her, relieved to discover her watching him with an incredibly serene expression. No suspicions. "Pardon?"

"You mentioned earlier about all the history that was lost when your parents passed. While memories of Edward are still clear, I think you should write what you remember as a legacy to your heir and all who follow. Otherwise, how will they ever know him?"

"I'm not certain they need to know him."

"I realize he was a bit of a rapscallion, but based on the stories he told, he led a fascinating life."

"He embellished."

"You say that as though it is a bad thing."

"Another word for embellished is lied."

She held up her book. "All stories are lies, but there is always a thread of truth in them."

"You are the last person I expected to be his champion." She had him kicked out of the London residence, for Christ's sake. It was the reason he had his own residence in London. Although he had to admit she'd done him a favor, as he preferred having his own place, being able to do what he wanted when he wanted.

"I'm not serving as his champion, but I do think your son should know him. You should write down all you remember while it's still fresh in your mind. Memories fade, even though we think they won't. There are times when I can barely remember what my parents looked like."

"Perhaps you're right. I should record what I remember about him. Maybe you can add your memories. Reveal what really happened that night I caught the two of you in the garden."

She blinked, but held his gaze. "I told you. We were discussing the trip." She tilted her head to the side. "What did you think happened?"

Taking a sip of scotch, he considered, then said, "I thought perhaps he'd kissed you."

Her expression changed not one iota. Her gaze remained latched on his. "Why would I allow him to be the first man to kiss me when that honor was yours?"

She might as well have picked up the poker and hurled it through his chest. She'd never kissed anyone before him? Had never before had a tryst in the garden with Albert? Albert had been courting her for weeks.

Edward had assumed his brother had taken advantage, that Julia had encouraged him—

But no. Their relationship had been chaste. Not even a kiss exchanged before that night. Little wonder she detested him. From her, he'd stolen what she'd intended to give another. Had his brother been a saint or a fool? On the other hand, he supposed a gentleman didn't compromise a lady he wished to wed. Edward didn't know if he'd have had the fortitude to resist her. He was having a hell of a time doing it now.

"Apologies, Julia. I wasn't questioning your morals, but my brother was not one to resist temptation."

"I assure you that he never found me tempting."

"Every man in London found you tempting."

Her cheeks flaming red, she looked down at the book in her lap. "You flatter me."

Did she really not know how fetching she was?

She lifted her gaze to him. "You are the only one who ever tempted me."

Dear God, but at that moment he rather wished those words were truly spoken for him. "What a fortunate man the Earl of Greyling is."

"My attraction had nothing to do with your title. You know that."

He tossed back what remained of his scotch. "Still, a man is his title—if he has one."

"You could have been a pauper and I'd have married you."

He grinned. "If I were a pauper, I doubt I could have afforded to wed."

She smiled. "You'd have found a way. You're too smart to let me go."

He wasn't as smart as he'd always thought. If he were, he'd have appreciated her before now, would have realized she was far more than a flint to spark his passions.

"I've missed this," she said wistfully. "Our sitting here in the evening sharing whatever thoughts occurred to us. While you were away, I'd often sit in here alone. I think because this room more than any other reminds me of you, belongs to you. I always felt your presence here more than anywhere else."

Interesting. He wondered how Albert would have felt about that. As for himself, he'd want his presence felt in the bedchamber, in the bed, when she settled beneath the covers and laid her head on the pillow.

"It is a room designed for an earl," he acknowledged. If she were correct, it would one day belong to her son.

"I suspect each earl made it his own."

He wondered which room she might have made her own. A reading room, no doubt. Although she had nearly brought him to his knees with her kiss in the bedchamber last night.

She sighed. "Well, you've finished your drink and I've finished my chapter. I suppose we should retire."

He didn't much like the anticipation that rocketed through him with that suggestion. He'd located his brother's nightshirts, had contemplated for all of half a minute that perhaps he should wear one to bed this evening, but he'd already offered an excuse to her for why he no longer wore one. He much preferred having his skin within easy reach of her fingers. He regretted that he'd not have a night with her when she also wore no nightdress—a night that she had hinted would come when she was no longer with child. But when the babe was born, he would reveal the truth and she certainly wouldn't welcome him into her bed then—clothing or no.

He should make an excuse, say he needed to recheck the ledgers or wasn't yet sleepy. But then he was prone to not doing what he ought. Setting his glass aside, he stood and held his hand out to her, feeling a quiver of need as her palm slid against his, skin-to-skin. He might ignite if their entire bodies glided together. This was Julia, his brother's wife, he told himself, not someone he lusted after. It was only because he'd gone so long without a woman. A few more weeks and he could have all the women he wanted.

Except the one he desired.

Putting his other arm behind her, he provided her with the leverage she needed to stand. Then her arm came around his in a smooth motion that gave him no choice except to accompany her to her bedchamber. Too late for excuses. Too late to avoid another night with her in his arms.

He shouldn't have limited his scotch. Dulled senses would make the night easier to endure. But it was too late for that as well.

Chapter 7

THE only thing Julia had ever lied to her husband about was that blasted kiss in the garden. Why had he brought it up tonight? Had Edward confessed when they were trekking through the wilds?

Avoiding her gaze in the mirror as Torrie braided her hair, she couldn't imagine that he had. While it might have caused a rift between her and Albert, it would have caused a greater one between Albert and Edward. Edward had to know that. It was the reason he'd not contradicted her lie that awful night.

She didn't like thinking about that kiss. It had been her first, and the wonder of it had taken her by surprise. It left her wanting another. Later, when Albert first kissed her, she had been disappointed that his mouth was not as hungry, as demanding, as raw with need. Because she was a lady, he'd held himself in check. Thank God that had changed after they married and the kisses deepened.

But she'd never been able to forget that first kiss. Or forgive Edward for deceiving her, for being the one to gift her with her initial taste of passion. That privilege had belonged to the man she loved—Albert. They were perfect for each other. A wayward kiss certainly didn't change that.

"Will there by anything else, m'lady?" Torrie asked.

"No, that will be all." Only after her maid left did she meet her gaze in the mirror. It was unkind to think ill of the dead. At least she was reassured that Albert would never learn of her betrayal. She'd always worried that Edward—during one of his drunken stupors—would blurt out what had occurred among the roses. She'd been ever so grateful when he'd taken up residence in his own London town home.

"You did nothing wrong," she reassured her reflection. Except fail to distinguish one brother from the other. She'd not repeated her mistake since that night. Now it was no longer a possibility. What struck her was how much Edward's passing saddened her. She didn't think he'd really meant any harm. It was simply his mischievous ways. Her pride had been pricked, she was embarrassed, and she certainly never wanted her husband to know. She might strive to think of some memories to share with him, but that night in the garden would never be one of them.

Rising, she glanced at the door that led into her husband's bedchamber. *I'll see you in a bit,* he'd said before leaving her to prepare for sleep.

This morning she almost instructed his valet to toss out his nightshirts, to ensure that he no longer wore one to bed. It was heavenly having so much skin easily accessible to her touch. She walked to the bed, used the low steps to climb up, then lay beneath the covers, stared at the canopy and listened to the quiet in the next room. Heard the click of the door opening. Turned her head to the side. Smiled at the sight of his skin revealed by the V of his dressing gown.

"Are you warm enough?" he asked, glancing quickly at the dying fire before looking back at her.

"I will be." She patted his side of the bed.

He extinguished the flame in the lamp before settling in beside her, lying on his back, staring at the canopy that only a moment before had held her attention.

"It's quite boring," she said.

He rolled his head toward her, and she rather wished he hadn't extinguished the lamp. There were too many shadows now, and she couldn't see his eyes as clearly as she'd like, couldn't determine what he was thinking. On the other hand, the grayness made it easier to say words that caused her to feel vulnerable. "You haven't kissed me since you arrived home."

Enough light remained for her to see his brow furrow. "I kissed you last night."

"No, I kissed you. Granted, you returned the kiss with fervor, but you've not begun one."

"The babe—"

"A kiss is certainly not going to hurt the babe. Whereas not kissing me causes me to doubt, to fear far more has changed while you were away than I realized. We used to kiss so often. We've not kissed once all day."

Rising up on an elbow, he cradled her face, stroked his thumb over her cheek and held her gaze. "We can't have you doubting your husband's devotion to you."

He lowered his head. Her eyes slid closed as she welcomed his warm lips brushing over hers just before he settled his mouth in to plunder. That was the only word to describe the force and surety with which his tongue swept through her mouth, claiming every corner, crevice, and hollow. The kiss last night had weakened her knees. This one weakened her entire body, caused warmth to sluice through every inch of her. She turned toward him, sliding one of her knees between his thighs, relishing the echo of his growl.

She skimmed her hands over his bare chest and shoulders, along his back. So firm, so hard, although not quite as hard as the part of him that pressed against her belly. She trailed her fingers down his stomach, his hip, around until she cupped him.

His head came up sharply, his hand tightened around her wrist. "We're not going there. I'm on a weak tether as it is."

"I want to touch you, all of you."

"No."

Taking her hand, he flattened it against the center of his chest, held it there. "You can touch anything not covered in cloth."

"That's hardly fair when I'm willing to let you touch anything you like."

She heard his sharp intake of breath, felt it as his ribs expanded beneath her palm. He squeezed his eyes closed, pressed his forehead to hers. "I shall play by the same rules."

She could not miss how rough and raw his voice sounded, as though he'd dredged those words up from the soles of his feet. He wanted her. She had no doubt that he wanted her. She nipped at his chin. "Spoilsport."

He chuckled low. "I'm working here to be a good

husband. Considerate. Mindful of your delicate condition." He leaned back. "Besides, imagine how mad we'll be for each other after the babe comes."

"I'm mad for you now."

With a low groan, he blanketed her mouth, kissing her with such abandon that she went light-headed. He kept to his promise of touching her only where cloth did not separate her skin from his. Thank God he noticed that the hem of her nightdress had risen up to her thigh. He stroked her calf, the sensitive area behind her knee. All the while he kept his mouth plastered to hers as though he drew the will to live through her.

She grew warm, so warm, wanting to toss off the covers, yearning for much more as her nerve endings thrummed with unbridled desire. She became aware of the dew between her thighs, an aching in her breasts. The power of his kiss astounded her. All the sensations it elicited. They'd shared a few chaste kisses while he was courting her. The more sensual ones had always accompanied their lovemaking, were part and parcel of the whole, and she'd been so lost in the moment that she never noticed all that a kiss stirred to life.

Everything.

He tasted of scotch, smelled of bergamot. His groans caused satisfied pleasure to ripple through her. She tingled, grew warmer, became lethargic and energized at the same time. She wanted to unbutton her nightdress, have his hands slip between the parted material to fondle her breasts, but considering where that action would no doubt lead, she had to acknowledge the wisdom of his rule. Touch nothing covered by linen.

He trailed his lips along the underside of her jaw,

down her throat. His mouth was hot, so incredibly hot. It was a wonder it didn't scorch her skin. His hand left her leg, cradled the back of her head and tucked her face into the hollow of his shoulder where his skin had grown damp. Beneath her cheek his heart pounded furiously.

"We should sleep," he murmured, his voice low and raspy.

She nodded, her arm resting along his side, her hand pressed to his back, her fingers creating soft circles on his skin. Had she known a trip to Africa would put him in the habit of sleeping without a nightshirt, she might have encouraged him to go sooner.

His rule regarding cloth seemed to no longer apply when his mouth wasn't on hers. His arms came around her, drawing her near, and she fell asleep inhaling a fragrance enhanced by the warmth of his flesh.

CONSIDERING how lethargic she'd been, she should have slept well. Instead, dreams of being kissed in a garden had jerked Julia from slumber every time she drifted off too deeply. When Albert had begun to stir, she pretended that she wasn't awake, didn't move when he left her bed and went into his chamber.

Now she sat at her dressing table and stared at her reflection, haunted by the dreams. She'd not thought of the details of that first kiss in years, had shoved aside all the inappropriate responses it kindled within her. She had reacted with such longing to that mouth pressed to hers because she believed it belonged to Albert. The shadows had caused her not to see clearly, to misjudge—

The rap had her shaking off the mad thoughts scurrying through her mind.

"Enter."

The man stepped inside. There were no shadows now. She knew those features. The square cut of his strong jaw, the knifelike edge of his nose, the brown of his eyes, the dark blond of his hair.

"Torrie said you didn't ring for breakfast. I wanted to make sure you were well."

The rough timbre of his voice.

"I've had a time of it getting going this morning."

He took a step nearer. "Are you ill?"

The deep furrow of his brow, the concern in his eyes. She knew these things about him as well as she knew the back of her own hand. She knew *him* as well as she knew herself. Although they'd both admitted to changing during the separation, the very essence of them shouldn't have. Yet something had spurred his reason for avoiding her, and it had nothing to do with sorrow over Edward. Could it be guilt for bad behavior? Out of sight, out of mind, and all that? "Did you practice while you were away?"

His eyebrows raised, his brow furrowed deeper. "Pardon?"

Mortified by her suspicions, she swallowed hard. "Did you kiss other women while you were away? I know it was a long time to be apart and that men have needs—"

"Julia." He was kneeling beside her, holding her hand in both of his before she was able to force out the remainder of the hideous words. The same pose he'd taken when he asked her to marry him. "Your husband would never be unfaithful to you."

"You're my husband. Why would you speak of yourself in the third person?"

"I simply meant that any man fortunate enough to be your husband would adore you to distraction and never stray. Any man. Including myself." He squeezed her hand. "Why would you think I would kiss other women?"

She looked down at his hands, darkened by weeks in the sun, a new strength to them, the veins and muscles standing out in sharp relief. "The kisses last night reminded me . . ." Memories were faulty. She knew that. Memories of her parents had become unclear. That kiss in the garden—it hadn't been like the ones last night, and yet something about it was similar. " . . . of hunger."

"We've been apart for some time. A bit of hunger is to be expected I think."

"But the night before—"

"Was tempered by grief." Lifting one of his hands, he cradled her face, tilted up her chin until her eyes met his. "I swear to you, Julia, on my brother's grave, that I kissed no woman while we were away. I bedded no woman."

She searched his expressive eyes, saw naught but earnestness and truth. "I feel such a fool."

"You shouldn't. You should always be able to share your worries and concerns with me. It is my job to reassure you that all is well."

With a self-conscious laugh, she pressed her fingertips to her forehead. "I don't know what I was thinking."

Wrapping his hands around her wrists, he lowered her arms, leaned in and brushed his lips over hers. "I shall strive to do a better job at restraining my passions."

"No, don't!" His eyes widened while heat scalded her cheeks. What a brazen wanton she was. "I enjoy your passion. That it seems more than it was before . . . perhaps absence makes more than the heart grow fonder."

"It certainly seems to, yes. Now, you should have some breakfast."

After rising to his feet, he walked to the door, paused in the threshold, glanced back. "Nothing ever stays the same, Julia, no matter how much we wish it."

Then he was gone, leaving her to wonder what exactly he'd meant by that.

THE kisses were going to be his undoing. As he riffled through the various drawers in the credenza in his brother's study, searching for any semblance of a will, the disturbing conversation he'd had with Julia rumbled through his mind. He feared that his kisses reminded her of the one he'd bestowed in the garden. A kiss was simply a kiss—

But he'd received enough to know that they differed. Yet he also knew that they changed over time, as a couple became more familiar. Or at least the kisses he gave at the beginning of the night seemed different by the end of it. His relationships with women were short-lived, as he had no desire for anything permanent. He was grateful that he'd been able to speak with complete honesty regarding the fact that he'd not been with a woman, not kissed a woman, while he was away. Still, he understood her suspicions. He wasn't acting like a man who was treading along familiar ground, but rather one exploring new avenues of discovery.

With a harsh curse, he slammed a drawer closed, frustrated by his lack of finding any mention from Albert regarding the arrangements he had made in the event of his death, as well as his own inability to completely embrace his deceptive role as a counterfeit earl. He dreaded tonight, when they would dine, sit in the library, converse. Damn Albert for loving his wife. It would be so much easier if they had shared a platonic relationship and welcomed *not* being in each other's company.

After taking a final walk through the room, searching for any hidden nooks or crannies, he decided he'd have to pen a letter to the solicitor. He could do it here, but he preferred the library. Once there, he poured himself a scotch, downed it in one swallow in order to shake off his lingering frustrations. So many things Albert should have told him that he hadn't. Why hadn't they ever discussed how Albert would want Julia cared for in the event of his demise?

At the desk, Edward tapped his finger on the mahogany wood, striving to determine how best to word the letter to the solicitor so he didn't give himself away. His gaze drifted to the ebony box. He was relatively certain that Julia would have sent acknowledgments to everyone who had offered condolences. The thought of reading them held no appeal, seemed a betrayal of sorts, as people were paying tribute to a man who still breathed. After shoving it to the very edge of the desk, he leaned back in his chair, studied the paneled ceiling.

Julia had the right of it. This room more than any

other reminded him of Albert. If he were to claim a room as his, it would be the billiards room. He wondered which room Julia might have claimed as her own. When he envisioned her, he always saw her in the bedchamber, which conjured up dangerous images of her stretched out on the bed with slumberous eyes—

Oh, he needed a woman. She was one he could not ever have. That he couldn't seem to stop thinking about her was a testament to his body's needs rather than her desirous state. She was swollen with child, for God's sake. Nothing attractive there.

Except her hands were so silken and warm when they traveled over his chest, his back. Her mouth was fiery and eager. Her moans were low and throaty.

Shoving back the chair, he got to his feet and stormed to the window. He was so hot that he was surprised he didn't ignite. He should go to the mausoleum, remind himself of the debt he owed his brother. Pressing his forehead to the cool glass, he realized that he needed to replace images of her in the bedchamber with those of her elsewhere.

The dining room, perhaps. Closing her lips around her fork, a look of sensual delight crossing her face. Her tongue quickly touching the corner of her mouth— No, not the dining room. If he wandered through the residence, he might find a place in which he could view her as unattractive and boring. He owed it to his sanity to give it a go.

The manor house was large, two wings. One could roam the halls for days and not come across anyone else. It had been relatively easy to avoid her when he would come to visit; except now he was supposed to be someone who yearned to be in her company. If he crossed paths with her, he could claim to have been looking for her. It would be a lie, of course, he wasn't wandering about, peering into one room after another because he *wished* to see her. Disappointment didn't punch his gut because he found each room empty. Rather, he decided, it was only because the rooms didn't suit his needs.

None reminded him of her. They seemed too harsh, imposing, not nearly as welcoming.

He should suggest she redo the residence so it reflected her more than any countess who came before her. It wasn't as though he had any sentimental attachment to anything. He didn't even know which rooms his mother might have decorated or if she had. When he was a child, most of his time had been spent in the day or night nursery except when he and Albert were paraded out to be inspected by their parents for a few minutes in the afternoon or evening. He had far more memories of his nanny than he did of either parent.

He was much fonder of Havisham than Evermore. Although many of the rooms there were locked, they'd been free to roam the hallways to their heart's content. While he and Albert had walked through every inch of this residence, most of it was still foreign to him. He was more at home in his London residence.

He needed to become more at home here. Albert would want his son raised within these walls, which meant much of his carousing was behind him. He'd have to set a good example, teach the boy how to be a proper lord. He'd never planned to marry, to have children, yet here he was on the cusp of raising a lad without enjoying any of the marital benefits. No woman in his bed every night. Not that he relished the warmth of Julia's body snuggled against his. Not that he was going to miss the sound of her breathing when his ruse was no longer necessary. Not that he drew solace from watching her in peaceful slumber.

At the end of a long hallway, he peered into a corner room papered with yellow flowers. Floor-to-ceiling windows along one wall provided a view of the rolling hills. There was an absence of clutter and, for the most part, furniture. A small settee sat before the fireplace, with a large table behind it decorated with an assortment of drawings. Near one of the windows, Julia sat on a plush bench, an easel in front of her, watercolors on a small stand beside her.

He could see only a portion of her profile, but she appeared so serene, so calm, a direct contrast to the wind battering the trees and the dark clouds rolling ominously across the sky. He would like to see her bathed in sunlight. He suspected she had chosen this room because of the days when the sun would warm her.

And she was singing, a soft, lyrical song about angels watching over a wee one as the babe slept. He imagined her holding that child, rocking it, and singing the same tune. He doubted he would ever see the sight. She would banish him from her life when she learned the truth. He didn't understand why his chest suddenly felt as though it might cave in.

He would be in the child's life, would insist on it, but he could not force himself into the mother's. Whatever time he would have with her would be fleeting, moments shared only until the birth, only until no reason existed for him not to reveal his deception.

But until that moment he was her husband—if not in truth, then in deceit, for a greater good. To honor a vow he'd made without considering consequences.

He tried to imagine what Albert would do at this moment, but then what did it really matter? She and he had acknowledged that changes had occurred during their separation. He had to stop treading too lightly, had to stop worrying over mimicking Albert. He could be himself, within reason. So he decided to give in to temptation.

As quietly as possible, he crept over the thick Aubusson carpeting until he was directly behind her. He cupped his hands on either side of her waist. She gave a start, a tiny gasp. He pressed his lips against her nape. With a soft sigh, she dropped her head back.

"I didn't hear you enter."

He trailed his mouth to the silken sensitive spot below her ear. "I wanted to surprise you."

Standing, she turned, her eyes glittering like the finest sapphires. "I'm glad. I was missing you."

She rose up on her toes, and he lowered his head, taking her mouth as any devoted husband might, with hunger and need. His response should have been forced, should have been the result of playacting. Instead it felt as natural and real as the woman in his arms.

If he didn't distract himself, he was going to lure her to the settee and take advantage of her enthusiasm. He might be a scoundrel but he had no plans to be completely rotten where she was concerned. She had been given into his keeping, and while it required an unconventional approach at the moment, he had no plans to betray the trust his brother had placed in him.

Leaning back, he smiled. "You do have a lovely way of making a man glad he sought you out." Lowering his gaze, he allowed regret to lace his voice. "But we must behave."

She winged her eyebrows and pressed her teeth into her lower lip. "I'm very much looking forward to the time when I can be naughty."

His lungs ceased to work as he was bombarded with images of her writhing beneath him on satin sheets, their heated bodies entangled, covered in dew. With great effort, he slid his gaze to the canvas, fully expecting to see a naked goddess.

Instead a mouse wearing trousers, shirt, waistcoat, jacket, and a perfectly knotted cravat greeted him, thankfully dousing his rampaging desires. "Interesting. I didn't think ladies liked mice."

And he hoped to hell that she hadn't shared this little creature with Albert before he left.

She laughed. "I know you're accustomed to my landscapes, but of late I've just had these whimsical creatures fluttering through my mind."

He walked over to the table with its scattered papers. She had created an entire menagerie of animals dressed in clothing. "They're very good."

Stepping up beside him, she rubbed his arm. "Do you think so? You don't think they're too silly?"

"I think they're marvelous."

As marvelous as the blush that swept over her cheeks.

"I thought to have them bound." Sadness touched her eyes. "I'd considered asking Edward to write a story to go along with them."

"He'd have liked that." When he rose from the dead, he would do it. For her, for his brother's child. He glanced around. This was her room. Even when it was dreary out, it was sunny in here. He was glad she had this room, hoped it would bring her solace in the days to come.

Chapter 8

A WEEK later, galloping his horse through the freezing rain, Edward ignored the sleet that pricked his face and cursed the weather for turning foul so quickly, cursed the farmer who had needed help pushing a wagon out of the mud, cursed his need to have an active role in managing the estates, to check on the tenants, to ensure all was well.

He considered for all of a heartbeat returning to the farm and taking shelter there until the storm passed, but he knew Julia would worry, and his entire purpose behind his ruse was to ensure that she didn't fret.

And blast it all, he didn't want to go another moment without seeing her. He wanted to enjoy an evening spent in her company, dining and conversing. Going to bed.

That he was content just lying with her had been a revelation. He liked listening to her breathing, enjoyed inhaling her fragrance when it became laced with the scent of sleep. It was a little different than when she was awake.

Sometimes she snored, more of a soft snuffling sound.

Whether she faced him or had her back to him, her feet always managed to work their way between his calves. And they were bloody cold when they first made their way there. He might have yelped if he didn't fear discouraging her, as he was fond of having her body oddly interwoven with his.

It was dangerous, so dangerous, how much he enjoyed being in her company. It didn't matter her reason for being with him. It only mattered that she was—

His horse screamed. He was aware of nothing surrounding him and then pain ricocheting through his shoulder, along his ribs, air refusing to come into his lungs, his eyes tearing up. Rolling to his back, he found himself in danger of drowning from all the rain. *Relax, don't fight the pain. Draw in a little air. Just a little.*

It wasn't the first time in his life that he'd taken a tumble. He doubted it would be his last, but it certainly couldn't have happened at a more inopportune time. Darkness was descending. And he was so bloody cold.

He thought of the warm fire waiting for him, the warm brandy, and the warm woman.

Pushing himself to a sitting position, he was grateful that his lungs seemed to be working again, even more grateful to see his gelding standing, although it was favoring its left front leg. Damnation. Making his way to his feet, he cautiously approached and knelt before his steed. Gently, he ran his hands over the leg. "Doesn't appear to be broken. That's good, but I assume you've gone lame." Taking the reins, he stood and guided the horse forward. It limped but at least it wasn't screeching in pain.

Edward glanced around, trying to map out the countryside in his mind, calculate distance. When he and Albert had reached their majority, they returned to Evermore and their first order of business was to ride over every inch of land that belonged to them, to introduce themselves to the tenants, to understand exactly what had been left to Albert. Edward had felt no jealousy, no envy, no desire to hold what had been placed in Albert's keeping. He was content to be the second son, to receive an allowance, to be free of responsibility. Even now he was merely the heir presumptive until Julia delivered her child, hopefully his brother's heir.

Although he could no longer be completely without responsibility. He would have to see after the raising of his brother's child. One day he would take the lad on a ride over this land, would introduce him to the tenants, would speak to him of his father. And he would hope that in time he would be able to forget how right it had felt to hold Julia while she slept.

With a frustrated sigh, he realized he was probably as close to the manor house as he was to any tenant lodging where he might be able to leave his horse and borrow another. He was not looking forward to the next couple of hours, but there was no hope for it. "Going to be a long walk, old boy. We'd best get to it."

More than once, as he began to lose feeling in his hands and feet, he considered stopping, lying down, taking a rest, but he feared if he ceased moving for even a few minutes he would cease moving forever. And that wouldn't do. Not with Julia waiting for him. Rather, waiting for her husband.

He pictured her working with her watercolors, sporadically looking through the windows toward the hills, striving to spot his dashing figure astride the gelding as it loped down the slope. Edward had deliberately gone in a direction that ensured she would be able to catch sight of him when he returned. But that wasn't going to happen now. Full darkness was almost upon him.

If he had grown up here, if he knew this land as well as he knew every hill and dale that surrounded Havisham, he might be more confident that he was trudging along the correct path. The sleet and snow obscured the stars. The compass he always carried in his pocket was of little use without light, and he doubted that if he struck a match, he could keep the flame going long enough against the wind to get a bead on the arrow of the compass.

Yet he was determined that one way or another he would make his way back to Julia, he would give her no reason to mourn for a husband she had already lost.

JULIA had done very little that afternoon except stand at the window and watch for her husband's return. She shouldn't have let him go out. Had she asked, he would have stayed. She knew he would have. He'd become more solicitous than he'd ever been, given her more attention than he ever had. He'd never really been lacking in either regard, but there was more devotion now— which she'd hardly thought possible.

His touches came more frequently, his interest in her more intense. He seemed to care about every aspect of her. She thought she'd loved him as much as it was possible to love any man. Strange to realize that she loved him a little bit more each day.

Before he left for the safari, it was as though their

love had plateaued, as though there was nothing additional for either of them to give to the other. But now she realized how wrong she'd been. There would always be more, something new to discover, uncover. A reason for their feelings to be reignited with a passion that surpassed what it had been.

So she was striving not to worry because the sun had disappeared but her husband had not yet reappeared over the rise. She'd never before noticed how dashing he looked riding away from her. She'd anticipated him looking far more dashing returning to her, a smile spreading across his face as he saw her. But it was growing too dark for her to see anything.

After ringing for the butler, she returned to her post at the window. If his travels hadn't ended in tragedy, she might not be so worried, but it could have easily been him the gorilla attacked rather than Edward. Life was precarious. She heard the click of the door opening, the fall of Rigdon's footsteps.

"You had a need, m'lady?" he asked.

"His lordship went over that rise this morning. As he's yet to return, I fear he might have suffered a mishap."

"He's an excellent horseman. The weather is no doubt slowing him or perhaps he took shelter for the night."

He wouldn't do that. He wouldn't leave her to worry. She turned from the window. "Gather up the outdoor servants and send them to search for him."

Surprise flickered across Rigdon's face before he could prevent it, but he quickly returned his expression to its stoic state. "It's rather nasty out there, m'lady."

"Which is the very reason they need to find him."

While Rigdon moved not a muscle, she was rather certain that deep inside, he was shifting his weight, possibly shuffling his feet. "I'm not certain he would approve of that action."

He wouldn't. Placing servants at risk. He wouldn't like it at all. "Then he should have returned sooner. Send them out."

"As you wish, m'lady."

He left, and she gave her attention back to the gloom. It was dreadful out there. She was being selfish to care about only her own happiness. Albert was not going to be pleased with her, even if he'd taken a tumble and was in trouble. But she could not bear the thought of him languishing—

A shape in the distance, an odd silhouette, caught her notice. Not a man on a horse, but she was relatively certain it was a man and quite possibly a horse.

"Rigdon!" Her heart hammering, she rushed from the room and nearly slammed into a footman. "Find Rigdon, let him know that someone is coming over the hill. Could be his lordship."

"Yes, m'lady."

He took off, his long legs quickly separating him from her, and she was suddenly quite grateful for tall footmen. She was pacing the entryway when the front door finally opened and a familiar figure stepped through.

"Albert!" She was suddenly in his arms, aware of his trembling and the cold of his skin as he placed his cheek to her temple.

"You shouldn't be touching me," he said. "I'm filthy."

Only his grip on her was so sure, so tight, she wasn't certain she could have broken away even if she'd wanted. Which she didn't. "I was so worried."

"Sorry, sweetheart. I helped a farmer whose wagon had become stuck in the mud. On my way home, my horse went lame. It was a day of mishaps."

"I was afraid you'd gotten lost."

Gently, with a gloved hand, he tipped up her face. "Not when you're my north star."

Then his mouth was on hers as though they'd been separated for years rather than hours, or as though a parting was on the horizon that couldn't be avoided. He was worried about the dangers of her giving birth, she knew that. But this seemed to be more, was woven with urgency, with need. She wondered if he'd feared never making his way back to her, if the storm had caused him to doubt that he'd ever again have the chance to hold her, to kiss her.

Drawing back, he held her gaze. "You warm better than any fire."

She smiled. "I should hope so. Rigdon, have a bath prepared for his lordship."

"Have already seen to it, m'lady."

Nodding, Albert released her. "Then I shall take advantage of that."

"I'll come with you, assist—"

"No need. I shan't be long. I'm as hungry as I am cold." He folded a hand over her shoulder. "I'll join you for dinner shortly."

"I'll be waiting." Always she would wait for him.

Watching him trudge up the stairs, she couldn't shake off the feeling that she might have lost him tonight, that tragedy seemed to take delight in visiting this family.

WITH a shudder of pleasure, Edward sank into the steaming water. He would have preferred sinking into Julia, which was the very reason that he forced himself to decline her invitation to assist him. His passions were on a short tether.

During each grueling step, he had envisioned her face, her smile, her soft voice urging him forward. When he had opened the door and seen her standing there, seen the relief, the joy wreathing her features, everything he felt for her that he had spent years denying—burying beneath caustic remarks and asinine behavior, drowning in drink—burst forth like a volcano spewing ash and lava. And just as the molten magma covered everything near it, so he had wanted to envelop her, to take true possession, complete possession.

Julia wouldn't have denied him, would have given him anything he asked. He saw it in the glittering of her eyes. But she would have thought she was giving it to Albert. Her joy at his return wasn't truly for him. And that knowledge had chilled him more than the winds and snow blowing beyond the walls. But it didn't lessen his desire for her, and that was the damnable problem.

He heard the door click quietly open. "I'm not yet ready for you, Marlow."

"How lucky you are then that I'm not he."

Pushing himself up from his lounging position, causing the water to ripple around him, he glanced back over his shoulder to see Julia standing there, holding a glass.

She smiled sweetly. "I thought you might like some scotch."

"You're a godsend." He held out his hand, fully expecting her to give him the glass and depart.

Instead she came around and knelt beside the tub before extending the glass to him. He took a healthy swallow, savoring the heat that settled deep within him. He cast her a sideways glance. "I shan't be much longer."

"I'd like to wash your back."

"It's not necessary."

She took a cloth and the soap from a nearby stand, dipped them in the water, and began to rub them together. "I want to."

"Julia—"

She arched a brow. "You know better than to argue with me when my mind is set."

He knew nothing at all, except that it was very unwise for her touch him when his mind had careened into lascivious thoughts during his trek in order to keep his legs moving forward. Another swallow of scotch, larger than the one he'd taken before. Steeling himself, he placed his elbows on his upraised knees, allowing his back to curve slightly. "Do your worst."

The light tinkling of her laughter echoed through the room as she moved behind him. "I've long wanted to do this," she said as she placed both her hands on either side of his spine.

What had become of the bloody cloth?

Then another thought dawned. She'd never done

this for his brother. He tossed back what remained of the scotch, clutched the glass in fingers that wanted to reach back and bring her forward, cradle her face, kiss her. Do something to distract himself from the light press of her palms as they glided down his back, up and over his shoulders. God, but it felt marvelous.

"Whose wagon got stuck in the mud?" she asked.

How was he supposed to think with her fingers dancing over his skin? "Beckett, I think. Yes, Beckett."

Why did his voice sound as though he was strangling? Perhaps because he was having a devil of a time drawing in air.

"Am I hurting you?" she asked.

"God, no."

"Should I stop?"

Yes, yes, please in the name of all that is holy . . .

"No." He squeezed his eyes shut. "Unless you want to."

"I don't. It's as lovely as I thought it would be, the water and soap creating a slickness as my hands glide over your skin."

The glass in his hand was in danger of breaking with the exertion he was placing on it. It was a risk, but he had to ask. "If you wanted to do this before, why didn't you?"

"Because I didn't think you'd approve of my boldness. But then this evening, when I feared something had happened to you, that I might lose you, I realized how silly I'd been."

Turning slightly until he could see her, he said, "Julia, I've always liked my women bold."

Her brow furrowed slightly. "I thought you wanted me prim and proper, a countess above reproach."

"I want you to be however you are. You don't have to pretend with me." The irony of his words didn't escape him since he was pretending with her. And he hated it. Hated that he couldn't yet tell her the truth. Only a few more weeks. He could hold onto the ruse a bit longer, but there was no reason for her to be anyone other than who she was. He didn't like considering that perhaps his brother had caused her to hold her passions in check. He'd have not done it on purpose, but of all the hellions, Albert had been the most upstanding, avoiding Society's censure while the others embraced it.

She scooted around until he could see her more clearly. With the pads of her palms she began creating small circles over his shoulders, carrying them down his arms, back up, her eyes focused on the movements of her hands rather than on his face.

"I've missed the intimacy," she murmured so low that he nearly didn't hear her.

"We agreed that for the sake of the child—"

"Yes, I know," she cut in, lifting her gaze to his, "but that doesn't extinguish the want, does it." A statement, not a question.

He should banish her now, announce that he was ready to dress, but her eyes, her voice, held such raw need, he could no more dismiss her words than he could dismiss her. "No, it doesn't."

His words rang with far too much truth.

Her hand slowly dipped below the surface of the water, closed around him, her lips curving into a slow, sensual smile, no doubt because she'd discovered him hard and ready. He wrapped his fingers around her wrist, stilling her. "Julia—"

"Please, let me do this for you," she rasped with such longing that everything in him tightened with unbearable need.

"I'm not in the habit of receiving without giving." Dear God, the words were out before he'd given them any thought. How could he think when she was tempting him so? He could only hope that he hadn't revealed himself, that she wasn't going to call him a liar.

"One of your unspoken rules, no doubt, but rules are meant to be broken. It would give me so much pleasure to break this one."

"The pleasure would be all mine, Julia."

She shook her head. "No, it wouldn't. I promise I would take equal delight from watching you. It's been so, so long. Allow me to grant you release. Please."

She would despise him when she learned the truth, but how could he deny her what she so obviously yearned for without causing her to doubt her husband's attraction for her, his love of her? When weighed against what the future held, all that mattered was this moment, ensuring that she was happy, that she was secure in her belief that her husbands' regard for her had not changed.

Slowly, he relaxed his fingers, lifted his hand to her cheek, not caring that water dripped onto her gown. He brought her nearer, settling his mouth over hers. Her lips parted on a quiet sigh, his tongue stroked hers with the same determination that she caressed him. He brought up his other hand, cradling her face, not bothering to keep his passions in check, falling into the depths of sensations that she created so masterfully.

She was correct. It had been so long, too long. While

he wanted her out of the blasted gown, wanted his hands gliding over every inch of her, he kept them where they were—knowing it was imperative that he lessen her regrets. Oh, but it was difficult when she sighed so softly, when his body was betraying him, when she was so very skilled—

He trailed his mouth along her neck, dipped his tongue in the hollow at her throat. "Jules, dear God, Jules."

"Shall I stop?" Her voice seemed to come from far away, another world, another sphere.

"Not unless you want me to die."

She nipped at his chin, took his right lobe between her teeth, worried it for a bit before pressing her mouth to his ear. He could feel the heat, the moisture—

"I love your hot cock straining against my hand," she murmured in a low, throaty voice.

Christ! He nearly reacted, nearly exploded then and there, but he caught himself just in time, recalling Albert's bad hearing in one ear. Right ear. Deaf ear. She thought he couldn't hear her words. How was a man not supposed to react to that? He was a bloody saint.

Hungrily, he took her mouth, craving as much intimacy as he could allow without being eaten by guilt. But it would come later. He knew it would. But for now, for this moment, he was lost in the sensations she brought to life with deft fingers and wicked palms and naughty suggestions. Her other hand journeyed over him as though she were an explorer who had discovered a lost continent and needed to map out every trail, every valley, every rise.

His body bucked with the force of the orgasm slam-

ming into him. His groan was feral and deep, even as
his mouth remained latched onto hers, swallowing her
soft moan, her triumphant cry. He very nearly dragged
her into the copper tub with him.

Instead, breathing heavily, he pressed his forehead
to hers. "Damn you."

Her laughter was the sweetest sound he'd ever heard.
Leaning back, she cradled his face. How could she look so
blasted innocent, so sweet, when she uttered such naughty
words about his cock? And he had to carry on as though
he hadn't heard them when they were in fact burned into
his brain and being repeated like a favorite ditty.

"I knew it would bring me as much pleasure," she said.

She had truly enjoyed it. It was reflected in the scin-
tillating glow of her eyes. "You should be more selfish."

Smiling tenderly, she shook her head. "I love you so
much."

Reality came crashing back with a vengeance that
very nearly doubled him over. He wasn't the man she
loved. He'd taken advantage of the lies, and all his reasons for doing so seemed to mock him now. "Julia—"

Leaning in, she kissed him deeply before pushing
herself to her feet. "We're going to be late for dinner."

She strode out, leaving him to sink beneath the
water, knowing that one day she would hate him for
what had just transpired. What a bastard he was that he
couldn't seem to regret it.

He'd been intimate with countless women, yet every
moment with them paled when compared with what he'd
just experienced. Dammit all if with Julia he didn't want
a full and complete coupling, a full and complete sur-
render. With her, he wanted what he could never have.

Chapter 9

"PLANNING to look smug all night?"

Sitting beside her husband at the small dining table, Julia couldn't help the immense sense of satisfaction that continued to roll through her. "I like that after all this time, I'm still able to surprise you."

Albert lifted his glass, took a sip of wine. "You did manage to do that."

"I enjoyed it immensely."

His eyes grew warm. "I suspect I enjoyed it more."

Reaching across, she placed her hand over his. "Having lost three babes, I understand the caution and that we must do everything to ensure we don't lose this one, but I have missed the intimacy, dreadfully."

His gaze darted over to a footman before coming back to rest on her. "Perhaps we should discuss this later."

She bit her lower lip. "I don't know. I'm feeling a bit naughty."

Intertwining his fingers with hers, he brought her hand up and pressed a kiss to her knuckles, holding her gaze. "I rather like when you're naughty. And while our servants are paid to be discreet, I suspect it's best not to give them cause for gossip."

There was no censure in his voice, but there was wisdom in his words. Even though they were speaking quietly and the wind was howling beyond the windows, discretion was no doubt called for. With a nod, she worked their fingers free and returned her attention to the glazed chicken. "You've never called me Jules before."

"Pardon?" His brow was furrowed. He looked genuinely perplexed.

"During . . . your bath, you called me Jules."

"I can't be held accountable for anything I might have said during my . . . bath."

"I rather liked it."

"My bath?" Now he was teasing her, his eyes glinting with wickedness even though he'd called for them to be discreet.

She gave him a secretive smile. "Jules. It seems less formal."

"It was a rather informal moment."

"So it was."

The conversation drifted into how she'd spent her day, and she refrained from admitting she'd spent most of it worrying over his return. She told him about her latest watercolor: a rabbit with a walking stick. He didn't laugh or mock her, but seemed to think it was perfectly normal that she would give her imaginary creatures humanlike qualities.

"He's a rather solitary fellow," she said.

He didn't seem surprised. Simply nodded and said, "Locke, then."

She was taken aback, then considered the importance of his observation. "Yes, I suppose he is. I hadn't really thought about it in that way."

"All your creatures represent someone."

She took another bite of chicken, forced herself to eat peas for the baby's sake. "Really?"

He gave her a knowing look. "The badger is Ashe. Determined. Stubborn. The weasel is Edward, always striving to get out of his duties, to get away with something."

She opened her mouth to protest, closed it. "That was the first one I did, right after you left. I suppose I was a bit cross with him for taking you away. I should tear that one up."

"Nonsense. It would have pleased my brother inordinately to see how you portrayed him."

"It just seems rather petty now."

"Creativity often mimics life. He'd applaud your efforts."

She wasn't quite certain he'd appreciate them as much as Albert implied. "Which one is you?" she challenged.

"You're the fox," he said. "Clever." He arched a brow. "Quite pretty. Although the color is wrong."

"But foxes are red."

"Not all of them. Once I saw a black fox out over the moors at Havisham. They're rare, which suits you even better, for you are a rare find."

She felt her cheeks warm. It had been so long since he'd flirted with her. She rather felt like a young girl again, innocent and waiting breathlessly for her first dance. How was she to have known then that her first dance would be with him and would lead her into his arms forever? "I've never heard of a black fox."

"Then you'll have to take my word for it."

"I rather liked pretending my hair was red."

"I like your hair just as it is. It brings out the blue of your eyes."

"I always thought it rather boring."

"Nothing about you is boring."

She angled her head, narrowed her eyes. "Are you courting me, my lord Greyling?"

He scoffed. "A man does not court his wife."

"Then you're avoiding answering my question. Which of the animals represents you?"

Taking a deep breath, he tapped his blunt-tipped finger against the bowl of his wine glass, seemed to consider. "Not the rat. At first I thought he was Edward, rummaging around in the rubbish, but then I caught sight of the weasel with his little beady eyes."

"You don't know which is you," she announced, somewhat surprised that he couldn't see it.

"The horse. Noble. Strong. Can be depended upon. Not much for laughing, but it won't let you down."

"Only yours did tonight."

He shook his head. "My fault there. I was riding him too hard, trying to get home. Snow was beginning to cover the ground. I'm lucky he didn't step into a hole and break a leg."

"You probably should have taken shelter somewhere for the night."

"I didn't want you worrying." He swallowed what remained of his wine as though he wasn't quite comfortable with that admission. Odd. He'd never had difficulty expressing his feelings, but then the past few weeks he'd been put through an entire gamut of emotions.

Every time she thought she knew exactly what to expect from him, she discovered she knew nothing at all.

THEY finished dinner and retired to the library. As she sat near the fire and read a book, Edward lounged back in a chair opposite hers, his finger tapping his glass of port. She'd seemed surprised that he'd been able to discern whom the animals in her drawings represented. He would have preferred being a squirrel, something lively and fun. Or even a promiscuous rabbit. But then weasels were known for stealing things, and he'd stolen a kiss from her, stolen away her husband. Was stealing these moments with her now.

He should have made an excuse. He needed to work, go over his ledgers, study his accounts. Instead he was sitting here enjoying the slope of her neck as she bent her head to read, enjoyed the fact that she still wore that damned smug smile.

As well she should. He didn't know if he'd ever reacted so viscerally to a woman's touch. He wanted to blame the intensity of his reaction on his recent abstinence, but he suspected if she got up from that chair, walked over to him and pressed her hand to his cheek, he'd draw her down to his lap and claim her mouth with a feverishness that would send most young ladies scurrying from the room. But she wasn't one to scurry. She would return it in equal measure.

Just as she had that night in the garden, just as she did each time they kissed.

Because she'd believed then and now that he was Albert.

Were they so alike in all things that she couldn't tell them apart? It was what he'd prayed for on the ship the entire time it had traveled over rough seas to return to England. *Don't let her figure out that it's me, the sneaky bastard who takes what isn't his. Don't let her realize that I'm not her husband.*

He'd repeated the mantra a thousand times while he sat in the hold and watched over the simple pine box, kept his brother company. He had expected it to be hard to not give anything away, to pretend to be Albert.

He hadn't expected it to be hell.

She lifted her gaze to his, her brow furrowed as though she'd felt the path of his thoughts. Part of him hoped she'd say, *I just realized who you are.* Part of him was beginning to hope she never would. How could he destroy such a remarkable woman?

"The servants were wondering if they should decorate the residence for Christmas."

He studied the port remaining in his glass. "Hard to believe it's that time of year already."

"December did seem to arrive with us hardly noticing. I wasn't certain what to tell them since we're in mourning."

"Have them brighten up the place."

She closed her book. "I didn't mean to be insensitive. I know you're probably not feeling very festive."

"I had two months of mourning him before I ever arrived here. I shall be jolly for Christmas. What gift would please you?"

Her lips pursed into a little moue of displeasure. "You know what I want."

Damnation. Had they discussed Christmas gifts before Albert departed? How the devil was Edward to deduce what she might have asked for? Had Albert already purchased it? He needed to go through every nook and cranny in the master bedchamber and the library. And if he didn't find it—

He studied her, sitting there, looking at him as though she were confident that he knew exactly what she desired. What would she want? What did any woman want?

Jewelry.

Necklace? Ear bobs? Bracelet? All three.

Rubies. No. Sapphires to match her eyes. No. Onyx. Black pearls. He'd only ever seen them on an island in the South Seas. They were as rare a find as she was. So kind, nurturing, but with a streak of wickedness in her that he would like to explore more fully. But that was an exploration forbidden to him. Instead he would have to be content with memorizing her laugh, her smile, the way her eyes sparkled with mischief, darkened with passion, softened when she rubbed her stomach as she was doing now.

"A healthy child," he murmured with conviction. Not jewels, not trinkets, not baubles. "That's what you want for Christmas."

Her smile would ward off the dark, turn back the cold winds, provide shelter from the rain. "It's what we agreed to give each other. We may have misjudged, as according to the physician, he won't arrive until around the first of the year. But it won't be much longer. I do hope he'll have your hair."

"I hope he has yours." He didn't think that was

unfair to his brother, as he saw Albert every time he looked in the mirror.

"Brown eyes."

"Blue."

"Are you going to disagree with me on everything?"

"In truth, Julia, I don't give a fig what he looks like. As long as he's strong and healthy." And a boy. A boy would ensure Julia's place in Society, ensure she would not be beholden to Edward for any kindnesses.

"It's silly to worry over the other aspects," she said, "but it's fun to speculate. I can see him so clearly in my mind. I suppose it's a mother's intuition."

"I think you're going to make a wonderful mother."

"I shall endeavor to be so. It's a rather daunting task."

"I have no doubt you will succeed."

She placed her hand over her heart. "You've never been so vocal in your belief in me. Not that I needed the words. You showed me often enough, but still it is nice to hear them."

He loved Albert, but his brother had always been quieter, less verbose. That she would welcome words that would have been left unsaid pained him, and he didn't know why. Actions were all well and good, but she deserved the actions and the words. She deserved a good deal more than he could ever give her, than he would ever have the right to give her. It was important not to forget that her enjoying his company was only temporary. He finished off his port, stood. "We should probably retire. It's been a long day, and I'm quite weary."

Pushing herself to her feet, she placed her hand on his arm. He fought not to remember where that hand had been earlier, how her fingers had danced over him. It had been a mistake to give in to her pleas, although he was having a difficult time feeling remorse.

They traversed the hallways, ascended the stairs in silence. At her door, he raised her hand, pressed a light kiss to her knuckles. "I'll see you in a bit."

"Undress me."

Everything in him froze, tightened. He stared at her inviting smile, her smoldering eyes.

"It's late," she added. "I hate to disturb my maid."

"She's paid to be disturbed." His voice sounded scratchy and raw, not at all like his.

She flattened her palm against his chest, and he wondered if she could feel the thundering of his heart. In truth, he wanted nothing as much as he wanted to disrobe her, but that course was fraught with dangers. "I'd rather you do it."

"I'm not certain that's wise. I'm on a short leash here, Julia."

Lowering her hand, she tilted up her chin, a challenging glint darkening the sapphire of her eyes. "I think you're simply being prudish."

Prudish? Him? He'd removed clothes from a thousand women. Well, at least a dozen. He didn't know why his sexual exploits suddenly shamed him, made him wish he'd been a bit more discerning, more deserving of her. As though he could ever deserve her. But he'd be damned if he'd shrink from a challenge, especially one offered by her.

He could be strong, even if it meant being stronger than he'd ever needed to be. He could resist her, could ensure that nothing happened to put her babe at risk. Even as he cursed the vow he'd made to Albert, he reached past her, turned the knob, shoved open the door, grabbed her hand, and drew her into her bed-chamber.

 THE door slamming in their wake should have had Julia wondering if she'd pushed him too far. Instead, as she stood in the center of the room, her back to him, her body thrummed with anticipation.

She felt the tug on the lacings of her gown, then the slow parting of the cloth as he took his sweet time to loosen the bindings. He skimmed one finger across her shoulders and back, lingering on her spine, before trailing it down one side, up the other. He pressed his lips to her nape, and she felt the heated circle of dew formed by his open mouth. Everything within her turned molten. She wanted that dew covering every inch of her body.

He eased her gown down, and she stepped out of it.

"I'll leave the remainder to you," he said.

Disappointment slammed into her. Turning, she saw that he was already at the wardrobe in the process of hanging up the gown. Hanging it up when she would have preferred he discard it on the floor because he was too impatient to unveil the rest of her. How silly she was to think he found her the least bit attractive in her current state. She'd long ago ceased wearing corsets or anything binding, so she had little left to remove except for her chemise and drawers. Her maid had left a night-dress laid out on the foot of the bed. Julia was incredibly tempted not to put it on, to force him to look at her nudity, to acknowledge all the changes in her body.

Knowing what they risked didn't lessen her desire

for him. If anything, since his return, she wanted him more than ever. He was more forthcoming with his feelings, his praise. And the way she sometimes caught him looking at her—as though he were on the verge of ravishing her any minute—caused her to yearn for him all the more.

So it wasn't her swollen body that had him turning his back on her. It was his desire for her. Taking solace in that, she slipped into her nightdress and spun around to face him. He was still at her wardrobe, standing before it as though striving to make sense of her gowns.

"You might as well undress in here," she told him as she walked to the dressing table and sat upon the cushioned bench. Reaching up, she began removing pins from her hair.

"I'll do that."

In the mirror, she saw him step behind her, his jacket, neck cloth, and waistcoat already gone, his cuffs and two buttons on his shirt undone, leaving him looking rather uncivilized. He was much quicker at undressing himself than he was at undressing her. Lowering her hands to her lap, she reminded him, "You've never done this service for me before."

Within the reflection, his eyes captured and held hers. "I've thought a thousand times of doing it."

She furrowed her brow. "Why didn't you?"

"I wasn't confident you'd appreciate it."

"I've never known you to lack in confidence."

"Perhaps you don't know me as well as you think."

Sifting his hands through her tresses, he began removing the pins, carefully placing them in the china dish on the dressing table.

"It's odd, isn't it, that after all this time we still discover things about each other," she said.

Her hair tumbled down and he buried his hands in the abundant strands, gently massaging her scalp. "I suspect an entire lifetime wouldn't be long enough to discover every facet of you."

"I'm not such a mystery."

A corner of his mouth hitched up. "You are to a man who wants to know everything."

"I don't keep secrets."

His gaze was far too knowing, his expression that of a man who could uncover hidden depths that she hadn't even known she possessed. "Every lady has at least one."

Swallowing hard, she strove not to look flustered by the accuracy of his statement as that long ago night in the garden with Edward raced through her mind. She'd never given herself leave to examine it fully, fearful of what she might uncover about herself.

Reaching past her, he snatched up her brush and began dragging it through her hair. "A hundred strokes, isn't it?"

"I'll be content with a dozen tonight."

"I might not be satisfied with less than two hundred."

"I thought you were tired."

"Not too tired for this. It's rather soothing, actually."

He took such care, was so gentle. She could fall asleep right there if not for the fact that she didn't want to miss a single moment of his attentions. How could she be so greedy for his touch, his nearness? Perhaps every now and then it was good for them to spend a few months apart.

"You're awfully skilled. When you were a bachelor, did you treat other ladies to your talents with a brush?"

"Bit late to be jealous of them."

"I'm not. I'm just curious."

"I've never done this for another lady. I never wanted to."

Such conviction in his words. She didn't doubt him, she never had. But all these changes in her body seemed to play havoc with her mind, her thoughts. Some days she wept for no reason at all. Some nights she questioned her ability to hold his interest. And other times she was as confident as ever. Although presently she was yearning for an abundance of affection.

She took delight in watching his hand gliding over her hair, observing the concentration on his face as though he were as lost in the sensations as she was. She couldn't recall him ever being so astonishingly absorbed by so simple a task. He had returned to her a man who seemed to take nothing for granted. She appreciated this new aspect to him.

Gathering up her hair, draping it over one shoulder, he leaned down and pressed a kiss to the side of her neck, just behind her ear. It seemed he'd also grown rather fond of her neck.

"Don't plait it," he said in a low voice that sent a shimmer of want through her. He set the brush aside, moved to the sitting area, dropped down into a chair and began tugging off a boot.

The masculinity of the act took her by surprise, as did the realization that she had never actually watched her husband dress or undress. He'd always come to her fully prepared to face the day or to enjoy the night. He took care of his toilette in his bedchamber with the assistance of his valet.

Getting up from the bench, she headed toward the bed, casting furtive glances his way. He was setting the other boot beside the first. She reached the steps she used to clamber into bed. His stockings were joining the boots.

She climbed onto the mattress. He stood, reached up, grabbed the back of his shirt and began dragging it over his head. Little by little his skin came into view. Was there anything more sensual than the unveiling of the male torso—even one with which she was remarkably familiar? Her mouth went dry.

She brought the covers over her as though they could protect her from everything she was feeling. They could not travel where her mind wandered, not without risk to the babe. She was rather certain of that. A few more weeks before she gave birth, a few weeks of healing, and then she could have this in all its glorious splendor. She would lie beneath him, spread her thighs, truly welcome him home.

He lowered his trousers, stepped out of them, tossed them without care onto the pile of clothing that rested on the settee.

Don't stop there, her mind urged, and it was all she could do not to voice the words aloud. What would he think of so brazen a command? He would be appalled by some of the improper places that her imagination took her. A proper countess did not desire a liaison in the garden that went beyond a kiss. A proper countess did not fasten her eyes on a man's firm backside as he crouched to stir the fire, wishing that she were near enough that she could cup his buttocks. She did not entertain thoughts of easing her hands beneath the cloth, setting his throbbing manhood free, pushing him onto his back, lowering her mouth—

He was striding toward her. Fearful her lustful thoughts were readable on her face, she rolled onto her side, presenting him with her back. So many fantasies rambled through her mind. His objections in the copper tub had been meek at best. Perhaps he would be open to her being a little more adventuresome after the child was born.

The room descended into darkness as he lowered the flame in the lamp. The bed creaked, dipped as his chest met her back. He swept her hair aside and once more his lips made their way to the nape of her neck near her shoulder. One of his hands stroked her side, her hip. Back up. Back down. Lulling her so deeply into the sweet fondling that it took her a while to realize that each caress journeyed a little farther down.

Just above her knee. Her knee. Slightly below it. Her calf. Where the hem of her nightdress had gathered.

This time when his hand came back up, it was beneath the linen, skimming over her knee, along her thigh.

"What are you doing?"

"Shh," he whispered, his breath wafting along her ear. "I told you that I don't receive pleasure without giving it."

"But the babe—"

"I'll be gentle. I'll be so gentle, Jules." He cupped the apex at her thighs. "I'm only going to give. Slowly, leisurely." His fingers parted the folds. "Until you sigh with pleasure."

Sigh? She might very well scream. It had been too long since she'd been touched with such intimacy, such tenderness. His own burgeoning desire pressing against her backside served to increase the power of the sensations rippling through her as his fingers taunted her with the magic they were so skillfully weaving. He took her earlobe between his teeth, and heat swarmed through her.

He somehow managed to work her nightdress down just enough so his hot mouth could travel over her bared shoulder. Her toes curled, uncurled. Her fingers tingled. He had always been gentle with her, respectful, but there was something different tonight, an almost feral need shimmering through him that she could sense at the furthest recesses of her consciousness.

It was like smoke, appearing and disappearing. She couldn't latch onto it, not when most of her awareness was centered on her own body, his hand between her legs, his mouth on her shoulder. It was almost as though he were weaving a web of pleasure between the two points. Only, the sensations spread beyond that to encompass everywhere. So deeply, so powerfully. Until they consumed, overwhelmed. Her back arching, she cried out with the long denied release.

His fingers stilling, he pressed her more closely against him, seemed to wrap himself more securely around her.

Then the unexpected tears came in great gulping sobs she couldn't control.

He pushed up onto an elbow. "Julia?"

Placing trembling fingers over her mouth, shaking her head, she rasped, "I'm sorry. It's just that . . . we haven't been this close in ages." Not since the physician had confirmed she was with child. He'd been so fearful of hurting her. He'd leashed all his passions, and she had tried to do the same with hers, but they had hovered near the surface, constantly taunting her with want and need.

"It's all right, Jules," he said, his voice low, comforting as he gently turned her until her face was nestled against his chest, his arms around her, one hand soothingly stroking her spine. "It's all right."

"I've grown so cumbersome, I was afraid you didn't want me anymore."

"I've always wanted you."

The sincerity in his voice caused another hideously wrenching sob to escape. "I'm being so silly. This sudden aching loneliness—I don't know where it came from."

He pressed his lips to the crown of her head. "I'm sorry. I didn't realize—"

She blinked back the tears. "Please don't leave me again."

"I won't." His hold on her tightened. "Ever."

Swiping at the dampness on her cheeks, she released a strangled bubble of gratitude and dismay. "I have such a time of late controlling these tears."

"I was afraid I'd hurt you."

Leaning her head back, she studied his face in the shadows. "It was marvelous. So intense. It took me off guard." She buried her face back against his chest. "But it felt glorious." Swallowing, she circled a finger around his nipple. "Was it as nice for you earlier?"

His chortle was short, nearly self-deprecating. "It very nearly killed me."

She laughed lightly. "It felt as though I'd died, and then I was more alive than I'd ever been."

"Considering our reactions, we should probably refrain from pleasuring each other for now."

Nodding, she snuggled more closely against him. He was right, but she was grateful for tonight. It would see her through the next few weeks until they could make love madly once again.

Chapter 10

PLEASE don't leave me again.

I won't. Ever.

What the bloody hell had possessed him to make that promise? It had kept him awake most of the night, with Julia nestled securely, trustingly, against him, while his mind reeled with the ramification of his words. He'd made a vow he could not possibly keep.

Now, he stood at the window, gazing out on the storm that continued to whip snow over the land and very much mimicked his own inner turmoil. Rising earlier, he'd drawn on his trousers and shirt but he was reluctant to go to his bedchamber until she'd awoken. Her shattering from pleasure in his arms had been the most satisfying moment he'd ever experienced. Her passions were so easily ignited, her response so gratifying.

He wanted to feel those muscles closing around him while he was buried deeply within her. Something else that would never happen.

"Considering going out?" she asked, her voice raspy with sleep, causing a tightening in his groin.

Damn, but he wanted to return to that bed. Instead he merely looked over at it, at her, with her hair cascading in a tangled mess around her. "No. Can barely see into the distance at all. I'll work indoors today."

Pushing herself to a seated position against the pillows, she smiled, and the reason why he had been so quick to vow to never leave her struck him hard. He loved the way the corners of her mouth quirked up, the manner in which her eyes warmed with pleasure. He wished he'd be able to honor every promise he made to her since his return.

He was barely aware of striding toward the bed until he reached it and sat on the edge of the mattress. She smelled of sleep and faintly of sex, a seductive perfume. He combed the dark strands back from her face. "I should brush out your hair."

"I should let you, but it might lead to other things."

He pressed a brief kiss to her forehead, her lips. "It no doubt would."

"We have to behave."

"Pity."

She giggled, the echo of a young woman filled with joy. He couldn't recall ever hearing her make such a whimsical sound. "I don't know why I doubted. Being with child has caused havoc with my emotions."

"Don't doubt." Cradling her face, he took her mouth as tenderly as he could, holding his own needs in check. Her fingers went up into his hair. It was tempting to just sink onto her.

Instead, he pushed back, stood. "I should probably be about my day. I'll see you at dinner."

Her look was sly, provocative. "If not before."

WHY were ladies served their breakfast in bed?

Edward had pondered the thought while eating his own breakfast in the smaller dining room and staring at an article in the newspaper that Rigdon had dutifully ironed. The paper was a couple of days old, having arrived with several others the day before. Now, sitting at the desk in the library, staring at the snow that continued to swirl beyond the window, he doubted deliveries of anything would be made today.

He finally had a handle on the land, the tenants, the potential for income. At least for this estate. In the spring, he would need to travel to the other two that were temporarily in his keeping until the heir reached his majority. He wondered if he should invite Julia to accompany him so she could see what her son would inherit. Although his brother had no doubt already shown her. Besides, come spring, she might still be rather cross with him.

Leaning back in the chair, drumming his fingers on the mahogany desk, he knew that all the pleasant moments he had to spend with her would soon be coming to an end. So why the devil was he sitting here going over ledgers, calculating sums, and striving to determine how to make the estate more profitable? He would have ample time to do all that when his days and nights were filled with little save his own company. Odd that he didn't envision himself filling his nights with women and drink.

Spending so much time in her company had ruined him. Only fair, he supposed, that suffering was in his near future. But it wasn't yet time to step out of his brother's shoes. Yes, all this could bloody well wait. For now, he needed to stock up on memories.

And he knew just where to begin, where he would find her.

Only she wasn't in the room where she worked with her watercolors. Not that he blamed her for not seeking solace here when one could barely see the landscape beyond the windows. When was the blasted weather going to quiet and still?

On the other hand, it was perfect weather for sitting before a roaring fire with a bit of warm brandy. Perhaps he would ask her to read aloud from *Madame Bovary*. He smiled with the image of her finding that book in his room—

His mouth went flat. Surely she wasn't in there now searching for something provocative to read. He had yet to go through his trunk, to go through Albert's. It was not a chore he was welcoming. He kept telling himself that tomorrow he could get to it. So many tomorrows had already passed, and still he hadn't taken care of matters.

No, she wouldn't go there. The residence was so large, she could be in any one of a hundred rooms.

He strode into the hallway. Why did they need a residence this large anyway? As far as he knew, royalty hadn't visited since Elizabeth. Wasn't that what Marsden had mentioned one night? How a previous earl had been one of her favorites? What did it matter now? It didn't. Finding Julia mattered.

"You there!" he called out to a passing footman, who stopped and faced him. "Do you know where I might find Lady Greyling?"

"No, m'lord. I've not seen her today."

Could she still be abed? Not that he would blame

her, when the weather was so dismal. Joining her there, though, could lead to things. It seemed neither of them had much willpower when it came to being pleasured. He waved his hand at the footman. "Carry on."

And he did the same, glancing in one room after another, finding each absent of her. Not even her scent lingered. He was not on the correct trail.

When he reached the foyer, he bounded up the stairs to the wing that contained the family's bedchambers. He rapped on her door. No answer. He shoved it open. Empty.

Back into the hallway. He walked briskly toward the bedchamber at the end that had been designated as his whenever he visited. The door was open. Not a good sign. He'd instructed the servants not to go in there. He'd given no such instruction to Julia.

Crossing the threshold, he came up short at the sight of her sitting on the floor, the lid of a trunk raised, her head bent, a leather journal in her lap.

"I said I would see to his things," he snapped, immediately regretting the tartness of his tone.

She looked up. "Edward's, yes. But this is yours." She lifted the book. "All your journal entries begin 'My Dearest Darling.' You wrote to me every day while you were away. Why didn't you share this with me?"

Because I didn't know it bloody well existed. "I was saving it to give to you for Christmas." Liar. God, he wanted to bite off his tongue at her crestfallen expression.

"I've ruined your surprise."

"Doesn't matter." He crossed over to her, crouched, placed his elbows on his thighs. "You shouldn't be messing with this. I'll get to it eventually."

"I know, but you've been so busy, and I knew you hadn't gotten to your things, so I thought to help out." She placed her hand on his wrist. "I'm in the strangest mood. I feel as though I need to do something, and I'm not sure what. Do you know I actually made my own bed this morning? The poor maid didn't know what to make of me. I tidied the nursery when there was nothing to tidy. I just wanted to do something a bit more productive. And I've only managed to upset you."

"I'm not upset. I simply don't want you putting yourself out. I suppose we could go through it together." Although he truly wanted to do it alone. He had no idea what he might find in his brother's trunk. Nothing that would reveal the truth, that was for certain, but still he would be reliving the memories. Best to do those on his own.

Shaking her head, placing her hands to her lower back, she arched. "I'm losing interest. My back has been aching all morning. I must have slept on it wrong."

"You should be abed, then."

"I don't feel like lying down. Perhaps I should walk."

"You are aware there is a storm outside?"

She smiled. "I can walk through the residence. We have an abundance of corridors here that would suffice."

Reaching around her, he pressed his hands against the small of her back, rubbing gently. She moaned softly. "Oh, that feels good."

"Let's go to your bedchamber. You can lie on your side and I'll massage your back for a bit."

"Thought you had business to see to."

"None of my business is more important than your comfort."

"You've convinced me." She nibbled on her lower lip. "May I keep the journal?"

Where was the harm? Obviously, Albert had intended for her to have it, since it was a series of letters to her. "Of course. Now let's get you up."

As gradually as possible, providing her with all the support he could, he helped her get to her feet. She took a step, released a small cry, bent and slapped a hand on her stomach. "Oh my God."

"What is it?" he asked, circling an arm around her shoulders, fighting off his alarm that something might be terribly wrong.

"A pain shot through me." She looked at him, horror in her eyes. "There's . . . something wet trickling down the inside of my legs. Oh, my word—"

He swept her into his arms. "It's all right. Everything is going to be all right."

"It's too soon." Her voice was thick with tears, laced with panic.

"It might not be what we think." He hoped with everything within him that it wasn't. With long strides, he carried her out of the room, down the hallway, and into her bedchamber. Tenderly, he placed her on the bed. "I'm going to have a look, all right?"

She nodded, but the fear reflected in her eyes was tearing him apart. He didn't have to push her skirts up far before he saw the dampness tinged with blood. Before he could say anything, she cried out, her hands balling around the covers as she squeezed her eyes shut.

He felt helpless and powerless, able to do little more than watch as she struggled through the pain.

When she opened her eyes, tears were welling and

she was gasping. "He's coming. The baby's coming. It's too soon. It's far too soon."

Dropping her head back down onto the pillow, she began to cry in earnest, the tears leaking onto her cheeks.

"Look at me, Julia, look at me."

She rolled her head from side to side, once again squeezing her eyes shut. "I'm scared, so scared."

He was terrified as well, but he couldn't let her know it, couldn't let so much as a drop of his terror seep out of him. It would only serve to reaffirm her fears, cause her to panic. "Julia." He placed his hands on either side of her face. "Look at me, look in my eyes."

Finally she did, and he had never been more sure of anything than he was of this. "You will not lose this child. And I will not lose you. I won't allow it."

"You cannot control fate."

"Fate owes me on this. I will not let anything happen that will cause me to lose either of you."

Blinking back the tears, she nodded, her mouth going into a firm line signaling that she was as resolute as he. "Yes, all right. But it's not time."

"Apparently this little one is of the opinion that it is. So let's have a little faith here. Relax. Be strong. Be brave. We have a child to bring into this world."

Chapter 11

$\mathcal{H}$ow could she not believe him when he sounded so certain? A calm settled over her as she watched him yank on the bellpull that would summon her maid.

"Do you think it's because of what we did last night?" she asked.

He looked at her, conviction mirrored in her eyes. "Absolutely not."

"How do you know?"

"I should think this would have happened last night."

She wanted to believe him, so at least she could sweep away the guilt. "He's coming a month early."

He sat on the edge of the bed, took her hand. "Maybe not quite. How can a physician accurately determine the date of delivery when he doesn't know the exact moment of conception?"

"I suppose you have a point."

"Trust me, Jules, you're not going to lose this one."

Wanting to believe him with every fiber of her being, she nodded. "Yes, all right." Another contraction hit her, and she squeezed his hand, almost certain she heard bones crack, although since he didn't yelp, but only folded his other hand over her shoulder, she had to be mistaken.

The pain receded, she breathed deeply. The door opened and Torrie stepped in.

"Have someone ride into the village to fetch the physician," Albert barked.

"In this weather?"

"In this weather. Find a servant who knows something about delivering babies. Then get yourself back up here to help your lady change."

Torrie pressed her hand to her mouth. "Oh, my dear lord. Is she—"

"Yes, now go tend to matters."

Torrie ran from the room, her pounding footsteps echoing up the stairs.

"I do so love it when you're forceful," Julia said.

Laughing, he leaned down and pressed a kiss to her forehead. "Later, we'll discuss less dramatic ways for you to encourage me to be forceful. For now, let's see about getting you into your nightdress, shall we?"

By the time Torrie returned, he had all the fastenings undone on her dress. Stepping aside, leaving Torrie to help her with the final stages of getting into her nightdress, he went to the fireplace and stoked the fire.

As Julia was settling beneath the covers, Mrs. Bedell, the housekeeper, walked in. "It's been a good many years since I helped me mum deliver her last bairn, but I was young enough that it made an impression." She turned to Albert. "You go on now, your lordship. We'll see to Lady Greyling and the little one."

"Not bloody likely," her husband said as he shoved a

chair nearer to the other side of the bed, then dropped down into it and took Julia's hand.

"It's not proper for you to be here, m'lord."

"It's proper for a husband to get his wife with child but not to be in attendance as the child is born? That's rubbish." Reaching up, he stroked the hair back from her face. "Unless you want me to go."

He hadn't been with her when she'd lost the other three. She didn't know what to expect here, what he might witness, but she needed his determination, his sureness. "No, I want you to stay. You're my strength."

He pressed his mouth against her knuckles. "We'll get through this."

Sometime later she realized those words were extremely easy for him to say when he wasn't the one with pain ratcheting through his body. But bless him, he never flinched, no matter how hard she squeezed his hand. He merely cooed encouraging words and wiped a cool cloth over her brow. And he told her stories, about his childhood, his travels. He made her laugh when she'd thought the act impossible, made her believe that before the day was done, she'd be holding a squalling babe in her arms.

Beyond the window it began to grow dark. "Where's the doctor?" she asked.

"He's no doubt delayed by the storm," her husband told her. "You don't have to wait for him."

She forced a laugh. "As though I could."

He brushed back her hair. "You're being so brave."

"Only because you're here. I don't mean to be awful, but I'm so glad it wasn't you who died in Africa. I don't know how I would manage to get through this if not for you."

"You're not awful. You couldn't be awful if you tried. The first time I laid eyes on you I knew you were special."

"I fell in love with you almost immediately."

"Almost immediately? Why the delay?"

"It was only a few minutes. From the moment we were introduced until we had our first dance. You were so serious. I thought, 'He won't be any fun at all.' And then you smiled at me, and I was lost."

"So you were won over by something as simple as a smile."

"You have a most charming smile. I hope your son has your smile."

"I hope he has your strength of character."

Another pain ratcheted through her. He was standing now, hovering over her. She was growing so tired, so weary.

"If I die—"

"You're not going to die," he insisted.

"But if I do, you must promise me that you won't abandon our child the way Marsden abandoned his. You won't blame this child for my death."

"Julia—"

"Promise me."

"I promise that the child you carry shall never know what it is not to be loved."

Nodding, she knew she couldn't yet give in to her need to rest. Not until their son entered the world, not until she gave Albert his heir.

"I think he's almost here, m'lady," Mrs. Bedell said encouragingly. "I can see the top of his head. Black hair he has."

She smiled at her husband. "Black hair."

Tenderly, he pressed the cool cloth to her temple. "He's going to look like you."

Wearily, she shook her head. "No, he's going to look like you. Only with black hair. Will that please you?"

"Any child you deliver will please me."

"I think you're going to want to push the next time the pains start up, m'lady," Mrs. Bedell said.

"Yes, all right."

The pounding of footsteps on the stairs caught her attention, and suddenly Dr. Warren was rushing into the room. "Apologies for the delay," he announced. "Weather's atrocious. Let's see what we have here."

The servants scurried back. She couldn't have been more grateful that Albert stayed as he was, serving as her sentinel. Dr. Warren began to lift the hem of her nightdress. "You should leave, my lord."

Albert sighed deeply, irritation shimmering off him. "I've already been through this with the servants. I'm not leaving."

"It's best if some things between a husband and wife remain a mystery."

"And it's best if a man I can flatten with one punch concentrates his attention on my wife and child."

"Yes, of course. M'lady, you're going to need to push—"

He didn't have to tell her. Her body was doing a marvelous job of that. Mrs. Bedell and Albert both lifted her shoulders so she'd have better leverage as the pain made its way through her. She couldn't stop herself from crying out but at least she didn't scream at the top of her lungs, even though she dearly wanted to.

"My brave, brave girl," Albert cooed near her ear, standing, still holding her hand.

"We're almost there," Dr. Warren said. "Next one should push the shoulders out and we'll be done."

Setting her jaw, grunting a little louder, squeezing her husband's hand, she pushed as hard as she could.

"That's it," Dr. Warren encouraged. "She's here."

Dropping back down, breathing heavily, Julia asked, "She?"

"You have a daughter."

A daughter? But she was supposed to be a boy, the heir to Greyling. And yet strangely, she experienced no disappointment, no regret. She looked at Albert, certain she'd never seen more love reflected in his eyes. "He's a girl."

"So he is."

"Can you see her?"

"Right now all I see is you. You're so beautiful, Jules."

She didn't see how she could be. "Why isn't she crying?" she demanded of Albert, as though he were the one in charge of life and death. "She should be crying."

Then the wailing started, and Julia had never heard a more beautiful sound in her entire life. She began laughing and weeping with joy and gratitude and love. This tiny creature was making a powerful statement. "I want to see her."

"Here she is," Mrs. Bedell said, placing the child, wrapped in swaddling, in Albert's arms.

He leaned over so she could see her daughter, her child screaming her lungs out. She met Albert's gaze. "I'm sorry I didn't give you your heir."

A veil of tears glistened in his eyes as he touched the babe's fist. Their daughter unfurled her hand and took hold of his finger. "I promise you, Julia, your husband could not be more pleased. She looks just like you. What father would find fault with that?"

A GIRL. His brother's wife had given birth to a daughter. Not a son. Not an heir. Which meant the title came to Edward. The role he'd been playing for weeks now was no role at all, but was the unvarnished truth, his reality. He was and would remain the Earl of Greyling.

Grabbing a bottle of scotch, not bothering with a coat, hat, or muffler, he strode out through the library terrace door into the snow, wind, and sleet. Into the blistering cold. But he barely noticed the frigid ice pattering his skin or the flakes gathering on his lashes.

He was the earl. It was not what he wanted, not what he'd ever wanted.

Yet how could he resent his newfound position when that delicate bundle of new life had wrapped her tiny hand around his finger? With her black hair, her chubby cheeks, and her face scrunched up as she squalled? How could a creature so tiny, so innocent, capture his heart with such ease?

Trudging through the blanket of snow, he took a swig of the scotch, welcoming its warmth spreading through his chest, a warmth that paled when compared with what he'd felt as he held his brother's daughter in his arms. Julia's daughter.

He hadn't bothered with a lamp, but nearly three-quarters of a moon was brightening the sky. In spite of it being near midnight, the snow reflected the light and illuminated his path. It could almost be day for how well he was able to see. The howling wind pushed against him, but he pushed back. Nothing was going to prevent him from reaching his destination. Julia and the babe were both sleeping. They needed their rest, while he needed to be elsewhere.

The mausoleum came into view, an ominous scepter in the night. Shoving open the heavy door, he pushed his way inside, welcoming the muted screeching of the wind when the heavy wood banged back into place. A lantern, burning eternally, lit his way as he crossed over to the newest burial vault, placed his back against the cold marble tomb and slid down to the floor.

"She's beautiful, Albert, your daughter and your wife." He held the bottle aloft. "Well done on both counts, brother." He took a long swig, banged his head against the marble. "God, Albert, I wish you'd been here to see her. A bit nervous to start, but so courageous, so strong when it mattered. I can understand why you loved her as you did."

He indulged in another long swallow of amber. "The two of you created a marvel. We're naming her Alberta, after you." He squeezed his eyes shut. *We* sounded as though they were together, as though Julia belonged with him—when she never would, never could. English law would see to that. "Your daughter has the blackest hair, the bluest eyes, the fattest cheeks. She resembles her mother but I can see some of you in her."

Which meant he could see some of himself as well. Why did that cause an ache in his chest, make him wish he were the one who had planted the seed? He would be as a father to her, even though that privilege rightfully belonged to his brother. "You'd be busting the buttons on your waistcoat if you were here. I've no doubt. Raising a toast as well, to their health and happiness."

While he would be doing what he was doing now. Striving to drink himself into oblivion so he could forget they weren't his. That all the emotions churning in his chest—the pride, the affection, the joy—should be tempered by the fact that he was a brother by marriage and an uncle. Not the husband, not the father.

But damn it all to hell, he'd felt like both as Julia had squeezed his hand when the pain became too much, as the housekeeper laid the babe in his arms and he had presented her to Julia, placed her on her mother's bosom. Actions he'd never thought to experience.

They had touched him so deeply, so profoundly.

He had kept his promise, honored his vow, ensured that Julia delivered her baby. No more reason for secrets existed.

But a thousand reasons existed for getting drunk.

"Cheers, brother!"

And he gulped down the contents of the bottle until there was no more, until he could forget why he was here, until he managed to convince himself that he shouldn't tell Julia the truth until she'd recovered fully from the ordeal of childbirth.

*H*E awoke cold, aching, and stiff, his head heavy and pounding. At least he'd managed to make it back to the library before collapsing; otherwise he might have been joining his brother, although Albert was in heaven, while he would no doubt be heading in the opposite direction. He wished he'd at least made it to the sofa instead of settling for the floor. Shoving himself to his feet, he cursed soundly as his skull protested.

It was difficult to believe that it had once been his morning ritual to begin his day feeling utterly and completely awful, with his stomach roiling and his surroundings spinning. What an idiot he'd been, although at the time it made perfect sense, as he'd seen no alternative.

It hadn't been the answer then, it wasn't the answer now, although now it wasn't only he who suffered. He had to remember that.

He hadn't meant to completely abandon Julia, although he suspected she'd sleep for a week following her ordeal. Her daughter less likely to sleep as long. Not that he knew anything about a baby's sleeping habits. He'd managed to avoid them until now.

But as of yesterday he was an uncle, and he had to give serious thought to being a good one.

He was also an earl. Officially, unequivocally.

All the work he'd done to oversee his brother's estates—suddenly, he'd been doing it for himself. All the responsibilities regarding the title were now his burden to carry, including providing an heir. Hell and damnation. Getting married had never been in his plans. Now he would have no choice.

But that was for considering another day, perhaps in another decade. Presently, he still needed to take care of Julia, ensure she recovered. It wasn't uncommon for women to fall ill shortly after they'd given birth, so his decision last night to delay telling her the truth was for her health. And he had a child to look after.

First things first. A bath and breakfast.

After he was finished with both he felt more like himself and better able to face the day, to face Julia. When he walked into her bedchamber, she was sitting up in bed, Alberta nestled in her arms. They were perfection, both mother and daughter. Torrie got up from a chair beside the bed, gave him a quick curtsy, and discreetly left.

"You look awful," Julia said, her brow furrowed. "Are you all right?"

Perhaps he wasn't quite as much himself as he'd thought. Guilt gnawed at him for making her worry. "I took a bottle of scotch to the mausoleum to celebrate Alberta's birth with my brother. We'd always planned to have a drink on that most auspicious occasion. I got carried away." Leaning over, he brushed a quick kiss across her lips. "Sorry if I worried you."

"I'm sorry he wasn't here to celebrate. I should have realized how hard it would be for you—"

"Don't concern yourself. You had enough to worry over." He sat on the edge of the bed. "How is your daughter this morning?"

"She's yours as well."

Damn. The fog from his mind wasn't entirely lifted. "Our daughter. Difficult to believe we actually have her."

"Would you like to hold her?"

The correct answer was no, because if he fell any more in love with her, if Julia wasn't willing to share her when she learned the truth, his heart might break. But at that moment he was pretending to be her father, not her uncle, and what father would refuse? To be honest, what uncle worth his salt would refuse? Besides, the truth was that he was desperate to feel her in his arms again. "I'd like that. Yes."

Alberta did little more than mewl as Julia transferred her over to him. Standing, he began swaying back and forth. "Hello, Lady Allie."

"Allie?"

"Alberta seems a bit grown-up for one so small, don't you think?"

She smiled softly. "I suppose you're right. Are you certain you're not disappointed that she isn't a boy?"

"I promise you with all my heart that I'm not disappointed in the least."

"I was just so sure, but then I guess one never truly knows. Next time."

He swallowed. "Next time, yes." If she had a next time, it would be because she'd remarried. She would give another lord his heir. He didn't want to think about Allie going to live on another estate, growing up in the shadow of a different residence. She belonged here. It was the home of her father.

Both he and Albert should have grown up here, but fate had denied them that privilege, those memories. He didn't want a childhood on these grounds stolen from Allie. Albert wouldn't want it either.

"What's wrong?" Julia asked. "Your face is a storm cloud."

He shook his head, waved off the troubling thoughts. "I'm sorry. I was just thinking about how important it is that she have the opportunity to grow up here, and how it was denied to me and my brother."

"All of this must be bittersweet. Your childhood memories being stirred, Edward not being here."

"It's far more sweet than it is bitter, I promise you. And I haven't asked how you're feeling."

"A little sore, but happy. Dr. Warren ordered me to stay abed for two months, but I've already gotten out of bed to see to my toilette and I felt fine."

"You should listen to your doctor."

"I don't think it's good to stay abed. I won't be reckless but I don't see the harm in sitting in a chair. And I want to feel strong enough to go downstairs by Christmas. This will be our first as a family. I want everything to be perfect."

A perfect Christmas. That would be his gift to her. Then he would tell her the truth.

Chapter 12

SITTING in the parlor, watching as the servants finished trimming the tree, Julia could hardly believe it was Christmas Eve, that three weeks had passed so quickly. Allie slept in a nearby cradle that was decorated with holly and red velvet ribbon. She was such a delight, but still so small. Dr. Warren had decided she needed to be fed formula rather than mother's milk.

"I feel as though I'm failing her," she'd told Albert.

"You only fail her if you don't heed your doctor's advice," he'd assured her.

She hadn't expected her husband to be so attentive or to spend so much time holding his daughter. With winter upon them, there was little need for him to go out and check on his tenants, but she still hadn't anticipated that much of his day would be spent entertaining her. They played cards. Sometimes he read to her.

He would get a bit miffed when she insisted upon walking through the residence. "I would think your physician has good reason for encouraging you to stay abed."

"I can think of none when I feel so much better after I walk."

He always accompanied her, provided an arm, and didn't harp on his displeasure with her. Their strolls were her favorite moments of the day. Sometimes they were silent. Sometimes they shared memories of their youth and spoke of their plans for Allie, all the things they would show her, teach her. Following in her father's footsteps, she would travel the world. Their daughter most certainly was going to have a singular upbringing.

Julia had always thought she loved Albert as much as it was possible to love a man. Strange to discover that with each passing day she loved him more deeply.

He stood by the fireplace with its evergreen boughs, his elbow resting on the mantel as he slowly sipped his scotch, his gaze on the activity near the tree. He was so incredibly attractive and masculine, every inch of him calling to her wantonness. From time to time he would glance over at her, smile, then his gaze would dip to the cradle, his eyes would soften. They were a family. They would have so many moments like this. A lifetime's worth.

"Is it to your liking, m'lady?" Mrs. Bedell asked as the servants who had been assisting her stood at attention, hopeful expressions mirrored on each of their faces.

"Yes, thank you, it's beautiful."

The housekeeper ushered out the servants. Albert walked over and took the chair beside hers. "I'm surprised you weren't in the thick of things, assisting them."

"I did put up a couple of baubles while you went to retrieve your scotch."

He laughed. "You are a stubborn wench."

"I'm not going to spend any more time abed."

He turned in the chair so he could see her more easily. "Julia—"

"I'm fine, Albert."

Reaching out, he took her hand, his expression deadly serious. "I don't want anything to happen to you."

"I feel best when I'm up and about. Now that I'm no longer nursing, my body doesn't need all the rest."

"I don't suppose there's any real harm in it. I did once see a woman in Africa give birth and then immediately return to skinning hides."

"You didn't think that was worth mentioning before?"

"I'm not going to give you ammunition for your arguments."

She slapped playfully at his arm, glad to see his eyes twinkling with humor. "I should be cross with you."

"Not on Christmas Eve."

"No, not on Christmas Eve."

He leaned toward her. "So what present did you get me?"

She wrinkled her nose at him. "I'm not telling, but it should be arriving any time now."

His brow furrowed. "You're having something delivered here today for me?"

"In a manner of speaking, yes."

He pursed his lips together. "What is it?"

"Patience, my husband. I've been planning this for a while. I'm not going to ruin the surprise now by telling you what it is." Taking his hand, she settled back against the chair. He finished off his scotch, set the glass aside, stared at the tree.

"It's so quiet," he said solemnly.

"I know you miss him."

"More than I can say. It would be a difficult Christmas indeed, if not for Allie."

"Then I'm glad she came early, even if she is a bit small."

"She's growing. She's getting heavier in my arms. Next Christmas she'll be climbing all over that tree."

Julia heard the front door opening, voices in the entryway, and fought not to change her expression, not to give anything away.

"Who's that?" Albert asked, coming to his feet. "Carolers, do you think?"

Julia rose as well. "Perhaps. Should probably go see."

He offered his arm. They'd taken only two steps when the Duke and Duchess of Ashebury and Viscount Locksley crossed the threshold.

"Happy Christmas!" they all said in unison.

"What the devil are you doing here?" Albert asked.

"We were invited," Ashebury announced.

Clearly confused, Albert looked at her. She smiled. "Your gift arrives at last. Merry Christmas, my love."

"You could not have given me anything better."

Then he hauled her up against him and took her mouth.

$\mathcal{H}$E hadn't kissed her since just before she gave birth, and he knew he could not have chosen a worse moment to do so—with an audience. But he'd been dreading the holidays, known they were another moment that would hammer home the absence of his brother. And he was truly touched by her gift of his friends.

He welcomed the excuse to show his appreciation by

plastering his lips to hers. He suffered through the agony of holding her every night, chastely, his arm around her diminishing waist. Each day, the evidence that she'd given birth dwindled. And he found himself wanting her all the more, fighting to keep his desires in check.

The fight was raging now—again with an audience.

Breaking from the kiss, he strode toward their visitors. "This is a marvelous surprise." He gave the duchess a hug, a kiss on the cheek. Shook Ashe's hand, clapped his back, did the same with Locke before asking him, "What about your father?"

"He's never liked Christmas," Locke said. "You know that. I doubt he'll even notice I'm not there."

"Well, I'm glad to have you here. Allow me to introduce you to Lady Alberta."

Minerva hadn't bothered to wait for him to lead them over. She was already at Julia's side, cooing over the child whom Julia now cradled lovingly in her arms. He'd never before realized how much a mother could love a child, had never considered what he and the others had missed out on by not having their mothers about as they grew into men.

"She's gorgeous," Minerva said.

"We think so," Julia admitted. "And Albert is a wonderful father, rocking her in the middle of the night when she awakens."

He could feel the gazes of both Ashe and Locke bearing down on him, knew what they were thinking, that they were judging him. He hardly blamed them. Once they'd given adequate attention to Julia and the babe, he suggested they retire to the library for a quick brandy before dinner.

The library door had barely closed behind them when Ashe said, "You haven't told her yet."

Not a question, a statement. Edward strode to the sideboard, poured brandy into three snifters, turned to hand them each one. "She wanted a perfect Christmas. I didn't think her knowing she was a widow would accomplish that. I'll tell her after."

"This seems an incredibly unwise course."

Not the first one he'd ever traveled. Ignoring the censure and a need to respond, he raised his glass. "To Lady Alberta and Julia's health."

The gentlemen drank, Edward downing far more than either of them. Now he needed to think of another toast, give them reasons to continue drinking so they'd leave off the inquisition.

"And the kiss?" Ashe asked.

Edward fought not to reveal his irritation that Ashe was acting as though he were a chaperon. He didn't want them reading anything into his displeasure other than what it was: annoyance at having all his actions questioned. "A husband kisses his wife when she does something to please him, doesn't he?"

"Not always with quite so much enthusiasm," Locke said. "The two of you generated more heat than the logs burning in the fireplace."

"Bugger off, both of you."

"You've grown to like her," Ashe said, clearly befuddled.

"I might appreciate her more than I once did." No harm in admitting that. They'd always liked her, thought he'd been a fool not to feel the same.

"The longer you wait—"

"Damn you, Ashe, do you not think I'm aware that there will never be a perfect moment to break her heart? The holidays just seemed an unusually cruel time to do so. In the new year. She'll be fully recovered from the ordeal of childbirth and better able to cope with the grief. I'll tell her then."

Ashe tipped his head in acquiescence, sipped his brandy, his eyes narrowing. "Just see that you do or I shall."

"It's not your place."

"As Albert's friend, I disagree. He wouldn't want his wife taken advantage of."

"How pray tell am I taking advantage of her? I'm not bedding her. An occasional kiss is harmless. From the beginning, I've done nothing except strive to protect her. I gain nothing for myself by continuing the ruse."

"He does have a point," Locke said, tapping a finger against his snifter. "He's truly the Earl of Greyling now. The temporary role is now a permanent one."

Edward nodded, met each of their gazes, wanted to confirm the truth of his feelings. "I wish to God she'd had a boy. The title should go to Albert's son, not his brother, but that little girl has stolen my heart."

"She's the image of her mother," Locke offered.

"She is that. Albert would have been pleased."

"We need to make a toast to the new Earl of Greyling," Ashe said, lifting his glass. "Welcome to our ranks, my lord."

They all raised their glasses before downing the contents that remained in each one. Edward poured them more.

"You'll be a good earl," Locke said.

"I shall at least try." He chuckled. "I can't believe Julia invited you here and kept it from me."

"She feared you'd be melancholy."

"But you two shall stop that from happening."

"Absolutely. Whatever else are friends for?"

For holding secrets.

"WERE you really pleased with your surprise?" Julia asked as Albert joined her in the sitting area of her bed-chamber.

Dinner had been a smashing success, with more laughter and joviality than she'd heard in ages. It had lightened her heart to see her husband enjoying himself.

"You could not have given me anything better," he said as he sat beside her on the sofa.

She had already changed into her nightdress, while he was still dressed for the evening. She might have suspected that he and the other gents were going to play billiards if it weren't for the fact that their company had already retired for the night.

"I fear my gift to you will pale in comparison."

"You've already given me the journal, although I decided not to read it until after the holidays. It seemed like peeking into the box otherwise."

"You're deserving of something much more than a journal."

Before she could tell him that it was the very best present he could have given her, he slid a leather case out of his inside jacket pocket and set it on her lap. "Shouldn't this be beneath the tree so that I can open it in the morning?"

"You might think Father Christmas brought it to you. I'd rather you open it now while it's only the two of us."

Removing the lid revealed a bracelet of linked pewter roses. "Oh, it's beautiful."

"Whenever I see roses, I think of you," he said quietly.

She smiled at him. "They're my favorite flower, my favorite fragrance."

With one large hand, he cradled her cheek. "They became mine the first time I kissed you."

He took her mouth with such tenderness, such gentleness, that she nearly wept. As she was still recovering from childbirth, he had been incredibly patient, marvelously solicitous, not pressuring her, not insisting on exercising his husbandly rights. Not that he would have to insist on anything. If she were completely healed, she would lead him to the bed at this very second.

With a groan, he shifted, his arms came around her, and she suddenly found herself sprawled across his lap as his tongue lapped at her neck, her collarbone, the dip between her breasts, before trailing over the upper swells. Heat swirled through her, moisture gathered between her thighs. She began fumbling with the buttons on her nightdress. She wanted his mouth over her entire breast, one then the other.

His hand closed around hers as he raised his head, held her gaze. "I won't be able to stop."

She sank against him. She was still bleeding, hardly a tempting vixen. Scraping her fingers up into his hair, she fought to calm her erratic heart. "I want you so badly. A few more weeks seem an eternity." She slid her hand down, pressing her fingers just below his jaw where she could feel the thundering of his pulse. "At least let me make your Christmas merry."

Slowly, he shook his head. "You know my gentleman's rule. Besides, when we do finally come together, it will be better for having waited."

His glorious mouth returned to hers, a little less gentle than before, with a little more hunger, a little more heat. His hands behaved, daring only to stroke her back, her hips, her spine. But his lips, his tongue, behaved with complete abandon, caressing every inch of her mouth, drawing moans and sighs from her, causing heat to ebb and flow through her until she was mad for him.

She fought to keep her own hands equally chaste as they roamed over his shoulders, chest, and back, loosening his cravat, setting his buttons free, but never venturing below his waist, never traversing to the heart of his manhood, even though she could feel it pressed against her, straining against his trousers.

Slowly, so gradually that she was barely aware of it happening, he shifted position until they were stretched out on the sofa, her legs entangled with his, his strong arm cradling her the only thing that kept her from tumbling to the floor.

Tearing his mouth from hers, he erupted in deep, masculine, satisfied laughter. "Why the hell are we cramped together here on the sofa when we could be sprawled in the bed?"

"Because it makes what we're doing seem more forbidden."

Holding her gaze, he danced his fingers slowly along her cheek, her neck. "You like the forbidden."

Her cheeks warmed as she recalled all the inappropriate things she'd muttered in his ear, his deaf ear, words no proper lady should ever know, much less speak. Powerfully titillating, they were her little secret. What would his opinion of her be if he knew of them?

"You never have to hide anything from me, Jules," he murmured in a low cadence that thrummed through her, made her want to hear him purring unsuitable, suggestive statements. "You can always be yourself with me."

Only she couldn't, not on this matter. Once she spoke the words so he could hear them, there would be no taking them back. What if she offended him, shocked him, caused him to lose all respect for her? What if he didn't? The allure of whispering wicked things in his ear would dissipate. She liked doing it because she knew she shouldn't.

"I am always myself with you," she assured him, and part of being herself was keeping some delicious secrets.

She brought his head down until their mouths met, their tongues danced and their moans echoed around them. Until the passion soared and the hunger had them rolling off the sofa and onto the floor. How he managed to do it so he landed first, cushioning her fall, was beyond her.

She wanted him desperately, now, tonight. Wanted him moving inside her—

"Enough!" He scooted away from her until he was sitting with his back against the wall, one leg stretched out before him, the other raised, knee bent. Breathing heavily, he plowed his hand through his hair, tugged on his ear in that endearing way he had, and gazed at her with smoldering eyes that put the heat from the fire to shame. "You are a vixen."

With a self-satisfied laugh, she pushed herself up until her back was against the sofa. She brought her knees up against her chest, tucked the hem of her night-dress beneath her toes. "You want me."

"Of course I want you. With every breath I draw."

She almost giggled as though she were a young girl. He was disheveled, his shirt hanging half off. She'd done that. Made a mess of him. They'd never gone at it before out of the bed. He was correct. She did like forbidden things.

"You show remarkable restraint, my lord." She wanted to go to her hands and knees, crawl toward him like a cat stalking its prey, but until they could bring their passions to complete physical fruition, it seemed cruel to tease him too much.

"You've no idea."

She batted her eyelashes coquettishly. "Oh, I think I do."

Laughing, he dropped his head back. "You will be the death of me."

"They call it the little death, don't they?" she asked, feigning a shyness she didn't really feel. Lately she'd been bolder with him than she'd ever been. Perhaps it was giving birth that made her so comfortable with the needs of her body. And his. "That moment when the world falls away."

"Is that what it feels like for you?"

Nodding, she knew she was blushing. She would probably ignite if she ever shared with him the words she dared to utter that he couldn't hear. "And you?"

He released a long, slow sigh. "Makes me feel as though I could conquer the world. And it feels bloody marvelous as well."

She laughed lightly, and dared to repeat, "Yes, it feels bloody marvelous."

Shoving himself to his feet, he reached a hand down to her. "Come, my little vixen. To bed. We have company to entertain tomorrow, a feast to consume, and a day to enjoy."

Liking immensely that he considered her a vixen, she slipped her hand in his. "And one less day to mark off until we can be together completely," she told him as he pulled her up.

"One less day," he said, leading her to the bed.

She found it odd that he sounded a little saddened by the prospect. Keeping her observations to herself, she clambered beneath the blankets and was soon nestled in his arms. She wanted nothing to ruin what had been a most wonderful Christmas Eve.

"*You* gentlemen are absolutely no good at this game," Julia announced, crossing her arms over her chest, mimicking a pout that as it turned out wasn't as much of a mimic as it should have been. She was striving not to be cross, because they weren't taking the activity seriously.

After a Christmas feast filled with much talk and laughter, rather than letting the gentlemen retreat to the smoking room for port and a cigars, she insisted they join her and Minerva in the parlor for a few games.

Presently they were all sitting in a circle. The object was not to smile. Generally, people had a very difficult time not twitching their lips or even chortling when they knew they weren't supposed to. But not these gents. So far, she and Minerva had alternated losing rounds while the men just sat there stoically, their mouths not even quivering with the need to lift up.

To make matters worse, staring at Albert's beautiful mouth, waiting for him to smile, only made her recall how heated his kisses had been last night, which in turn made her want to get up, settle on his lap, and latch her mouth onto his until he carried her from the room.

"Actually, we're very good at it," he said now, his face set in a smug expression that she thought her kiss would utterly destroy. "We've yet to smile."

"But you're supposed to!" she screeched in frustration.

"Except you told us not to."

Minerva started laughing, and Julia glared at her. "Help me out here."

"Perhaps we should give charades a go."

"We don't have an even number for charades." She flung her hand toward the viscount. "If Locksley would only marry—"

He made a choking cough that strongly resembled a strangle. "Now you sound like my father."

"Has he been after you to marry?" Minerva asked.

"Relentlessly. I was hoping that here, at least, I might find some respite from the constant nagging."

"Only marriage will accomplish that," Julia assured him. "Minerva and I shall make it our mission this Season to find you a woman to love."

"Oh, I'd never marry a woman I could love. If I learned anything at all from my father it is that along that path lies madness."

Julia shuddered at the words. "Only if she dies young."

"Which always is a possibility."

"That's a morbid way to go through life. No wonder you're atrocious at this game."

"As Grey pointed out, we've been winning."

At a loss for any other words she released a deep breath of frustration.

"You have to understand, Julia, we didn't play parlor games on Christmas," Albert said kindly.

In the past, it had been only her, Albert, and Edward here for the holiday, which was the reason she'd invited his friends. There was no hope for it. This year would be different from years past. She just hadn't wanted the difference to be melancholy. "What did you do?"

He shrugged. "Ran wild mostly. No parlor games, no tree, no evergreen boughs or ribbons, no feast. No Father Christmas. For us it was a day like any other."

"Carolers from the village certainly never ventured to Havisham," Ashebury said.

"That makes me sad." She shifted her gaze to her husband. "You knew it would. I suppose that's why you never told me about it before."

"You shouldn't be sad. We weren't."

"But you must have had memories of Christmas with your parents."

"We did. They were magical, special. Marsden offered us nothing to replace them. In a way that was a gift."

She looked at Locksley. "So you were grown before you experienced a Christmas celebration?"

Appearing uncomfortable, he shifted in his chair. "This is actually my first opportunity to partake in the traditions of the season, and to be quite honest, I'm not particularly fond of the parlor games."

She fluttered her hand in the air. "Off with you all! Go have your port and cigars, while Minerva and I—"

"Join us," Albert said, standing and extending his hand. "It's Christmas; let's start a new tradition."

As hostess, she needed to ensure her guests were comfortable. She glanced over at Minerva. "Are you willing?"

"Absolutely. Rather than parlor games, in the future might I suggest poker?"

Ashe was suddenly at her side, helping her to her feet. "Only if you won't cheat."

"My dear husband, I wouldn't dare consider it—unless something I wanted was at stake."

Laughing, he began escorting his wife from the room. Locksley followed.

Julia placed her hand in Albert's and he drew her up until she was in the circle of his arms, his mouth moving insistently over hers. Winding her arms around his shoulders, she returned his kiss with equal fervor.

A clearing of a throat had them jumping apart as though they were young lovers caught doing something they shouldn't. Ashe stood in the doorway, eyebrow arched. "Joining us?"

"You're irritating, Ashe," Albert said as he offered her his arm before leading her from the room.

"Trust me, I could be more so." He spun on his heel and headed to his wife, who was waiting for him.

"What did he mean by that?" Julia asked, sensing a tension in her husband that hadn't been there before.

"As the highest in rank and the eldest, he's always felt he had the right to boss us around, so he's just being Ashe."

"But you're glad he's here."

"Very glad he's here. You've given me a wonderful gift today."

When they reached the smoking room, they discovered Locksley handing out the glasses of port he'd poured while waiting for them. He raised his glass. "To new Christmas memories."

"No, wait!" Julia said before anyone could take a sip. "That's lovely, but I want us to take just a moment to remember Edward."

"Julia—"

"Albert, I don't mean to bring in sadness, but I thought it might be nice if we all silently reflected on one moment when he made us smile."

"Did he ever make you smile?"

"More often than he realized, which would have irritated him, no doubt, but that makes me smile even more. It's no secret that we had our differences, but I do hope he's at peace." She lifted her glass. "So to Edward."

"To Edward," they repeated far more solemnly than she wanted before taking a sip of the port.

"Now," Minerva announced, "I'd like a cigar."

As Ashe and Locke turned to the wooden box on the sideboard that held the cigars, Julia faced her husband, cupped his cheek, rose up on her toes and kissed him sweetly, tenderly. "Merry Christmas."

"Merry Christmas, Jules."

"And may the coming year bring us nothing but happiness." Lifting her glass, she finished off her port, watched as her husband did the same, and wondered why he suddenly seemed remarkably sad.

Chapter 13

TONIGHT. Tonight was the night that he told her the truth. While he watched her sip her wine as she waited for the next course to be served, he knew he had to tell her. He'd delayed long enough.

It had been a little over three weeks since Christmas, since their guests had departed. Their nights had become filled with heated kisses and exploring hands. His nights had become filled with frustration. He wanted her with a desperation he'd never known. Wanted to unveil her completely, wanted to worship her from the top of her head to the tips of her toes.

Instead he dove into the pork and tried to turn his thoughts elsewhere. "I thought I might go riding tomorrow if the rain stops." It had started just before twilight. Hard, heavy, and chilled.

"To see the tenants?"

"No, just for pleasure. Perhaps you'd like to come with."

He could tell her then. No, he had to tell her tonight. Get it over with. Get it done.

"I'd enjoy that. I haven't been on a horse in close to

a year. Can we stop by the tea shop in the village for some strawberry tarts?"

He thought of her eating them, getting the jam on her lips. He could kiss it off her. "I don't see why not. It'll be a day for doing whatever we like."

"I wish it were warm enough for a picnic."

He imagined her stretched out over a blanket, slowly unbuttoning her bodice, peeling the cloth back so the sun could kiss her where he had not. With a silent curse, he grabbed his wineglass, gulped its contents. "When it's warmer."

Of late it didn't matter what the bloody hell they talked about, he saw her stretched out before him, luring him in, tempting him. If he wasn't careful, he was going to go as mad as the Marquess of Marsden.

Suddenly, he pushed back his chair and stood. "I'm in the mood for billiards. Care to join me?"

She stared up at him. "We haven't finished dining."

"I've had my fill." And he had to do something so he wasn't watching her lips closing provocatively around eating utensils. She had the most sensual addicting mouth that he'd ever known. Get her away from the dining table, away from the servants, and he would tell her who he was. Her reaction would no doubt get his mind off what he'd like to do with those lips.

"You've never asked me before."

"Then it's high time I did, don't you think?" Pulling out her chair, he helped her to her feet.

"Will you think less of me if I confess that while you were away I went into your billiards room and smacked some balls around?"

"Why would I think less of you for wanting to enjoy the game?"

"The room was always your sanctuary."

"Now it will be ours." He offered his arm.

As they wandered from the dining room, she admitted, "I'm not certain I was doing it correctly—hitting the balls."

"Did they go into the pockets?"

"What pockets?"

"The holes along the sides."

"Oh, yes, sometimes. Why are they called pockets?"

"Nicer than holes don't you think?"

"I suppose."

As they entered the billiards room, she said, "I'm always struck by the masculinity of this room. All dark woods and burgundy, the scent of cigars. I never thought it was fair that men got to smoke, drink, and play games while ladies poked needles and pulled thread through cloth."

He'd always thought it rather shortsighted of men not to invite the ladies into their sanctum, which was the reason he'd asked her and Minerva to join the gents at Christmas. He moved away from her, went to the sideboard and poured himself a glass of scotch. He glanced over his shoulder at her. "Did you want to indulge?"

"Yes, I believe I will. I'd like to try brandy."

He handed her the glass, watched her throat work as she sipped. Tonight she was wearing a dark burgundy that suited the room, bared her shoulders and the upper swells of her breasts—which suited him.

"It's quite nice," she said.

"It can fool you. Don't drink it too quickly lest it go to your head."

"What happens then?"

"You'll lose all your inhibitions."

"We're married. It doesn't matter if we lose our inhibitions with each other, does it?"

"Depends what those inhibitions are protecting, I suppose." He walked to where the cue sticks were lined up along the wall. He took two, handed her one. "That should be a good length for you. Let's see what you learned while I was away."

Standing off to the side, watching as she worked to properly hold the cue, Edward knew that she had no idea how dangerous it would be if he lowered all his inhibitions, if he knocked down the walls that warned he could only go so far and no farther.

He had to distract himself before he did something he really shouldn't. She was concentrating so hard, her brow so deeply furrowed, that it had to hurt. "Wait," he ordered.

She lifted her gaze. Christ, why did she have to look at him as though he were the answer to everything? Why did she have to make him wish he were?

Setting his glass aside, he walked over to her. "You're not holding the cue properly. You want to hold it like this." Using his own, he demonstrated.

"Oh, I see." And she did. She was a quick learner.

"Then you bend down so you can see your mark clearly and envision the angle of the strike."

She did. Her backside sticking out enticingly. He was only a man, not a saint. He shouldn't look, but he did, taking his fill of her lovely form.

"Slide the stick between your fingers like this," he said.

"That's rather erotic, isn't it? Especially if you imagine your fingers represent a woman and the cue a man."

"Jesus, Julia." He shoved himself away from the table. The things she sometimes said.

"Sorry. It's the brandy."

Turning, he gave her an incredulous look. "You had one sip."

"Perhaps I should have another?"

Laughing, he shook his head. "Not if one loosens your tongue that much."

Leaning back against the table, she set her hands behind her, arching just enough to offer him an enticing image. "Why don't you come over here and see just how loose my tongue is?"

So brazen, so bold, so damned tempting, but within her eyes he saw the barest measure of doubt, a whispering fear of rejection. He didn't have it within him to turn away from her, to give those seeds of uncertainty a chance to bloom, not when he desperately wanted her and all she was offering. He wouldn't take all, but he would take a kiss, and make sure it was one she never forgot.

Before he could change his mind, before he could think better of it, he pulled her into his arms and slammed his mouth over hers, growling low and deep when she opened her mouth and her tongue darted between his lips to parry with his. She clung to him with a feverishness she'd yet to exhibit, an urgency that implied she would die without more.

Lifting her up, he placed her on the billiards table,

put his hands behind her back to offer support as he carried her down to the green tabletop. He trailed his mouth over her throat, her shoulders, those lovely plump swells of her breasts, while her hands made a mess of his hair, his cravat.

He was between her legs, where he had longed to be for too long, where he had no right to be. Pushing himself up, he looked down on her. She was flushed with desire, her bosom heaving with each breath she gasped.

"I want you," she rasped. "Take me. For God's sake, please take me."

"Julia—"

"I'm recovered. Completely, absolutely. Have me right here."

He could lift up her skirts, unfasten his trousers—

He had to tell her the truth. But not here.

"Not when I have waited so long," he growled, drawing her up into his arms and carrying her from the room.

One of her arms was around his shoulders, while her other hand tugged the knot of his neck cloth free as she nibbled on his ear. He took the stairs two steps at a time while she laughed softly.

Into her bedchamber he went, slamming the door in their wake. The bed loomed large and inviting, called to him. Gritting his teeth, he ignored it and set her feet on the thick carpeting.

"Julia—"

"I want you so badly. I have for the longest."

Holding her face between his hands, he looked deeply into her blue eyes. He had to tell her the truth. Now. Before they went any further. Before she despised him fully and completely. Before he despised himself. He had to confess his sins, his duplicity. He had to be honest with her.

He had to lose her forever.

Or he could hold his tongue. Continue on with this role for the remainder of his life. Be Albert until he drew his final breath. Keep his promise to her that he would never again leave her. It was the only way to keep that promise.

To never hear his name on her lips, crying out with passion.

To never be the man to whom she was actually married.

To never be the man she truly loved.

To live the remainder of his life with his brother's leavings.

But in the end he would have her. He would always have her.

Whatever sacrifices he endured would be worth it to keep her happy, to keep from breaking her heart.

He knew his motives weren't purely unselfish, but then he'd never claimed not to be selfish. Because in the end, his silence would keep her with him, and he wanted her more than he'd ever wanted anything in his life.

He claimed her mouth. And he was lost.

THE ferociousness of his kiss didn't frighten her. It merely ignited every ounce of passion she possessed. He'd been right. Holding back, merely teasing each other with what was to come, was making every touch, every sigh, every moan all the sweeter.

Clothing came off in a frenzy of popped buttons and ripped seams. Never before had things between them been so wild, so untamed. It was as though Africa had changed him, stripped him of his civilized veneer.

Her hair tumbled down around her shoulders, and only then did they take a moment to appreciate what they had unveiled.

"My God, but you're beautiful," he rasped, his eyes smoldering with hunger, glinting with need.

He was all lean sinew and corded muscle. Strength and purpose. Familiar and yet not. There was a rigid scar that angled down from his hip. She trailed her finger over it. "Africa was not kind to you." Leaning down, she pressed a kiss to it.

With a low groan, he had her back up in his arms and was striding toward the bed. Once there, he set her on the mattress and followed her down, covering half her body with his, running his hands over her as though she were unchartered territory. Then he was flicking his tongue over her skin, tasting, tantalizing. She scraped her fingers over his scalp, along his broad shoulders. He fondled her breasts, her nipples puckered, and he closed his mouth over one, tugging gently, and she very nearly came up off the bed.

"Oh, God," she breathed shakily as pleasure skidded through her.

He kissed the underside of one breast, then the other, before giving the same attention to each of her ribs, climbing down her body inch by marvelous inch. He circled his tongue around her navel, pushed himself down farther until her thighs were resting on his shoulders, his hands cupping her backside.

"What are you—"

"Shh." He lifted his heated gaze to hers. "I want to worship all of you."

He lowered his head, his mouth. His tongue licked the very essence of her, velvet to silk, sultry heat to sultry heat. Clutching his hair, she arched up, offering him more. And he took.

With slow strokes and tiny nibbles and teasing flicks. Slow journeys up and slower ones down. Her body strained against him, begging for release. He increased the pressure, and just when she was on the cusp—

He retreated, went gentle and tender. She cried out in frustration. He merely laughed, low and dark, and with promise. She would make him pay. When it was her turn, she would make him pay.

Again he brought her to the cusp. Again he retreated.

She was quivering with need. "No more," she begged. "No more."

"Once more." He raised her hips slightly as though she were an offering to the gods of decadence and desire. His mouth worked its magic, suckling and nipping, swirling until her world fell away, until there was nothing except sensation, nothing beyond raw nerve endings and need. Pleasure erupting with such force that her shoulders came up off the bed, she dug her fingers into his shoulders, looked down to see him watching her with quiet satisfaction and a burning need of his own.

With a gasp, her body trembling, she dropped back down, swallowed hard, fighting for control. He glided his body up hers until he burrowed his face in the hollow between her neck and shoulder. She loved the sensation of his slick skin sliding over hers.

"I can't wait to have your cock buried deeply inside me," she whispered in his bad ear.

"Oh, you are such a wicked girl," he growled.

Everything within her froze and she stiffened. He went equally still. She pushed on his shoulders until he came up just enough that she could look into his eyes. Eyes that a moment ago had been smoldering with desire and were now cautious, waiting. "You heard me."

No question but a statement as panic threatened her. "You said the words aloud did you not?"

"I whispered them in your bad ear."

"You must have spoken louder than you thought."

She shook her head. "No. Still, you heard me." Her heart began pounding. Her stomach recoiled and she thought she might be ill. "You heard me." Shoving on him, she scrambled back, nearly fell off the bed, catching her balance as her feet hit the floor. Snatching up her dressing gown from its place at the foot of the bed, she jerked it on and held it in tight at her waist. It couldn't be and yet she knew it had to be true. "You're not Albert. You're Edward."

He held out a hand imploringly. "Julia—"

No denial, no laughter at the absurdity of her claim. *I'm sorry that I'm not the man you married.* How many times had he told her that? "Oh my God! Oh my dear God!"

It was difficult to draw in a breath, She thought she might suffocate. Right here. Right then. All the air had been sucked from the room. All the life had been stolen from her limbs.

He pushed himself into a seated position. "Julia—"

"It's true, isn't it?"

He said nothing, merely looked at her, the guilt etching the truth over his features.

"Oh, my God! Albert! Albert!" Her bare feet padded over the floor as she ran from the room, ran from the truth, ran from the memories of all that had passed between her and Edward since he'd returned from Africa. She raced down the stairs and out of the house, into the cold rain, into the dark night, into the horrendous knowledge that Albert was dead.

Chapter 14

*H*ELL and damnation.

He'd been so lost in desire, so lost in the heat of her, that he'd forgotten he was supposed to be partially deaf. He knew of no other woman who could stir his passions to life as she did. When she had whispered those wicked words, he'd hardened to such an extent that he was unable to think clearly.

And now she knew the truth. He'd been a fool to think he could keep it from her forever. But he certainly hadn't meant for her to find out like this. Rolling out of bed, he snatched up his clothes, donned trousers, shirt, and boots. Rushing into his bedchamber, he grabbed his coat, shrugged into it, and headed out. He was fairly certain he knew where she was going.

In the cold and the rain. Silly woman. No, not silly. Grieving. Her heart would be breaking, shattered, not only by the death of her husband but the betrayal of his brother. Running through the rain, he cursed himself for not bothering with a hat, but his own discomforts mattered not at all.

The only thing that mattered was Julia. Finding her

and doing what he could to lessen her pain. Although he doubted anything he did would accomplish that goal. He'd seen the look of horror on her face, the revulsion. So much had transpired between them that shouldn't have. He despised himself for his weakness where she was concerned. Imagined she despised him even more.

He found her in the mausoleum, draped over Albert's vault as her great, heaving sobs echoed through the chamber. He'd never felt so helpless, so lost, when it came to knowing exactly what to do. In dismay, he watched as she slumped to the floor, her weeping lessening in intensity but no less heartbreaking. Never before had he wished so desperately to trade places with his brother. He crouched beside her. "Julia."

"No," she rasped. "No. He can't be gone. He can't."

But he was. Forever and always.

Edward settled his coat over her. "You can't stay out here. You're soaked to the bone; you'll catch your death. You must think of Allie." Gently, he slid his arms beneath her, hefted her against his chest and struggled to his feet.

"I hate you," she said, her scratchy voice filled with the pain of loss and betrayal.

"I know." But no more than he hated himself.

The rain pelted him as he fought to shield her from the frigid wind and rain, knowing his coat could only offer so much protection. She was shivering from the cold, the damp, the grief. Why hadn't he told her sooner? Why had he thought he could live a lie for the next fifty years?

In her bedchamber, he came up short at the sight of Torrie standing by the bed, rubbing her hands together.

"I saw her ladyship running out of the manor, you after her. I thought I might be needed when you returned."

One did not explain oneself to servants. Therefore, after giving Torrie little more than a nod of acknowledgment, he set Julia on the sofa, crouched before the fireplace, stirred the embers, added a log. As the fire took hold, he shoved himself to his feet, looked at her. She was shivering, pale, her gaze focused on the fire.

"I need a hot bath," Julia stated flatly.

"Yes, m'lady," Torrie said.

"And change the bedding. It reeks of the earl."

The maid's gaze jumped to him. He knew she was wondering how best to respond to her ladyship's request without insulting his lordship and losing her position in the household. She settled for a quick bob of her head, a curtsy, and a dash from the room.

He knelt on one knee. He wanted to hold her, offer comfort as she had for him, but he knew she wouldn't welcome his touch, his words, his solace. "Julia, I beg of you to say nothing to the servants until we determine how best to handle this situation."

Her sorrow-filled eyes remained focused on the fire. "Get out."

For the servants, it mattered only that they served the earl. It didn't matter who the earl was: Albert or Edward. For them there would be no transition. Everything would remain the same. *The earl is dead. Long live the earl.*

"Julia—"

Slowly, she shifted her gaze to him. He didn't know if he'd ever seen so much hatred. "Lady Greyling. Get. Out."

She was filled with too much grief to fully understand all the ramifications, but he had to trust that she wouldn't say anything. And if she did, then he would have to deal with it. He pushed to his feet. "I never meant to hurt you."

He walked out, knowing that things between them would never again be the same.

SHE waited until she heard the door close in his wake, then curled into a ball on the sofa and let the tears flow. Albert was dead. Dear, sweet, wonderful Albert was dead. Gone. And she hadn't known.

Her chest ached, her throat knotted. How could he be gone? How could she have not known?

Albert was dead.

Absent from her life for more than six months in total, two during which she had laughed and teased and desired the man who had pretended to be her husband. A forgery. An imitation. A counterfeit.

But my word he had been a good and clever one.

That more than anything she could not forgive. These past weeks her love had grown deeper, she had been happier than she'd ever been. And it had all been false.

What made it so truly awful was that she wanted him here now, holding her, consoling her, promising her that everything would be all right. She'd believed him when the labor pains had begun too soon. She'd trusted him.

Edward. How could she have been such a fool? So blind. How could she have not seen?

He drank scotch but not to excess. She hadn't actually seen him drunk, although she suspected he had been the night Allie—

Alberta. Named for her father. He had insisted. What had he said?

We'll not name the Greyling heir after such a self-ish bastard. He's to be named after his father, as he should be.

Selfish bastard. He'd been talking about himself.

It made so much sense now. How deeply he'd mourned, the guilt he must have felt because he was the one who insisted Albert travel with him. All the times he had referred to himself as her husband or the earl when she asked him a question.

We can't have you doubting your husband's devotion to you.

I promise you, Julia, your husband could not be more pleased. She looks just like you. What father would find fault with that?

She had thought it odd but had only once questioned it.

She buried her face in her hands. All the times she had made the advances, all the naughty things she'd whispered, thinking that he couldn't hear them. Oh, the bastard. How would she ever look him in the eye again?

Lowering her hands, she knew she would do it with all the hatred and indignant fury that coursed through her at his betrayal. She would never forgive him for this. For making sport of her, for taking advantage of the situation.

She would find a way to make him pay, to make him suffer. He was worried about her telling the servants?

She intended to tell the whole of London.

*D*ON'T *let her lose the babe.*

    Be me. Be me. Take care of her.

    Take her to Switzerland.

His brother's dying words. Odd at the end. As though taking his wife on holiday was of prime importance. Maybe he regretted never taking her. It was a beautiful country.

On bended knee, Edward knelt before Albert's vault. It had been three days since Julia learned the truth, and he had yet to speak with her. She took her meals in her bedchamber. He wasn't certain she ever left the room. Twice he had gone into it, only to have her turn her back on him and demand that he leave.

The servants knew something was amiss, as he'd moved into the other wing. He couldn't be certain she wouldn't run a poker through him in the dead of night. Although he couldn't deny that he deserved it, and worse.

"I mucked things up, Albert. Stupendously. And stupidly."

He should have told her right after Christmas. No, right after Allie was born. Better yet, when he arrived at Evermore. She was stronger than Albert gave her credit for. Yes, she had lost three babes, but he believed that was nature's folly. Nothing Julia could have done, nothing any of them could have done, to change that. She would have grieved over Albert's death, yes, but not in a way that would have endangered her child. She would have seen to it. She was smart and wise and . . . blistering mad at him.

Hearing the groan of the door opening, he looked over to see her standing in the doorway, dressed the part of a grieving widow. Black gown, black gloves, black hat, black veil, black cloak.

But even through the black gossamer, he could feel her hard-edged glare. He was surprised he didn't ignite into a ball of flames. Slowly, he came to his feet, walked quietly toward the door. She stepped aside when he neared, as though he were a leper.

He stopped. Considered. "When you return to the residence, come to the library. We need to talk."

"I have nothing to say to you."

"That may be, but we must consider how best to move forward, how to protect your reputation and do what is best for Allie."

"Lady Alberta."

Dear God, she wasn't going to make this easy, was she? Not that he blamed her. "Lady Greyling, you and I have been living as husband and wife for well over two months. We must coordinate our story. I'll be awaiting your arrival in the library."

He could feel her hatred burning a hole in his back as he strode out. He had to make her understand—at least what had prompted his ruse in the beginning. Why he hadn't ended it before the situation went too far was another matter. He didn't expect forgiveness there. He wasn't even going to ask for it.

JULIA waited until the door slammed in Edward's wake to kneel before the vault, press her forehead to the cool marble. The closest she could get to her husband. God, it hurt.

Her heart, her soul, her body. The pain was nearly unbearable.

"Why did you have to die?" she whispered. "Why? Oh, Albert, I miss you something terrible. When I think about how long you've actually been gone, I feel cheated. There's this chasm that I can't seem to cross. This looming abyss. Why do I think it would have been easier to deal with if I'd known sooner?

"I've been a widow for more than four months. I wasn't even wearing black any longer."

She understood so much now. Understood why the man she'd believed was her husband had come here the night Alberta was born.

"I know he told you about your daughter, but it should have been me who told you. I hate him for that. I hate him for everything. I know I tell you this every time I come here, but it's eating at me. You cannot possibly imagine how much I miss you."

Shaking her head, she flattened her hand against the marble. "I just want to hold you one more time. Want you to hold me. Want you to tell me what to do, how to go on."

The grief was devastating, but Edward's betrayal made it all the worse. She didn't know how she would survive it all, but survive it she would.

Because only survival ensured the possibility of retribution.

SITTING at his desk, Edward began to scribble out a strategy for how best to handle explaining this unconscionable situation to the nobility. That was the key, the core problem. It required a delicate balance. He would express his contrition for the deception, but he could not be too contrite. After all, his actions had come about at the behest of his brother. He would reassure them that nothing untoward had transpired, that because of her delicate condition, their relationship has been chaste. He didn't think it would be difficult to convince anyone of that possibility. He'd never made a secret of the fact that he could barely tolerate his sister-by-marriage. She'd never pretended to find him anything other than obnoxious. That common knowledge could now be used for the good, to save her reputation, her standing within Society.

Leaning back in his chair, he realized that he might very well come out of this a hero. Ladies would fawn over a gent who had been so considerate as to spend his time in the company of a woman he couldn't tolerate. He would be applauded for his unselfishness, for his caring, for his devotion to his brother and his sister-by-marriage. Ladies would find him gallant, sing his praises, arrange trysts in dark gardens to sample the flavor of his kiss. He would gain more attention that he had ever dreamed.

Yet he wanted none of it.

As Julia marched through the doorway, her hands balled into fists at her sides, her face set in unforgiving lines, he knew that she would never view him as a hero. She would never see him as anything other than a sly weasel who played unkind tricks.

Straightening, he got up from his chair, prepared to face the tigress. "Would you mind closing the door?"

She stood unmoving.

Right. She wasn't of a mind to make any allowances or do him any favors. Already this discussion did not bode well for a favorable ending. He strode toward the threshold, walked past her and shut the door. What they had to say to each other needed to be said without servants overhearing anything. Earlier he'd sent the footman who usually saw to the opening and closing of doors on his way. Edward swung around.

"Why?" she demanded, firing the first volley of what was bound to be a combative exchange. "Why did you do it?"

"Albert asked me to."

"He asked you to deceive me?"

"He asked me to ensure that you did not lose the babe. 'Be me,' he said. 'Take care of her.' He feared, as did I, that the grief over his death would cause you to miscarry. So I pretended to be him."

"I don't believe you."

And he had no way to convince her except with words. "Why would I do this if not for his asking? Why would I pretend all these weeks to be Albert?"

"Because you feared I was carrying a son. You wanted the title, the estates, the power, the prestige. That's the reason you weren't disappointed I gave birth to a girl."

"I did not want the title."

She shook her head vigorously. "And then to carry on with the farce. There can be only one reason for that: to humiliate me, to make sport of me, to gain what you'd been denied in the garden, to make me pay for that slap."

"You think me that petty? To take advantage of my brother's death in such a vile manner?"

"What else am I to think when you had ample opportunity to tell me, and yet you carried on with the pretense. The things I said to you, the *things* I did to you. Oh, you must have had a jolly good laugh."

She wasn't listening, wasn't hearing what he was saying. "I swear to you, Julia, I laughed during none of this."

She placed her hand over her mouth. "The things you did to me. How could you?"

"I was trying to mimic your husband. I could see no good coming from turning you away. I feared you becoming melancholy, causing the very outcome I was trying to prevent."

She pounded her fist into his shoulder, nearly causing him to stumble back. In righteous anger, she possessed quite the wallop.

"What rot! You enjoyed it. You enjoyed deceiving me."

"No."

"You've always been jealous of Albert. You wanted the title. If I gave birth to a boy, you would never have it, so you took preemptive measures to ensure your position."

"No. It's as I said. Albert asked—"

"Liar. It was your plan all along to take everything. His title, his estates, even his wife, his child—"

"No! I never planned to take any of it. It was my intent to tell you everything as soon as the babe was born."

"As soon as the babe was born? It's been six weeks! What the devil were you waiting for?"

"To fall out of love with you."

Chapter 15

REELING from his declaration, Julia took a staggering step back and gawked in disbelief at Edward. She expected him to burst out laughing any minute now, but he remained solemn, stoic. He had to be striving to trick her, to gain sympathy or forgiveness or something nefarious that she couldn't identify. "But you've never even liked me."

"Dear God, if only that were true."

Striving to make sense of him, she continued to stare as he walked past her to the sideboard, poured scotch into a glass, brandy into another, and held the one containing brandy toward her. Another way in which the brothers were so vastly different. Albert never would have offered her spirits. Why had she thought a journey to Africa would change his basic philosophies?

But she couldn't take it, couldn't seem to force her feet to move. Nothing was making any sense.

Setting her glass aside, he carried his to the window and gazed out. "It's very important that Allie—Lady Alberta—grow up here," he said quietly.

She blinked, trying to focus on the words he'd uttered. She'd expected him to elaborate on his earlier comment, needed him to explain himself. He'd made her feel a fool that night in the garden. Was he striving to do the same now?

"That experience was denied to Albert and myself. He would never forgive me if it were denied to her. I've moved into the other wing. God knows the residence is spacious enough that we could go years without catching sight of each other. I will, of course, spend as much time as possible at the other estates or in London so you are not burdened by my presence."

An hour ago, five minutes ago, she would have expected him to say, *So I am not burdened by* your *presence.* But he claimed to love her.

Reluctantly, she moved closer, stood far enough away that she couldn't inhale his familiar bergamot scent but near enough that she could see every tiny line that had been carved by the weight of his burdens into his face. "You hardly ever spoke to me."

He closed his eyes. "Julia—"

"If I walked into the room, you walked out."

He bowed his head, clenched his jaw.

"You never had a kind word for me. Although to be fair, neither did you have an unkind one. It's just that they were all rather . . . dutiful-sounding, as though dragged out of you because they were expected."

"It was easier that way." Turning, he pushed back against the edge of the window as though he needed something sharp biting into him. He pressed the flat of one foot to the wall, his knee bent slightly. He was a picture of raw masculinity, and she hated herself for noticing. "It was easier if you looked at me with loathing, because what manner of man would desire a woman whose eyes flashed with disgust whenever she saw him? And when that wasn't enough, I drank and drank and drank to dull the yearning, to make myself obnoxious so my brother's wife would not welcome me into their residence, because God forbid Albert ever realized the hunger I felt for the woman he loved, the one he had married."

That long? He'd carried feelings toward her for that long? How had she not known? How had Albert not guessed? She pressed her back to the casement, needing the support as her knees threatened to give out at the unexpectedness of his revelation. It hardly seemed real. "When did you begin to feel this way?"

He lifted his glass, downed what remained of his scotch, and shifted his gaze back out the window. He squinted. "Oh, it was lurking about for a while. That night in the garden sealed it. I thought, 'You're only interested because she's forbidden. Kiss her, have your taste, and be done with her.' Instead that blasted kiss only made me want you all the more."

She squeezed her eyes shut and rasped, "That night in the garden I thought you were Albert."

"I know. I didn't realize it until after the kiss, actually convinced myself that you'd been waiting for me. More the fool was I. When you called me Albert, it was like a kick to the gut, but it didn't lessen the tumult that you created within me."

Opening her eyes, she discovered him studying her once more, his expression an impassive mask, and yet within the brown depths of his eyes was the want, the need. How had she been so blind before? Because he'd been so incredibly unpleasant that she'd never bothered to look beyond the surface.

"Since you mistook me in the garden, I thought there was a chance that after a four-month separation from Albert you might mistake me again and I could pull off what he asked of me."

From the moment she had walked into the library, she would have sworn he had been more honest with her than he'd ever been, but part of his story made no sense. Was he merely striving to weasel his way out of what he'd done? Was everything he'd said merely a lie to gain her favor, her forgiveness? How could she trust his words when he'd done something so untrustworthy? She furrowed her brow. "When did Albert ask you to do what you must to ensure I didn't lose the child?"

He blinked. "Pardon?"

"I assume the story about the manner in which Edward was killed was truly Albert's, that he died instantly. Is that correct?"

He nodded solemnly.

"Then how did he have a chance to ask anything of you? How can any of this that you've done"—she flung her arm out to encompass weeks of deception—"have been at his request?"

He raised his glass, scowled at its lack of content. "One night as we were sitting by the fire, he said that if anything happened to him I was not to let you know until after the babe was born. He feared the news would cause you to miscarry. He had a premonition, I suppose."

"Once again, I don't believe you." It was too far-fetched. He was either lying about Albert's request or lying about how he'd been killed. She thought she might be ill. "He didn't die straightaway, did he?"

Lowering the glass, his hold on it so tight that his knuckles were turning white, he met and held her gaze. "It's as I said. He died with the first blow."

He didn't flinch, didn't look away. She wanted to believe that Albert's death had been quick, that he'd been spared any pain, but it seemed unlikely. "So some night, during a random conversation, he just happened to ask you to pretend to be him if he should die?"

"Two nights before we spotted the baby gorilla."

The tale of a premonition was preposterous. Yet she wanted it to be true, wanted to believe Albert didn't suffer. But Edward would know that, wouldn't he? If he truly cared for her as he claimed, he would want to ease her pain.

She didn't know what to make of his declaration, his confession. It confused her, made her feel as much the betrayer as the betrayed. She didn't like all the tumult he was creating within her. "I loved Albert. I love him still."

"I know. I'm not asking you to love me, Julia. I'm not even asking you to think kindly of me or forgive me for the duplicity. I understand that you're angry, furious. You have every right to be. I'm merely asking that you not do anything rash that might have an adverse effect on Alberta's future."

Damn him, damn his deception. Originally she had wanted to hurt him in some manner, publicly humiliate him, but she did have to take care not to ruin her daughter's future chances for a good match. "I don't know that I can stay here," she admitted, not certain she could trust her feelings, trust him. The wounds of his betrayal still festered. Her grief, her loss of Albert, seemed to suck the very life from her.

"Where will you go? To your cousin's? Can he provide for you any better than I can?"

She despised that he understood the truth of her situation, used it to his advantage to keep her and Alberta near. Her parents were gone. She had no siblings. The cousin who had inherited her father's titles and estates had been pleased beyond measure that she'd married at nineteen. "Albert must have made some provisions for me."

"Ironically, I believe I'm it. I've been unable to locate a will."

Apparently, all the hours he'd spent in the library had not been solely about managing the affairs of the estate. "Surely his solicitor has a copy."

"I wrote him asking if Edward had left a will and to advise me regarding mine. I worded it in such a way that it wasn't obvious the earl was completely unaware as to whether he even possessed one. His response was that Edward had left no will—which, of course, I knew, being Edward, after all—and his advice regarding the earl's will remained what it had been for some time now: One needed to be prepared with all due haste and diligence."

She sank against the wall, then straightened, to avoid showing any disappointment or weakness. "It seems I'm dependent upon your kindness."

"I will be more than generous with an allowance, and I shall ensure that Lady Alberta never wants for anything." He seemed to hesitate, sighed. "There is a cottage in the Cotswolds. Based upon notes I've uncovered, I believe our father intended it to be the dower house for our mother. Apparently she liked the countryside there. It's not part of the entailment. I could gift it to you, but as I mentioned, I truly believe with all my heart that Albert would want his daughter raised here."

Unfortunately, she was of the same opinion. He had often spoken of how he longed to have his children grow up within the shadow of Evermore, how much he'd regretted that he'd been denied the same. "As I have a good deal to consider, presently I can't commit to any decisions or a course of action, but I do agree that we must take care in how this situation is managed—for Alberta's sake. What are you going to tell the servants?"

"They serve the Earl of Greyling. I am Greyling. I'm not going to tell them a damned thing."

"They'll be suspicious with your move into the other wing."

His smile was self-deprecating. "They'll think we're having a bit of marital discord, and if they value their position here, they'll keep their suspicions to themselves."

"And Society?"

"I think it will be best if we wait to make any sort of admission until all the lords and ladies are in London for the Season. I shall be there as well and can personally handle any repercussions that might arise with the revelation of my duplicity. That gives us time to determine exactly what we wish to say."

With a nod, she turned her attention to the winter

gardens beyond the window. "Your wife won't be too pleased if Alberta and I stay on here."

"My wife?"

"As you said, you are the Earl of Greyling. You require an heir."

"That won't happen for years yet, decades, if ever. Not until Lady Alberta is well situated. She matters above all else."

She touched the pane. It felt as cold as her soul. She wondered if she'd ever know warmth again. "We shall remain here for now. I shall not take meals with you, nor spend time in your company in the evenings. If you must communicate with me, please do it through a servant."

"If you need to speak with me—"

She quickly faced him. "I shan't."

With that, she spun on her heel and marched from the library, wondering how it was that two brothers could each break her heart in vastly different ways, and wondering why it was that her heart ached painfully in equal measure for the loss of each brother.

STANDING at the window, savoring his scotch, Edward watched as darkness fell. One glass was all he was going to allow himself. He didn't want to dull the sting of her parting words that he so justly deserved or the ache in his chest because he had opened his heart to her. A tiny part of him had hoped, prayed, wished that she would claim her love for him when he had professed his for her, even as the greater part of him had known it was a fool's errand to travel that path.

He wasn't even certain he'd completely understood

the depth of his feelings until the words had burst forth. He didn't know exactly when he'd fallen in love with her. He knew only that he had. Unequivocally. And he feared she would forever hold that place in his heart. While to her, he would remain little more than a rodent, striving to make off with the scraps to which he wasn't entitled.

"Dinner is served, my lord," Rigdon announced.

He had bathed, shaved, and dressed in his finest evening attire, just in case her anger with him lessened a bit and she took enough pity on him to dine in his company. He didn't care if she didn't speak with him. It would be enough just to have her near. They could eat in the formal dining room. Dressed in her widow's weeds, she could sit at the far end of the table, yards away from him. He suspected she would join him if she understood the extent of the agony that sight would cause him.

"The countess . . ." If he waited a bit longer, perhaps she'd show.

"Informed Torrie she would be dining in her rooms. I believe she's feeling a bit under the weather."

He had to give his butler credit for at least striving to pretend that all was right with the lord and lady of the house.

"I'll be there in a moment." Dear God but he was a sorry excuse for a lord, sniveling about. He'd had a little over two months with her. He was going to have to make due with that for a lifetime. With a sigh, Edward finished off his drink and headed to the small dining room.

He didn't know why he expected to see her there,

why he felt like he'd taken a punch to the gut when the only ones waiting for him were the butler and a footman. The heart was a cruel mistress, always giving one hope.

Taking his seat, he stared at the flames burning in the candelabra in the center of the table while his wine was poured and soup was served. The room was so blasted quiet, the only sound his silver spoon periodically clinking against china. He'd never thought to miss the screeching winds of Havisham Hall, but at that moment anything was better than being surrounded by the silence of Julia's absence.

Chapter 16

My dearest darling,

How I wish you were here to enjoy this adventure with us. Edward is quite the tyrant, constantly pushing us forward. He seems to be in his element, thriving on his role as leader of our little expedition. He does not drink as much. I have yet to see him inebriated. Perhaps it is because he is at home here. Or maybe it is that he is fully aware that once our stores of liquor are depleted there is no more to be had within these jungles. If the latter is the case, he is showing remarkable restraint.

Although we have made many journeys together and he has always ordered people about, I don't know why it is that this time I am appreciating the manner in which he takes charge. Watching him, I cannot help but believe that he is better suited to being the earl than I. I have always found being responsible for others a chore, while he revels in it. It seems to me

that something more than exiting the womb first
should determine who inherits a title.

CLOSING her husband's journal, Julia set it carefully in her lap and gazed out her bedchamber window. She was a dozen days into their journey. She didn't want to read about how Edward made him laugh, or taught him how to prevent blisters, or ensured they were served proper tea in the teeming wilds. She wanted to read about how much Albert missed her. She wanted to read a passage that said, "I had a premonition last night. I want you to forgive Edward for what I am going to ask him to do. Know I do it out of love for you and our unborn child."

But as of yet, she discovered no such revelation. He'd penned no words of comfort, no words to confirm that he had known he would die. No final words reaffirming his love for her, no parting message, no tender goodbye. Everything was inconsequential, nothing of import. It was as though he had fully expected to write in his journal a thousand more times.

While she dearly wanted to read the final entry, she refused to read the entries out of order. She wanted to experience his last few weeks as he had lived them. While she had never had any interest in traveling, she suddenly found herself wishing that she had been at his side the entire time he'd been away, as though her presence would have been enough to prevent the horribleness of what had transpired.

She was a widow, had been one in truth for more than four months. Yet time with Edward had tempered her sorrow. She thought she might hate him for that most of all. When she should be thinking about her husband she was thinking about his brother. The way he had made her laugh, the way he had held her, how he hadn't left her side as she had brought her daughter into the world. The admission that he had fallen in love with her.

If he truly loved her, how could he have allowed her to live a lie, how could he have withheld the truth? Perhaps she could forgive him for the weeks before Alberta's birth, but the ones after—

The rap on the door barely caused her to stir. "Enter."

Torrie cautiously strolled in, looking somewhat wary, and handed her a note. "From his lordship."

Julia took it, unfolded it, read the words inscribed in his neat, precise script, almost identical to Albert's but not quite. Now she found herself searching for the most mundane differences between the brothers, swearing beneath her breath each time she noted one, wondering how she'd missed it before.

I shall be in the nursery from two until half past.
                                       —Greyling

She wasn't surprised. He'd had the same message delivered every day for the past week. And she knew that he knew she couldn't deny him visiting Lady Alberta without causing speculation and gossip among the servants as to the reason she would not allow the child's *father* to spend time with her. While staff was not supposed to blather about what went on upstairs, Julia wasn't fool enough to think they held everything they observed to themselves. With a harsh unladylike curse, she'd torn the first note into tiny shreds. She'd ripped the second in half. Balled up the third. Did little more than sigh and refold all the others.

At least he forewarned her about his intentions so she wouldn't cross paths with him in the hallway or the nursery and have to endure seeing him.

"Would you like me to deliver a message to him?" Torrie asked.

Go to the devil was probably not what her maid had in mind. "No. Let Nanny know that she should prepare Lady Alberta for the earl's two o'clock visit."

"Yes, m'lady. Shall I press a gown for you to wear to dinner?"

That question had also become part of her daily ritual. "No. Have dinner brought to my room."

"Yes, m'lady." She heard the disappointment and sorrow in Torrie's voice. Her maid knew something was wrong. The entire staff no doubt knew something was wrong. They simply couldn't imagine what it could be. Why would they—why would anyone—suspect the truth when it was preposterous and unfathomable?

"It's not the nanny, m'lady," Torrie suddenly blurted.

Julia looked at the young woman who was rubbing one hand over the other as though apprehensive she'd said something she shouldn't. "I beg your pardon?"

"Everyone knows he goes to the nursery each afternoon. The scullery maid, she's a bit dimwitted, she said he fancies the nanny and that's why he goes, that no father takes that much interest in a baby. But he sends the nanny down to the kitchen for a cuppa when he's in the nursery. He's just spending time with Lady Alberta. He's not being unfaithful to you."

She'd never considered that he would be; perhaps she should have. He was a young, virile man—

What was she thinking? He owed her no faithfulness. Why did that thought bother her? What did she care who he might bed? She looked back out the window. She did wish spring would arrive, that the weather would warm, that she could go riding.

"He likes to go into your relaxing room."

Into the room where she worked with her watercolors. She'd once told Torrie that it relaxed her, and the maid had taken to calling it her relaxing room. And now she was offering up this tidbit as though that would somehow redeem him in Julia's eyes when the poor woman didn't even know what he needed redemption for. "When?"

"Different times, but at least once a day."

Was he hoping to find her there, stumble across her? Well, she wasn't going to allow it. Julia surged to her feet. She would have her maid deliver a missive instructing Edward to stay out of her room—

Only it was no longer hers. It was his. The entire residence was his, every room, every painting, every knickknack, every bauble, every statue. She couldn't order him about. He would simply laugh. She was here by his good graces. Everything he gave her was only because he deemed it worth her having. She sank back into her chair. Suddenly she desperately wanted to watercolor. Since she'd learned the truth of her widowhood, she'd only left her bedchamber to visit the mausoleum and Alberta. The remainder of the time she'd remained in seclusion, grieving a loss that often made it difficult to even consider climbing out of bed. Now there was a chance she would run into him in her sanctuary, if she should decide to go there. How easily he took things from her.

"Thank you, Torrie. You may go."

"Wish I knew why you were so sad, m'lady."

She offered her maid a solemn smile. "I discovered the earl was not who I thought he was."

Honest, but cryptic. The words no doubt failed to satisfy the young woman's curiosity, but they did cause her to make a hasty retreat. Julia rose and walked to the cheval glass and studied her reflection. The black made her appear so somber. The staff probably wondered at her change in attire. She'd seldom dressed in mourning when it was Edward supposedly in the mausoleum, but now she wore only black. Thank goodness she did not have to explain her actions to the servants. It was difficult enough to explain them to herself, especially when the clock on the mantel neared the stroke of two and she pressed her ear to the door.

He was always so punctual. She didn't know why she had this insane urge to listen for his footsteps. They were muffled by the carpet but still she heard them, marking off his long strides. They went silent, and she knew he had stopped right outside her door. He always did. It was madness to think that she could feel his gaze on the wood, hear his breathing. Madness to believe his scent somehow permeated the room to tease her nostrils.

Not wanting him to know she was there, she held

her breath, and yet she feared that he did know, that he was as aware of her on this side of the door as she was of him on the other. She wondered if he was tempted to knock, to call out to her, to flatten his palm against the wood—in the same spot where her own hand rested.

She heard the unmistakable sound of him carrying on, his steps brisk and quick. Releasing her breath on a little shudder, she pressed her forehead to the door and waited. Waited until she heard the rapid click of the nanny going down the back stairs. Yes, she knew the nanny always left.

Slowly, carefully, she opened the door, peered out into the empty hallway. With far more confidence than she felt, she straightened her shoulders and stepped out. After glancing around once more, she lifted the hem of her skirt and crept on bare feet down the carpeted hallway to the nursery. The door was open. It always remained open.

She got as close to it as she could without being seen and pressed her back to the wall. The creak of the rocking chair wafted through the doorway, and she envisioned him holding her daughter cradled in his arms as he swayed back and forth. She closed her eyes and listened.

THE half hour that Edward spent with Allie in his arms was his favorite time of the day, and not just because his niece blinked up at him with such big blue eyes. Her mother's blue eyes. But because he had her mother's attention as well. He could see a quarter of an inch of black skirt creeping past the doorjamb, and he knew before he was done it would be a full inch as Julia leaned closer to the threshold in order to hear him. It wasn't until the third day that he'd noticed the edge of her gown. Until then he'd given all his attention to Allie, but on that particular afternoon she'd fallen asleep. He'd looked up, seen the bombazine, and continued waxing on.

"Let's see, Allie, where were we?" He was so tempted to call out and ask Julia where he had ended yesterday's tale, but he knew her well enough to know that she wouldn't appreciate the teasing. She would no doubt cease her scurrying down the hallway to secretly join them as he wove his story. That she was there gave him hope that perhaps at some point they could at least get on civilly. They needed to, for Allie's sake.

"Ah, yes, the great and magnificent steed that oversees all the animals has discovered that trouble is afoot. I think we should give him a name. Shall we call him Greymane, the Grey in honor of your father? I think he'd like that. Badger, who is in fact a badger and wears a green waistcoat, is telling Greymane that he saw Stinker the Weasel, with his beady eyes and his sharp jagged teeth and his long pointy nose, lurking about behind the trees. They think he's up to no good, planning to ruin the picnic that Princess Allie is planning to have for all her forest friends in the clearing with the yellow wildflowers."

He continued to weave the story of the beautiful princess and her noble friends. And the jealous and selfish weasel that wanted to ruin everything. Rocking, he talked until an inch of black skirt became visible. He did wish it was red, blue, or green. But she was truly in mourning now, fully aware that she was a widow.

Each morning, an hour before dawn, unknown to

her, he quietly followed her as she made her way to the mausoleum. Hidden within the trees, he would stand guard. By the time she headed back, the sky was lighting to a pale blue so he couldn't follow her as closely. At least she was making the trek when the servants were too busy to notice. It might make them wonder why she was suddenly devoted to early morning walks and time spent within the family's resting place.

Other than that, he only caught a glimpse of her skirt when he rocked Allie. He was more the fool for taking pleasure in a scrap of cloth simply because it belonged to her. He continued to eat alone, to sit in his library alone, to play billiards alone. In the late hours of the night when sleep eluded him, he worked on the story he was writing for Allie about whimsical creatures that wore clothes, spoke, and behaved in a manner that very much resembled humans.

Looking down on her now, asleep in his arms, he knew he would write her an entire bookshelf of stories. Out of the corner of his eye he saw the skirt disappear. Three seconds later he heard the rapid tapping of the nanny's shoes as she entered the corridor just beyond the door.

Standing, he carried Allie to her crib and carefully set her down in it. She opened her eyes wide, waved her arms and feet. "See you tomorrow, little one."

With a final word to the nanny, he walked into the hallway. Julia's scent was stronger now. Like a desperate man, he inhaled deeply, taking his fill. He carried on until he reached her door. Halting, he placed his hand on the wood. He didn't know why it made him feel closer to her. It was a silly, stupid thing to do, yet he couldn't seem to stop himself.

Then he headed down the stairs into the lonely emptiness that was now his life.

HER heart thundering, Julia awoke to crying. For a moment she thought perhaps her own sobbing had disturbed her sleep, because her cheeks were damp and now there was only silence so it must have been her crying out that brought her from the depths of slumber.

Laying there in the dark, in the quiet, she stared at the canopy, striving to determine what was amiss. During the past week, she'd slept fitfully. She was tired of the sorrow, the ache in her chest that felt like a physical bruising, the doubts, the guilt. Tonight she'd had enough and gone to the bedchamber previously designated for Edward and taken a bottle of brandy from the little cabinet where he kept spirits. She'd sipped until she was barely able to keep her eyes open. Then she'd clambered into bed and succumbed to the allure of welcome oblivion.

But now she was awake, and she had the sense that something important had lured her from the dream in which she was continually running toward Albert only to have Edward constantly stepping in front of her, blocking her path. Or was she running toward Edward? She couldn't even tell them apart in her dreams.

Sitting up, she pressed her elbow to her knee, her forehead to her hand. Her thinking was muddled, as though she were striving to make her way through a ball of cobwebs. In her dream, she'd heard crying in the distance. She'd begun racing toward the sobbing but the faster she ran the farther away it became, until it faded to nothing. And the silence, a portent of bad tidings, had terrified her.

Alberta. It had been Alberta bawling. In the dream? No, outside of the dream. Bawling until her cries invaded the dream. If not for the brandy dulling everything, she would have woken up sooner, would have realized where the crying originated. Flinging back the covers, Julia scrambled out of bed. She was certain Nanny had soothed Alberta, but still she had a strong need to hold her daughter to her breast, to comfort her, to let her know that nothing would hurt her.

She flew out of her bedchamber, down the hallway to the nursery. Nanny was sitting in a chair with a lamp burning low and a book in her hands. Not Alberta. She wasn't holding Alberta.

Edward was. Lying on Nanny's bed, his eyes closed, Alberta on his chest, her knees tucked beneath her so her tiny bum was sticking up in the air. Pillows formed a barrier on either side of his body so if she rolled she wouldn't roll far. Not that Julia thought she was likely to move at all. One of his large hands was splayed over her back, holding her in place.

Setting the book aside, Nanny got up and approached her, tiptoeing. "She was crying something awful. I couldn't soothe her. The earl came in, none too happy. Said he could hear her howling in his library. Thought he was going to sack me on the spot. Instead he took her, placed her against his chest, and she quieted right down."

He'd come to her rescue, Julia realized, while she had been suffering from too much drink to do anything but stir to life sluggishly. How had Edward managed to live like this for years, drinking to excess every night? Waking up was most unpleasant.

"Go find a bed in another chamber so you can get some sleep," she told the nanny.

"I shouldn't leave her."

"She's fine."

"Thank you, m'lady."

Julia waited until the woman was gone to sit in a chair near the bed. The sight of the tall, powerful man sprawled over the small bed with her daughter resting near his heart made her want to weep. She did not want to be so moved. Damn the weasel for coming to the princess's rescue. Damn her own heart for its gladness at seeing him—she thought it might swell beyond the confines of her chest—when she hadn't caught so much as a glimpse of him for days.

He'd lost weight. Shadows rested beneath his eyes. Even though he was asleep he appeared tired. Was it fair to punish him for doing what Albert had asked of him? No, the punishment was for the six weeks when he'd held the truth from her and charmed her instead.

If you got to know him better, I think you'd like him, Albert had once told her. The problem was, she liked him far too much.

She wasn't going to ask for the cottage in the Cotswolds, because he was correct, blast him. Alberta belonged here. Nowhere else would she be more loved, more protected, more spoiled.

Unfortunately, she feared that nowhere else would she herself be more miserable.

Chapter 17

IT had been a wretched winter. Edward cursed the frigid winds that whipped around him as he dismounted in front of the village tea shop, then chose some rather strong words to fling at himself for braving what surely had to be the last storm before spring for something as whimsical as strawberry tarts. They weren't even for him. As nearly a week and a half had passed and Julia had yet to communicate with him in any manner whosoever, he knew she was still grieving, and he was hoping the tarts might cheer her, lessen her disgust with him. Or they would make her angry, but her fury was better than her sorrow.

The bell atop the door tinkled as he stepped inside and welcomed the warmth. The only other customer was a young boy, barefoot without a jacket. What sort of parents would be so negligent? He was of a mind to have a word with them.

"Please," the boy pleaded, holding up a fist that appeared to be closed around a coin. "Me mum's hungry."

"Sorry, love," Mrs. Potts said, "but a ha'penny isn't going to buy you a meat pie."

"But she's gonna die."

"I'm sure she'll be fine." Mrs. Potts looked at Edward. "Good day, Lord Greyling. What would please you?"

He understood no profit was to be made in giving away food, but surely exceptions could be made. On the other hand, if she gave something away, she'd have all manner of beggar at her door.

Edward knelt before the boy, who he put at around six years of age, surprised to see how flushed his face was. It wasn't that warm in here. "What's wrong with your mother, lad?"

"She's sick."

"Probably influenza," Mrs. Potts said. "Lot of people coming down with it."

He touched his palm to the boy's forehead. "He's far too hot."

"He shouldn't be in here, then. Be off with you, lad. Go on home."

Edward held up his hand to halt her hysterics, wrapped his other hand around the child's bony shoulder. "What's your name, boy?"

"Johnny. Johnny Lark."

"How many in your family?"

"Four."

"Box up four meat pies, Mrs. Potts. Put them on my account." Removing his coat, he wrapped it around Johnny Lark and lifted him into his arms. The lad weighed nothing at all. Taking the box Mrs. Potts placed on the counter, he said, "Box up four strawberry tarts. I'll return for them shortly." He turned his attention to the boy. "Show me where you live, Johnny."

It was a small cottage at the edge of the village.

Based upon the lines of rope strung along the back that he could see as they neared, Edward assumed Johnny's mother was a washerwoman. Setting the lad on his feet on the stoop, he knocked on the door. When no one called out to him, he opened it and was nearly knocked back by the foul stench of sickness.

"Mrs. Lark," he announced as he stepped inside.

On a bed in the corner, a woman with tangled red hair pushed herself up. "What'd ye do, Johnny?"

Her voice was scratchy, raw, and weak. Her face glistened with sweat; her eyes were dull.

"He acquired some food for you. I'm the Earl of Greyling."

"Oh, m'lord."

Edward rushed forward, placed a hand gently on her shoulder, taken aback by the heat emanating through the flannel. "Don't get up. I'm here to see after you."

"But you're a lord."

"Who was rather impressed by your son's resourcefulness." Turning away, he took his coat from the boy, draped it over the back of a chair at the table. Opening the box, he set a meat pie on the table. "You need to eat, Johnny."

"But me mum—"

"I'll take care of your mum."

A little red-haired girl slightly younger than the boy crawled out from beneath the bed. Edward placed a pie on the table for her, lifted her onto a chair. He found spoons for them. The fourth member of the family was still in the cradle. He was going to have to mash up the meat pie for that little one. He needed to locate some milk as well.

He took a pie to the woman, offered it to her.

She shook her head. "It won't stay down."

"You need to try, even if it's no more than a couple of bites. What does the doctor say about your condition?"

"He won't come here. I got no way to pay him."

"He hasn't been here at all, then?"

She shook her head. "Wouldn't even come when me husband was dying last week. Said there weren't nothing he could do. Ben died. Undertaker came, took him and the last of me coin. Then I got sick. Who's going to take care of me bairns when I'm gone?"

"You're not going anywhere." He placed the pie in her hands. "Eat what you can. I'm going to fetch the physician." He grabbed his coat and headed toward the door.

"I'm telling you—he won't come."

Edward stopped and looked back over his shoulder. "For me, he'd better damn well come."

He stormed out of the house, barely noticing the drizzling rain that had started. When he'd seen the sickly woman, the babe, the little girl crawling out from beneath the bed, a near panic had hit him as Julia flashed through his mind, alone and sentenced to squalid conditions. He knew that if she decided not to remain at Evermore, she would not be living in a hovel. She would have the cottage in the Cotswolds, an army of servants, and funds to ensure that she and Allie never went without. He would set up a trust. He needed to see to that immediately. As well as a will. He needed to ensure they were provided for. It didn't anger him that Albert hadn't seen to those details. He'd been a young, virile man. Why would he think death would come before he even reached his thirtieth year? But Death honored neither calendar nor clock, and Edward had no plans to be caught unawares when his time came.

He'd been striving to get all his holdings in order, to take stock of all that came to him with the title. His brother had left things in relatively good order, but still he had so much to learn, so much to comprehend. While he was not lord of the village, he could not help but feel as though he had a role in the care of its citizens. He was the largest landowner in the area, the only man for miles with a title. Those two aspects alone came with responsibilities that he had no intention of shirking.

When he arrived at the physician's residence, he pounded on the door. It was opened by a small woman with hair the color of corn silk. Her eyes widened.

"Lord Greyling, you shouldn't be out and about in weather such as this. Come in."

Removing his hat, he stepped over the threshold. "Is your husband home?"

"He's at Mr. Monroe's lancing a boil. He shouldn't be long if you'd like to wait."

"I shall do that, thank you."

"Would you like a cup of tea?"

"I don't wish to trouble you."

"It will be no trouble."

"Then, yes, thank you, I would welcome it."

"Please, take a seat."

"I'm drenched, Mrs. Warren. I have no desire to ruin your furniture. I'll stand."

"As you wish; I shan't be long."

Warren on the other hand seemed to take his time. It

was nearly an hour and two cups of tea later before he walked through the door. His eyes widened. "Greyling, this is a pleasant surprise."

"Not so pleasant. I've just come from Mrs. Lark's. She's unwell."

"Yes, influenza."

"How would you know? You haven't seen her."

Warren raised his chin. "Half the village has succumbed to the disease."

"What is the treatment?"

"There is none except to let it run its course."

"Her husband died."

He lowered that chin that Edward had a good mind to punch. "The disease can be quite . . . unforgiving."

"She has three small children. I believe the boy to be fevered as well."

"It is contagious, I'm afraid."

"So is it her lack of funds or your lack of courage that prevents you from going to her?"

The chin up again, the nose at a haughty angle. "I resent the implication that I am a coward."

"Good. Then it's lack of money. I can deal with a man who is absent of compassion. You will go with me now to see her. You will then call on anyone who is ill. If they cannot afford to pay for your time, then you will come to me for payment. You will also let it be known that I will pay handsomely anyone who is willing to nurse those who have no one to care for them."

Warren shook his head. "To put the well with the unwell will only spread the disease."

"So your solution is to leave them to die?"

"Not everyone dies."

"Then one is merely inconvenienced for a time. You will do as I demand or come spring there will be another physician in the village." Regardless of whether Warren did as he'd insisted, there would be another physician come spring. A little competition always brought out the best in people. "Shall we be off?"

Warren sighed. "As Mr. Lark just died, I don't know that I'll have any luck finding anyone willing to go into the house and take care of Mrs. Lark and her children. Death tends to make people uncomfortable, as though if it visits once, it'll visit again."

"You don't have to find anyone for her. I'm not going to ask others to do what I am unwilling to do. I'll see to Mrs. Lark. I just need you to examine her and tell me how best to help her."

SITTING on the sofa before the fireplace in her bedchamber, Julia stared at the clock on the mantel, watching as the hour hand neared two and the minute hand came ever closer to twelve. No missive alerting her to the earl's afternoon visit to the nursery had been delivered. Did he assume that after nearly ten days it was understood that he had established a ritual and would be attending to her daughter?

Or had he grown tired of his visits, weary of giving time to Alberta? Had he been using Alberta to manipulate her, and when she failed to rise to whatever bait he was dangling, decided to cast her daughter aside like so much rubbish?

Even as she had the horrid thought, she couldn't envision it of him, not after witnessing him with Alberta perched protectively on his chest two nights ago.

Torrie was no doubt at fault, lounging around some-where instead of seeing to her duties. Shooting to her feet, she crossed the room and yanked on the bellpull. Then she paced, wondering why she felt strung as tightly as a bow. When the knock finally came, relief swamped through her. "Come in."

Torrie entered, gave a little curtsy. "You rang for me, m'lady?"

"Did you not have a missive to deliver to me?"

"No, m'lady."

Julia was unprepared for the disappointment that struck her. "The earl did not give you a note for me?"

"I don't see how he could. He's not here."

"What do you mean he's not here?" Where was he? London? Another estate? Havisham Hall? He couldn't just leave without telling her.

"He rode to the village this morning and he hasn't returned yet."

"In this weather?" She raised her hand. "No need to answer. It's not our place to question him." But why did this man have such a penchant for traveling about in dreadful weather? No doubt it was the adventurer in him. Pity his poor wife, who would in all likeli-hood spend an inordinate amount of time worrying over him. Not that Julia was worried. He could catch his death for all she cared. Served him right for never saying anything when she whispered naughty things in his ear. It still mortified her to know he'd heard every shameful word she'd spoken.

"That'll be all."

"Shall I alert you when he returns?"

"That would be splendid. I'm going to spend half an

hour with Lady Alberta, and then I'm going to work with my watercolors." She'd been envisioning a new character for her menagerie, and she was anxious to begin working on him.

Torrie smiled as though Julia had just announced she was going to set her up with a house and she wouldn't have to work for the remainder of her life. "Very good, m'lady. That room's been lonely without you."

"Don't be absurd, Torrie. A room can't be lonely."

"You'd be surprised, m'lady."

Perhaps not, as this room at night felt incredibly lonely. Near midnight last night she'd gone into the master's bedchamber seeking some sort of solace that she couldn't understand. Failing to find it there, she'd gone to the chamber that had been designated as Edward's whenever he visited. The trunks were still there, untouched since her last sojourn into the room. Sinking to the floor, she'd opened Albert's trunk and wept as his familiar scent circled about her. Then for reasons she failed to comprehend, she opened Edward's and wept all the harder.

What a difficult task Albert had set before Edward. So many of her conversations with him since his return randomly ran through her mind, and she saw them in a different light, saw a man striving to remain as honest as he could with her while at the same time deceiving her.

With a shake of her head to scatter those disturbing thoughts, she put on her slippers and wandered down to the nursery. No need to creep about trying to be quiet.

Nanny immediately jumped to her feet. "M'lady."

"Go enjoy a cup of tea. I'll watch Lady Alberta for a while."

Nanny's brow furrowing deeply, she looked toward the door. "Is his lordship not coming, then?"

"Perhaps later." She walked to the crib and picked up Alberta. "Hello, my darling." The infant's face scrunched up as though she were on the verge of bellowing in protest. "I know I'm not who you were expecting, but he's been delayed. I'm sure he'll come see you as soon as he returns home."

Holding her daughter close, she sat in the rocker. "I haven't your uncle's gift for storytelling. What do you suppose that naughty weasel is up to? Do you know what I think, Allie? I think the weasel—who is supposed to be the villain of our tale—may just turn out to be the hero."

ℋOURS later she set her watercolors aside and walked to the window. It had grown dark and he had yet to return. She was considering whether to send the stable lads out to search for him when Torrie walked in and handed her a missive.

Lady Greyling,

>   *A widow in the village is in need of my assistance. Not certain when I will return. Kiss Lady Alberta for me and give her my love.*

>   *—Greyling*

With a scoff, she crumpled the paper. Did he think her a fool? She knew precisely what sort of assistance he was delivering. He was a man with needs, and they would be met most willingly with a night in the arms of a widow. Assistance, indeed.

Julia took her meal in the dining room, the first time since that fateful night when she'd discovered the truth. She was kept company only by the ticking of the clock on the mantel, the footman occasionally removing one dish to place another before her. While she had dined alone within this room many a night while Albert was away, she couldn't recall ever feeling quite so devastatingly alone.

Following dinner, she enjoyed a glass of port in Edward's library, sitting in a chair, listening to the crackling of the fire, imagining him here by himself night after night while she remained in her bedchamber seeking to ensure he understood her displeasure at all he'd done, hoping to make him miserable. In the end, being the one who was miserable.

It was after ten when she went into the billiards room and, using her hand rather than a cue, rolled balls back and forth over the table, remembering how easily he had lifted her onto it, the devilish smile he'd given her. She thought of all the times he had looked at her with desire and hunger, all the times he made her feel as though he had no interest in any other woman, made her believe that no other woman would satisfy him.

What a fool she was. She kept envisioning him with the widow. She wanted her to be old, wrinkled, with half her teeth missing. No, all her teeth missing. But in truth, she suspected she was young and pretty, more than willing to provide an evening of comfort to a man as strappingly built and handsome as he.

She understood now why he had drunk, why he had

sought to dull his senses. Thinking of him in the arms of another woman made her want to weep when she knew she had no right to him, no cause to expect him to be loyal to her.

For all she knew he had sought out dalliances before now, only he'd been incredibly discreet and now there was no need for discretion. But even as she thought it, she rejected the notion that he'd been with others before now. Strange that she had known Edward as a drunkard, a womanizer, a gambler, and yet had no doubt whatsoever that from the moment he returned from his travels until this evening, had been faithful to her.

The fact that he was with another woman should not have caused the ache in her chest that it did. She should not be missing him.

But she was grateful for tonight, for the reality of it, because it made her realize that she might not be strong enough to stay here after all.

Two afternoons later Julia was convinced that the widow was not only young, but incredibly skilled at pleasuring his lordship and distracting him from his duties. As she splashed watercolors on her canvas in order to create tempestuous skies, she was half tempted to ride into the village and remind the Earl of Greyling that he had responsibilities. Although perhaps he had moved on to tavern wenches. He did tend to take his vices—whether it be wine, women, or wagering—to excess.

She'd thought he had changed, thought he was different, but he was falling into his old habits.

Torrie opened the door and walked in carrying a tea service on a tray. She set it on the low table before the fire. "I brought your afternoon tea."

Julia took a seat on the sofa and smiled with delight at the sight of four strawberry tarts. "Please give Cook my regards. I had no idea she could make tarts that look just like the ones at the village tea shop."

"In fact, m'lady, they are from the village tea shop. His lordship brought them."

She jerked her head up. "The earl has returned?"

"Yes, m'lady. Not more than twenty minutes ago. Gave the tarts to Mr. Rigdon, with orders to serve them with your tea, and dashed off straightaway to his chambers."

He was back and he'd brought her a gift. She was touched that he'd remembered how much she enjoyed strawberry tarts, almost enough to overlook that he had spent the past three nights keeping a widow company.

Biting into the pastry, she moaned with the pleasure the taste brought her. It was so decadent, and now she was beholden to him. She would have to thank him.

Torrie turned to leave.

"Press my red gown. I'll be dining with the earl tonight."

Her maid's smile was so wide and bright as to be blinding. "Yes, m'lady. With pleasure."

She fairly skipped out of the room, while Julia took another bite of pastry and wondered if Edward would come to this room today, if he would pay a visit to Allie.

$\mathcal{E}$DWARD leaned against the wall near the window while his valet oversaw the preparation of his bath and the building of a fire in the fireplace. He'd never in his life been so bloody tired. The widow's fever had finally broken late last night, her son's this morning. Both of the other two children had seemed to escape the disease—at least so far. As chills were racking his body, he didn't think he'd been as fortunate.

As he'd ridden back here, he thought it was exhaustion coupled with the weather. But now he wasn't so sure. When the servants finished with their chores, his valet stood at attention by the door. Edward had already ordered him to keep his distance. "After you walk out of here, you are not to come back in."

"My lord, I don't think you're well."

"Very observant. I'm going to bundle my clothes into a blanket and set them outside the door. Touch them as little as possible. Burn everything." That was probably an extreme precaution, but he was going to take whatever means necessary not to cause anyone else to fall ill. "Every two hours you are to leave a pitcher of water and a bowl of broth outside the door. If they remain untouched for two days, you may enter."

"My lord—"

"If you enter before that, you'll be sacked. And you're not to breathe a word of this to the countess." Not that he thought she would ask after him, but again a precaution was needed. He didn't need her praying for his hasty demise.

"I don't feel right about this, my lord."

"It's only influenza. I'll be miserable for a few days and then I'll be fine. No need for anyone else to be bothered by it."

"As you wish, my lord."

"Good man. Now be off with you."

With obvious reluctance, Marlow opened the door and slipped out. Edward pulled a blanket from the bed and dropped it to the floor, tempted to follow it down and stretch out right there. Instead he began the laborious process of removing his clothes.

He did hope Julia enjoyed her strawberry tarts.

SHE dined alone, blast him. He hadn't come to her room where she worked with her watercolors. Nor had he visited Allie. His absence there was odd, as he had seemed to adore the girl. Had he only been pretending in order to get into Julia's good graces?

She didn't think so. From the moment her daughter was born, he could not have been more tender or expressed a more sincere interest in her well-being. Perhaps he was simply worn-out from his escapades. She knew firsthand that he poured a great deal of effort and himself into the act of pleasure. As hard as she tried, she had no success not envisioning his powerful muscles bunching and cording as he glided his body—

Damn him. Damn him for giving her a taste of what she could not have. Damn her own weak body for wanting to be worshipped.

She spent most of the night writhing on the bed. Every time she drifted off to sleep, she dreamed of him reaching for her. Even though he and Albert looked exactly alike, she knew it was Edward, because of his devilish smile and his smoldering eyes.

She awoke in a foul mood, with a need to confront him, to face him, but feared he'd take satisfaction in her need to see him, that he would know he had sparked jealousy in her by spending multiple nights with another woman. Which was ridiculous, as she had no hold on him. She was a widow, in mourning. The last thing she should be thinking about was another man.

Still, she needed to thank him for the tarts. It was unconscionable that she had yet to do so. Taking breakfast downstairs would allow her the opportunity to express her appreciation.

However when she entered the breakfast dining room, Rigdon informed her that the earl was taking breakfast in his room. First dinner and now breakfast? He was secluding himself as she had been. Why?

"Is he planning to have all his meals in his bedchamber?"

Looking somewhat guilty, Rigdon shifted his feet. "For the present time, yes."

She narrowed her eyes. "What aren't you telling me?"

"Nothing m'lady."

Oh there was something. Otherwise he wouldn't have averted his eyes. Why was Edward staying in his room? Oh, dear Lord! Had he brought the merry widow home with him? Had he sequestered himself away because he was coupling with her?

And what if he had? It wasn't her business. She couldn't forbid him from bringing women into his own home, not like before when it was hers. Except that everyone thought he was Albert being unfaithful to her. And that she could not tolerate. He was disparaging Albert and her relationship with him.

Rigdon suddenly straightened his stance, squared his jaw. "It's not right, m'lady. On this matter, his lordship is being most foolish."

Oh, God, she was correct and the servants knew he was carrying on with some other woman. Why the devil couldn't he have been discreet? The anger swept through her on such a rush of heated indignation—

"He ordered us not to tell you but I fear for him."

As well he should. She was going to do all within her power to ensure Edward was never able to show his face in a fancy parlor. To humiliate her like this was beyond the pale. She might even take a poker to him in his most private of areas to ensure he pleased no other widows.

"He has yet to retrieve the broth or water that Marlow left out for him," Rigdon told her.

Broth? He was serving his mistress broth? Hardly the most charming means of seduction. Yet he'd brought her strawberry tarts. None of this made any sense. She shook her head. "Marlow is leaving broth *where*?"

"In the hallway, outside his lordship's chamber door."

"Why?"

"Because he's forbidden anyone from going inside— unless the broth sits there for two days, at which point someone may enter. I suppose because Lord Greyling will be dead."

Did one die from excessive sex? She supposed it was possible, and wasn't an entirely unpleasant way to go . . .

"Rigdon, I'm not quite sure I follow."

"Of course not, m'lady, because we're not allowed to tell you."

"Then I suggest you tell me."

"He'll sack me."

"I shall sack you if you don't."

He released a big heavy sigh. "Very well. Lord Greyling is ill."

"Ill?"

"Yes, madam. Influenza. He feared that if he did not isolate himself . . ."

The remainder of his words faded into the background because she'd already run out of the room and was rushing down the hallway. Her parents had died of influenza. How had this come to pass? How had he gotten ill? He was too strong, too bold, too young to be taken down with an illness such as this.

Not until she reached his wing did she realize that she had no idea which room he had claimed as his own. Broth. She merely had to find the broth in the hallway. She sprinted up the stairs. At the landing, she headed toward the left.

She didn't need to locate the broth after all. Marlow was sitting in a chair at the end of the corridor. As she neared, he came to his feet. "Lady Greyling."

She went past him.

"His lordship doesn't want—"

But his words, too, were lost as she shoved open the door and dashed over the threshold, coming to a staggering stop as she saw Edward, lying in a tangle of sheets, the upper half of his body exposed and covered in sweat.

He pushed himself up, waved his hand. "You can't be in here."

"And yet I am."

As she crossed over, he flopped back onto the bed. "You need to leave."

Ignoring him, she pressed the flat of her hand to his forehead. "You're fairly on fire."

"Which is why you need to leave."

Which was exactly why she wouldn't. Turning, she was grateful to see Marlow had followed her in, hovering just inside the doorway. "Have someone fetch Dr. Warren."

"There's nothing he can do," Edward muttered.

"Oh, and when did you become an expert on medicine?"

"When I was caring for Mrs. Lark and her son."

Who the devil were Mrs. Lark and her son? And where was Mr. Lark? Good Lord, was it conceivable that he hadn't been fornicating with a widow but caring for one? "Is Mrs. Lark a widow?"

He gave a slight nod. "Her husband died recently. Fever. She was ill. The boy was ill. I shouldn't have returned here. Should have stayed in the village, but I was just tired. Thought I was cold because of the weather."

"Doesn't matter. You should be home when you're ill. But why were *you* caring for this woman and her child?"

"No one else would."

He'd stayed in the village to do good, and she'd assumed the worst. How much longer was it going to take before she accepted that the man with whom she'd been living for nearly three months now was the true Edward Alcott? She turned to Marlow. "Send someone to fetch Dr. Warren. He's to come as quickly as possible."

As Marlow left to do her bidding, she looked back at Edward and prayed that quickly as possible would be soon enough.

"*Y*OU need to prepare yourself, Lady Greyling," Dr. Warren said solemnly as he turned away from the bed. He reminded her of a dog that had been kicked. "It's unlikely your husband will survive."

He might as well have bludgeoned her. She couldn't breathe, couldn't feel her fingers, her toes. "There must be something you can do."

Slowly, he shook his head. "I'm sorry, but there is no remedy I can offer for this illness."

"The woman he cared for, Mrs. Lark, did she die?"

"No."

"Her son?"

"He recovered as well."

"What did he do for her?"

"It doesn't matter what we do. Some people die, some don't."

"Then what bloody good are you?" She spun away from him, trying to contain the tremors of anger and fear that were cascading through her. Whipping back around, she glared at him. "Be off with you."

"I'm sorry—"

"I don't want to hear it. Just go." He shuffled out. She wanted to be sympathetic. He'd probably helplessly stood by while many died, but she could work up no sympathy when he wasn't even willing to try. She looked over at Marlow, who stood just inside the door, a silent sentry. "Fetch me a bowl of cool water, some cloths, ice chips from the ice box, and some fresh broth."

He turned to leave, and she was struck with an idea. "And Mrs. Lark."

He spun back around. "I beg your pardon?"

Unlike Dr. Warren, she did not intend to stand help-lessly by while some disease ravaged this man who was far more noble than she'd ever given him credit for. In her mind, she'd accused him of fornication when he'd actually been caring for the ill. She was ashamed of the thoughts she had. She always expected the worst of him, but for nearly three months now he had shown her the best of himself. "Send a footman to the village to ask Mrs. Lark exactly how Lord Greyling took care of her. Have him write it all down. Even the smallest thing may be important."

"My mum always recommended a hot toddy."

Edward would certainly welcome that. "Thank you, Marlow. Fetch it as well."

Leaving, he closed the door in his wake. She gave her attention back to Edward. He seemed to have drifted off. She couldn't help but believe that time was of the essence. And now that they were alone, she could address him far more intimately. "Edward, Edward, I need you to wake up for just a bit."

His eyes fluttered, closed.

"Listen to me. I'm sending a servant to talk with Mrs. Lark. But can you tell me what you did to help her get better?" She shook his shoulder. He failed to respond. She shook harder. "Edward, can you tell me what you did?"

Opening his eyes, he blinked at her. "I killed him. I killed Albert."

Chapter 18

SHE would hate him now, hate him more than she already did, hate him as much as he hated himself. She would leave. He needed her to leave as much as he needed her to stay. "The story I told you about how . . . Edward died. It was how Albert died."

"Yes, I assumed that," she said softly.

He felt so hot and clammy he could be walking through the jungle at that very moment. He had to tell her. She had to know the truth, but it was so hard to think, so hard to focus. Yet the guilt had been gnawing at him. He couldn't take this truth to the grave. He would never tell her how Albert had suffered, suffered because of him. But she had to understand that what happened wasn't Albert's fault.

"I didn't tell you precisely what occurred. I, not Albert, was playing with the baby gorilla. Albert merely stood off to the side and warned me—"

Don't get too close.

We're fine. She's a sweetheart. Look how eagerly she came to me.

"But as usual, I ignored his concerns. The huge ape that

barreled out of the jungle was coming for me. I was his target, because he perceived me to be the threat. Except Albert stepped in front of him. Don't you see? It should have been me who was hurled about, who died. I never meant to take everything from Albert. Forgive me."

Sitting on the edge of the bed, she wrapped her fingers around his hand. Hers was cool, so very cool. He wanted it on his brow, his chest.

"There's nothing to forgive," she said softly. "You were his younger brother. Of course he was going to try to protect you."

"Younger by only an hour." He swallowed hard, ignoring the pain in his throat. "I should have saved him. I never should have insisted he come on the damned safari with me."

"He wanted to go. He wanted to be there. I'll read his journal to you, shall I? You'll see. He thought it a marvelous adventure. He wouldn't have missed it for the world. Every night he wrote fond remembrances of your time together."

"Every night he spoke of you."

"When you're well, you can tell me what he said."

"He wanted me to take you to Switzerland."

She blinked, shook her head. "Why would he want you to do that?"

"I assumed because it was someplace you wanted to visit."

"Not particularly. Maybe he wanted to take me there as a surprise, but it's not anyplace I yearned to visit."

Staring at her, he fought through the fog, striving to remember Albert's exact words. Had he misunderstood them? "Makes no sense."

"Neither does blaming yourself for his death. He would be bitterly disappointed if you continue to do so. It happened as it happened. It's no one's fault. There were a thousand steps along the way where a different choice would have changed everything. We always believe a different path would have brought something better. But the reality is that it could just as well have brought something worse."

She was right, and he could be bringing her something worse at that very moment. "Please don't stay in here with me. If you fall ill, if Allie does—"

"We won't. I won't allow it. Neither will I allow you to die."

He could not help but give his lips an ironic twist. "My words."

"Your words. Now don't make me a liar."

She wasn't going to leave. He cursed the weakest part of himself that was glad, that wanted the last thing he saw to be her face, the last thing he heard to be her voice, the last thing he knew to be her touch.

Today we saw a magnificent waterfall. The thunder of the water crashing down was remarkable. We were standing at the edge of a cliff, just watching its incredible power, when Edward suddenly said, "Wouldn't Julia love that? Wouldn't you like to share such beauty with her?"

I could not help but think that he'd left unsaid that it would pale beside you.

While I miss you terribly, I have enjoyed this journey and have no regrets that I decided

to take it. You were correct. Once our child is
born, I would never discard my responsibilities
for something as selfish as this, and yet it is
an experience I will look back on with great
fondness.

It's the oddest thing, Julia, but every night
we speak of you. At first, I shared some of my
favorite memories of you because I thought if
Edward could see you as I do, then he would
care for you just as much.

Yet as we sit by the campfire talking late into
the night, if I don't mention you, at some point
he does.

Looking up from the journal entry she'd been reading aloud, Julia studied the man lying so motionless on
the bed. She'd forced him to eat ice chips and broth.
The hot toddy he'd taken without complaint. No surprise there. But he seemed to grow weaker with each
passing hour.

Beyond the windows day fell to night, dawn
emerged, night returned. Occasionally she napped for
a few minutes in the chair. She opened a window to
bring in some fresh air—how could the staleness of the
room be healthy? Sometimes she stood there inhaling
deeply, considering what she had learned of how he'd
cared for Mrs. Lark and her son. The widow told her
footman that Edward had made them drink until she
thought they'd drown. Purchased oranges for them to
eat. Boiled up a soup with chicken and assorted vegeta-
bles. She couldn't help but wonder how much he might
have learned during all his travels, what he might have

done for himself in order to survive. He would survive this.

Sometimes he was awake while she read, but mostly he slept. She'd arrived at the very last entry in the journal, the final night when Albert had dipped pen into inkwell and scratched his thoughts over the parchment. She couldn't read these words aloud. She needed some that were for her and her alone, and she couldn't help but believe that he'd written these only for her.

> *I'm beginning to suspect that he doesn't dislike you at all. But I have yet to determine why he makes such a grand show of pretending to do so.*
>
> *I have to admit to being rather relieved by the discovery. I've put off drawing up a will, as I was concerned he might not see after your care as well as I might. I knew he would take offense if I did not name him guardian of my heir, and yet based on his reckless behavior the past few years how could I place those I love in his keeping?*
>
> *I'd considered Ashe, but while he is a brother of my heart he is not of my blood. He would take on the burden I hoisted upon him without complaint. My father passed our care on to a friend, who did not do poorly by us, and yet I forever longed for Evermore.*
>
> *I did not wish that for my child or for you. But for you, I want more than a roof and food and clothing. I want you to have happiness.*
>
> *I feared under Edward's care, you would find naught but misery.*

> *But now I am of the belief that I could leave
> you in no better hands.*

She traced her fingers over the final words. Had he truly known that he would not return to her? Or had he merely been speaking in generalities?

Even knowing nothing had been written on the next page, she turned to it. The sadness that engulfed her was nearly overwhelming. She wanted more words, more insight, more absolution that he would not find fault with her for having these confusing feelings toward his brother.

> *I could leave you in no better hands.*

She read permission in those words. In his entire journal she had read love. He had loved her just as she'd loved him. Had wanted her happiness. To find it without him seemed at once impossible and a betrayal. Yet it was almost as though he expected it, was encouraging her to be happy, to find love again, to move on. He knew what she was just discovering: She had to do as he wanted if she were to be the best possible mother to Alberta.

Setting the journal aside, she closed her hands around the linen resting in a bowl of water on the bedside table, wrung it out and began to wipe it over Edward's brow, neck, and shoulders. He went so still, so quiet, his breathing so shallow as to be nonexistent. His skin was so hot to the touch that it was nearly frightening. Leaning in close, she whispered, "Fight for me, Edward. Albert would want you to. Would insist on it, in fact. And fight for Allie. She needs to know how the story ends."

His eyes slowly fluttered open. "Top right drawer of my desk. The story is there, written out, waiting for her."

Would he forever make her think that he couldn't hear what she was saying? "You went so still that you gave me a fright."

He smiled slightly. "I know you want to know how it ends as well. I could see the edge of your skirt from where I sat in the rocker in the nursery."

So she'd been caught, had she? She angled her chin. "Could have been a servant's."

"Why didn't you come in?"

Averting her eyes from his, she pressed the cloth to his neck. "I didn't want to give you the satisfaction of knowing I was interested in your silly story."

"They were all for you, you know. All the stories I told in your parlor."

She studied the familiar contours of his face, wishing he didn't look so haggard, and wondering how it was that although he looked exactly like Albert, when she looked at him she didn't see Albert. She was somewhat mystified that she ever had. "Get well and I'll invite you to tell more."

"Don't go to the Cotswolds."

"This is neither the time nor the place."

"I'm weakened, have your sympathies. It's the perfect time."

Needing something to do, she dipped the cloth into the water again, wrung it out. "I haven't decided what I'm going to do, and I won't make a promise to you now that I'm not certain I can keep. I would appreciate, however, if you would hasten your recovery."

"And give up having you in my bedchamber?"

She snapped her attention back to him, grateful to see a twinkle in his eyes, when she had feared for two days now that they would dull as the life left him. "You're being inappropriate."

"You like that I'm inappropriate."

She did, damn him. "You must be feeling better."

"Somewhat." He closed his eyes. "I'm not going to die, Julia."

"The staff will be relieved. They've met your cousin who would inherit."

He chuckled low. "You'll be relieved as well."

"A little I suppose." She placed the cloth on his chest, near his heart.

He wrapped his fingers around her wrist. "I'm sorry I didn't tell who I was right after Allie was born. That was wrong of me. I want you to know—I need you to understand—that if things between us that night had gone further, Edward would have remained buried."

She sank back, not certain what to make of that. He'd been willing to be Albert for the remainder of his life, in order to have her. Perhaps she should have been flattered. Instead her temper was pricked. She would have been unwittingly caught in a deception. "I should have the choice."

"With English law there is no choice."

Because a woman could not marry her deceased husband's brother.

"We always have a choice. To live within the law

or to break it. You should not presume which I would choose."

"You're right. I was thinking only of what I wanted and how best to keep you happy. I can see now that it was unfair to you."

"It was unfair to us both. Would you really want to live with a woman who thought she was giving her love to someone else?"

"I've never loved anyone before. I'm not wise in its ways."

She was his first. Of all the women he'd been with, he'd loved none of them. She found it both sad and flattering. "I think it would have been a hard lesson. Eventually you would have resented both me and Alberta, and your life and mine would have become miserable."

"I'm so sorry."

She placed her finger against his lips. "It doesn't matter any longer. What matters is how we move forward."

"Will we move forward?"

"I suppose you'll have to recover in order to find out."

"Unsympathetic wench. Will you not even give me hope?"

"I'm here, aren't I?"

That seemed to satisfy him as he closed his eyes and drifted off to sleep. She was half tempted to crawl into bed with him, rest her head on his shoulder and succumb to slumber, but she feared that if she didn't remain vigilant he would slip away when she wasn't looking. She remembered that both her parents had seemed on the mend, talking with her, assuring her all would be well. In both cases, they were gone by morning.

His fever broke near dawn. She nearly wept with relief. After summoning Edward's valet to assist him as needed, she walked into the bedchamber across the hall and fell into the bed, certain she'd never been more tired in her life.

For two days straight she slept. Then she bathed twice. She looked at Allie from the doorway as Nanny held her up. She didn't dare stand too close, just in case she was on the verge of becoming ill. She would give it a week, after which she would hold her daughter close for two days straight.

She enjoyed a hearty breakfast, ate until she could barely move. But movement was in order. Gathering her cloak about her, she walked to the mausoleum. Within these marble walls, she had poured out her heart and soul to Albert, wept uncontrollably, wiped away tears, cursed him, cursed herself, cursed Edward.

Now she knew he had died not because he was careless enough to play with a wild creature, but because he'd been intent on saving his brother. She placed her hand on his effigy. "I finished reading your journal. You thought of me every day as I thought of you. I still think of you every day. I wake up and think—he's already gone down to breakfast. Only you haven't. You never will again, and I have to keep reminding myself of that.

"It's difficult to believe that it's been a little over seven months since we parted, since I last kissed you or held you or spoke to you or looked at your beloved face. The grief over losing you hasn't lessened. I don't know if it ever will. It's a fact of my life now, no matter how much I wish it otherwise.

"I don't know if you knew that you weren't going to come back, but I do believe, with all my heart, that you would understand everything I'm feeling right now without my having to tell you. Everything I feel for you. And everything I feel for Edward. I think you would approve. I think that's what you were trying to tell me, why you wrote to me. So I would know that you cared for my happiness above all else."

She stroked her hand over the marble, wishing she could touch him one last time. "I love you, Albert. Always I shall love and miss you."

She remained only a few minutes more before walking back to the residence. She hadn't seen Edward since his fever had broken. It was time she did.

He was lounging on the sofa in the sitting area in front of the window. The draperies were pulled aside, allowing the sunlight to stream in. Based on reports from the servants, she knew he had yet to venture out of this room, but as he came to his feet, wearing only trousers and a loose fitting linen shirt, she knew he was on the cusp of feeling well enough to go about his business.

"You don't have to get up," she said.

"Of course, I do."

Making her way around the sofa, she went to the chair that rested between it and the window. "You look as though you're feeling much better," she said, dropping into the chair.

"You look tired." He returned to his place on the far end, as though he feared he might spook her if he got too close.

"I'm rested. Feeling well. So far no one else in the residence has taken ill."

"I pray everyone else is spared."

"I'm remaining optimistic." She glanced at the clock, the fireplace, the perfectly made bed. "It appears we're going to have a lovely day."

"Winter should be behind us soon."

She nodded, not really here to discuss the weather.

"Would you care for some tea?" he asked, and only then did she notice the tea service in the center of the table, the cup and saucer resting on the corner near his knee.

What she really craved was some brandy, except it was far too early for that. She shook her head. "No, thank you."

They sat in silence for a few minutes. Finally he said, "I'm glad you came by. I've not had a chance to thank you for tending to me."

"My parents died of influenza."

"Yes, I know. I'm sorry."

"It was some years back."

"Still, it must have been difficult for you to be in here."

"It would have been more so not to be here. I'm sorry that you didn't feel you could let me know."

"I didn't want you to worry." He gave his head a little shake, his smile self-effacing. "To be honest, I think I was more afraid that you wouldn't worry, that you would rejoice, consider it deserved."

"I'm sorry for that as well. That you would think I'd take pleasure in your suffering." She hated this inconsequential prattle. "Do you have any brandy?"

One of his eyebrows arched up. "Within this room, no. But I can have some brought up."

She shook her head, waved her hand. "Not necessary, but can you give me a moment?"

"Of course."

Although she was studying her gloved hands clutched tightly in her lap, she could feel Edward's gaze on her. The words had spilled forth so much easier when she was walking back from the mausoleum. "I think I knew."

"That I had no brandy?"

She delivered a pointed glare that had him sitting back as though she'd punched him.

"I see."

"I'm not certain you truly do." Taking a deep breath, she squeezed her hands until the bones ached with the danger of cracking. "I knew something was different. I convinced myself that Albert and I had both changed during the months that we were apart. That it was natural for someone who wasn't in another's company every day to forget exactly what the other person was like. That our memories become faulty with absence. But I know he would never have approved of my reading *Madame Bovary*."

"He may have."

"No, he would not have. He was quite prim in his beliefs regarding what was proper. He would not have welcomed my advances when he was taking a bath."

"I think you're wrong there."

"No, you knew him as a brother. I knew him as a husband. I assure you he would have been shocked had I insisted upon pleasuring him during his bath. He was good to me. Kind. I never regretted marrying him. Never. I never didn't want to be married to him. But sometimes—" She inhaled deeply, let the air siphon out slowly. "Sometimes, I remembered a long-ago kiss in a faraway garden. And I would wonder things a married woman shouldn't wonder. So I told my husband that I didn't like his brother with all his bad habits staying with us. It was easier than acknowledging that his brother caused a whirlwind of confusing feelings within me.

"When you returned from Africa as Albert, the way I felt around you was very different. I loved Albert. Love him still. I didn't want him to be dead. It was easier to ignore the nagging doubts. And by being too weak to face the truth, I betrayed him."

"You didn't—"

"I did. I have spent hours at the mausoleum talking to him, explaining myself, sorting out my thoughts and my feelings. You must never doubt that I love him."

"I don't. I never have."

She nodded. This was so damned hard. "The problem, you see, is that I fell more deeply in love with the man who recently shared my bed, helped me bring my daughter into the world. So to be completely fair and honest, I have to subtract the depth of my love for Albert when he left and acknowledge that what remains is yours."

"Jules—"

She held up her hand. "Please don't say anything yet."

He bowed his head slightly, acquiescing to her request. That should have made things easier. It didn't. "When you were ill, so dreadfully ill, when Dr. Warren told me to prepare myself, that my husband would probably die, because of course he believes you to be Albert . . . I thought, 'How will I possibly go on if he dies?' There was a part of me that wasn't sure I would want to, and yet I knew I must for Allie."

"I promised I wouldn't leave you."

Tears burned her eyes. "But I'd hurt you. I made you think I didn't want you."

"Still, I've yet to fall out of love with you."

A horrendous sob escaped. She covered her mouth, looking at him through the veil of tears. "What are we going to do?"

Moving to the other end of the sofa so he was nearer to her, he held out his hand. She should get up now and leave, she told herself, end this madness. Instead she intertwined her fingers with his.

"I am the Earl of Greyling," he said. "To the servants, lords, and ladies, that's all that matters. The title. Whether it is held by Albert or Edward, they don't care. You are the Countess of Greyling married to the Earl of Greyling." He lifted a shoulder. "I don't see that we need to tell anyone that it wasn't my hand that guided the pen that signed the marriage contract."

"That seems sordid, unfair to you."

He squeezed her fingers. "If we acknowledge that Albert is dead, British law will not let me marry you."

She breathed in a deep sigh. "Yes, I'm aware."

"Any children we have will be bastards. I'll never acquire an heir."

Pulling her hand free of his grip, she folded her hands in her lap. "We need to end this now. You need to send an announcement to the *Times* explaining what has occurred."

"And your reputation?"

"Doesn't matter. You need your heir."

A corner of his mouth tilted up. "I'm never going to marry, Julia. It would be unfair to her when my heart will always belong elsewhere."

"So we live a lie?"

"Within that lie is the truth. I love you. I want to be your husband."

She shook her head. "I need time, Edward, to be sure. If we take this path, we can never leave it. Already we risk Allie's future by delaying the truth."

"We have until the Season, until we go to London. But if we present ourselves as man and wife there, we will have to carry on."

"When were you thinking of going to Town?"

"Sometime in May. We can delay until June. After all, I'm mourning the loss of my brother."

And she was mourning the loss of her husband. How could she possibly consider pretending otherwise? She felt a great deal for this man; she simply didn't know if it was enough or if what she felt was prompted by believing for two months that he was her husband. "You should remain in this wing so I am not unduly influenced by your nearness."

"You want to be courted."

"I want to be sure."

"Know this, Julia. If you feel for me even a thimbleful of what you felt for Albert, I would be content. For the sake of propriety, to the world, I am willing to pretend to be Albert. But never again will I pretend to you."

Chapter 19

JULIA didn't feel quite comfortable not wearing black, but neither did she want to go down to dinner wearing the austere bombazine, with buttons secured up to her throat and at her wrists. So she chose a gown of black silk and lace, an off-the-shoulder style that was at once elegant and respectful, and if she were honest with herself, also seductive.

She saw the approval in Edward's eyes when she joined him in the library before dinner, was very much aware of it during dinner. In the small dining room, she sat at the foot of the table that would accommodate eight, so she could look at him head-on, rather than his profile.

She wanted—needed—whatever it was they might be moving toward to be different from what it was they were edging away from.

"I was thinking of rearranging the family wing," she announced during their third course.

Studying her over his glass of red wine, he nodded. "Rearrange the entire residence if you like."

"Not the furniture so much as the people. I thought to move into another set of suites."

Where she had no memories of being with Albert, where everything would be fresh and new and different.

His gaze never wavered from hers. "Splendid. But I also want you to feel free to replace any furniture, any art, anything that isn't to your taste. Neither my brother nor I ever had any sentimental attachment to anything here. We never knew much of the history behind the items. A consequence of not living here in our youth."

"I've always found the residence welcoming. I want only to move to another set of suites for a bit of a change."

"As you wish."

She hadn't expected that he would deny her; she didn't think he would deny her anything she asked.

Their conversation during dinner wasn't as lively as it had once been. They were both treading lightly. She worried now about revealing something to the servants she shouldn't, slipping up. She couldn't call him Albert. She knew differently now. Although she knew wives who referred to their husbands by their title, she'd always found it a bit odd, Grey being so formal and distant.

When they were finished with their desserts, he invited her to join him in the library. As she walked into the room that no longer reminded her of Albert, but rather of Edward, she strolled over to the shelves, studied the volumes lined up like well-disciplined soldiers. "I thought I might read aloud tonight."

Having some form of planned entertainment would remove a little of the strain of striving to come up with conversation.

She was suddenly acutely aware of him at her back, the heat radiating from his body warming her exposed flesh. Her breath held, she waited, even as her heart pumped with a madness that made her light-headed. He reached up toward a bookshelf, the opening of his jacket barely floating over the curve of her shoulder, as light as a butterfly's fluttering wings just before it landed on a petal. Inhaling deeply, she took in his purely masculine fragrance, wondering why she had ever thought his scent was the same as Albert's. His was more tart, more bold. He was not one for subtlety.

"This one would prove interesting," he said, his voice low, provocative, hypnotic.

She wanted to turn into him, press her cheek against the center of his chest, have his arms close around her. But it was too soon for such intimacy. She needed to be more certain of her feelings, that they were not influenced by grief and the prospect of loneliness. So she stayed as she was, watching as he slowly tipped back the leather-bound book, brought it down and placed it in her hands.

He stepped away. "Brandy?"

"Yes, please." Why did she have to sound breathless, why was it that he always managed to so easily send her nerve endings rioting?

Cursing the unsteadiness of her legs, she made her way to a chair near the fireplace. He handed her a snifter, and she studied the reflection of the flames in the glass, in the amber.

"To new beginnings," he said, raising his own snifter.

She looked over at him, lounging back in the chair, so casual, so comfortable. Always at ease with himself, always confident as to his place, even when that place had been as second son, younger brother. Even when that place had been pretending to be Albert.

After taking a sip of her drink, she set it aside, turned her attention to the book resting in her lap—and burst out laughing. "*The Husbandry of Sheep*?"

"There's an excellent chapter on breeding, quite titillating."

"You've read it?" She didn't bother to hide her skepticism.

"At Havisham Hall it was the most risqué reading we could find. I was quite good at embellishing the narrative whenever I read it to the others." He held out his hand. "Would you care for me to demonstrate?"

Smiling, she shook her head. "How did I ever believe for a single second that you were Albert?"

"Because the alternative was unthinkable, and that's what I was counting on."

And now the thought of him being dead was unthinkable. She set the book aside, picked up her glass, took another sip. "What if Allie is the only child, healthy and strong, I shall ever bring into the world?"

"I don't want you for your breeding capabilities."

But he should. Now that they knew the troubles that plagued her, she was an awful choice for him, for a man who needed an heir.

"That said," he began slowly, "I very much want you for the act that leads to breeding."

He spoke of mating as though it wasn't something that should be limited to beds and darkness. Her face warmed with the thought of them finishing what they had merely begun. "You're a bad influence."

"You like that about me."

She did, but it was more than that. "There are aspects to myself that cause me to experience a sense of shame. I am left with the impression that in a similar circumstance, you would experience no humiliation."

Leaning forward, he braced his elbows on his thighs, his hands cupping the bowl of the snifter as though it were an offering. "I've always been of the opinion that what people do in private is of no one else's concern."

His gaze was so intense, practically boring into her, and she had to fight to hold it. "What if I wanted to do something that you found disgusting?"

"Such as?"

Why had she traveled here? "You are already quite familiar with my penchant for whispering naughty words."

"Based on my reaction that unfortunate night, I should think you would be well aware that I have no objections to any words you would utter. Some of my favorites are naughty ones. Words should bring you no shame. What else?"

Taking another sip, she realized she hadn't really considered his reaction that night. She'd been angered by his deceit, mortified that he'd heard her words, but it was her own shame that had prompted her reaction. He'd never given her any cause to experience a sense of degradation. He'd never teased, chastised, nor tormented her for the folly of her actions. She circled her finger around the rim of the glass. "Sometimes, I think about putting my mouth where I shouldn't."

"Where exactly?"

"Your—" She nodded toward his lap, or tried to.

"My cock?"

She glowered at him. "You say the word with such ease."

"It's a good word. Trust me, I would not take offense if you put your mouth there."

"I'm not talking about putting it on the word, but on the object. And I don't know why you make me think such wicked things."

"Look at me."

It was much easier to stare at the fire. Mayhap she should leap into it.

"Julia," he prodded far too insistently.

She shifted her gaze over. He was sitting back, his elbow on the arm of the chair, his chin on his hand, one finger slowly stroking just below his lower lip. She wanted to kiss him there.

"There is no place upon my person against which you could press your lips, your tongue, that I would find fault."

"It's not proper."

"Would it bring you pleasure, joy, satisfaction?"

She fought not to squirm. "I think so. I don't know for certain, as I've never been quite so bold. I've only thought of doing it."

"Then it is not improper."

"How does one learn what is proper and what is not?"

"By experimenting, I suppose."

"It's easier for men. You can visit brothels. I suspect you've had a thousand women, and if you make a fool of yourself with one you simply move on to another."

"Not quite a thousand."

"A hundred?"

"I truly didn't count, but I suspect the number is far fewer than that. The important thing is: I would never make you feel a fool." He held out his arms in supplication. "You may do with me as you will, and I shall be ever grateful for it."

"If I wanted to flog you for keeping things from me?"

He grimaced. "I would probably object to that. I'm not of the opinion that pain equals pleasure. Although I think I'm relatively safe, as I promised not to keep anything else from you." He looked toward the fire. "And yet already I have done so."

Her chest tightened a fraction. "What have you kept from me?"

He slid his gaze over to her, a wicked gleam in his eyes. "Shall I gave it to you now?"

She furrowed her brow. "It's an object, not a secret?"

"It's a secret if I haven't given it to you yet."

"You're being difficult."

He grinned. "I am, but then you expect that of me, don't you?"

To tease her, to cause mischief, to be playful. Strange how the facets to him that had once irritated her now charmed her. "Perhaps I don't want it."

"Fear of you tossing it in the fire is actually why I haven't given it to you yet."

She pouted, sighed, rolled her eyes. "I won't toss it into the fire, but it's not fair to tell me about it if you're not going to give it to me."

"I suppose you have a point. Wait there." He drained his glass before getting up, striding to the desk and pulling open a bottom drawer. Reaching inside, he pulled out an oblong shape wrapped in brown paper, secured with a string. Walking back over, he held it out to her. "I was going to give it to you for Christmas, but I had second thoughts, was afraid it might give me away."

Taking it from him, she set it in her lap, watched as he returned to his chair and went incredibly still, his focus on her as though this item and her reaction to it were of monumental importance. She tugged on the string until the bow unraveled and the paper fell away to reveal a glistening rosewood box with a small crank on one side. "Oh, Edward, it's gorgeous."

"It opens."

Lifting the hinged lid, she smiled at the exposed mechanisms, protected behind a veil of glass. "What does it play?"

"Wind it up and see."

Slowly, gently, she turned the small handle, afraid something so delicate might break. When it would turn no more, she released her hold and "Greensleeves" began tinkling around her.

Memories washed over her, of ballrooms and waltzes and being held inappropriately close, yet never objecting. She hadn't even realized she held those remembrances, and yet there they were, so vivid, as though the moments had occurred only last night.

"You always waltzed with me when the orchestra played this tune," she said quietly.

"I wasn't certain if you noted that it was always the same song." He still hadn't moved, didn't appear to even be breathing.

"I'm not certain that I really did until just now. Why the same song?"

"If it was a pleasant experience for you, I wanted you to associate it with me. And if it wasn't, I didn't want to be responsible for ruining every tune for you."

Closing the lid, she stroked her fingers over the polished wood, the vibrations of the tune thrumming through it. "I always enjoyed dancing with you. It seemed to be the only time that we weren't at odds. I thought it was because we were concentrating on not stepping on each other's feet."

"Having the opportunity to dance with you is the only reason I ever attended any ball."

It wasn't so much that she wanted to be wooed as much as she wanted to ensure she saw him clearly, the man he truly was and not the man he'd been pretending to be. She needed to be certain she could separate one from the other, that any feelings she possessed for the man sitting across from her were sentiments he rightfully deserved. But when he uttered words such as those, how could she not be wooed, flattered, enticed? How could her heart remain unaffected? "We never spoke when we danced."

"I wanted nothing to distract me from the sensation of holding you in my arms. Dance with me now."

She glanced around wildly, wanting what he offered, yet strangely fearful that it might prove her undoing. "What? Here? Or are you suggesting we go to the grand salon?"

"The grand salon is too large." He stood and extended his hand. "The foyer would serve better. More intimate but with enough room that we won't bump into anything. The box can serve as the orchestra."

"It's madness."

"Then be a little mad."

He was looking at her seriously, solemnly, and yet there was a challenge in those brown eyes. Neither of them had put on their gloves following dinner. His hand in no way reminded her of Albert's graceful one. Edward's appeared stronger. He had a callus on the pad below his index finger. Months here, and yet still his hands were those of someone who preferred the outdoors and exertion. She slipped her hand into his. As his fingers closed around it, before she could rise, he grabbed the box that would have required two of her hands to hold it securely and was then pulling her to her feet.

"I haven't danced since last Season," she said as he escorted her from the room.

"I haven't danced since I last danced with you."

"But you did dance with other ladies," she pointed out. She'd seen him dancing with them, and each one had looked completely infatuated.

"I did, but I usually retired to the card room after I waltzed with you. I liked having your scent lingering around me, which in retrospect was rather masochistic on my part."

"I truly had no idea."

"That was the whole point in my unforgivable behavior." They reached the foyer, and he released his hold on her. "Now I need you to see and trust that the man I was before is not the man I am."

He wound up the music box, his large hand dwarfing the small mechanism, then set it on a table that hugged a wall. The music filled the area. He stepped up to her and drew her into the circle of his arms.

And then they were waltzing. Closer than was appropriate, more securely than he'd ever held her, as though he would never let her go. Or perhaps he merely wanted to ensure that she didn't knock into any of the tables or statuettes or flower vases. How he managed to avoid them was beyond her, as his gaze never left hers.

She realized that during all the years when they had shared a single dance, he'd always given her his full and complete attention. She simply hadn't seen it because devotion to her was not what she expected of him. She'd assumed he was striving to make her feel uncomfortable or mock her in some way, and yet still she'd enjoyed circling over the floor with him because he was one of the most graceful dancers she knew. Perhaps because he'd spent time balancing along cliffs or hazardous trails. He'd skirted obstacles to reach his destinations—

But he'd walked away that night in the garden because his brother loved her, and she loved his brother. And he loved Albert.

The music stopped and yet still seemed to hover on the air, reluctant to go away completely. As reluctant as Edward seemed to release his hold on her. He lowered his head.

She pressed a finger to his lips. He stilled, his eyes searching hers.

"If you kiss me, I'll be lost," she told him.

"I'll find you, lead you back."

"I have to lead myself back. Edward, I must be sure that what I'm feeling is not influenced by what I no longer have."

"I promised you time and you shall have it." Stepping away from her, he went to get the music box.

She was a silly woman to mourn the distance that now separated them when she had been the one to insist upon it.

He offered his arm. "I'll escort you up."

They were silent as they went up the stairs, and yet there was nothing uncomfortable in it. He wasn't resentful or angry, nothing untoward shimmied off him. At her door, he handed her the box.

"Sleep well, Julia."

Then he was gone, jogging down the steps at a steady clip, the click of his footsteps echoing up. She went into her bedchamber, walked to the window and sat in the chair. Holding the music box on her lap, she wound it up, leaned back, closed her eyes and let the music and the memories overtake her.

She had no plans to compare brothers. Still, what she felt for Edward was unlike anything she'd ever before experienced. It was vibrant, alive, intense. It frightened her, if she were honest. It was as though he had the power to reach into her and expose every secret she'd ever possessed—without shame, remorse, or guilt. Surely it could not be healthy, surely they would burn up if they gave in to their desires. But it was more than a touch of the flesh, it was a touching of souls, a commonality of passion.

She had loved once, loved still, but the stirrings in connection with Edward were vast, encompassed more than the whole, seemed to reach beyond what was safe and secure. Yet how could she contemplate not surrendering?

Chapter 20

$\mathcal{A}$s he tossed back his scotch, Edward considered stripping down to his trousers and racing barefoot over hill and dale, taking a plunge into an icy river, finding a wolf or wild hog to wrestle. He took small comfort in the fact that she was not immune to his charms, that she did desire him, otherwise she wouldn't be so wary regarding where his kiss might lead.

Straight to her bed if he had his way with it.

The odd thing was, he understood her reluctance, had no wish to be a substitute for his brother. He wanted her feelings to be for him, separate from what she'd felt for Albert. He didn't expect them to ever be as strong or as large in scope, but he did want to be the one in possession of them.

He could honestly admit that he had never felt for any woman what he felt for her. It bloody well terrified him, and yet walking away was not even a consideration. Her company from a distance was better than not having her company at all.

Patience had never been his strong suit, but for her, he would bide his time. For her, he would have unique musical boxes crafted. For her, he would drink less. For her, he would give whatever was within him to give.

For her, he would toss and turn a good bit of the night, and wake up in a foul mood that required a cup of coffee stronger than his usual. He'd taken one sip that nearly blistered the roof of his mouth when she strolled into the breakfast dining room, wearing a black dress that was comprised of too much material and far too many buttons. She was done up tight, but still a sense of welcome relief washed through him. He shot to his feet. "Good morning. Is something amiss?"

She smiled sweetly. "I decided it was silly of me to eat alone when I could enjoy breakfast in your company. If you don't mind if I join you, that is. I suppose I should have asked first. Perhaps you prefer to begin your day in solitude."

The way she was prattling on, he wondered if she were nervous, fearful that he might not welcome her presence. She could join him in his bath if she wanted. "I've never much cared for solitude. By all means, please join me."

She wandered over to the sideboard, made her selections, and took her place at the foot of the table. Smart girl. If she sat within reach, he would touch her. Wouldn't be able to help himself. Just gliding a finger over her hand, her cheek would suffice to lessen his need to possess her.

Fool, nothing was going to lessen that.

Resisting the urge to pick up his plate and move nearer to her, he dropped into his chair, sipped his coffee, aware that it was now too strong, as his mood had improved considerably.

"Did you sleep well?" he asked.

"Not really. You?"

"Horribly."

She bestowed upon him a gamine smile. "Why does that please me, I wonder?"

"Because you're a little witch, and you know you're the cause for my restless night."

"I would not presume—"

His laughter quieted her. "You deny me a kiss and you don't think you're responsible?"

She glanced around as though hoping the servants had all suddenly gone deaf. He wished he could make her completely comfortable discussing their passionate natures. Then the full weight of her blue gaze fell on him. "Would a kiss have made it better?"

He released a deep sigh. "No. I suspect it would have made it all the worse, but a small price to pay for the flavor of your lips upon my tongue."

Even at this distance, he could see the deep crimson blush creeping up her face. He rather imagined that it began at her toes. He'd like to kiss those toes, the arch of her foot, her ankles, and journey all the way up to the haven between her thighs.

She looked past him to the windows. "Appears it's going to be a lovely day outside."

Her change of topic was no doubt intended to take his thoughts off their wayward path—although that wasn't likely to happen. Still, no harm in allowing her to believe he was easily distracted. "I was going to ride into the village today. I wanted to check on the health of Mrs. Lark and her family. Perhaps you'd care to join me. I seem to recall promising to take you riding."

Her face blossomed, wreathed with joy. "I would dearly love to go riding. I've missed it so."

"We'll stop for some strawberry tarts."

Her smile grew. "Even better."

"We'll leave following breakfast, shall we?"

"I'll need to change."

"Thomas," he said, directing his attention to one of the footmen. "Send word out to the stables to have our horses readied."

"Yes, m'lord."

After Thomas walked out, although two other footmen remained, she leaned across the table and whispered, "And you'll behave."

"I'll be the perfect gentleman."

But even a perfect gentleman could find a way to steal a kiss if he put his mind to it.

$\mathcal{I}$T felt so marvelous to be on horseback again. Her chestnut mare seemed equally pleased. While a groom had been riding and exercising her, Julia liked to think that the old girl had missed her and was glad to have her mistress back in the saddle.

It had turned out to be a rare warm day that required neither coat nor cloak. She'd never before had occasion to ride beside Edward. He kept them at a sedate pace, while she yearned to race over the fields. On the return home, she would take matters into her own hands, but she didn't wish to arrive at the widow's appearing bedraggled with her hair askew.

The village came into view. They plodded down the main narrow thoroughfare that cut through the center of the town, shops and buildings lined up on either side.

At the far end, they approached a small weathered cottage that had most certainly seen better days. The door was so small that Edward would have had to duck to cross the threshold. She imagined that he had fairly filled whatever space there was inside, couldn't envision the dwelling as having more than one room.

Edward brought his horse to a halt and dismounted in a graceful movement that made her mouth go dry. Why did the most common of actions, when performed by him, have to affect her as though he were the most extraordinary man she'd ever seen?

He came around and held his arms up to her. The moment she had both anticipated and dreaded. His powerful hands spanning the breadth of her waist, closing around it, his eyes latched onto hers, her hands coming to rest on his broad shoulders. He lifted her up slightly, brought her down, leaving her with the impression that he could have held her aloft all day, without his muscles once quivering with fatigue. Her feet came to rest on the dirt, her knees feeling somewhat weak—no doubt because she'd gone so long without riding. Not because he looked at her as though he might sweep her into the cottage and have his way with her.

"Your lordship!" The youthful voice echoed around them.

Edward broke out into a wide grin, released her and spun around just as an urchin leapt on him, the boy's legs circling his waist, his scrawny arms wrapping around the earl's neck as Edward closed his arms around the lad. Not that Julia thought that action was needed. The boy clung so tenaciously to him that she didn't think Edward would be able to extricate himself from the hold, even if he wanted to.

A slender woman with a babe in her arms and a little girl clutching her skirt scrambled out of the house. "Johnny Lark! Get off his lordship this instant. You can't be crawling all over your betters."

"It's quite all right, Mrs. Lark," Edward said. "I'm just glad to see he appears to be doing well."

"Too well if you ask me. He is a handful. I was sorry to hear you took ill, m'lord."

"I'm fine, completely recovered, no lingering ill affects."

"Ye lost weight. I can tell that. Come inside for a cup of stew."

Julia knew it was ridiculous to experience a pang of jealousy because this woman with her worn clothes, her untidy hair, her rough raw hands, knew Edward well enough to note that he had indeed lost weight.

"I appreciate the offer, but I promised the countess some pastry." He turned to her. "Lady Greyling, allow me to introduce Mrs. Lark."

She smiled kindly. "It's a pleasure."

Mrs. Lark curtsied three times, as though she wasn't quite certain when she'd paid enough homage. "M'lady. Sorry I'm such a sight. Wasn't expecting company today. But I've got enough stew for the both of you."

"That's very kind of you, but I rather have my heart set on the pastries. I possess a bit of a sweet tooth."

The woman smiled winsomely, as though she and Julia shared a little secret, then she scowled, reached out and swatted her son's backside. "Johnny, get *off* his lordship."

Like a little monkey, the lad scrambled down. Mrs. Lark's face fell. "Oh, look what you did. You got dust all over his clothes. I'll be happy to give 'em a good washing, Lord Greyling."

"Actually, Mrs. Lark, that's part of the reason I've come today. I deduced by the lines strung up at the back of your house that you're a washerwoman."

"Yes, m'lord. I'd be pleased and honored to do your laundry free of charge for an entire month to thank ye for taking care of us."

"Not necessary. However, we are in need of a washerwoman at Evermore. I wondered if you might be interested in the position."

The woman's eyes widened. "You mean, working for you?"

"For the estate, yes. The countess recently gave birth to a daughter, and as I understand it, the present laundress's workload has increased somewhat. You would assist her, live within the residence, have three rooms available for you and your children. They would be tutored. Meals and clothing would be provided to your family. I'm also in need of a boot boy if Johnny is interested. You and he would both receive a salary."

She staggered back. "Caw! Blimey!"

Julia wasn't surprised by her reaction. Edward was offering them an incredible opportunity to better themselves. She realized while he may have wanted to assure himself that they were well on the road to recovery, his main purpose in coming here was to take further care of this widow and her children.

"I'd be honored, m'lord."

"Very good. I'll send a footman along Thursday next to assist you and the children in packing up and moving to Evermore, if that gives you enough time to prepare."

"Oh, it does indeed." Tears welled in the woman's

eyes. "I didn't know how we'd make it with my man gone. Can hardly afford the cottage and food."

"Well, now you no longer have to worry about it. I'd say a celebration is in order. What say Johnny accompany us to the tea shop for some meat pies?"

"I like pastries," Johnny announced.

"Johnny, don't be asking for things," his mother admonished.

"Nothing wrong in asking, Mrs. Lark," Edward said. "Worse that'll happen is that I'll say no." He winked at Johnny. "Then again, I might say yes. Come on, lad."

After grabbing the reins to their horses, Edward offered Julia his arm.

"It was lovely to meet you, Mrs. Lark," Julia said before placing her hand in the crook of Edward's elbow.

Johnny hopped on one foot, then the other, darting in front of her before settling in to walk beside Edward. "I can do more than polish your boots," he assured Edward. "I can take care of your horses and your dogs, if you have dogs. Do you have dogs?"

"We have some hunting dogs, yes."

"Don't take care of cats, though. Don't like cats."

"Think the cats pretty much take care of themselves. Would you rather work in the stables than in the manor?"

The boy nodded feverishly. "Can I pet your horse?"

"You may."

"If I work hard will you tell me some more stories?"

She watched Edward's profile as the corner of his mouth lifted. "I may very well indeed."

"I liked the weasel best."

Edward's laughter echoed around them. "Yes, I imagined you would."

"Think he should have a sword, though."

Edward shifted his gaze to her. "What do you think, countess?"

"I don't know that I see him with a sword. A rapier, perhaps. Or maybe we need another character entirely." Another one was beginning to take shape in her mind. "You shared the story with him."

"Seemed the best way to keep the children calm."

She wondered how many lords would have given two figs if the children were rambunctious. But then how many lords would have stayed with a recent widow and cared for her?

She bid her time until they were sitting at the same table they'd sat at before, strawberry tarts and cups of tea in front of them. Before sending Johnny on his way, Edward had loaded him up with meat pies and enough various pastries to give the entire family a bellyache. "How did you come to know Mrs. Lark?" Julia asked.

He shrugged. "Johnny was in here, trying to purchase a meat pie for his dying mum. He didn't have enough money so I bought them, escorted him home, and discovered his mother was indeed ill."

"You remained to take care of them."

"Her husband had recently died. People are suspicious about death. Some believe it lingers, searching for another victim."

"But you don't?"

"There's not a good deal that I fear. Losing my parents when I was so young caused me to become a bit reckless. Then, of course, living at Havisham where we were told that a ghost would snatch us up at night if we went outside made us all rather intrepid. You can only live in fear for so long before you say to hell with it."

"A method to the marquess's madness?"

"Possibly. I hadn't considered that, but yes, I suppose it's quite possible."

Sipping her tea, she considered his earlier actions. "Offering Mrs. Lark a place at Evermore was very generous."

"We can well afford to be generous."

It touched her that he included her in that statement, that he made her feel as though she had been generous as well when she had in fact had nothing at all to do with it.

"I'm thinking you should publish your stories," she said.

"Only if you're willing to include your watercolors."

She laughed, pleased and embarrassed by the notion. "They're not that good."

"They're very good. They bring my words to life. I wished I'd had them with me when I was recounting my tales to Johnny and his sisters."

She shook her head. "I never meant to share them with anyone other than my child."

Placing his elbows on the table, he leaned forward. "Why would you limit them to bringing only one child joy when they could bring happiness to so many?"

"You never struck me as someone who cared so much about children." Yet, she'd seen it in the attention he gave Allie and the camaraderie he'd developed with a young lad who had no qualms whatsoever in climbing over a lord of the realm.

He grinned. "It's a fault of having never grown up."

But he had grown up. She'd seen that as well. He was a caring landowner. He took care of people. He possessed a kindness that he'd kept hidden from her; yet it had been there all along when he tried to ensure that Albert never became aware of his feelings for Julia. When he'd allowed himself to be disparaged and disliked in order to protect her and Albert.

"We would have to give the story a name," she told him.

"*The Adventurous Friends of Havisham Hall.*"

She laughed. "We should probably disguise it a bit more."

"We'll think on it, then."

It was as though they were planning a future. Whether or not they decided to spend their life together, they would have the stories, the books to connect them. They would have something that they had created together. But she doubted it would be enough to sustain her.

She needed more.

As they rode back toward Evermore, the words echoed with the plodding of her horse's hooves. She needed more. Needed more.

She needed the wind in her face, the freedom, the danger, the chase. Before he could caution her against it, she yelled, "I'll race you to the top of the distant rise," and prompted her horse into a sprint.

Without any doubt, she knew she was being reckless, but he seemed to call out that aspect of her. She'd spent her entire life striving to be the good daughter, the good cousin, the good wife. She regretted not a single moment of it, yet with him she felt no need to judge her actions before she acted. She experienced a certain independence that had never characterized her behavior before. Originally she'd credited it to changes within her while her husband was away, but she realized now it had more to do with Edward taking on a significant role in her life—even before she realized he was Edward.

She heard the pounding of his horse's hooves and urged her own into a faster gallop. She felt young, happy, unburdened. For the first time in weeks, sorrow was not dogging her heels.

His horse's labored breathing sounding so very close signaled that he was catching up, but she was almost there. Just a bit farther. Then she crested the rise, drew her mare up short, spun around. Her laughter echoed through the copse of trees, up to the heavens and over the land surrounding her.

He was grinning broadly as he brought his own beast to a stop. "Well done."

"I can't remember the last time I rode with such abandon."

"We need to give the horses a rest." He dismounted, walked over to her and held up his arms.

His nearness still caused a fluttering in her belly, but her triumph overrode the sensations. She'd controlled her horse; she could control him. As soon as her feet touched the ground, she broke away from him and, with a teasing giggle, dashed over to a nearby tree. His deep laughter floated toward her, and she heard the thud of his footfalls.

Whirling around, she pressed her back to the tree. "No touching, no kissing," she ordered, knowing that with the barest of caresses she would find herself ceding control over to him.

Before she was even aware of his intent, he was leaning in, his forearms raised and resting against the bark, his head bent, his cheek nearly but not quite touching hers. "Not touching," he rasped, his raw voice sending a shiver of desire through her.

"But if I were allowed to touch you," he said on a seductive whisper, "I would begin with your gloves, slowly unbuttoning them before peeling them off, one at a time, stuffing them in the pocket of my jacket. I would press a kiss to the knuckles of your left hand, the palm of your right."

Her eyes fluttered closed as she imagined the heat of his mouth coating her skin in dew.

"Then I would free two buttons of your bodice—only two—just enough so I could dip my tongue into the hollow at your throat."

Her breath grew shallow, heat surged through her.

"I would lap at your skin, three times, four, before trailing my lips up to the underside of your jaw. I would inhale the rose fragrance tucked away behind your ear, and skim my mouth over your neck, from one side to the other and back to center."

"Edward—"

"Shh, I'm not done yet."

But she nearly was. She didn't know how she continued to stand when her legs had become unsteady.

"Two more buttons I would loosen; nay, three. I would slip one finger between the parted cloth and glide it slowly, lightly, provocatively over the swells of your breasts, aware of your sharp intake of breath as you lifted them higher, yearning for a surer caress, one that encompassed the whole of my hand reaching inside your corset, your chemise, to cup your entire breast—"

"Oh, my Lord," she breathed out on a whisper.

"—my thumb and forefinger pinching the tight little bud of your nipple as it puckered for me."

She swallowed hard. She'd thought she was in control, but he had easily reversed their roles until she was little more than his puppet. Dampness formed between her thighs. Her nipples were not the only buds reaching for him, desperate for the pressure of his hand stirring sensations to life, eclipsing the fantasy with reality.

"If I had leave to touch you—"

"Don't," she pleaded in a raw voice that sounded as though it belonged to another woman.

"If I had leave to touch you, I would go to my knees and lift your skirt high, exposing the pink heart of your womanhood. I know it's glistening with dampness at this very moment. Even without being able to touch you, I can feel the heat of passion radiating from you. I suspect your breasts are straining against the cloth, desperate for the caress you're denying them. You're throbbing between your thighs. My tongue could offer surcease, with just the right amount of pressure I could have you screaming."

Her eyes flew open. "You're the very devil."

He laughed darkly. "Tell me I'm wrong."

"You know you're not, damn you."

"I've never wanted a woman as much as I want you. You torment me. It's only fair that I torment you."

"And once you've had me?"

"I'll want you again."

"How do you know?"

Pushing back, he held her gaze. "Because I love you."

"What if it's just that we were lost in the pretense?"

"The pretense is gone now, yet still the emotions remain. Why do you doubt?"

"Most are lucky to be loved once. Why should I be fortunate enough to be loved twice, to have happiness twice? I'm afraid fate will snatch it away if I reach for it again."

"So I'll be denied because you don't trust fate? Fate can go to the devil, Julia. Place your trust in me."

Reaching up, she brushed his hair back from his brow. Somewhere along the way he'd lost his hat. "A little more time, Edward."

"I'd be lying if I said I'm in no hurry. I want you with a desperation that threatens to unman me, but I want all of you, without guilt, without shadows, without ghosts. And for that I will wait with all the patience I can muster."

He understood her, comprehended why she struggled. She didn't want to lose her past, but she had to let go of it in order to reach for a future with him. But always he would be inextricably tied to Albert. "I'm closer to saying goodbye to what was. I enjoy the time I spend with you. I'm glad for the opportunities to get to know you better. You're not at all as I thought you were. You may be the least selfish person I've ever known."

"Don't make me into a saint."

"Oh, I'm not so much taken with you that I would mistake you for anything other than the devilish sort. It's only that I'm coming to realize I like the devilish sort."

Chapter 21

WINTER finally gave way to spring, the appearance of the first buds filling Edward with hope as he took his morning walk with Julia. They frequented the mausoleum less often. Sometimes they simply strolled past it. Some mornings, Julia indicated she wished to go in a different direction.

While their time together remained relatively chaste, he wasn't above trailing a finger along her exposed skin if the opportunity arose as they were going into dinner, pressing a kiss to the nape of her neck as he leaned over to help her set up her billiards shot, bussing his lips over her cheek as he handed her brandy before they sat in front of the fire within his library.

"Will you be riding out to see any tenants today?" she asked as the mausoleum came into view.

"It's too fine a day for that. I was thinking a picnic was in order."

"Let's go this way," she said, indicating a detour and a day that focused only on the present, not the past. "A picnic, then?"

"Yes, I thought we should take Allie on her first one."

"She won't remember it."

"But we will."

As usual, her hand was on his arm. She pressed up against his shoulder. "Oh, Edward, I think a picnic would be lovely."

"Grey," he reminded her.

"There's no one out here to overhear."

"But if you are in the habit of using my title, you are less likely to slip up as I did with my hearing. At least until you have made up your mind concerning our course."

"I've caught a couple of the servants looking at me oddly. I'm not sure they know what to make of my no longer calling you Albert."

"It is not their place to make anything of it, nor should we concern ourselves with what they think."

"I know, but if we go to London together, I think others will find it odd as well."

If they went to London together. He wondered how much longer it would be before she said *when* they went to London together. "People notice far less than we think."

"Not among the nobility. Especially among the ladies. They're all searching for gossip."

"Did you?"

She laughed, the joyous sound that always traveled straight into his soul. It was becoming more difficult not to take her in his arms and kiss her. He wanted to give her the time she required, but damnation, it was torment to keep his desires chained. But then most widows mourned for two years. The Queen still mourned the loss of her husband, and nearly twenty years had passed since his death.

"Of course I did. Especially my first Season. Not

so much now. It's a game the ladies play. Who can uncover the best gossip? Anyone who uncovered our story would be heralded." The laughter was gone, her voice tinged with sadness.

"No one will suspect anything sordid of you," he assured her. "You are too well liked, too respected. They won't even be looking."

"You don't know ladies as well as I thought if you believe that. The taller one's pedestal, the more determined they are to find a way to knock her off it. Besides everyone loves a scandal."

"We don't have to go to London."

She stopped walking and faced him. "Of course you do. You now sit in the House of Lords." Reaching up, she cradled his face. "I don't fear London."

"What do you fear?"

She looked out over the rolling hills that were now covered in wildflowers. "Stepping onto a path that will lead to Allie's ruination."

"If she is half as strong as her mother, there is nothing that will ever cause her ruin."

"I hope you're right." She smiled brightly. "Let's take her on that picnic, shall we?"

$\mathcal{H}\text{E}$ chose a spot near the small pond where he and Albert had fished as lads, where he had shoved his brother into the frigid waters for declaring that Edward would always have to follow his commands. To Albert, he'd proven his point that he wouldn't be ordered about. To himself, he'd proven that he'd always be there to get his brother out of trouble, even if he was the one who originally got Albert into it.

When Albert partially lost his hearing, Edward had learned there were consequences to his actions. That lesson had not served him as it might have.

Had he told Julia the truth shortly after she'd delivered, he might not have lost her trust, might not now be stretched out on a blanket with her sitting feet away from him—instead of nestled against him—and Allie resting on her stomach between them, periodically pushing her head up so she could gaze at her surroundings. She had the sweetest smile, and he suspected she was going to break many a heart.

Unfortunately, he feared her mother was going to break his.

The nanny was reading several yards away, her back resting against the trunk of a tree. He wondered if Julia had wanted her in attendance not such much to care for Allie should the need arise, but to ensure that he didn't take advantage. Although why she thought he would now when he hadn't yet was beyond him. Except that maybe she could tell he was skirting the limits of his patience.

He wanted her—badly.

She was wearing a dress of dark blue. A wide-brimmed hat shaded her from the sun, and had hidden much of her face from his view until he'd gone down on an elbow, with the excuse of wanting to be nearer to Allie. But whenever he brought his face in close to his niece and made her smile, he was able to lift his gaze just enough to see her mother's serene expression.

He liked that she appeared happy, liked that perhaps the darker days were behind her. He didn't fool himself into believing she wasn't mourning or that she would ever be grateful to have lost Albert in order to gain Edward. He understood his place in her heart. But coming in second when he had no hope of being first was something with which he could live.

All that mattered to him was that *for him* she would always be first. Every other woman didn't even come in a close second. Each was dead last. He wasn't willing to settle for less than what he wanted, even if it took a lifetime to acquire her. Without her, his life had no anchor, no purchase, no direction. Even being the Earl of Greyling gave less purpose to his life than she did.

For her and her daughter, he would rule a kingdom. Without them, it was merely land to be looked after.

She took a sip of wine, nibbled delicately on some cheese, and while she appeared to be occupied with something in the distance, from his lower vantage point he could see how often her gaze flicked to him. She was not as immune to his presence as she wanted him to believe.

"It's unseasonable warm today," he said.

"I hadn't noticed. I find it rather pleasant. I do hope you're not taking another fever."

"Could be that I'm just warm because you're near."

She laughed, a tinkling that would open the gates to heaven. "Please don't ruin our afternoon with trite flattery."

"For two months, Julia, I've been as steadfast a friend as possible. How can I win you over without flattery, without seducing you? How much longer must I behave?"

Her gaze darted to Nanny.

"She can't hear us," he said. "Besides, she believes

me to be your husband. She would think nothing of it if I were to take liberties."

Julia took another sip of wine, touched her tongue to the bow of her upper lip. God help him, but he wanted to dive across the distance separating them and place his own tongue there. Pushing himself up, he shirked out of his jacket and tossed it near the spot where he'd earlier pitched his hat.

"What are you doing?" Julia asked.

"I told you that I'm hot. Stiflingly so. I feel as though I'm suffocating." He tugged on his neck cloth.

"Wait." Her voice held no panic but there was something primal in it that caused his lower extremity to stir. Not that it generally took much from her for that to happen. "Nanny! Take Lady Alberta to the nursery. I fear it's growing much too warm out here for her."

"Yes, m'lady." She placed her book in the bag that contained Allie's things, slung it over her shoulder, marched over and plucked the child into her arms. Allie squealed with delight. "You are flushed, little one. Let's leave Mummy and Daddy to enjoy the picnic while we enjoy a nap."

With the nanny's parting words, he felt Julia's mood change as though a shroud had been dropped over her. Neither of them spoke nor moved until the woman had disappeared over the rise.

"Would we ever tell her about her father?" Julia asked quietly, her gaze directed where they had gone as though she had the ability to follow their progress to the manor and into the nursery.

"When she's old enough to understand the import of keeping it a secret."

"Until then she'll believe you're her father. How will she feel when she finds out differently?"

"We don't have to tell her."

With a sigh, she looked at him.

He rose up on a knee, held out a hand. "Come here."

She took the time to remove her hat before coming into his arms.

"It's not perfect, Julia, but the alternative is that we shall never have this." Gently, tenderly, holding all the hunger and need at bay, he angled her back over his raised knee and lowered his mouth to hers. It was as though he had finally come home. As though all his journeys, all his adventures, had been simply a quest for what he could not identify. But here it was at last, with her fingers cradling his jaw, her sighs filling his ears, her mouth moving over his with wild abandon.

No other woman made him feel whole, complete. No other woman touched the very essence of him. No other woman made him want to put away his roguish ways. How much simpler life would be if he could walk away, but he could no more do that than he could cease to breathe.

She twisted in his arms, changing the angle so he could more easily deepen the kiss, and he did just that, sliding his tongue over hers, threading his fingers through her hair until he could hold her head. He wanted to take her down to the blanket, take her as though she belonged to him. But that step had to come from her. He wanted her to have no doubts, no regrets. Once they were as one, there would be no turning back.

She was not a woman who gave herself lightly. It made him want her all the more, made him determined to be what she deserved.

Breaking off the kiss, he held her gaze, her eyes pools of limpid blue. "I could give you the vows."

Her gaze roamed over his face as she feathered her fingers lightly through his hair. "I want to show you something I've done in watercolors."

Not what he'd expected. A profession of love was more what he had in mind. Not a desire to share whimsical creatures with him. He cursed his foolish heart for misjudging her readiness, for believing that a kiss and a few well-placed words could turn the tide in his favor.

Helping her straighten, he said, "I'd like that very much."

"I've heard more enthusiasm from someone on the verge of having a tooth extracted." She gave him a teasing smile. "But trust me, you're going to be ever so glad that I showed it to you."

*A*s Julia watched Edward pack up their picnic, she could no longer deny the strength of her feelings for him. She'd almost laughed aloud watching him strive for a look of innocence that barely passed muster while he removed his jacket. She was fairly certain the neck cloth and waistcoat were going to join it in the pile quickly enough. A few loosened buttons, the rolling up of his shirtsleeves to expose those corded forearms, and he'd have had her mouth watering.

She wasn't averse to being taken on a blanket in a field by a pond—on another day. On this one, she needed something different.

He offered his arm, and she wound hers around it. Strange how he made her feel small and delicate. He'd regained the weight he lost during his illness. He was out riding every day, assisting tenants where he could. He thrived in the outdoors. She wondered if he would ever be truly content serving as lord of the manor, or if a time would come when the wanderlust took hold again.

"Do you have any plans to travel?" she asked as the wide front steps of the manor came into view.

"Not presently. Is there somewhere you would like to go? I'll book passage wherever you want, whenever you want."

"I've always found the idea of being on the sea rather daunting. To look out and see nothing stretching into forever." She'd seen it from the shore. She couldn't imagine being in the center of it.

"Ah, but then you sight land after days or weeks of travel, and the joy of it can almost make a man weep."

"I shall take your word for it."

"You have no desire to travel?"

"Not while Allie is so small."

"We could take her with us."

She laughed. How like a man. "Have you no idea what all is required to travel with an infant? Even our journey to London will require extra planning and room for her things."

"We can purchase whatever she needs when we get to London."

"She will require things along the way. And you like to go to remote, unpopulated places. How will you provide for her there?"

"I can be most resourceful."

She didn't doubt it. To be honest, she would like to be with him somewhere far away beneath the stars where they would not be subjected to Society's censures. No matter what choice she made, it came with a cost. The gossips were not prone to listening to reason, to making allowances, to understanding circumstances that warranted unprecedented actions.

Inside the residence, they walked the familiar hallways until they reached what had once been her favorite room. Now she was torn between the nursery, his library, and the billiards room. She enjoyed each one with equal measure.

Still, this room and what she did within it brought her peace. She led him to a table where an assortment of drawings were scattered. The one she wanted was on the bottom, hidden away. Bringing it out, she set it on top. "A new character for the stories."

"A wolf in a linen shirt, knee britches, and boots. And you've given him a rapier. That'll please Johnny."

Mrs. Lark and her children had settled in at Evermore. From time to time Edward would take the lad for a ride. She suspected he wove his tales for him then.

"I suppose it will. What do you think of the new addition to our menagerie?"

"People don't generally like wolves. They're wily. I take it he's another villain."

"No, he's on par with the steed. He's noble, protective. Strong. The others look up to him."

"I'll work him into the next story."

She smiled. "You don't recognize who he is?"

He shook his head, clearly baffled, and she didn't know why his reaction caused her to love him all the more. "Yet you saw yourself so easily in the weasel."

"That's supposed to represent me?"

"Not supposed to. It does."

He brought his gaze to bear on her, and she saw the torment and doubt woven there. "Julia, I am not noble."

"Yes, you are." She placed her hand against his jaw. "Protective." She slid her fingers up until they could toy with the hair at his temple. "Strong. I was wrong. You're not the weasel. You were never the weasel. That was just a façade. You are a good and honorable man." She stepped forward until her breasts flattened against his chest, took delight in his sharp intake of breath, the darkening of his eyes. "If the only way that I can have you is to live a lie, then I choose to live a lie."

"Jules." He tugged her in closer, locked his arms around her, pressed a kiss to her neck, her cheek, her temple.

She held him tightly. She'd struggled with this decision, but she knew it was the right one, the only one. She wanted him in her bed, wanted to give him children, wanted to be his wife.

Leaning back, he took her face between his hands, burned his gaze into hers. "I, Edward Alcott, promise to love, honor, and cherish you as long as we both shall live. I shall be as good a husband as a man can be."

"I, Julia Alcott, promise to love, honor, and cherish you as long as we both shall live. I shall be as good a wife as a woman can be."

Reaching down, he took her left hand and placed his fingers on the ring. "May I?"

Swallowing hard, she nodded. He gently pulled off her ring and set it in the palm of his hand. "I could purchase you a new ring, but I know how much love this one represents. I don't want to take that away from

you. I want to add to it. So if you've no objections—"
He slid the ring back onto her finger. "—with this ring,
I thee wed."

Tears burned her eyes at his unselfishness, his willingness to let her honor what she had once had. "I love you, Edward."

His mouth came down on hers with such passion, such power, such urgency, that she might have stumbled backward if his arms hadn't clamped around her at the same time. His tongue slid like velvet over hers, stirring everything she felt in her heart for him until it was whirling through her body. Her limbs went weak, she went weak. Yet she didn't know if she'd ever felt stronger.

They'd been teasing each other for weeks now. It was only natural that her awareness would be heightened, and yet she felt as though he had struck a match to the kindling of her desires.

Quite suddenly he swept her into his arms and began striding from the room. "I want you on a bed," he growled low, as though he were providing a message to himself as well as her.

With a laugh, she wrapped her arms around his shoulders, buried her face in the curve of his neck and began to press kisses there, tasting the saltiness of his skin. She wanted him with an unyielding fierceness that terrified and excited her. He made her feel alive, no longer numb.

When they arrived at her bedchamber, it was much as it had been before—with clothes being removed in a mad rush, abandoned to the floor. Only it was different. He was a different man, a man she'd never been with completely, and yet she felt none of the awkwardness, none of the doubt that had characterized her wedding night. Perhaps because she was no longer an innocent. Perhaps because she'd been with him as intimately as one could be without being joined.

When he shucked his trousers, she reached out and touched the scar at his hip. He froze. "You didn't get this in Africa, did you?"

"No. The Orient. Some years back."

There was still so much to learn about him, but so much that she already knew. Stepping forward, she pressed her body to his, stroked her hands over his broad shoulders down his sinewy arms. How was it that she had believed only four months in Africa would sculpt a man into such perfection? This had taken years of trekking through rugged terrain, climbing mountains, hoisting gear. He was a man who would spend as little time sitting behind a desk as he could. He would take her rowing on the Thames, riding in Hyde Park, galloping over the hills. He would help tenants manage their livestock, their fields. He would nurse a widow and her son back to health.

He would brave cold weather to bring her strawberry tarts.

"I love you, Edward," she repeated, knowing she would never tire of saying it, could never say it enough.

His eyes slammed closed, his head dropped back. When he opened them, she saw enough love to humble her. He marched her backward until her knees hit the bed. With his mouth latched onto hers, his arms holding her close, he tumbled them back onto the mattress. His roughened hands journeyed over her, eliciting sensations wherever they touched.

He shifted, nestled between her legs. Raised up on his arms, he hovered, looking deeply into her eyes. "Say something naughty."

The scalding heat of embarrassment rushed through her entire body. "You were never supposed to hear those things."

"And yet I did and they inflamed me." He leaned down, took her mouth, released it. "I told you that you never have to pretend with me."

Christmas Eve. By then he knew her tawdry secret. She turned her head to the side.

"Look at me when you say it. See how much I love it."

She ran her fingers into his hair, held his head in place, licked her lips. "I want your cock inside me."

Growling low, feral, he thrust his hips forward, plunging deep, stretching her, filling her. He never took his eyes from hers. "I love how hot and wet you are, the way you close around me."

Laughing, she pulled him down, opened her mouth to him until their tongues were following the same ancient ritual as their bodies. Being with him was liberating. She felt no need to hold anything back, to keep any secrets. He accepted her wholly. She scraped her fingers up his back. He groaned low, increased the rhythm of his thrusts.

Sensations swirled through her, leaving no part of her untouched, unloved. He was giving her everything of himself, allowing her to do the same. She'd experienced their connection during their kiss in the garden and it had terrified her. Now it only emboldened her.

She could touch him however she wanted, say whatever she wanted. No holding back for fear of censure. No withdrawing for fear of judgment.

With him, she could be herself completely and absolutely.

Was herself completely and absolutely. Was more than herself as the world fell away. She was herself with him, with this man who accepted her openly, naughtiness and all. Who made her his own.

Crying out his name, she tumbled through the void where pleasure dominated. Fell fast and hard, her body arching, clutching him close as he bucked against her, her name a growl forced through his clenched teeth.

They landed together, a tangle of glistening, sweating bodies, their breaths coming in short gasps.

Rolling off her, he brought her in against his side, holding her close with one arm, while his hand trailed up and down her arm. They lay in silence for long moments, simply catching their breath, basking in the glow of lingering pleasure.

"Did you think of him?" he asked quietly.

She trailed her fingers across his chest. "No."

"Not even a little?"

Rising up on her elbow, she looked down on him. "What are you really asking?"

"When you look at me, do you see him?"

"I see only you, Edward. I have for weeks now. I know the two of you looked alike, but I can see little mannerisms in you that I never noticed before, that he didn't have. I love him."

He squeezed his eyes shut. "I know that. I shouldn't have even brought him up."

She placed a finger over his lips. "Open those lovely

brown eyes of yours." When he did, she said, "I love
him and I love you. The love I felt for Albert is different than the love I feel for you. It's not more or less. It's
not better or worse. It's simply different. I can't put it
to words. You said if I loved you a thimbleful as much
as I loved him, it would be enough. I love you so much
more than a thimbleful. I can't compare or contrast
what I feel for either of you. Now and then of course I
think of him, but not during moments like this. You've
been with other women. Did you think of them?"

"Of course not."

"Then there you are."

The corners of his mouth hitched up. "None of them
said naughty things."

"I bet you know a whole host of words and phrases
to teach me."

"I'll teach you anything you like."

"I was afraid he wouldn't enjoy it, that he would dis-
like me for it, that's why I only whispered it in his bad
ear. You know me better than he did, and I fear that
wasn't fair to him."

"He loved you, Julia. He loved what he had with you.
Don't second-guess any of it now. That you and I have
something different doesn't make it better or worse. As
you said, it just makes it different."

She was glad she had something with him that she
hadn't had before. "I think I love you three thimble-
fuls."

He laughed. "Let's see if I can get it up to four."

Rolling her over, he enthusiastically threw himself
into the challenge.

Chapter 22

As the first of their four coaches pulled to a stop in front of the London residence, Julia took a deep breath. It was one thing to carry on a ruse when they were seldom visited. It would be another thing entirely here. Every day someone was bound to call on them. Not to mention the whirlwind of parties, balls, and dinners they were expected to attend.

She felt Edward's—Greyling's, Grey's, she had to remember to think of him as Grey—hand close around hers and squeeze.

"It's not too late if you've changed your mind. I can help you and Allie get settled in here, and then I'll carry on to the residence I began leasing last year."

Leaning in, she kissed him. "I haven't changed my mind. I'm married to the Earl of Greyling."

"No one will know otherwise."

The footman opened the door. Greyling stepped out and handed her down. He seemed so confident, self-assured, and yet she suspected he had to be experiencing some trepidation regarding the gauntlet that he—that they both—would be passing through. Far too many opportunities existed for a slip, which would destroy their one chance to be together as well as their reputations. But the love she held for him was worth the risk.

She was unable to envision her life without him in it. A chaste relationship seemed hardly possible when she was fully aware of the passion that existed between them. It still amazed her that he'd been able to hold it in check for so many years.

As they walked up the steps, another footman opened the door. "My lord, my lady, welcome home."

"Thank you, John," she said. Edward had memorized the names of the main staff, but distinguishing one tall, dark-haired footman from another was going to take time, because she'd been unable to provide him with any descriptions that would make that task easy. Not that he needed to know the names of most of them.

Stepping into the residence, she inhaled deeply the familiar fragrances of their London residence. Flowers adorned the entryway, the floor glistened with a recent polishing, stairs on either side led up to the next level.

"Lord and Lady Greyling," the butler said with a slight bow. "We're glad to have you in residence. Allow me to offer the staff's condolences on the loss of Mr. Alcott."

It hadn't occurred to her that everyone in London who hadn't been at the funeral might feel a need to offer their sympathies on the death of Edward. And each offering simply served as a reminder of their deception.

"Thank you, Hoskins," Edward said. "I'll be going back out shortly. See that a horse is readied."

"Yes, my lord."

Taking her arm, Edward began escorting her toward the stairs that led up to their bedchambers.

"I didn't realize you would be leaving so soon," she said.

"I need to go speak with Ashe."

"That seems rather risky. I should think if anyone could discern the truth—"

"He already has."

At the top of the stairs, she turned to face him. He gave her a laconic grin. "He and Locke both figured it out the day of the funeral. For what it's worth, Ashe was rather insistent that I tell you the truth then and there. Which is why it's imperative that I speak with him as soon as possible. He needs to know that you know, before he takes it upon himself to tell you." He touched his fingers to her cheek. "Don't look so worried. He won't object once I explain things to him."

"Perhaps I should go with you."

"It's best if I go alone. I'm sure he'll have some choice words for me, the sort that should never touch a lady's ears."

"Will he think ill of me?"

"Not unless he wants a bloodied nose."

She forced a light laugh. "And Locke?"

"He's not coming to London for the Season. Perhaps we'll stop at Havisham on our return to Evermore."

It hadn't occurred to her that anyone would know what she and Edward were up to, but she knew he trusted his childhood friends.

"When I return, we'll go for a ride in the park," he said. "Ease our way back into London Society."

"I shall look forward to it." A little lie. She rather dreaded it, feared she would give them away.

Leaning in, he took her mouth, and she melted against him. She always melted against him. How was it that after a hundred kisses, he still had the power to completely undo her with little more than the persistent press of his lips, the swirling of his tongue over hers?

Drawing back, he grinned. "I'll return posthaste."

"I'll be waiting."

"I love when you utter those words."

He dashed down the stairs before she could stop him, before she could suggest that perhaps he should join her in her bedchamber for a bit. God, what a wanton she was. He sent all her good sense to perdition.

As Edward trotted his horse through the familiar streets, he hoped that taking Julia to the park later would reassure her that no one was going to look at him and *see* Edward. They had no reason to doubt the veracity of his identity. He had no reason to lie. He was the Earl of Greyling. That was whom people would see.

The closer they'd come to London, the tenser Julia had become. He'd tried to distract her with kisses but even they had failed to relax her once they entered London proper. One of the things he loved about her was her awareness of her reputation and its impact on her daughter's prospects for a happy life. Scandal was a scourge that could ruin any bright future, and unfortunately, ladies could get away with far less inappropriate behavior than men. Perhaps because they cared so much more about their positions, but then it was more important for them. Few had the means to support themselves. Marriage was their occupation.

Edward now had a rank, power, and wealth. Mothers would overlook his transgressions if it meant a good match for their daughters. But a ruined woman made a favorable mistress, and men would often settle for that when desire was all that drew them.

But more than desire drew Edward to Julia. He admired her strength, her dedication to the right path even if she was willing to tiptoe along the wrong one for him. Actually, that made him love her all the more.

Drawing his horse to a halt in front of Ashe's residence, he quickly wrapped the reins around the hitching post before darting up the stairs, taking them two steps at a time. He wasn't anticipating this confrontation, but it had to be done. He knocked, waited. The door opened.

"Lord Greyling," the footman said.

Edward still had a moment of wanting to look around for Albert whenever someone spoke that address. He wasn't certain if he'd ever grow accustomed to it being directed at him. For Julia and the sake of their relationship, he had to.

Handing his hat, riding crop, and gloves to the footman, he asked, "Where might I find the duke?"

The earl's presence here was the natural order of things. Staff was well aware that he didn't require an announcement.

"He's in the library, my lord."

Edward carried on down the hallway. The library door was unattended, which suited him just fine. He didn't need anyone to overhear the coming conversation, and he suspected part of it might entail a raised voice or two. Although he had no intention of being goaded into shouting.

Ashe was sitting behind his desk, apparently in the process of inscribing some missive. Looking up, he shoved back his chair and stood. "Edward. I was just writing to you to see if you were planning on coming to London."

"Why wouldn't I?"

"You told her, then?"

"I did."

With a brusque nod, which Edward took as a sign of approval, his longtime friend walked over to the sideboard and splashed scotch into two glasses. He handed Edward one. "How did she take it?"

"As you predicted. Her heart shattered, she wished me dead, and she went into mourning."

"That could not have been pleasant for either of you, but being forthright is always the least complicated path. I suppose your next step is to dispatch a letter to the *Times*."

"No, actually." Edward took a long slow swallow of the scotch, holding Ashe's gaze the entire time. "My next step is to tell you to keep what you know to yourself."

Ashe angled his head thoughtfully, his mouth pressed into a hard, firm line. "I beg your pardon?"

"I love her, and she loves me. We're going to continue on as we have been, with people believing Edward is dead and I am Albert."

"Have you gone mad?"

"Our positions in Society prevent us from going off to some parish where we're not known and getting married. We are known among the nobility. Good God, we're known among royalty. The only way we can have a marriage that is not questioned is if Albert remains alive. Tell me that I'm mistaken."

"But you're not Albert. This is not legitimate; you're not legally wed."

"No one other than you, Locke, Marsden, Julia, and I will ever know that."

Ashe spun around, paced halfway across the room, stopped, turned back. "If even one person should suspect—"

"No one ever will. Why would they? Why would anyone suspect I am not Albert? The entire notion is ludicrous—that I would pretend to be my brother. That Edward would want as his wife a woman he abhorred. Why would anyone even postulate such a scenario as Edward not being the one laid to rest in the vault at Evermore? I'm the legitimate heir, Ashe. There is no reason for this ruse other than keeping at my side the woman I love. Who is harmed by us going on as we have been for a little over half a year already? I submit that we will cause more harm if the truth is revealed."

Ashe dropped into a chair, hung his head. "Are you certain you love her?"

"It is the one thing I am completely, entirely certain of. And I love her with all my heart. Will you deny us a lifetime of love because of a stupid law?"

He looked up. "We could work to get it changed."

"How long will that take? What if we have children before the law is changed? Do we deny ourselves each

other's company? Would you tell Minerva, 'Someday
we will be together but not now'?"

"Damn you."

Edward realized he should have asked him that
question in the beginning. It was no secret that Ashe
adored his wife, would do anything to have her.

Ashe stood. "If you love her even half as much as I
love Minerva . . ."

Edward was willing to wager his entire fortune that
he loved Julia as much as Ashe loved Minerva—if not
more.

The Duke of Ashebury raised his glass. "Edward, I
wish you and Julia all the happiness in the world. You'll
have my silence, and from this moment forth I will recognize you as Grey. I pray to God that you have better
luck keeping your secrets than I had keeping mine."

Edward tossed back his scotch, ignoring the shiver
of foreboding that skittered up his spine.

"DON'T look so terrified, Julia."

Perched atop her horse, at the entrance to Hyde Park,
she glanced over at Edward. "I feel as though I'm wearing a huge sign that reads 'Imposter.'"

"You're not the imposter. I am." He said it so casually, with such ease, as though he wasn't at all bothered, but then he had been ensconced in the role for a
good long while now.

"I'm afraid I'll give us away."

"We've exchanged vows. I'm your husband as much
as I can be your husband. Remember that. And remember that I love you to distraction."

She held out her hand. When he placed his within it,

she squeezed hard. "I love you as well. So much. Bearing witness to our devotion to each other, people will surely not suspect the truth."

"I promise you that no one is looking for Edward."

Nodding, she released his hand. "Don't forget that you're deaf in your right ear."

"Few will take note of that. Albert was self-conscious about his loss of hearing. Only those closest to him knew he had difficulty hearing."

She smiled with a memory. It was becoming easier to think of him without the pang of sorrow. "I'd forgotten about that. He told me just before he asked me to marry him—as though his inability to hear in one ear would dampen my love for him."

"I liked to tease him about it."

"No! You were not that cruel."

He nodded. "When we were in a group of people, I could tell when he didn't hear the comments because he would just nod and smile, so I would make some ludicrous retort as though it was in answer to something someone said, and Albert would respond in kind until we had those around us thinking we'd lost our minds."

"That sounds awful."

"It was funny, but you had to be there to appreciate it. He'd always laugh afterward. 'You got me again, Edward,' he'd say. Then I'd discover he filled my scotch glass with some bitter brew of tea that had me spitting it out. God, I so enjoyed the tricks we played on each other."

"I'm glad we can talk about him now, so openly."

"I'm glad to see you smiling. We can carry on now, I think."

She realized he'd used his tale about Albert to distract her, to put her at ease. With a gentle flick of her riding crop, she prodded her horse forward into the park and the mash of people who thought it was incredibly important to make an appearance this time of day. Tomorrow she would begin making morning calls, and ladies would make them on her.

For now, she simply focused on how much she enjoyed the company of the man riding beside her. "Will you be going to the club tonight?"

"No. I doubt I'll ever go to the club again."

With a teasing smile, she looked askance and skeptically at him. "That would raise suspicions. A gentleman not going to his club. That's rather expected."

"Not of a man who is madly in love with his wife."

She did feel like his wife, in manner, deed, and commitment. "You make me blush."

"I intend to make every inch of you blush later."

"Your mind always travels to the bedchamber."

"Who said anything about a bedchamber? I was thinking on the desk in the library."

"Grey!" She didn't know if she'd ever become accustomed to calling him that.

"Or perhaps in the garden among the roses." He was smiling wickedly. She could clearly see herself stretched out on the verdant grass, him raised above her, the stars a backdrop behind him while she—

"Lord and Lady Greyling."

At the sound of the deep voice, she very nearly squeaked like a frightened mouse and jerked on the reins. She managed to bring the mare up short without causing her to shy away from the couple, on matching black horses, who had drawn even with them. The Duke and Duchess of Avendale. He, dark and foreboding; she, fair, but with a shrewdness in her eyes that indicated not much escaped her notice. The one thing that Julia took comfort in was the knowledge that Rosalind Buckland, a commoner by birth, had only recently entered the ranks of the nobility and didn't know her or the Earl of Greyling well enough to discern if anything about them was different. They were the perfect couple for easing her back into social situations.

"Your Graces," Edward said.

"Our condolences on your loss," the duke said, and Julia wondered how far into the Season they would have to go before people stopped offering condolences. Not that she didn't appreciate them, but they made her feel uncomfortable, as they believed Edward was dead. Their sympathies were more for the earl on the death of his brother because they didn't realize she had lost a husband.

"We appreciate your sentiments," Edward said.

"We also hear that congratulations are in order," the duchess said, smiling kindly at Julia.

"Yes, the countess gave birth to a beautiful daughter just before Christmas," Edward offered, and she was conscious of the fact that in this instance he was careful not to refer to her as his wife. At the time, another had been her husband. "She greatly resembles her mother."

"I can see shades of her father in her," Julia assured them. "Especially as she is beginning to move about more. I believe she's going to be quite the adventuress."

"Traveling the world?" the duke asked.

"I hope so. I hope she's fearless."

"There's no reason she won't be," Edward said, and she knew what she'd known all along: With his guiding hand, her daughter would be fiercely independent, able to hold her own in any situation. *Her daughter?* Theirs. Hers, Albert's and Edward's.

The duke and duchess lingered a few more minutes, talking about the weather and the gardens and topics that suddenly seemed incredibly trivial, subjects that Julia had once taken delight in expounding on. But now she couldn't seem to work up the enthusiasm.

As the other couple trotted away, Edward guided her in the opposite direction.

"Do the condolences bother you?" she asked. "They don't know who they mourn."

"They're not really mourning. They're simply being polite."

But they would be mourning if they knew they'd lost one from among their ranks. Someone from among the royal family would have no doubt attended the funeral. She didn't want to travel this path, didn't want to consider the unfairness of it. People were offering words without realizing the truth of it all.

"Julia, it's all right," he said, and only then did she realize how deeply her brow had furrowed, how tightly her hands clutched the reins.

"In the country, we'd moved beyond mourning. I don't know why I didn't realize that here people would remind us of it. I'm trying not to be troubled by it."

"In a couple of weeks it'll all pass."

And that would be when they could truly settle into the lie that they were husband and wife.

Chapter 23

TONIGHT would be the real test. Ladies were much more discerning than gentlemen, and while Edward had managed to run the gauntlet of the House of Lords without mucking things up, and Julia had handled morning calls with aplomb, he knew the Ashebury ball would prove a challenge, as they would be appearing as a couple at the well-attended function. Especially troubling was the notion that Albert may have had discussions with people, and those people might expect him to know what they were talking about when he wouldn't have a bloody clue.

Watching Julia put on her ear bobs, he'd much rather stay here and take them off, along with her gown. "We don't have to go."

She caught his gaze in the reflection. "It's the Duke and Duchess of Ashebury's first ball since they married. People will find it odd if the Earl of Greyling doesn't make an appearance."

He moved up behind her, pressed a kiss to the nape of slender neck. "Then we shan't stay long. How does that suit?"

"We might have a marvelous time. I want at least two dances with you."

"Only waltzes."

"I would expect nothing less."

Tonight she was radiant in a gown that shimmered between black and blue, depending on the light. It gave her a sleek look, certainly not the body of a woman who a little over half a year ago had given birth. He knew some women who seemed to grow wider with each child, but Julia looked as though she'd only recently had her coming out. Slender and svelte.

"Keep looking at me with so much heat in your eyes, and we might not even make it through two dances," she teased.

"I'm familiar enough with Ashe's residence to know where every dark corner lurks. Don't be surprised if I decide we should make use of one or two before the night is done."

Rising, she gave him a seductive smile. "I think we should try for three or four at least."

He pulled her into his arms. "Is it any wonder I love you?"

He leaned in, only to find her gloved finger proving a barrier to his destination. "I know what you're thinking and I know where it will lead—to my having to redress and have my hair put back up. We'll be late. The Earl of Greyling is never late."

The Earl of Greyling needed to consider changing some of his habits. Perhaps he could chalk it up to being a new father.

"So be it." He offered his arm. "But you'll make it

up to me later by screaming my name until it's echoing off these walls."

She looked at him through half-lowered lids. "I was thinking tonight that you would be screaming mine."

"Bloody hell." Grabbing her hand, he began dragging her toward the door. "Let's get this over with. I want to be back in this room within the hour."

Her laughter followed them out.

꜀ULIA had known that once they arrived there would be no hasty leaving. This was one of the first balls of the Season. Much gossip was to be caught up on, news to be shared, debutantes to speculate over, matches to predict.

She managed to enjoy one dance with Edward before she was snagged by a trio of ladies whose first Season had been rather unremarkable and who were hoping for better with their second.

"I was so sorry to hear of Mr. Edward Alcott's passing," Lady Honoria said. "I wanted to attend the funeral but Mama said it wouldn't be appropriate."

"I shall miss dancing with him," Lady Angela offered.

"I shall miss his stories," Lady Sarah murmured on a sigh, as though he'd recounted them just for her. "And his dashing good looks."

"How can you miss his dashing good looks when you have only to look at his brother to see him again?" Lady Honoria asked.

"I suppose you have a point."

"I nearly fainted dead away tonight when I first saw

Lord Greyling," Lady Angela admitted on a laugh that grated on Julia's nerves. "Until I remembered they were twins. I thought he was a ghost for a moment there."

"It must be so odd to have someone look exactly like you." Lady Sarah gave Julia a pointed look. "Did you ever confuse them?"

"No," she lied. "The more one was around them, the easier it was to tell them apart."

"He was such a scalawag," Lady Honoria said. She glanced around as though she expected that scalawag to jump out of the crowd at any moment. Then she leaned in and whispered in a conspiratorial voice, "He gave me my first kiss."

"No!" Lady Angela exclaimed.

"Yes. In a dark corner of a terrace at a ball."

Julia did not want to hear this, did not want to hear the details of Edward's exploits, although to be fair neither had she wanted to hear those of Albert. It wasn't a bad thing for a man and wife to keep some mystery about them.

"I wish he'd kissed me," Lady Sarah whined in a high-pitched voice that was rather like silver scraping over silver. It sent an awful skitter up Julia's spine.

"He might have this Season," Lady Honoria said. "He would only take you out if he knew you weren't trying to trap him into marriage."

"I would have tried to trap him," Lady Regina confessed.

"Not I," Lady Honoria told her. "He was jolly good fun and I enjoyed his company, but he wasn't titled and I don't think he was the sort to take his vows seriously."

"He takes his vows very seriously," Julia blurted

before she could consider the ramification of her words. "I mean, he would have had he had the opportunity to marry."

"I'm not sure," Lady Honoria insisted.

"I'm absolutely positive," Julia said, unable to bear the thought of these silly girls thinking the worst of Edward, of not truly comprehending the decent, good person that he was. "He was an honorable man. And as I am—was—his sister-by-marriage, I had the opportunity to know him far better and observe him in many more situations than you did."

"There was certainly nothing honorable in his kiss. It was frightfully wicked. He promised me another one this Season and now I shan't have it." While the other two girls giggled, Lady Honoria produced an exaggerated pout.

Julia had an insane urge to pull that jutting lower lip down to the girl's knees. "Yes, well, we certainly want to concentrate on how inconvenient his death was for you."

"I meant no offense."

Yet she'd taken offense. They were disparaging him, mocking him, and she hated it, hated that they didn't know him as she did. They saw him as offering little more than kisses in the garden. "My apologies. We're still mourning his passing." Not that she thought she had anything for which to apologize. She simply wanted these girls gone from her presence before she said something rash, before she did something to threaten the new life she was striving to build.

"We just wanted to express our sorrow over your loss," Lady Sarah said, before ushering the others away as though she were a mother hen and they were her chicks.

Thank God. She needed another dance with Edward to help settle her nerves. Or a glass of brandy. She wondered where she might find that. She'd been to the refreshment room earlier and there was only lemonade and sparkling wine to be found there. Still, wine was better than nothing.

"Julia."

Turning, she smiled at the friendly and familiar face. "Ashebury."

"Surely after all these years you can call me Ashe."

"I'll try."

He glanced around as though seeking a secluded spot. "Let's dance, shall we?"

"You're in luck, as my dance card isn't filled tonight." It had been before she married. Every ball had been a whirlwind of dances. Tonight she hadn't even bothered to bring an extra pair of slippers.

She'd waltzed with Ashe a dozen times, had always been comfortable with his presence, but for some reason tonight words escaped her. He knew the truth, and she didn't know quite how to respond to that. "It's a lovely ball. So well-attended. It speaks to how much you and your wife are loved."

"I suspect it speaks more to curiosity. Minerva and I seem an odd match."

"I never thought so."

"Speaking of odd matches—"

"Don't," she commanded in a low sharp tone.

"I just never saw the two of you together."

"He's changed." Only he hadn't really, had he? She simply saw him differently, saw him as he truly was.

She shook her head. "It's not that. I never really knew him before. Don't think he really knew me. We're quite compatible. More than compatible. I love him."

Drawing her closer, leaning in, he swept her in a circle as he whispered, "He is not Albert."

"I am very much aware of that. He resembles him not at all. I wouldn't be with him if he did. He is not a substitute for . . . what we have is very different. But it's what I want. What I need."

"I don't want you to get hurt. I don't want him to get hurt."

"Life offers us no guarantees against being hurt. He would not hurt me, not on purpose."

He grinned wryly. "That I know to be fact. Even at his worse, when he is three sheets to the wind, there is good in him."

"People don't seem to truly know him. I think it's because he never wanted to outshine his brother. He accepted his place as the second, the spare. In his journal, my husband wrote that fate had made a mistake in allowing him to be born first. It's funny how we sometimes allow Society and our place in it to determine our behavior, even if it goes against the grain. You're his friend; you grew up with him. You must know how incredibly worthy he is."

"His worthiness has nothing to do with my misgivings. I would defend him to the death, and I will stand by him on this. And by you. If you ever need me for anything, do not hesitate to call on me."

"Although I am sorry that you lost your parents when you were a child, I am grateful for your place in Albert and Edward's life."

"And now in yours."

"And now in mine."

The music drifted into silence. He kissed the back of her hand. "Fortunate men, my friends."

Laughing, she arched a brow. "To have your friendship?"

"To have your love."

*I*T was an odd thing to find himself at a ball, not flirting with young single ladies, not making matronly ones blush, not arranging trysts in the garden—although he had thought numerous times about slipping Julia out for a rendezvous among the roses.

He'd danced with her because it was his favorite thing to do at a ball, danced with Minerva out of politeness—and curiosity. She seemed to have no suspicions regarding his true identity. He'd listened to a couple of lords debating some political question; he'd spoken to one lord about the changes in agriculture. He'd introduced a young swell to an even younger lady, which left him feeling as though he were matchmaking. Strangely, he enjoyed it all. He didn't miss the marriageable women batting their eyelashes and fans at him. He didn't miss the flirtation or sneaking out for a forbidden encounter behind an ivy-covered trellis.

He was content in his new role of earl and husband.

But that didn't mean he was completely satisfied with the activities in the ballroom. He was in need of a drink and a hand at cards. Just one.

*A*FTER Ashe left her, Julia skirted the edge of the ballroom, greeted one person, then another, avoided lingering. She couldn't quite settle in. Recalling her earlier thought regarding refreshments and the benefits of champagne, she decided a trip to the refreshment room was in order. She was halfway there when the Duke of Lovingdon approached her. "Your Grace."

"Lady Greyling, I understand congratulations are in order. I spoke with your husband earlier. One would think he thought he was the only man to ever have a daughter."

She smiled. Edward couldn't love Allie more if he had fathered her. His feelings toward her were honest and true. "He is rather fond of Lady Alberta."

"Can't say I blame him. Daughters tend to wrap themselves around our hearts so easily. I mentioned to Greyling a bill I'm working on that is designed to better protect infants. He made some rather good observations, and I have the impression he's willing to work on it with me. Perhaps sometime soon we could get together for dinner. I won't talk politics during the meal, but I'm not adverse to getting a man's opinion over port."

Edward told her things had gone well in Parliament but he hadn't shared any specifics. For him to be working on a bill with one of the most powerful men in Great Britain was certainly worth mentioning, would elevate his status and good opinion among his peers. Not that the Earl of Greyling required any elevating, but after listening to those silly girls earlier, she wanted Edward to stand out on his own, to stand apart from the title, even though no one would realize he was Edward. She felt as though she were spinning in circles, that she couldn't quite grasp what was and what should be.

What she did become incredibly aware of, however, was that the duke was waiting for an acknowledgment to his earlier comment. One did not require dukes to wait while she sorted out her thoughts. "We would be most delighted to dine with you and your wife."

"You'll no doubt receive an invitation in the next few days. Protecting children is a passion of ours. I'm looking forward to working with Greyling. Through our combined efforts, I've no doubt we can make an incredible difference. Please forgive my rudeness in not immediately offering my condolences on the death of Mr. Alcott. The loss of one so young is always a tragedy."

"Thank you, Your Grace. I appreciate your kindness."

"Now if you'll excuse me, I must find my wife. I believe her next dance belongs to me."

As he walked away, she couldn't help but think that it would be Edward helping him to make an incredible difference, but he would receive no credit for it because people thought he was in a grave. He'd settled for a life of never being recognized, in order to have her as his wife. As much as she wished it so, as easy as it had been to live this life while they were in residence in the country, here she was finding it extremely difficult to hold onto the illusion that she was his wife. Here there were constant reminders that she alone might be the only person who knew the true worth of the present Earl of Greyling. One of the few who knew that the seventh earl had died and the eighth actually now held the title.

In the refreshment room, a table was spread out with an assortment of dishes, yet none of the offerings appealed to her. The champagne didn't satisfy as it once had. As soon as they returned home, she would have a brandy. She was standing by the window looking for a moment of quiet reflection, instead seeing her own reflection in the glass, not certain she even recognized herself any longer, when Lady Newcomb arrived in a swath of pink taffeta and the cloying fragrance of lavender left too long in a bottle.

"Lady Greyling, I'm so glad to see you came to London for the Season. What with Mr. Alcott's passing and all I wasn't certain if you would make your way here. An accident out in the wilds, wasn't it?"

She would wager her monthly allowance that the woman knew exactly how he had died, but Lady Newcomb tended to fancy her own cleverness at saying one thing while conveying something else. Simple condolences were all that were required, not dredging up the unfortunate circumstances of one's death. "Yes, unfortunately, untamed beasts are not to be trusted."

"Ever so glad it wasn't Greyling."

"I would have preferred it not be either brother."

"Of course, of course, but you must be thanking your lucky stars that it wasn't your husband. I daresay that man was an absolute godsend to the female population, the most upstanding of those hellions, setting an example for them. How fortunate you were to snag him."

Only it *had been* her husband, and she had to stand here and talk with this woman as though it hadn't been. "I've always considered myself blessed."

"I know one isn't supposed to speak ill of the dead, but if one of the brothers had to go, the right one did."

Her words were a punch to gut. Julia could barely

draw in a breath. She wanted to shake the woman. "Why would you say such a horrid thing?"

"My dear, I'm merely speaking what so many are thinking. I daresay many a mama is quite relieved that she doesn't have to keep quite as close an eye on her daughter this Season. It was only a matter of time before he ruined one of them."

"Edward didn't take advantage of proper ladies, so I don't see how he could have ruined one. But if he did give in to temptation, he would have done right by her."

"Oh, I don't think so. He was all about the chase, not the capture. I dealt with many a such scoundrel in my youth."

"You're mistaken. He was a good, honorable man."

Lady Newcomb shook her head, her jowls quivering. "Well, the argument can hardly be proven one way or the other now. He was a man who failed to leave a mark. A sad state of affairs was his life. Even his obituary said so. If you'll excuse me—"

It was all Julia could do not to stick out her foot and trip the beastly woman. How dare Lady Newcomb assume to know Edward at all! How dare the ladies be gossiping so unkindly about him? She hated it, hated what people said, thinking that circumstances were different than they were, thinking they were talking about a dead brother when they were, in fact, talking about one who was very much alive.

Fresh air. She required fresh air. Opening the doors to the terrace, she stepped out, walked to the railing and closed her gloved hands around it. She drew in a deep breath, striving to clear her mind of all the unkind thoughts that had been voiced tonight. She had an insane need to recall the words of his obituary. She'd barely given it a passing glance. What was the wording?

Failed to accomplish anything of note . . .

Why did those who wrote obituaries feel compelled to point out perceived shortcomings? She recalled a notable poet's obituary a few years back mentioning that the world would have been better served if the man had never taken pen to paper. They tried to be so damned clever. And they were wrong.

She had enjoyed the poet's works. And Edward had not failed to accomplish anything of note. He had traveled the world, scaled mountains, explored remote regions. He had led expeditions, seen things, experienced things that few people did. He had shared his adventures, entertaining people with his tales. He had separated himself from his brother in order to ensure that he did not interfere with the relationship that existed between herself and Albert. He'd been a loving brother, and in retrospect a loving brother-by-marriage, even if he had gone about his endeavors in a rather unfortunate way, with drinking, carousing, obnoxiousness. But his intentions had been well-intentioned.

At great cost to himself, Edward had honored a vow he made to his brother. He'd helped her bring her daughter into the world. He was caring for that child with all the love her father would have given her. He was going to work with a duke to bring about changes in English law. That was only the beginning of what he might accomplish. Who knew how far he might go—as Albert, the Earl of Greyling.

It wasn't right. It wasn't fair. And she knew with every fiber of her being that they'd made a terrible mistake.

Chapter 24

EDWARD had planned to play only a hand or two but he was having such amazingly good fortune that it was incredibly difficult to push back his chair, bid the gentlemen good-night, and walk away. He'd never spent much time in the ballrooms because he wasn't one to lead ladies on regarding his attentions. He never danced with the wallflowers, as he didn't want to give them hope that he could make them blossom, which left those who saw themselves as excellent marriage prospects, and he'd never been in the mood to go prospecting.

He was holding three queens when she walked in. He didn't see her as much as he felt her presence, felt her gaze landing on him, and when he looked up, she was standing in the door, pale and unsmiling. As he stood, he tossed down his cards. "I'm out for this hand, gentlemen."

The ladies and gents who had been standing around watching the various games made a wide berth as he plowed through them, determined to get to Julia. Something was amiss, terribly amiss. She looked on the verge of weeping, and she was not one who easily wept.

When he reached her, he placed his hands on her shoulders. "What's wrong?"

"May we please leave? My head hurts."

"Yes, of course. Straightaway." He turned toward the doorway, made to follow her out—

"Greyling, your winnings!" one of the lords shouted.

He turned back. "Donate them to a charity." Grinning broadly, he winked. "Just make certain you're not the charity."

Laughter trailed after them as he guided Julia from the room. In the parlor, he retrieved her wrap, his hat and walking stick. Together they went out and waited in the drive while a footman ran off to notify their driver that they were ready to depart.

It wasn't until they were inside the carriage, with her against his side, her head on his shoulder, his arm around her, that he asked, "What happened?"

"I just needed to leave, to think, to find some quiet."

Settling back to provide her with just that, he tempered his alarm. He would get it out of her eventually, before they retired. Nothing good ever came from sleeping on troubling thoughts.

She spoke not a word as they entered the residence, kept silent as they looked in on Allie, although Julia seemed reluctant to leave her daughter. Had she had a premonition? Had someone threatened the child?

At the door to her bedchamber, he made to follow her in when she stopped and faced him. "Will you bring me some brandy?"

"Of course. I won't be but a minute."

"Allow me enough time to prepare for bed."

"Julia—"

"I also need to gather my thoughts."

That didn't bode well. As he stood in the library sipping on his scotch, he didn't think that boded well at all. He shouldn't have left her alone at the damned ball. Something had obviously been done or said to upset her. But what husband never left his wife's side?

They'd have all thought he was besotted. While he was, it would have been out of character for the Earl of Greyling to hover over his wife all night. Although neither did the earl generally sit down to a game of cards, at least not since he'd wed. He'd explained that away as "one hand in memory of my brother."

Of course, one hand had turned into several. He had to take more care. Maybe coming to London so soon after he and Julia had committed themselves to each other had been a mistake.

With his scotch in one hand, her brandy in the other, he made his way to his bedchamber and stripped down to his trousers and linen shirt. Then he entered her room. She was sitting at her dressing table staring at her reflection in the mirror. He set down the glasses and said in a low, gentle voice, "Come to bed."

If he could only hold her, comfort her, he could reassure her, make whatever was troubling her go away.

Pivoting on the bench, she lifted her gaze to his. He hadn't seen that much sadness since she'd discovered she was a widow.

"I can't do this, Edward. I can't live a lie. I thought I was prepared to do so, but I'm not and I shouldn't be. It's not fair to you or Albert or Allie."

He knelt before her. "Julia, whatever happened—"

"They think you're a scapegrace." She shook her head. "Edward, they think Edward was a scapegrace."

"He was. I was." It was confusing, the person he'd been versus the person he was now. He touched her cheek. "Before you."

"No you weren't. You liked to have fun. You were a bachelor, young, having a good time. You never ruined anyone. You never 'didn't amount to anything.' But no one will ever know that. No one will ever know you as I do."

"I don't need for them to. The only opinion I care about is yours."

Her eyes held such sorrow, such remorse. Her brow knitted, and he could see her struggling to explain what he truly had no desire to understand. He didn't want things between them to change. He didn't want to lose her.

"The Duke of Lovingdon told me that he had approached you about working on a bill with him."

"Yes. He thought as a new father I would have a keener empathy toward the plight of the poor and a newfound understanding of how children needed to be protected."

"You will do good things and everyone will credit Albert."

While he appreciated that it bothered her, that she wanted more for him than he rightfully deserved, he was not willing to pay the price that came with any recognition he might receive in his name. He sighed. "As long as good things are done, what does it matter who gets the credit?"

"That's exactly why I love you and why I want them to know the man you are. What you do is your legacy, not Albert's."

"The only legacy I care about is having a life with you."

With an almost frantic nature to her movements, she shook her head. "It's not fair to Albert either. Don't you see? He will never have a funeral or a memorial service or even his own obituary. He will never be mourned."

"He will when I die."

"The man they mourn will be your version of Albert. It won't be him. His life, his legacy, came to an end last year. All that he accomplished until then will be lost in the life that you lead for him."

"Julia, you're not thinking clearly."

She placed a cool hand against his cheek, and a coldness settled in his chest. "I'm thinking more clearly than I have since I discovered the truth regarding who you are. Allie will never know her true father, what he was like. Because of our selfish desires."

Shoving himself away from her, pacing four steps one way, four the other, he plowed his hands through his hair before halting to face her. "It is not selfish to want something."

"It is selfish if gaining it hurts others. We're stealing her father from her, stealing his daughter from him."

"When she is a young woman, we can tell her, explain things."

"We have no idea how she will react, what harm we might inflict. If she decides we betrayed her, that her entire life was a lie and hates us or tells someone—the life we led until that moment will be completely unraveled. People will know we lived in sin. Any children we have will be declared bastards. Even if she holds our secret, it is one thing for us to choose to live a lie. But it is wrong for us to choose for her that she must live one as well."

Why did she have to make such convincing arguments? Why did she have to be so blasted right about this?

"Julia, no one will believe that nothing passed between us, not when we have been portraying ourselves as the Earl and Countess of Greyling. Not when we've been seen in each other's company at the park and attended a ball together. By revealing the truth, we will create an unprecedented scandal that will follow us for years."

"But at least it will be an honest one." Tears welled in her eyes, rolled over onto her cheeks. "I cannot live a lie for the remainder of my life. I cannot stand by silently while people think ill of you and give you no credit for being the decent man you are. I cannot allow Albert's life to be absorbed by yours. I wish I were strong enough to say it doesn't matter, but it does." A sob escaped. "I know I am giving up a life with a man I love, but you deserve to be recognized as something more than a scoundrel. I'm sorry, so sorry, but I can't live this lie that we're creating."

And that was the reason he loved her, damn it all to hell.

She began to cry in earnest. Going back to his knees, he put his arms around her. "It's all right, my love. It's all right."

"I know they'll hate us, ostracize us—"

"Shh, no. I'll take care of it. I'll make it right, determine a way to limit the damage."

She pushed back, swiped the tears from her cheeks. "How? Will you write a letter to the *Times*?"

He brushed the loose strands of hair back from her face. "You leave it to me. I'll figure something out. I spent a great deal of my youth getting in and out of scrapes. I have a wealth of experience to rely on."

Taking her hand, he stood. "Now come to bed and let me hold you."

Once they were settled in beneath the covers within each other's arms, she said quietly, "I know you must be disappointed that I'm not stronger."

"In many ways this path will be harder, and you know that, yet you're willing to travel it. That takes an incredible amount of strength."

"Not so much. I'm really rather cowardly. I can't live in sin with all of London knowing."

"I wasn't expecting you to." Men could be forgiven for all sorts of bad behavior. Women were forgiven for nothing. Even now he had to devise some means to protect her, to ensure she didn't carry the brunt of his actions. "You must promise me that Allie will grow up at Evermore. I won't live there, but I will visit from time to time."

"You must promise me that you will marry and provide an heir for Evermore."

He had sworn to never again lie to her, but he had also vowed to make her happy. "Eventually I will. But for now, let me give you a proper goodbye."

He rolled over until she was partially tucked beneath him and he could rise up on an elbow to gaze down on her. The lamp, still providing a low light, allowed him to see her clearly within the dancing shadows. Never had he enjoyed so much simply looking at a woman. He was going to miss her terribly.

She was young, too young to spend the remainder of her life alone. Eventually she would marry again. He was not going to think about that, wasn't going to focus on what he wouldn't have. For now, he wanted to only concentrate on what he did have: her in his arms, in his bed for one more night. For now, he intended to catalogue every aspect of her, hoard the memories so they would never fade, so he would always have them to visit, to remember, to relive.

"I do love you, Edward."

He'd planned to go slowly, but with her words, he crushed his mouth to hers, his tongue delving deeply, possessively. He would always think of her when he tasted strawberries, heard the sigh of the wind, felt the warmth of the sun. She encompassed a myriad of sensations. With her, everything was always richer, more intense, more compelling.

Her hands were as frantic as his, divesting him of his clothes while he did the same with her nightdress. Then they were flesh against flesh, beginning with their toes and traveling upward. He knew if he'd been granted a thousand years with her, he'd have never tired of her, never tired of this, but all he had was a few more hours, until the lark sang at dawn. He would leave her bed in the morning for the final time. He didn't know where he would find the strength to do it, but he would.

*H*ow could she say goodbye to this? How could she say farewell to him?

Julia found herself praying that the sun would never again rise, that the passage of time would cease, that she and Edward could remain forever cocooned around each other. Selfish thoughts, but then where he was concerned, she seemed to be filled with selfish needs. It was one of the reasons she'd thought she could live a lie, that she hadn't considered all the ramifications, all the people affected.

She knew she would never again experience such uninhibited passion, be possessed by such rampant yearnings, be obsessed with one man. Something deep within him called to a place within her that had been unchartered, undiscovered. She could have lived her entire life without being aware of it and she would have been content, happy. But now that it had been revealed, how could she ever forget that it existed? How could she ignore it?

Oh, she would miss him.

The way his heated mouth left a trail of dew over her skin, along her throat, across the swells of her breasts. The manner in which his mouth closed over her nipple and suckled gently while his hands continued to explore, his fingers to tease. His thigh provided the right amount of pressure between her legs, causing her to writhe against him.

His groans delighted her ears; his tangy scent filled her nostrils. His skin was salty against her tongue. She was striving to hoard every sensation even as she was becoming lost in them. How was it that she could be so aware and yet so disoriented? She was ascending and falling at the same time. Every time they came together it was the same and yet different.

She pushed on his shoulders until he fell onto his back. Straddling his hips, she glided her hands up his arms until she reached his wrists, then shackled her fingers around them. She guided them above his head, pressed them into the pillow. "Don't move them," she ordered.

"What are you going to do?"

She gave him her sauciest grin. "Have my way with you."

"Christ, Ju—"

Her mouth captured his lips, her name, his breath. She was the one who had determined they needed to end the farce. He capitulated because of his love for her. She knew that. She also knew that he had the power to change her mind; knew that he knew as well. Yet he had surrendered, accepted defeat because her happiness was more important to him than his own.

She wanted people to know that he put others before himself. He wasn't a scapegrace; he didn't take advantage. She wanted people talking about Edward with the respect he deserved. It wasn't right to live one's life in another's shadow.

She skimmed her mouth along his bristly chin. She loved this time of night, when his face was roughened with whiskers, when he appeared slightly uncivilized, a little barbaric. So very, very masculine.

He groaned low, and she felt his chest vibrating where her knees rested against his ribs. She loved how tortured he sounded. She placed her lips against his ear. "I'm going to take you in my mouth."

His hips reared up. "Jesus."

"Do you want that?" she asked in a silken throaty voice.

"Yes."

Lifting up, she met his gaze. "What do you want?"

"For you to take me in your mouth."

"Then keep your hands where they are."

Above his head, he interlocked his fingers so tightly she could see the knuckles turning white.

"I want you to remember this night," she whispered.

"I will remember every moment I ever spent with you."

She kissed him thoroughly, controlling the depth and tempo of their movements. She felt powerful, strong. Equal. She could drive him as mad as he drove her. She nibbled on his chin, his neck, his collarbone. Watched as the muscles in his arms bunched and flexed as he struggled not to reach for her.

She slid her body down his. He moaned. She flicked her tongue over his hardened nipple. He growled.

Ah, yes, she could taunt and tease to her heart's content. His other nipple received her attention. His breaths became labored, his stomach tautened. She kissed a path along his ribs, down his flat abdomen, which quivered beneath her lips. The tension radiating through him was palpable.

She took her mouth over his hip, across the scar, along an outer thigh to his knee, up the soft inner thigh, up, up until she reached her destination and closed her lips around him. His snarl was that of a man tormented as he held her captive between his legs, squeezing her tightly as his soles caressed her.

Lifting her gaze to his, she took immense satisfaction in the heat burning brightly in his eyes.

"You are a witch."

Smiling, she returned her attention to revealing just how much of a witch she could be. He swore harshly as she took her sweet time driving him mad. Licking the long length of him, tasting, suckling. If this was to be farewell, she wanted to brand every inch of her over every inch of him.

In the morning, he would leave her bed for the final time. She didn't know where she would find the strength to let him go, but she would somehow. Tonight would become a demarcation in her life, the point where her life parted. On one side was her life with him, on the other side her life without him. One was marked with laughter and love. The other with loneliness.

He would marry and she would find a way to survive it, to live with the knowledge that another lived her dream of warming his bed and bearing his children. Part of her thought it might have been easier to have never known what life with him could be, yet how could she regret a single moment when they would provide sustenance for the coming years?

Suddenly his strong fingers were in her hair, massaging her scalp. "I can't go any longer without touching you."

He shifted until he was nearly sitting, pulled her up until his mouth was nipping at hers. As he fell back down, she realized she was once again straddling him. Lifting her hips, he guided her until he was buried deeply inside her. She nearly wept at how wonderful it felt to be filled by him.

As she rocked against him, he kneaded her breasts, the sensations rolling through her like waves upon the shore. Crashing and retreating. Powerful, then calm.

She braced her hands on either side of his wide shoulders, her hair draped around them, creating a further intimacy, blocking out the world. If only they could block it out forever.

He cradled her hips, providing the support she needed as his thrusts came more quickly, more powerfully. He raised his head, his mouth latching onto her breast, driving her mad as he tugged, as pleasure spiraled until she was crying out his name.

He lifted her up, set himself free, pressing her close against his chest until she was splayed over him, as his body bucked beneath her and he growled her name. He trembled as she quivered, as the remnants of passion had its way with them. Their breathing finally calmed, their bodies stilled.

"Why did you do that?" she asked. "Why did you leave me?"

"I can't risk getting you with child now."

She squeezed her eyes shut. It was an aspect to coupling that she'd never before had to be concerned over. "Does it make it less pleasurable?"

He kissed the top of her head. "No."

Gnawing on her lower lip, she suspected he'd lied. "Does it make it less satisfying?"

"If you're asking if I'd rather be inside you, of course I would. But we do what we must."

She raised her head to look at him. "Are there other ways to ensure that I don't get with child?"

"There is no way to ensure it. What I did lessens the chances, but there are no guarantees."

Sighing, she settled her head back on his chest, listened to his heart thundering. "I'm going to miss being with you."

"No more than I shall miss you."

"Perhaps we'll spend our winter years together, in secret." When she was too old to have children.

His arms banded more tightly around her. "I shall look forward to growing old."

The tears formed, and she let them fall, because this man deserved so much more than she could give him.

Chapter 25

*J*ULIA awoke alone, his side of the bed empty, as it would remain for the rest of her years. She'd been fortunate enough to love two men in her life. There would not be a third.

Glancing at the clock on the mantel, she saw it was nearly one. She did wish Edward had awoken her before he left, for one more goodbye. But then after that one, she would want another. He had the right of it. Best to just move on.

It had been so easy at Evermore when it was only them, alone, not having to carry on conversations with people in Society. So easy to forget what was at stake, what mattered within the upper echelons they inhabited.

She slipped out of bed. Her stomach roiled. Pressing a hand to her mouth, she realized she probably should not have had the brandy on top of the champagne, especially when she hadn't eaten at the ball. Nothing had appealed. The thought of breakfast didn't appeal now.

As she went to ring for her maid, another wave of nausea rolled through her. She dashed across the room, hung her head over the washbasin and heaved. When she was finished, she poured water from the pitcher into a glass, rinsed out her mouth, grabbed a towel and wiped the perspiration from her face. She did hope she wasn't getting ill.

Starting across the room, intent on yanking the bellpull this time, she stopped, placed a hand on her stomach. Oh dear Lord. Closing her eyes, she began counting back weeks. She hadn't had a menses since welcoming Edward into her bed.

She sank to the floor. This changed everything. She couldn't bring a bastard into the world, not Edward's. Poor child. It didn't matter that his father was an earl. There would be no place for him in Society. If it were a girl . . . it would be so much worse. No good marriage.

Did she deny one child knowing the truth about her father in order to protect another? She didn't see that she had a choice. She had to protect both children. Edward would agree. She knew he would. She had to find him, talk with him.

But after she was dressed for the day, she discovered he was nowhere about. He'd gone out to see to some business. When he returned, they would discuss how best to handle this situation. Until then there was no cause for alarm or worry.

She was going through some of the things Albert had left in his study—another journal, notes regarding a bill he was considering presenting in the House of Lords, a ball of string, a bent penny, other little things that she desperately wished to know why he'd bothered to keep, wished to understand their significance—when the butler announced that she had callers and presented the cards of the Duchesses Ashebury, Avendale, and Lovingdon.

Walking into the parlor, she found them standing, a triumvirate of the youngest, most beloved, and powerful ladies of the next generation.

Stepping forward, Minerva took her hands. "My dear, as soon as we received word of what had transpired within the House of Lords this afternoon, we thought to come here and offer our support."

Julia's stomach dropped, a million possibilities, each one of them involving Edward, racing through her mind. "What transpired?"

"The Earl of Greyling stood before the assembly and announced that he was Edward Alcott. That it was Albert who was killed in Africa."

She shook her head in disbelief, her knees growing weak. It wasn't supposed to happen that way. He was to write a letter to the *Times,* he wasn't supposed to face his peers so publicly.

"He said you only learned of the truth last night. That it was time to bring the farce to an end."

"Farce?" she repeated.

"He swore that nothing untoward passed between you," Grace, Duchess of Lovingdon, said. "That you are an innocent in all of this."

Minerva studied her face. "But he lied, didn't he?"

She could only shake her head. Until she understood his plan, knew exactly what he was telling people, she could neither confirm nor deny anything. Why hadn't he discussed the matter with her before he did anything so rash? "Shall I ring for tea?"

"I think we should sit."

"Yes." She took a chair, while the ladies lined up on the sofa, with Minerva closest to her. Although she appreciated that they were offering their support, all she wanted was to usher them out the door so she could find Edward.

"I'm sure Ashe will be here presently," Minerva said. "I left word for him that I was coming straight over, although he will probably head here anyway. Grace was the one who first received word."

"Why now?" Rose, Duchess of Avendale, asked. "Why confess now and not before?"

She shook her head. "I'm rather baffled right now, ladies. I hardly know what to say." Not until she spoke with Edward.

The slamming of the front door had her jumping to her feet, nearly dashing from the room to greet Edward and ask him what the bloody hell he'd been thinking. Only it was Ashebury who barged into the room.

"Where is he?" he demanded. "Is he here?"

"No, I don't know where he is. What exactly happened?"

"He stood up in the House of Lords and declared himself to be Edward. He confessed that his original intent was to honor a vow he made to Albert to ensure you didn't lose the babe but then he realized it was to his benefit to continue on with the ruse, as he had considerable gaming debts and the unsavory men holding his markers were not the forgiving sort."

"Is that true?" Minerva asked before Julia could.

"Absolutely not. At least not what he told me," Ashe said.

"Would he have told you if he was in trouble?" his wife inquired.

Ashe sighed. "When it comes to Edward, who knows? He loves to tell stories, but I have no reason to believe he lied."

"So he lied to all the other lords?" Minerva seemed horrified.

"Apparently so."

"Why would he do that?"

"To protect me," Julia said.

"How does his story do that when you have been living together for months now?"

She had no response to that question.

"Edward explained that away," Ashe began, "by assuring everyone that his relationship with Julia remained chaste. Naturally, no one found that difficult to believe, as we all know he never had a kind word for you. He went on to say that you were growing suspicious, so he paid off his debts and he is once again free. Or some rubbish like that. I could scarce believe what I was hearing. Of course, the chambers erupted and he walked out."

"Probably in need of a stiff drink," Minerva offered.

He smiled at his wife, before looking at Julia. "I was waylaid, as everyone pounced on me to find out if I'd known what he was up to and if it was true."

"Why did you say?" she asked.

"What could I say? That I've never known him to lie. I just wish he'd bloody well told me what he planned so I would have been prepared and could have provided my support in a more effective manner. I'm rather certain I resembled a fish that finds itself flopping about on shore."

Which she suspected was the very reason Edward

hadn't told him. He wanted his reaction to be honest. "He didn't want to draw you into our mess."

"Well he should have. That's what brothers are for. I know I'm not his brother by blood, but I am, by God, his brother!"

"Darling," Minerva said, rubbing her hand up and down his arm, "you must calm yourself."

"I simply don't understand his strategy."

"Is anyone talking about me?" Julia asked.

"No, they're all . . ." He sighed. "He is the one they are speculating about. And not very flatteringly I'm afraid. Hiding behind his brother's death and a woman's skirts. Which I assume is what he meant to accomplish—painting himself as a villain."

"In a year or so he'll be forgiven," Minerva said.

"In all likelihood, yes," Ashe confirmed, before turning his attention back to Julia. "Should his words not be enough to protect you, know that I, Minerva, and Locke— even though he is not in London—will stand by you."

"As will we," the Duchess of Lovingdon said. "And Avendale. We've all been touched by scandal in one way or another. It's easier to ride out the storm if you're not alone in the boat."

"I'm going to pour us all a drink," Ashebury said.

"Scotch," the three duchesses said in unison.

The duke raised a brow at Julia. "Nothing for me, thank you," she told him. If she were with child, she wasn't going to indulge in spirits. Nor was she going to tell Edward. She didn't need to burden him when he already had so much on his plate. She would return to Evermore and, once there, determine how best to handle the situation.

Her guests sat in her parlor sipping their spirits. Julia had sandwiches and cakes brought in. Darkness fell.

Ashebury began to pace. "Where the deuce is he?"

"Gentleman's club?" Minerva asked.

"I don't think he'd be in the mood for the company of lords. If anything, he's probably in someplace like St. Giles, trying to get lost." He looked at Julia. "Do you have any clue as to where he might be?"

She had a fairly good one, but the fact that he wasn't here and Ashebury didn't know where to look told her that Edward wanted no company. "I'm afraid I don't. But I'm sure he'll return here when he's ready. I'll send word when he does. No reason for you to ruin your evening by staying and keeping me company."

He narrowed his eyes. "Why do I have the impression that you're trying to get rid of us?"

"Because I am. Nothing is to be gained by your being here, and it's quite possible that your carriages out front are keeping him walking the streets."

Ashebury looked as though he were contemplating what he might gain by throttling her.

"She's quite right," Minerva announced, coming to her feet. "We should be off."

Ashe pointed a finger at her. "Send word as soon as he gets here."

Minerva wrapped her hand around his finger. "It's rude to point, dear."

"I want to know that he's all right."

"I'll send word," Julia assured him.

He still seemed somewhat disgruntled as he escorted the ladies out.

Julia waited half an hour before ordering a footman to have a carriage readied.

He'd known she would figure out where he was . . . eventually. At half past nine she walked in to the library of the residence he'd begun leasing last year. He rose from his chair beside the fire. "I have brandy waiting for you."

He'd already set a glass for her on the table beside the chair opposite his.

She touched his cheek, held his gaze. "Why did you do it?"

"I told you that I would set matters right."

"But so publicly and in front of all your peers."

"It was the only way to protect you and Allie, to be seen as a weasel. Since according to my tale you only just discovered you are in mourning, there's no reason for you to remain in London. As a matter of fact, to give credence to my story, it would be best if I returned the mourning widow to Evermore posthaste. People will expect you to go into seclusion. I can come back here later to face the piper."

Rising up on her toes, she feathered the hair back from his temple. "I don't believe I've ever loved you more."

And then she kissed him.

Banding his arms around her, he held her tightly, angling his head so he could take the kiss deeper. He was going to miss this: the taste of her, the feel of her tongue, the press of her lips. The little mewling sounds she made before the passion took hold and she began moaning in earnest.

When she drew back, she settled in the chair, lifted her glass. "To my wolf."

He wasn't feeling much like a wolf. Still, he sat, took a sip of his scotch.

"Ashebury is worried about you," she said, setting her glass—barely touched—aside.

"That's why I came here. Knew he would seek me out, remind me that he had urged me months ago to reveal the truth of my deception. Didn't want to hear him gloating about being right."

"He wasn't gloating. I believe he's genuinely concerned that you're in need of a friend."

All he needed was her, and he could no longer have her. "Was he the one who told you?"

"No, I was visited by three duchesses."

"Ashebury and—" He arched a brow.

"Lovingdon and Avendale."

"Ah, yes."

"I won't leave London and have you face them all alone. I'll stand by you and confirm whatever details of the story you told."

He didn't want her here for the Season, the scandal. She was safe but he wasn't going to be welcomed anywhere for a while.

"Let me take you to Evermore. I won't stay in London. I'll go on to another estate. By the time you're officially out of mourning this will all be forgotten."

"That's what Minerva said. That it won't take long before you're forgiven."

He lifted his glass. "Let's hope she has the right of it. I'd like to stop by Havisham if you've no objection.

I know it's out of the way, but I want Marsden to meet Allie. He's the closest thing she has to a grandfather."

"Will it be difficult explaining things to him?"

"Locke already told him the truth. He wanted to ensure his father was mourning the correct brother."

"So we'll be welcomed."

"With open arms."

"That'll be nice. I'd like to stop by there, then." She glanced around. "Never been in your residence before, but it doesn't remind me of you."

"Most of the furnishings belonged to Ashe. As usual, I took the easy way. Simply purchased what was already here."

She scowled at him. "You don't take the easy way, Edward. I don't believe you ever have. You work hard to make people believe you're a slacker, but you're not."

"Ah, so you've figured me out have you?"

"Yes, I quite believe I have." She finished off her brandy, set the glass aside. "Has your residence a bed-chamber?"

"One more night?"

"One more night."

Chapter 26

*I*T was good to see Havisham appear on the rise. Edward hadn't realized exactly how much he'd missed it until he caught sight of it again. He had so many good memories of the place.

"We fought," he said quietly as the coach turned onto the long path that would lead them to the manor. "Albert and I smacked at each other the entire journey here. Drove the solicitor to distraction."

"Do you think your father knew that Marsden was mad?" Julia asked.

During the long sojourn here, they'd barely spoken, simply held each other. So much needed to be said, so much shouldn't be said.

"Surely not. I don't know if anyone really knew how much he was affected by his wife's passing, not until years later."

"But to go mad . . ."

He decided against revealing that he could understand it. He had become lost in drink, Marsden had become lost in the past, held too tightly to the memories. If Julia weren't here at all, he might do the same.

While their future relationship would be chaste, at least he could speak to her from time to time, could share a dance with her at a ball, could visit at Christmas and play St. Nicholas for her daughter.

"I've only been here once before," she said. "I don't think I slept a wink."

It had been many nights before he'd finally been able to sleep in the strange residence with its homages to the past and its haunting echoes. "The screeching is only the wind."

"But it sounds so mournful."

The carriage came to a halt. As Edward prepared to disembark, he leaned in and whispered, "If you get frightened tonight, come crawl into bed with me."

The footman opened the door before she could respond. Edward leaped out and then handed her down. Looking up at him seductively, she said, "I offer you the same invitation."

He thought he just might take it. If nothing else, he could simply hold her. Although the last time they were in bed together, they'd done a good deal more than that. Neither of them seemed to have much strength in resisting the other. But for her, he had to be strong, had to battle the temptation.

"Hello!" Locke shouted.

Edward looked over to see his friend charging down the steps of the manor. Visitors here were infrequent, and he'd sent word ahead that they'd be arriving. Obviously, Locke had been watching for them.

Reaching Edward, he embraced him, gave him a sound clap on the back. "Welcome, Grey."

Stepping back, Edward said, "Edward will suffice."

Locke looked at him, looked at Julia. "So you know."

"All of London knows," she admitted.

He grimaced. "That couldn't have been very pleasant."

"Might be a while before I again stand up in the House of Lords to make a statement," Edward assured him.

Shaking his head, Locke laughed. "I wouldn't put it past you to be telling them tales next year." Leaning in, he bussed a kiss over Julia's cheek. "Welcome to Havisham Hall. My father has been beside himself with the thought of your arrival. He's actually made a rare departure from his rooms and is waiting for us on the terrace."

As the Marquess of Marsden pushed himself out of his chair, Edward was taken aback by how frail he appeared, and yet he hardly seemed to have changed. His white hair hung past his shoulders in limp strands, his cheeks as sunken as they'd been the day he met him. His green eyes as sharp. They could fool a person into thinking he still had all his wits about him.

He held his arms wide. "Edward."

He went to Marsden, let him fold his arms around him. The marquess's hold was stronger, more powerful, than he'd expected, Marsden's arthritic hands gently patting his back.

"Sorry, lad, sorry," he rasped in a voice that had gone permanently hoarse from all the times he'd screamed his love's name as he'd raced over the moors, firm in his belief that he saw her, that he could reunite with her.

The tears of sadness threatened as Edward hugged the thin, bent man who had been like a father to him and Albert. "He went quickly." The lie on his tongue was beginning to resound as though it were the truth.

But when he leaned back, he saw in Marsden's eyes that the marquess recognized the lie for what it was: an attempt to spare him the pain of the truth. Giving his head an almost imperceptible shake, he patted Edward's cheek, censure in the flatness of lips. He'd forgotten that Marsden had always known when one of them lied, had never approved, but he knew the old man would hold the secret, that he understood it was for Julia.

Looking past Edward, Marsden smiled sadly and held out a hand. "My dear."

Julia went to him, placed her gloved hand in his. He brought it to his lips. "It is not easy to be the one left behind."

She darted a glance at Edward. "No, it's not, but Edward has proven to be a great source of strength."

"Albert was destined to go young, you know. Had an old soul, like my wife. I could see it in his eyes. But it doesn't make us miss them any less, does it?"

"It absolutely does not."

He raised a gnarled finger. "But he left you a precious gift."

Her smile was brighter than the sun. "Yes, he did." Taking Allie from the nanny who was standing nearby, she turned back to Marsden. "I'd like to introduce you to Lady Alberta."

"Beautiful child, beautiful." He lifted hopeful eyes. "May I hold her? I won't drop her."

"Yes, of course." Very carefully she transferred Allie into Marsden's arms.

He lowered his head. "Hello, precious."

Allie emitted a high-pitched sound that very much resembled a laugh.

Her eyes wide, Julia chuckled. "She's never done that before, has she, Edward?"

"No, she hasn't. Not that I've heard."

Marsden winked. "I have a way with the ladies." He looked at Locke. "You need one of these. Except it should be a boy. They could marry."

Locke merely rolled his eyes, crossed his arms over his chest and looked out over the vast expanse of land that stretched toward the horizon, as though he wished to distance himself from his father and his pointed words.

"Lady Greyling, have some tea with me and tell me everything about her," Marsden insisted.

"You must call me Julia," she said as she took a chair.

Holding Allie close, obviously not yet ready to relinquish his hold on her, Marsden sat. Edward and Locke joined them, although most of the conversation was carried by Marsden and Julia. He truly did seem to want to know everything about Allie, although at this point in her life there wasn't a good deal to tell. Still, Julia went to great pains to expand on any question the marquess asked.

It was a lovely afternoon. Troubles seemed far away, impossible dreams seemed possible. Edward half listened to the conversation. It was odd that he felt more at home here, but then he'd lived here longer than at Evermore. Some of his fondest memories of Albert had occurred here. When Allie was older he would bring her back, walk over the grounds and share stories of her father.

Julia was right about that. It wasn't fair to deny her an opportunity to know and appreciate her true father. Edward didn't want to take that away from her, or Albert.

She began to fuss. Standing, Julia took her from Marsden. All the men came to their feet.

"I'm going to take her for a little walk," she said. "Give you gentlemen a chance to catch up." Bouncing her daughter in her arms, she wandered away from the terrace into the sunshine, the nanny in tow.

"Fetch us some scotch, Locke," Marsden ordered. "I detest tea. Always have."

When the scotch was poured, Marsden raised his glass. "To love." After taking a sip, he arched a brow at Edward. "You do love her, don't you?"

"How can one not love that little girl?"

The wrinkles of his face shifted as he smiled. "I meant her mother."

Edward shouldn't have been surprised by Marsden's ability to recognize his feelings. The man might be completely mad, but he wasn't stupid.

Locke, on the other hand, straightened as though his father had walloped him on the side of the head. He leaned forward. "You love her? How the bloody hell did that happen? You've always disliked her."

Edward grimaced. "Not as much as I let on."

"Well, hell, that's unfortunate. What are you going to do?"

"What can we do? The law won't let us marry. Any children we have would be bastards. She would be ostracized. Allie's future would be compromised. So I'll deliver her to Evermore. She and Allie will live there while I'll reside at one of the other estates."

"Take her to Switzerland," Marsden said.

Edward released a burst of harsh laughter, then sobered. "Albert told me the same thing, as he lay dying. 'Take her to Switzerland.' I thought maybe it was someplace he and Julia planned to travel, somewhere she dreamed of visiting, but when I asked her about it, she had no interest in it whatsoever. Why would he and you tell me to take her there?"

Marsden looked at him as though he were the one who was mad. "Because you can marry her there."

Stunned by his words, Edward could do little more than stare at him.

The old man cackled. "Do you think you're the first man to want to marry his brother's wife?" He waved a hand through the air. "Oh, some people will turn their noses up at you, but to hell with them. These laws prohibiting those related by marriage from marrying are preposterous. The belief that a couple engaging in sex suddenly makes the entire family blood relations is madness."

The irony of the mad Marquess of Marsden calling anything madness was not lost on Edward.

Marsden pounded his fist on the table. "Do you not pay attention to what goes on in Parliament? Of course you don't. You've only just taken your place in the House of Lords. People have been trying to change those laws for years."

"How do you know?" Locke asked. "You haven't sat in the House of Lords since I was born."

Marsden scowled at his son. "I read the newspapers." He shrugged. "Sometimes someone might send me a letter asking my opinion. And I know a gent or two who took his lady to Switzerland."

Scraping back the chair, Edward stood and walked to the edge of the terrace. "We just go to Switzerland. Live there." He could manage the estates from there, periodically return to England.

"No," Marsden answered impatiently. "You marry there, because they don't care if people are related by marriage. Then you come back here. England recognizes the marriage. Julia is your legal wife. Your children are legitimate. One consideration: It is costly."

As though lack of money would prove any sort of deterrent to him when he loved Julia so much. But why would Albert spend his last breath telling him to take her to Switzerland? Why would he—

He slammed his eyes closed as the truth nearly knocked him to his knees. Albert had known, known about Edward's feelings for Julia. He thought he'd been so damned good at disguising them. All the drinking, all the sarcastic remarks, hadn't fooled his brother.

With his dying breath Albert had provided not only the answer to a question that Edward hadn't even known he'd be asking, but given his blessing as well.

JULIA watched as Edward strode toward her. She'd enjoyed watching him sitting and talking with the marquess and the viscount. It was obvious that for him this was home and they were family. They shared a very special bond, and she was extremely glad that he had it. She thought he might need them in the coming months, especially if being without her was going to be as difficult for him as being without him would be for her.

"Take a walk with me," he said when he reached her.

She handed the sleeping Allie off to Nanny, intertwined her arm with his and let him lead the way through what she assumed had once been a beautiful garden, but now consisted only of weeds and overgrowth. Weather and years of neglect had taken its toll on trellises and benches, leaving behind only rotting wood.

"A woman with a great deal of stamina and creativity might have fun putting this place to rights," she said.

"The challenge for her would be convincing Marsden to let her change anything at all. Every decaying inch of the place is a memorial to his wife."

"How can he stand to see everything deteriorating?"

"I don't believe he does. I think he sees it exactly as it was when she was alive. By never letting anyone touch it, he ensured that he never saw it any differently."

"He must have loved her immeasurably."

"To him, she was everything. I'm not certain if that's a good or bad thing."

She didn't want to even try to provide an answer to that question. "Is she buried here?"

Edward pointed off to his left. "In a small cemetery over that hill."

"I suppose you explored there."

"We explored everywhere."

He helped her step over a low bit of brush and onto what had once been a path. The boughs of the trees provided shade. She supposed he was worried about the sunshine causing her to have freckles, though she'd never had a single one in her entire life. Or maybe he wanted to escort her farther into the trees so he could kiss her.

But if that was the case, he was taking his sweet time, as he had yet to do anything more than face her and hold her gaze.

"Albert knew," he said quietly. "He knew I had feelings for you."

She blinked, shook her head, tried to make sense of what he'd said. "How do you know?"

"Because he told me to take you to Switzerland."

"I don't understand. As I told you before, I've never considered traveling there. He and I never talked about it. Why would he say that?"

"Because I can marry you there."

While her heart hammered, everything else within her went still, quiet. She'd heard the words but they made no sense.

"Marsden knows people, in our situation, who went to Switzerland to marry. Why would Albert tell me to take you there unless he knew I would want to marry you?"

"Perhaps he simply wanted you to watch out for me, and he thought it would be easier if we were married. He trusted you, Edward, and he hadn't left a will."

"Maybe."

"But you don't think so."

He shook his head. "I think he knew. I think he always knew. He was always encouraging me to spend more time with him, with you. I think he was aware of what it was costing me to keep my distance. Costing him, me, maybe even you. He understood that my love for him would ensure that I never did anything untoward where you were concerned. He was trying to give me permission to be more myself."

Possibly. She remembered the final entry in his journal, how she'd read silently instead of sharing it with Edward. "In his journal, he wrote that he had yet to write his will because he'd been struggling with whom to name as guardian of his child. During your time together in Africa, he came to the conclusion there was no one better than you to care for those he loved."

"I have to admit, Julia, that while we've been together, I have not been clear of conscience. A small part of me nagged that I was betraying my brother."

"I must be honest that I've not been completely clear of conscience either," she said. "Perhaps that's the reason London was able to open my eyes so clearly to the myriad ways that what we were doing was wrong."

"But if I am judging Albert's words correctly, he would approve of our being together." Taking her hand, he dropped to one knee. "So will you, Julia Alcott, honor me by becoming my wife? Our marriage will be legal. Our children legitimate."

As tears burned her eyes, she covered her mouth with the hand he wasn't holding.

"Not everyone will approve," he continued. "There may yet be some scandal, some gossip—"

"I don't care. Yes, I will marry you. I love you, Edward. I have been so miserable thinking of you leaving me behind at Evermore."

"I promised not to leave you." Standing, he pulled her nearer, cupped her face. "I love you, Julia. I believe I have since that night I kissed you in the garden."

His mouth was on hers before she took her next breath, his arms closing around her as though he would never let her go. She didn't want him to let her go, didn't want to let go of him. Ever.

They would live at Evermore together. They would have children together. They would be happy together. Maybe he was right. Maybe Albert had known. Maybe he did approve. All that mattered was that he and Marsden had given them a way to be together.

When Edward pulled back, his eyes contained no more sadness, no more sorrow.

"When do you want to get married?" he asked.

"As soon as possible."

Taking her hand, he began leading her back toward the house. "I'll start making the arrangements as soon as we return to Evermore."

"You must know, Edward, that I am marrying you because I love you."

He smiled down on her. "I don't doubt that in the least."

"Good, because I'm also with child."

That stopped him in his tracks. "Why didn't you tell me?"

"I'd only figured it out the afternoon that you made your announcement in the House of Lords. There was nothing to be done at that point except to make you worry."

He dragged her into his arms. "Christ, Julia."

"I would have kept her. I would have loved her. I would have done everything in my power to protect her."

He leaned away from her, arched a brow. "Her?"

"We're going to have a daughter. I feel it in my bones."

Laughing, he picked her up and swung her around in a circle.

"Edward!"

Finally he put her down, but he was still smiling brightly. "I'm going to make a huge wager in the betting book at White's that we're having a son."

"But I've told you. It's a girl. A woman knows these things."

SEVEN and a half months later, Edward Albert Alcott, heir apparent to the earldom of Greyling, made his entrance into the world.

Epilogue

London
Some Years Later

EDWARD stood in the hallway, right knee bent, foot
flat to the wall, waiting. He'd been waiting all morning.
No, in truth, he'd been waiting for a good many years,
anticipating and dreading this moment.

His marriage to Julia had been the source of immeasurable gossip. His son and heir, Edward Albert,
making his debut into the world only a few months
after the wedding of his parents took place, had been
cause for further gossip and speculation. But it didn't
take long for his love for Julia and hers for him to cause
even the most righteous and upstanding among the nobility to admit that perhaps they were a bit hasty with
their censure.

After all, how could a love as pure, unselfish, and grand as theirs be denied?

Slowly, they'd been welcomed back into the ranks of the elite. It was, however, years before they admitted that the beloved children's author and illustrator—J. E. Alcott—was not a distant cousin to Louisa May, as was often hinted, but was in fact the pseudonym for the Countess and Earl of Greyling. What he liked best about the stories was that he always felt as though he and his brother, along with Ashe and Locke, had been immortalized and would carry on with their adventures long after they each drew their final breath. Greymane was a favorite among the children, who often named their hobbyhorses after him. Edward liked that best of all: that his brother was still loved by so many.

Beside him, Edward Albert sighed, shifted his stance and stuffed his hands into the pockets of his trousers.

"I know you're anxious to be off, but Kilimanjaro isn't going anywhere."

His son, nearly his spitting image, smiled. "I daresay you want to go with us."

Ashe and Locke's sons were part of the group headed out on the morrow. Edward chuckled. "I'm too old to be scaling mountains. Besides, someone has to stay here and keep your mother from worrying."

"She's going to worry anyway, but not as much as she would if Allie were traveling alongside us. She was keen to go, too, you know."

"She'll be busy with her own adventures." If there was one thing true of Allie, it was that she dearly loved going on adventures.

"We'll be home for Christmas."

"See that you are." He wasn't going to admit to his own worry, but then he worried every time one of his children left the house. He wondered if he and Albert might not have seen as much of the world as they had if their parents hadn't been killed. He did know that their lives would have been different—not better or worse, simply different. Still, he and Julia had never wanted to hold their own children back. They'd come by their adventuresome spirits naturally.

The door to the bedchamber opened, and he shoved himself away from the wall as Julia stepped out. After all these years, his heart still kicked up a notch at the sight of her. She was dressed in pale lavender, her hair peppered with white that only made her all the more beautiful.

She walked up to him, touched her fingers to his cheek. "I'm going to weep a thousand tears today."

"I'm carrying extra handkerchiefs."

Her lips lifted into a soft smile. "Always looking out for me."

"One of my greatest joys."

"Honestly, if you keep this up," their son said, "people are going to think it's the two of you getting married today."

"If you're lucky, one day you'll have a love as grand as ours," Edward told him.

"Not for a while yet."

"When you least expect it," Edward said quietly, holding Julia's gaze, looking into the blue eyes that continued to enthrall him. "Where you least expect it."

"That's certainly true of Allie," Edward Albert said. "Never thought she'd marry."

"She loves him," Julia said. "And he loves her."

"Still, it's a surprise."

Not to those who knew love.

"She'll be out shortly," Julia said. "She just needed another minute."

"I'll be waiting," Edward said. "Son, escort your mother down to the carriage and on to the church. We'll follow shortly." He and Allie were going to arrive in a white open carriage drawn by six white horses, the lead horse possessed of a gray mane.

He watched as mother and son, arm in arm, descended the stairs. All in all they'd had a good life. His work in the House of Lords had gained him respect among his peers. He expected the church would be packed to the rafters with those who wanted it known that they were friends of the Earl and Countess of Greyling.

The door opened once more and another beauty stepped out. She wore a gown of white silk and lace, and he thought she'd never looked lovelier.

She smiled serenely. "Hello, Poppy."

"Papa" was reserved for Albert. Allie was seven when she announced that Uncle Edward wasn't the correct name for him. "You're more than my uncle. You're my papa, too. I'm going to call you Poppy because it's a bit like Papa but isn't. It's special."

"Hello, my darling girl," he said now. "Aren't you a beauty?"

"I'd wager you say that to all the ladies," she said sassily.

He grinned. "Only to you and your mother. I have a little something for you." Reaching inside his jacket, he removed a leather box.

She took it from him, opened the lid to reveal a gold locket on a gold chain. "Oh, Poppy, it's lovely."

"Inside, protected behind glass, are locks of your father's hair." He didn't know why he'd had the presence of mind to cut off a few of Albert's locks, but he was grateful that he had. "I thought you might like to wear it today so you're reminded that he is always with you."

Turning, she presented her back, held up the locket. Moving her flowing veil aside, he secured the necklace. Spinning back around, she rose up on her toes and kissed his cheek. "I never knew him, and yet I love him. You made sure of that. Because you did, I love you. It's not every girl who is blessed enough to have two wonderful fathers."

"It's not every uncle who is blessed enough to have a niece who is also loved as a daughter."

"And now you will give me away."

"Never. I'll place you in his keeping, but make no mistake, you are still ours."

"I love you so much, Poppy."

"No more than I love you. Now we'd best be off," he said, threading her arm around his. "The Earl of Greyling is never late."

One of Albert's habits that he'd never gotten around to changing.

He and Allie carried on down the stairs. A footman opened the door. As they stepped outside, Edward was nearly blinded by the brightness of the sun. As he put up his hand to shield his eyes, he could have sworn he heard a whispered, *Well done, brother, well done.*

"Poppy, are you all right?"

Lowering his hand, he realized the glaring light had

faded. No doubt merely the angle that had caught his eyes. "I'm fine. Let's go."

He helped her up into the carriage and then sat beside her. As the driver set the horses into motion, he looked up at the blue sky. What a glorious day.

"You know, Poppy, I've been thinking, no doubt because I'm madly in love myself, but I think in your next story, Stinker the Weasel needs to find a love."

"He did, sweetheart," Edward said, smiling. "He did."

Author's Note

My dear readers,

When I originally envisioned Edward's story, I knew it would be a challenge. First, I had to ensure that readers didn't fall in love with Albert before I did him in, and I didn't want him to be a nasty sort of fellow. I also knew that British law at the time prohibited a man from marrying his brother's widow.

But I also couldn't envision that the imagination of a romance writer was the only place where a man might want to marry his brother's wife. So I began doing some research. It was fascinating. I found an instance where a woman was imprisoned for marrying her deceased sister's husband. Not sure why the man got off scot-free, but there you are. I discovered some people married in parishes where they weren't known and didn't reveal how they were related, meaning they had the documents to show they were married but in truth they weren't legally wed. It took only someone objecting in order to void the marriage. And I discovered that the well-to-do would travel to and marry in Switzerland or Norway, where the laws were more lenient regarding whom one could marry, but it was costly, so those who could take advantage of this opportunity were few.

For sixty-five years members of Parliament battled to change the law. Finally, in 1907, the Deceased Wife's Sister's Marriage Bill was passed to allow the sister of a deceased woman to marry her brother-in-law. But it wasn't until 1921 that the Deceased Brother's Widow's Marriage Bill allowed a man to marry his deceased brother's widow. I like to think that Edward and Julia were still around and saw that law take effect.

To be quite honest, I'm not sure if their son would have been allowed to inherit, since they skirted the boundaries of the law by marrying elsewhere, but I write fiction, so I hope you'll indulge me in my belief that he would have become the next Earl of Greyling. Regardless, Edward and Julia wished only for their children to be granted healthy, long, and happy lives. In that regard, I assure you that their wishes were realized.

Happy reading,

Lorraine